PALETTE

OF

SECRETS

The Scottish novelist Joan Fallon, currently lives and works in the south of Spain. She writes both literary and historical fiction, and almost all her books have a strong female protagonist. She is the author of:

HISTORICAL FICTION:
Spanish Lavender
The House on the Beach
The Only Blue Door
The al-Andalus series:
The Shining City (Book 1)
The Eye of the Falcon (Book 2)
The Ring of Flames (Book 3)

LITERARY FICTION:
Loving Harry
Santiago Tales
Love Is All
The Thread That Binds Us

NON-FICTION:
Daughters of Spain

(all are available in paperback and as ebooks)

www.joanfallon.co.uk

JOAN FALLON

PALETTE

OF

SECRETS

Scott Publishing

Palette of Secrets

ISBN 978 0 9955834 5 0
First published in 2018
Scott Publishing
Windsor, England

ACKNOWLEDGMENTS

My sincere thanks to my editor Sara Starbuck for her advice. As usual she has helped me to both clarify my ideas and refine my prose. Thanks also go to Rachel Lawston of Lawston Designs for her compelling cover. The advice and support of both of them have been invaluable to me.

Palette of Secrets

CHAPTER 1

She stands at her living room window, looking out at the beach across the rooftops of old fishermen's cottages long since converted to bars and ice cream parlours. It is still only April, but already, two people are swimming in the sea—tiny, shapeless dots bobbing about in the waves. She has almost convinced herself that they are not people after all, but discarded buoys cut loose from the fishing boats that cruise inshore, sweeping up shoals of supposedly protected tiny fish. One of the swimmers starts waving. A line of poetry comes back to her, some half-forgotten piece she learned at school. Stevie Smith? Maybe. It was a long time ago. Now the other swimmer is waving.

Something is wrong. She sees a crowd beginning to form on the beach—agitated Lowry figures, gesticulating and calling to the bobbing heads in the water. She cannot hear anything for the double-glazed windows that keep her hermetically sealed in her warm little flat, but she can sense the agitation. One of the bobbing heads disappears under the waves. She waits for it to reappear. The crowd becomes more agitated, and one of the Lowry men rushes into the sea, fully clothed, and heads out towards the swimmers. Despite the double-glazing, the wailing cry of a siren penetrates her home as a car speeds along the beach. Someone has summoned the *Guardia Civil*.

Now the good Samaritan has reached one of the swimmers. It is hard to see what is happening—the two men appear to be dancing in the waves, a water ballet, alternately dropping below the water and resurfacing in a flurry of foam. She sees no sign of the second swimmer.

Cold grips her heart. Some treacherous underwater current has dragged him down, deep into the sea. She shivers. What must it be like? Are his eyes open? Does he see his life drifting away from him as he struggles for breath and only water fills his mouth, his nose, his stomach, his lungs? Does he fight against it? She turns from the window, trembling. She is determined not to let these thoughts take over. She has tamed them all these years. They must not resurface now.

Nancy walks over to her American-style kitchen. That is how the estate agent described it, conveniently disguising the fact that this bijou kitchen—another of his words—is sitting in the corner of her lounge. She fills the kettle and plugs it in. Martin made her replace her old kettle with this electric model after she left it on the gas and it burned dry. He accused her of nearly setting the apartment alight and insisted on removing the gas stove, so cheap to run and familiar to her, and installing the safer, more expensive, electric one. She asked him if he was going to pay her electricity bills for her. He scowled. She would be grateful in the long run, he said. She was still waiting for that feeling of gratitude to envelop her.

There is a light knock at her door. Who can it be? She looks at the clock; it is only nine-thirty. María comes at ten. She always comes at ten to make Nancy's bed and put the mop over the floor. María is Nancy's minder. Martin likes to think of her as a carer-cum-cleaner, but really she's his spy. Nancy doesn't trust Maria. She is overweight—fat even—and she treats Nancy as if she were mentally deficient. Nancy has never trusted fat people. Behind their jolly exterior, they hide a sense of superiority over the thinner members of the world. The knock on the door repeats, this time louder. She peers through the spy-hole. It's a young woman. She's wearing glasses and has the same long, silky black hair as all the other young Spanish women in the neighbourhood. But who is she?

Nancy retreats to her desk, a large round table that occupies most of the space in her living room. It is covered with books, newspapers, lists, and notebooks. Somewhere under it all is a diary. She finds it beneath a book about Van Gogh that Martin gave her for Christmas. Now the difficult part. What day is it? She glances back at the clock. It has a traditional face with large, clear numbers, and in the centre is the date: 23rd April 2014. She opens her diary to the appropriate page and there it is. The woman's name is Ana Álvarez. Underneath, she has scribbled 'bio.' Of course. She has come to help Nancy write her memoirs. She hurries to the door, pulls back the top bolt, then the bottom one, takes the key with its bright red lasso from the hook on the wall, and unlocks the door.

'*Buenas días*. Señora Miller?' the young woman asks. She shows no sign of irritation that it has taken Nancy such a long time to open the door. She smiles warmly.

'Come in, my dear,' Nancy says, smiling back. 'You must be Ana.'

'I'm sorry I'm a bit late,' the woman says. 'There was a hold-up on the beach road. There's been an accident, ambulances and police cars everywhere.'

She stops and looks around her. 'What fantastic paintings,' she says. 'Are these yours?'

'Yes, the ones I decided not to sell.'

'They are wonderful,' the woman says. She crosses the room to look at the one Nancy painted of the lighthouse at Fuengirola. 'They are so vibrant. The colour of the sea is extraordinary.'

'Someone drowned,' Nancy says.

The woman looks bewildered. 'Here?' she asks, pointing to the painting.

'No. This morning.'

Nancy locks the door behind Ana, then walks to the window. 'I saw it all from here,' she explains.

The crowd of people on the beach has dispersed, either from boredom or moved on by the *Guardia Civil*. The ambulance is still there, its doors open, the paramedics in their yellow jackets bustling about. Was the swimmer rescued, she wonders. What about the other one, the one fighting for breath? Is his body now drifting with the current only to be tossed up later on another golden beach?

'There were two of them,' she tells Ana. 'I think one drowned.'

'That's terrible. You saw it all from up here?'

The young woman's English is perfect, and she seems to appreciate art. She will do well, Nancy thinks. 'Would you like some tea?' she asks.

'No, thank you. I've just had breakfast. Would you like me to make you a cup?'

Surprised, Nancy snaps, 'I'm quite capable of making myself a cup of tea, thank you.' As if to collaborate her statement the kettle begins to boil.

'Sorry, I didn't mean it like that. I thought maybe you'd like to get your notes together before we get started,' Ana says, blushing with embarrassment.

'Oh. Well, don't take any notice of me. It's my son's fault. He makes me so defensive, always fussing around me. He has me only a step away from going into the funny farm.'

She sees the girl frown. 'Funny farm?'

'A mental home, a place for old women who've lost their marbles.' To help the girl understand, Nancy says, 'He thinks I should be in a home where I'll be cared for twenty-four hours a day. Then he would have a clear conscience and wouldn't have to come round to check up on me all the time.'

She knows this sounds ungrateful but she can't help it. Martin cannot understand how she needs her freedom. If she went into one of those places she would wither and die. She saw what happened to her own mother, and she doesn't want that to happen to her.

'I expect he wants the best for you.'

'No doubt about it. He brought me a glossy brochure of one of those "Residences of the Third Age" as they euphemistically call them. "Third Age"? I ask you! What are the other two ages, I wonder? Does anyone ever refer to the "First Age" or "Second Age"—apart from Tolkien that is? Of course not! And why stop at third? Why not fourth or fifth? Why not final? Or why not leave it as the good old "old age" everyone is familiar with? With luck, we know that will come to every one of us.'

She pours a little hot water into the teapot and swills it round before tipping it down the sink.

Cautiously, Ana asks, 'What is it like, the home?'

'Expensive. Luxurious. Martin is not one to be mean with money. "*El Paraíso*" it is called—"Paradise." My God, it wasn't *my* idea of paradise. Swimming pools, tennis courts, massage parlours, nursing staff on call—the only people under seventy are the staff. And, of course, there are social activities, designed to keep the inmates, if not happy, at least docile. Karaoke nights, bingo, musical evenings—not Beethoven and Bach, mind you. No—Barry Manilow and Perry Como. They alone could finish you off. I told Martin that if he put me in one of those homes I'd save up all my sleeping tablets and take an overdose.'

Nancy smiles. She can see that Ana doesn't know whether to laugh or look shocked.

'Don't worry, my dear. I'm not suicidal. I just like my personal space, and I mean to keep it.'

Nancy measures two spoonfuls of tea into the pot and pours in some hot water, stirring it briskly.

'Sure you don't want a cup?' she asks.

Ana shook her head.

'Right. Well, let's get started then, shall we? Where do you want to sit, on the sofa or at the table?'

The girl looks at the overloaded table. 'Don't worry about that,' Nancy says, 'I'll make a space.'

She piles the books at one end and sweeps the newspapers onto the floor, creating a small island on the shiny oak table top where they can work.

'Where shall I begin?' Nancy asks her visitor.

'Like all good stories, at the beginning,' Ana says with a light laugh.

Nancy warms to her. She is going to enjoy working with this woman.

CHAPTER 2

Andrew is already at home when Ana returns. He is in the kitchen, preparing their lunch. She can smell the fish as she comes through the door.

'Is that you, Ana?' he calls. 'You're late.'

She checks her watch. 'Not quite, still ten minutes to go,' she says kissing his cheek. 'That looks good.' She picks up a spoon and dips it into the fish stew, blowing to cool it before she tastes. It's delicious, and she tells him so.

'Make yourself useful and open some wine,' he says.

'Not for me, I've got to work this afternoon,' she tells him. 'I want to write up my notes while it's all fresh in my mind.'

'All the more for me then.'

Andrew likes his wine at lunchtime. He's not an excessive drinker, she tells herself, he just enjoys it.

It is too cold to eat outside on the terrace, so she throws a cloth over the kitchen table and sets out spoons and forks. He has already cut the bread into thick chunks, which she now puts in the bread basket in the middle of the table, then pours herself a large glass of water.

'The wine's in the fridge,' he says.

It's a Rueda, not her favourite, but Andrew likes it. The old lady likes her wine, too. She had pulled out a bottle at the end of their session. They both deserved a glass, she'd said. Ana declined, though she certainly felt it was true. It had not been easy interviewing Nancy. She kept wandering off the subject and forgetting what she was talking about. Then, when her cleaning lady arrived, she became quite paranoid about the woman, dropping her voice to a whisper every time she came near them, so Ana could not make out what Nancy was saying. Thank goodness she'd had the foresight to take her digital recorder with her, but even that had not been straightforward. 'Why is it necessary to tape me?' Nancy wanted to know. 'Who would hear it? Would Martin hear it?' It had taken Ana half an hour to convince Nancy there was nothing sinister about her actions, she was just trying to be efficient, to make life easier for them both.

'So how did it go?' Andrew asks, putting on the table two steaming bowls of *abacá de pescado*, a recipe he picked up when he was living in Cádiz.

'It's going to be hard work,' Ana tells him. 'She's very old and her memory is not as good as it should be.'

Andrew helps himself to a chunk of bread. 'Sometimes old people remember their past much better than they remember what they did that morning,' he says. 'It'll work out fine.'

He pours himself a large glass of the cold white wine while Ana sips her water.

'How much is she going to pay you?' he asks.

'We didn't talk about it,' she says. 'I expect it will be the usual rate.'

'So not enough to pay off our debts?'

'Maybe. It's too soon to say.'

Money is very tight at the moment. Ana had tried to plan her career wisely. With a degree in English Literature and an MA in Modern Languages it should have been easy to find work, but then the economic crisis hit, and there were no jobs to be had. She moved from Badajoz to the Costa del

Sol thinking she could put her language skills to use as a bilingual translator in a part of her country that boasted the highest percentage of foreigners. But though she was fluent in English, relatively fluent in Russian, which she had learned to cater to the recent influx of wealthy, sun-seeking Russians, and passably so in French and German, work has been all but impossible to find. All she has managed to get in recent months is a job teaching English to a couple of teenagers whose interest in the language is limited to translating pop songs, and a few days' work as a bi-lingual hostess at a big conference in Marbella. When her friend telephoned to say that she knew someone who needed a ghost writer, Ana had at first hesitated, protesting that it was a while since she had done anything like that, but then agreed, spurred on by the electric company's final demand that dropped into their letter box that morning.

Andrew is doing what he can but, as she discovered soon after their relationship started, he is not a very ambitious man. In England, he had worked as a bank clerk, a solid, steady job for which he was totally unsuited. On a whim he had given his notice, cancelled the lease on his flat in central London, and decided to tour the world. In fact, he got only as far as Spain, but he spent those first three years of freedom back-packing from the Pyrenees to Cádiz, where he met Ana. They have lived together now for almost a year, moving from Cádiz, first to Seville and then to Marbella. Sometimes she feels he still has itchy feet, and she lives with the sensation that one morning he will calmly tell her that he is on the move again. She doesn't know how she will react if that day ever comes.

'Are you working tonight?' she asks him.

'At nine o'clock,' he answers.

He is currently serving behind the bar in an Irish pub in Puerto Banús. The pay isn't very good, barely over the minimum wage she guesses, but the tips are generous. It restricts their social life somewhat as he is never home before three or four in the morning and doesn't surface until midday. Which is why it is usually Andrew who cooks the lunch.

'So who is this woman? Is she famous?' Andrew asks, helping himself to more wine.

'She's a painter. Watercolours. You may have heard of her, Nancy Miller. She's pretty good. She's had exhibitions all over the world: Paris, New York, Madrid. For a while, back in the eighties everyone was talking about her.'

'Did she tell you that?'

'I Googled her. According to what I read, she is very talented. Even while she was still at art school, she was selling her paintings. Then she managed to get her work into one of those posh galleries in London and never looked back.'

'If she's so famous why is she asking you to write her memoirs?'

Ana smiles. Andrew's outspokenness never ceases to amaze her.

'I was recommended,' she says. 'As it turns out, my friend Jenny is the niece of Nancy's agent—it was his idea that she write her memoirs.'

'So, jobs for the boys, then?'

She ignores him and takes more bread. 'She's an old woman, you know, and it seems she's reluctant to talk to anyone about her life, so her son said he wanted someone who would be sympathetic to her. Apparently she's become something of a recluse in the last few years, and her health's not too good. That's one reason why he wants his mother to write something soon, while she's still up to it.'

'So, what is she like? A batty, old woman with more money than she knows what to do with?'

'Not at all. She's articulate, and though she seems a bit frail, I wouldn't say she was ill. She's just getting old and a bit forgetful.'

'English, isn't she? Where's she from exactly?'

'Wallingford, in the Thames Valley. Do you know it?'

'Not really.'

Andrew is from Northumberland, near the Scottish border. He speaks disparagingly of all those who live in the south.

'You should see her flat' Ana tells him. 'It's amazing. Paintings cover every inch of the walls and they're all hers. She's even got them hanging in the loo. It's like living in an art gallery. They're stunning; I can understand why she's so famous.'

'Nice apartment is it?'

'Not really. It's not even as big as this place, but you can see she's been used to a better life style. The furniture is solid oak and much too large for such a small flat. The rugs are Persian—silk—but worn and stained, now. There are beautiful mirrors on the walls and bits of sculpture doubling as bookends. Books and magazines are littered all over the place. Everywhere you look it's a complete mess, but somehow it has style.'

'No painting things? Easel? Brushes?'

'I didn't see any. Maybe she has a studio somewhere else. I'll have to ask her.'

'Perhaps she's given it up.'

Ana wipes round her bowl with the remaining piece of bread.

'She's quite old, so you could be right.'

'Do you want some more *pescado*?'

'No, that was lovely,' she tells him. 'Now for coffee and a siesta.'

When Ana wakes, the flat is quiet. No sign of Andrew. Then she remembers he is playing paddle tennis this afternoon with a friend. She stretches and for a moment just lies there looking at the sunshine streaming through the half-closed blinds and crisscrossing the marble floor. The room is simple, with plain white walls and a fitted wardrobe at one end. It is rented, so she has never had the inclination to stamp it with her own personality. Who knows how long they will be there? The only additions she has made were a supersize duvet and a cover in electric blue—that, and she'd exchanged the crucifix that hung above the bed for a Picasso print.

Ana's thoughts turn back to the morning. It had gone well for a first session with a rather eccentric old woman, but there is something about Nancy that disturbs her. She seems somehow frightened of something or someone. That business about María was ridiculous. Is it a symptom of her age? Is it because her memory isn't as good as it once was? Or is it just an act for Ana's benefit? Ana sits up and routs in her bag for the recorder. They hadn't started at the beginning, Nancy had launched straight into talking about her painting. Ana sets the recorder to play:

'I've always loved painting, ever since I was a small child,' Nancy begins. *'I knew that was what I wanted to do,*

go to art school. My father thought it was a ridiculous idea but my mother was very supportive.'

Ana recalls how she had stopped to pick up a sepia photograph of a young woman.

'This was my mother. She was a romantic, always telling me tales about her past, about strange happenings in our family, and spirits that had appeared to her in dreams. I loved listening to her.'

There is a pause, then Nancy's voice continues:

'She said we all have a spirit guide, even my father, although she said he closed his eyes to it and that his spirit guide must have been very frustrated with him. She was so pleased that her daughter was artistic. She said that my spirit guide had chosen that path for me. I don't know whether she was right or not, but I knew I was never happier than when I was immersed in painting something.'

'Tell me about art school,' Ana's voice asks.

'What can I say? Let me show you some of my paintings instead. Do you know anything about art, my dear?'

'Not really.'

'Well, I will have to teach you.'

Ana hates the sound of her own voice coming out of the machine. She can hear her Spanish accent shushing its way across the English consonants despite the fact that she had spent every summer in England since she was thirteen. Her mother, whose brother had married an English woman, was insistent that her children learn to speak English. She was a forward thinking woman who realized how her country was changing. She knew her children would need many new skills to compete, and speaking English was one of them. So Ana and her sister spent every summer in a small village in Suffolk, learning the language.

Ana presses the pause button. It is time to start writing. She pulls out her laptop and begins. She is still typing when Andrew, hot and sweaty, returns from his match.

CHAPTER 3

Nancy pours herself a second glass of wine and settles in her favourite spot, on the sofa by the window. From here she can watch the world go by. Below her, people are returning to work. Shops that have been closed for lunch are raising their blinds and unlocking their doors. A group of school children are dawdling along the promenade, stopping every so often to check their mobile phones and compare messages. Their school bags hang from their shoulders or are dragged along the ground behind them. Two young lads on bicycles speed past them, shouting something that causes the children to momentarily scatter, then regroup as quickly as a school of fish. A man stoops to pick up his dog's faeces and place it in a black bag. She sees that a lot. Many people walk their dogs along this stretch. She wishes she still had a dog. Nowadays she feels invisible when she goes out, which isn't very often. Nobody notices an old woman. That's what she should do, buy herself a dog. A big beautiful black dog, one nobody could ignore. Then she'd have heads turning again. Then she would no longer be invisible.

Two women come out of the ice cream shop, eating ice cream cones and giggling like teenagers, although they must be middle-aged, the pair of them. Nancy finds her binoculars in their usual place by the window and focuses them on the horizon. A yacht is making its way back to harbour, heading for Puerto Banús. She cannot make out the name on its side but it's a big, expensive vessel with red sails. She wonders about the owner. Is he someone famous? An actor for example, or a politician. Maybe a pop star or a film director, maybe a bull fighter, maybe an Arab prince. They all come to Marbella, the rich and the famous, they buy expensive houses on exclusive housing estates, they moor their boats in the marina at Puerto Banús, they eat in the best restaurants, they drive Mercedes and Ferraris, they wear Cartier and Bulgari, their clothes are from Armani, Steve McQueen, Stella McCartney, and above all, they make a grand display of their wealth. That's what it's all about, in a world where everyone is rich and famous, letting the world know just how rich and famous you are. Nobody in this town hides their light under a bushel.

The yacht disappears from view. Nancy swings the binoculars on a group of swimmers, northern Europeans most certainly—it's only the foreigners who swim in this weather. A small group of people on the beach enjoy the last rays of the afternoon sunshine. They are there every day. She sees them arrive, usually about four o'clock. They look like Germans or Scandinavians, and none of them is young. They swim, no matter what the weather, then they sit on the beach and chat. The seagulls have decided it's time to rest. The fishing boats are back on shore, and there is no more opportunity for snatching up scraps from the nets. The gulls fly in, a noisy cloud of flapping wings and high-pitched cries, and land on the beach, all facing the same way. She thinks she might paint that scene one day. She likes painting birds, especially seagulls. They are greedy birds but brave and determined. They know what they want, and they go for it.

The sun is warm through the glass. Nancy is sleepy, but each time she closes her eyes something begins to worry her. She cannot remember exactly what she has told the writer woman. What did she say to her? Next time she comes, she must ask her to let her listen to the tape—if it is a tape, these days. Probably not. Probably some digital apparatus. She shuts her eyes. It's time she did some more painting. It's a long time since she painted anything worthwhile. They probably think she doesn't have it in her anymore. She's sure that's Martin's opinion. 'Take it easy, Mother,' that's what he's always saying to her. If only he knew what she had done for him. But he doesn't, and it's better that way.

Her mind begins to drift on a cloud of sunshine and wine. Such a long time ago. Water under the bridge.

It was 1957 when she fell in love, summertime. They were just about to take their end of year exams and then everyone would go their separate ways until September.

Nancy's class had finished early that day. Toby, their watercolour teacher, had a staff meeting, something to do with funding for a field trip he was planning. He had this idea of hiring two barges and taking the group through the Loire the following Easter. It sounded like a wonderful trip but she wasn't sure she would be able to afford it as her grant was very small and she couldn't ask her father for any more money.

'Hey, Ginger, where are you off to?'

It was that gangly youth who was doing a BA in Sculpture, always hanging around their class. Now what did he want?

'We're finished for the day. Toby's got a meeting,' she said.

'So you've time for a coffee then?' he said, with a grin.

'I suppose so.'

She followed him down the corridor and out into the light drizzle that had started to fall from a sky heavy with clouds. She was bored, otherwise she wouldn't have agreed to a coffee with him as she hardly knew him and she hated being called Ginger. Her dark auburn hair was cut short in the elfin style favoured by Audrey Hepburn. People occasionally remarked how much she looked like the film star. She had the same oval face and delicate bone structure and she would have dyed her hair black if she thought she could do it without her father knowing.

'Got anything planned for the holidays?' the youth asked her.

'No, just the usual, home to Mum and Dad. You?'

'I'm off to France with Nick and a few of the others.'

'Really?' She felt a pang of envy at this news but struggled not to show it.

'You could come with us. It'd be nice to have some girls along. We're taking the train down to the south of France and finding somewhere to camp.'

That sounded even better. She'd never been abroad. The farthest she'd been was Cardiff, on holiday with her parents when they went to visit her aunt.

'My dad would never allow it,' she said. 'But thanks for the offer.'

Anyway, they probably would expect her to do all the cooking and cleaning. Boys never did anything for themselves. Her own brother was a pain in that respect, and what was worse, her mother supported him. It was always Nancy who had to clear the table and wash the dishes, either because Ted wouldn't make a good job of it, or Ted had too much homework, or worst of all, it wasn't a man's job to wash the dishes. Her brother came up with that one.

The café was crowded. Half the campus seemed to have descended on the place. The atmosphere was dense with cigarette smoke, and wet coats dripped onto the black and white tiled floor. A boy she recognised from her class had his sketch pad out and was surreptitiously drawing the waitress, a pretty blonde who was desperately trying to clear away the dirty cups and saucers.

'Over here, Joe,' someone called from a table in the corner, one arm raised, waving at them.

She recognised the faces, all of them students at the college.

'Sit down,' someone said and pushed up leaving a small space on the end of the banquette for Nancy to squeeze into, while Joe grabbed a chair from another table and sat down next to her.

'So, who is this, Joe? A new girlfriend?' one of the students asked. He had a craggy face and bright blue eyes that stared at her intensely. He waved his cigarette at her and said, 'I've seen you before. You're one of the painters, aren't you?'

She felt herself blushing—his eyes seemed to be burning right through her.

'You know she is, she's the one you're always going on about, saying what a great arse she's got,' said Joe, his grin malicious.

Nancy was grateful for her voluminous duster coat, which was big enough that nobody could check if Joe's comments were true or not.

'Well introduce us then,' Blue Eyes continued.

'My name's Nancy,' she replied. 'And no, I'm not his girlfriend, although I don't see what business it is of yours.'

'A girl with spirit. Wow, I like that.'

'Pack it up, Nick. You're embarrassing her,' one of the other students said. He turned to her and held out his hand. 'I'm Kelly. We're all from the faculty of Three Dimensional Arts; in other words, sculpture. Budding Michaelangelos, every one of us.'

'Pleased to meet you,' she said, returning his handshake.

He had a soft Irish accent and a twinkle in his eye; his handshake was warm and firm. He brushed a lock of wet hair out of his eyes. 'We're planning our trip to France.'

'Yes, Joe told me about it,' she replied, looking to the gangly youth for confirmation.

'I bet he asked you to join us, didn't he? He's desperate for us to take some girls along, but so far he's had no takers, only his sister. Can't say I'm surprised. What girl in her right mind would want to go to the south of France with this lot? It'll be a month of sweaty socks and tinned beans,' Kelly said.

Blue Eyes was still looking at her. She could feel his stare eating into her. 'Don't listen to him,' he said at last. 'It will be a wonderful experience. They say the light in Provence is marvellous for painting. Come with us. I promise you won't have to wash any sweaty socks and I, for one, don't intend to eat baked beans.'

She shook her head. 'I don't have any money.'

'I've seen you working in the newsagents. Don't they pay you?'

'Of course they pay me, but that's to last me all next term. I can't spend it on a holiday. Anyway, my parents are expecting me home for the hols.'

'What a pity. And I always thought artists were free spirits.'

Maybe it was the reference to 'free spirits' that did it. Or maybe it was that the feeling of boredom had lifted now, in the presence of these young men. Maybe it was his eyes, still holding her captive. Suddenly she felt the need to do something reckless. The prospect of two months at home with her parents and her brother was bleak by comparison.

'Okay. Tell me more about your plans,' she said, not realizing those few words were about to change her life forever.

Nancy never told her parents the whole truth; she only said she was going to Provence with an art group. That part was true. She let them believe that Toby was organising it and that they were going by train and staying in a small hostel. 'It's very cheap,' she told them. 'I won't need a lot of money.' Much to her delight and shame, her father gave her £10 to pay for her train fare. Naturally they wanted an address and she readily obliged, taking one from an old guide book borrowed from the library.

She packed her paints and brushes into the bottom of her brother's rucksack, added the minimum of clothes, and a pair of stout shoes. She applied for a passport, took her savings out of the Post Office, and she was ready. She confided to her friend, Helen, that she was going with a group of sculptors but again managed to give the impression that it was an organised trip run by the college.

Her tutor had often spoken to them about Provence and the painter Van Gogh, so she asked him to tell her about the area. He caught her excitement and introduced her to the work of Matisse, Renoir and Cézanne, all of whom had loved the French Riviera and spent many of their most productive years there. The more she found out about where she was going, the more excited she became. The prospect of travelling abroad, painting in the same place as so many famous artists had before her, filled her with such delight that it bubbled away inside her until she thought she would explode.

There is a loud banging on Nancy's door, and someone is ringing the bell, insistently. For a moment she doesn't know where she is—she thinks she is back in the bed-sit, and Nick is clamouring for her to let him in.

'Mama, are you in there? It's Martin. Open the door.'

Martin? Martin, she cannot recall a Martin at college. Then it comes to her—it's her son. What's he doing coming round at this hour? And why is he making such a racket? He'll disturb the neighbours. Now she'll have that nosey German, Herr Braun, coming round to moan at her again. She gets up and smooths her skirt into place. There's a damp patch down the front where she must have spilled her glass of wine. Yes, there's the glass on the floor. How stupid of her. Thank goodness it was white wine. Nobody will notice.

'Mama.'

'All right Martin, I'm coming.'

Nancy unbolts the door and lets her son into the flat.

'I've told you before, Mama, it's not a good idea to bolt your door from the inside. What if something happens to you? How can anyone get in to help you?'

'I don't need any help. Anyway you're always telling me to be safe.'

She wanders back to the sofa, still feeling a bit woozy. It doesn't do to be woken up suddenly like that. She tells him so.

'Why are you here anyway?' she asks ungraciously.

'I wanted to see how you are. Sara sent you some homemade biscuits.' He puts a plastic box on the table and says, 'They're ginger biscuits. You like those, don't you?'

She nods and opens the box. 'I must have dozed off,' she says, biting into one of the biscuits.

'María says you haven't been eating much lately,' he says, staring at the wet patch on her skirt.

He thinks I've wet myself. Nancy chuckles. He'll be bringing me incontinent pads next.

'What's so funny?' her son asks.

She can see him struggling to remain calm. She knows she irritates him, but she can't help it. If only he wouldn't treat her like an imbecile.

'Nothing really. María's lying. I do eat. I made myself a *tortilla de patata* yesterday. She just says that because I don't eat what she brings me. Awful stuff. I think she's trying to poison me.'

'Mama, how can you say that? She's a good woman, who's just trying to do her best.'

'Mama,' he still calls her that, just like when he was a little boy. She looks at him suddenly with affection. What a lovely child he was. She really ought to make more of an effort to be nice to him.

'She only wants what's good for you. We all do.' Martin says, wandering across to the kitchen area and opening the fridge. The *tortilla* is still there, with only a tiny square of it removed.

'I'm going to have some more tonight for my supper.' She knows exactly what her son is thinking.

He closes the fridge door and comes to sit beside her.

'Have you thought any more about *La Residencia El Paraíso*?' He bends down to pick up the wine glass from the floor.

'I'll go to paradise when I'm dead and not before,' she snaps.

'But Mother, it's a wonderful place. There's plenty to do, and you'd have company. Look at you. You're stuck in this flat on your own all day long. If it weren't for María, you'd see no one.'

'That's not true. Herr Braun comes round sometimes.' She doesn't say that it is usually to ask her to turn the television down. 'And there's the woman upstairs, the Danish one. She often knocks at my door. Anyway I'm too busy now with my memoirs.'

'Oh yes, your memoirs.'

He has that patient look on his face as though he is talking to a child.

'I'm sure that young woman wouldn't mind visiting you at *El Paraíso;* it's only five minutes away.'

'You don't think I'll finish them, do you?'

'I didn't say that.'

'You didn't have to. I can hear it in your tone. You never could hide your feelings about anything, even as a child. You think I'm mad to have started them, don't you?'

'That's not true. If it gives you something to do, then it's a great idea. I just want you to be happy, Mama.'

'Well, stop trying to lock me away in a home with a lot of old biddies. I haven't got time for it.'

Her son puts his arm around her and hugs her.

'I just want what's best, Mama. I don't want anything to happen to you, and here you're stuck all alone, with no one to help you. Please tell me you'll at least consider it.'

He is remembering the time she had those chest pains and the doctor told him she had a slight heart murmur. That was years ago, but he has been expecting her to have a heart attack ever since.

'That place is too expensive,' she mutters. 'Anyway, I'm as fit as a fiddle. Nothing is going to happen to me.'

'I can afford it, Mama. Don't worry about the money. Just say you'll think about it.'

She looks at him. To think her little boy is a doctor now, an important man, well-respected and adored by the parents of the children he treats. But to her he will always be her little Martin, her little songbird—that's what she used to call him. 'Come here my little bird, my little songbird,' she would say, because he was always singing, scraps he heard on the radio, songs he learnt at school or things their Spanish neighbours taught him. She remembers the look on his face when he realized the birds nesting in the porch and making such a mess over the front step were martins. His namesakes. How he fluttered and swooped around the garden pretending to be one of them. He was such a happy child. She never could refuse him anything.

Nancy nods, suggesting she will think about it, although she has no intention of doing so, and says, 'Now let me get on. I want to go through the photograph albums tonight.

Ana asked me for some photos of us when we were younger.'

'I'll get them for you.'

He hauls the albums out of her cupboard and places them on the coffee table, then sits down again beside her.

'I haven't seen these photos for years,' he says. 'Look, is that really me? God, how skinny I was. And those glasses––I look a complete nerd.' He laughs and turns the page. 'I haven't seen this one before.' He slips the photo out of its mount and brings it closer to his face. 'It's a bit out of focus. Is that you?'

She takes it from him and puts it back without looking at it. 'That was a long time ago. We were all students at Kingston,' she says dismissively.

He picks it up again. He seems intrigued. 'But where is it? Are you camping?'

'I told you, it was one summer a long time ago. We all went to Juan-les-Pins, and camped on the beach. Yes, that's me, there.' Reluctantly, she points to the girl in the back row. She thought she had thrown that photograph out, years ago.

'So who's the man? The one with his arm around you?'

'Oh, I don't remember any of their names now.' She snatches it back. 'It doesn't matter anyway. Ana won't want to see that one.'

'I disagree,' Martin says. 'I think that's exactly the sort of detail she will be looking for.' But he turns the page anyway.

'Would you like a drink?' she asks him. She takes an opened bottle of wine from the fridge.

'Just a small one, I'm driving.'

He lets out a chuckle. 'I remember this one,' he says, pointing to another of the photos. 'This was when you took me to the zoo and that bloody peacock chased me. I must have been about three then.'

'Two,' she says.

As she looks at it, the years just melt away. Her little darling, standing there with a tear-stained face and his lovely blond curls flopping over his eyes, blood dripping down his leg from where he had tripped. It was the only time he'd been to the zoo.

'Look, I've got a peacock feather in my hand,' he says.

'Yes, that's why the bird was chasing you. You had just pulled it out. It was your own fault.'

'So who took the picture?' he asks.

'I don't remember. A friend, probably.'

Martin looks at his watch. 'I'm sorry, Mama, I've got to go. I promised Sara I'd pick her up from work.' He drinks his wine quickly and bends to kiss her. 'I'll pop round tomorrow if you like, and we'll look at some more photos,' he suggests.

'If you like.'

'Now lock up behind me.' There is no mention this time of the bolts. 'See you tomorrow, then.'

'Bye, Martin, drive carefully.'

Nancy locks and bolts the door behind him. So he wants to look at more photos tomorrow. Well, now she will have to go through the albums carefully to make sure there are no more photographs that shouldn't be there; she doesn't feel up to going through long explanations with her son. He probably wouldn't believe her anyway.

CHAPTER 4

Ana waits patiently while Nancy unbolts the door and lets her in. It is stifling inside; the air is stale and smells of bodily odours that she doesn't want to explore.

'Hello, Nancy,' she says. 'How are you today?'

'Come in, my dear. Just let me lock up behind you.'

Nancy goes through the usual routine, then joins her on the sofa.

'Do you think we could open a window?' Ana asks, taking her fan from her handbag and fanning herself energetically.

'Are you hot, my dear?' she asks, surprised.

'A little.'

'Of course.'

She opens one of the windows a mere crack.

'I don't want any draughts,' she tells her. 'My son would be annoyed if I caught a chill.'

'No, that's fine. Just a little fresh air.'

Ana takes the newspaper from her bag and says, 'I thought you might like to see this; it's about that accident that you saw the other day. You were right, there was another swimmer. His body washed up on a beach near Estepona. Quite battered, apparently.'

'All that way. Well fancy,' Nancy replies, taking the newspaper from Ana's outstretched hand. 'I told you I saw another one, didn't I.'

She glances at the paper and, as she hands it back, she mutters something that sounds like 'The dead always turn up, eventually.'

'What was that?' Ana asks and when Nancy doesn't reply she continues, 'They were holiday-makers, apparently. English.'

She thinks Nancy will be interested but the old woman is flicking through a large notebook. She has been writing down her memories, she tells her.

'I thought I'd put everything down; then we can go more quickly,' she says.

'That's an excellent idea,' says Ana. 'So what do you have for me today?'

It is disappointing. Nancy has covered three pages with an untidy scrawl that is difficult to read, so she hands the notebook back to her and says, 'Why don't you use it to remind you, and we'll carry on as before, recording what you tell me.'

Nancy looks a little disappointed at this but nods anyway.

'So where did we leave off?' Ana says. 'You were telling me about your paintings, weren't you? When did you have your first exhibition?'

She sits back and smiles encouragingly at Nancy.

'Not for some years. I was quite old before I had a proper exhibition, one of my own, that is,' Nancy replies. 'I'd had my work displayed in the college end-of-year exhibition and sold some while I was still studying, but it wasn't until I came to Spain that I had my own exhibition.'

'Really. How did that come about?'

She had imagined that Nancy's career had started in England, but here she is telling her that she was living in Spain before she became famous.

'You've heard of the Marbella Club?' Nancy asks.

'Of course.'

'Well, I'd been selling a few paintings through a small gallery in the town, just to holiday makers and a few of the locals, nothing much. Still, it helped to pay the bills. Then a friend said to me that I should talk to the manager of the Marbella Club, that he often had local work on display. So I took some of my best work and went along to see him. He was a charming man. Didn't know a thing about painting, but he said I could display them in the foyer for a couple of weeks.'

She smiles at Ana. 'Isn't it strange how something can hang on one chance circumstance? It was August, and it just happened that this well-known American art critic was in Marbella on holiday. He and his family went for dinner one evening to the Marbella Club. He saw my work and fell in love with it. Just like that. After that, it was a roller coaster of exhibitions and interviews. Some of the best galleries in the country wanted my paintings. The little gallery in Marbella, which had reluctantly stocked my work, was now desperate to buy it. A painting by Nancy Miller had become *de rigueur* for the wealthy Marbella socialite.'

'As easy as that?'

'I suppose so. I was told to get myself an agent, which seemed a bit excessive at the time but, looking back, I could never have managed without Harry.'

'What about the Marbella Club?'

'I'm grateful to the manager for giving me that opportunity. There's still one of my paintings hanging in the main dining room, a view over the bay. I presented it to the club the day my first exhibition opened in London. I often think how different my life would have been if it hadn't been for that manager.'

'But someone else would have discovered you, surely.'

'Not necessarily. I'm not conceited enough to think my work would have made its own way to the top. After all, there I was in southern Spain, miles from the cultural centres of the world, working alone, trying to make a living. What were the chances of my paintings being noticed? Very slim. I was just lucky.'

'And you never looked back?'

'I suppose not. My paintings sell particularly well in the States,' she adds, passing a glossy brochure to Ana. It is dated August 2000.

'The Millennium Exhibition?' Ana reads. 'Have you had any exhibitions since then?'

She knows that this was Nancy's last big success. She has read the reviews on the internet but wants to get Nancy's reaction.

'I'm retired now.'

'So you don't paint anymore?'

'Would you like some wine?' Nancy asks. 'Or maybe some tea? You like tea, don't you? My Martin likes tea— strong, with two sugars.' Her concentration is wavering, and Ana realizes she will have to let her rest a bit.

'I'd love a cup of tea,' she replies, 'and then maybe we could look at those photos you've been promising to show me.'

Ana pours herself some coffee and sits down at her computer. This writing project is a lot harder than she had imagined. She tries to write in Nancy's voice, but Nancy wanders off the point all the time. She rambles and then stops, forgetting where she is and what she's talking about, then off she goes again on a completely different tangent. Ana has to separate Nancy's thoughts and try to put them in a coherent form. Well, she had been warned about it.

When her friend Jenny telephoned to say Nancy was looking for a ghostwriter, she had told her that the artist had a problem with her memory. 'A tad forgetful,' she said. 'Nancy Miller's a very interesting woman. Lived here for years, one of the original ex-pats on the Costa del Sol. She moved here when Marbella was not much more than a village, you know. Anyway, my uncle Harry is—was—her agent. He has the idea that she ought to write her autobiography, but he knows that she can't do it alone. She's nearly eighty. He sent me an email last week to ask if I knew anyone in the area who would be able to ghostwrite it for her. So I immediately thought of you. You've nothing on at the moment, have you?'

What could she say? Jenny knew she was out of work. This had come along just in time. If she or Andrew didn't earn some money soon, they'd have to move out of the flat.

Ana switches on her digital recorder and sits back to listen.

'*So how many children do you have, Nancy?*' her own voice asks.

'*Just the one, Martin. He was born in 1961.*'

Nancy had checked in her notebook to give her that information, then pulled out a photo of a small boy with tousled hair and a sunhat.

'*And your husband?*' Ana had asked. '*What was his name?*'

Nancy had avoided the question. Instead she asked Ana, *'Would you like to see some more photos of Martin? He was a lovely boy. Never any trouble, you know.'*

So, she doesn't want to talk about the father. Ana flicks back through her notes. 1961. The boy must have been conceived around the time Nancy left art school. Not the thing in those days if you weren't married. Still, it's 2014 now; people won't care if she had been married or not. Ana has lots of friends who live with their partners, with no intention of ever getting married. It doesn't stop them having babies. It's a bit odd though, Nancy had given her the impression that they were quite a bohemian lot at the art college. She would have expected her to come right out with the fact that she'd had a child out of wedlock. Did she think Ana would be shocked?

'Any coffee in the pot?' Andrew is dressed for work in black trousers and a white shirt. His dark blond hair is sleeked back off his forehead and he has shaved. There's no mistaking that he's a foreigner, a typical Englishman, her mother had said when she first met him. Ana has never been sure exactly what she meant. Perhaps that his skin was so fair that it turned pink every time he stepped out into the sun, or his eyes so blue he even wore sunglasses in winter. Ana presses the pause button on the digital recorder.

'Yes, help yourself. I want to get this finished.'

'Problems?'

'Not really, but it's a lot more difficult than I thought it would be. It's okay when she's talking about her painting, but she gets really vague when I ask her for personal details. Sometimes I wonder if she's having second thoughts about writing it.'

'Well don't let her change her mind. If she's as rich as you say she is, this is a good opportunity for you to make some money out of her.'

'I never said Nancy was rich. I just said she was famous.'

'That's the same thing, isn't it?'

She shrugs. 'Maybe.'

'Well, you know we can't manage on the pittance that I earn. I don't know how they can get away with it—less than the minimum wage and no social security.'

'Employers know people are desperate, they'll work for anything,' she says.

'It's exploitation. I've been thinking of jacking it in and going on the dole.'

'Don't be stupid, Andrew. You know you won't get anything; you've already received all they are prepared to give you. Just stick it out until something better comes along. Things are bound to improve soon. They said on the news that the economy is on the upturn.'

'They've been saying that for a while, but unemployment is still rising. Nothing is going to get any better until they get rid of that government. We need a government that will stand up to those bloody bureaucrats in Brussels, not that load of thieves lining their own pockets all the time.'

Ana sighs. If Andrew gets started on politics, she will never get any work done.

'You'll be late,' she says, switching the machine back on.

Her boyfriend hurriedly drinks his coffee and bends down to kiss her cheek.

'I shouldn't be too late tonight.' His hand slides down her face and caresses her neck. 'Don't stay up all night, writing. It would be nice if you were awake occasionally when I get home.'

She smiles at him and nods. What is it that Nancy is saying? She presses rewind.

'Okay, darling, see you later,' she mutters.

The door closes behind him, and this time she listens carefully to her recording. '*I had to protect him. He was such a little chap, so vulnerable. Jealous. Unable to control it. Had to protect him.*'

Ana's own voice cuts in. '*Are you all right, Nancy? Would you like some water?*'

The old woman had drifted off into her own thoughts. Ana had been worried she was going to have a stroke or something, but then she smiled. '*No thanks, dear. I think I'll have a glass of wine. What about you? Would you like one?*'

So what had she meant? Who was jealous? The little boy? And who was he jealous of? Had she met a man? What had happened to her husband? She was going to have to ask her some straightforward questions, but would she get any straightforward answers?

CHAPTER 5

Nancy turns on the television. Whichever channel she switches to, it is the same. Everyone is talking about the king. Juan Carlos has decided to abdicate after forty years on the Spanish throne. She remembers when he became the king. How the people loved him then, him and his lovely Greek wife. He had saved the country from anarchy after Franco's demise. His was the voice of reason that steered the new democracy through its early years. He was a king to be proud of then. But things are changing. The old world is disappearing. A few months earlier, Suarez, the first democratically elected prime minister under the new regime, had died, and now the king is going, beset with poor health. Time for the old to bow out and make way for the younger generation, Nancy thinks. She puts the TV into mute, leans back and closes her eyes. So long ago.

They had stayed in Juan-les-Pins all summer, returning late September in time for the new term. It had been idyllic. She remembers the empty beaches and rocky coves where they had swum in water so clear and blue that you could see all the way to the bottom. They had scrambled over rocks, poking about in the seaweed, looking for crabs which they boiled in a bucket on a fire of driftwood. She had snorkelled for the first time ever, following schools of tiny bright fish as they darted to and fro among the rocks. She lazed in the sun until she was as brown as the locals, and drank too much cheap red wine. The only other female, Dorothy, was a pleasant, shy girl who would do anything for anyone, and it didn't take the boys long to realize that. She cooked and cleaned; she went to the market and shopped. Nobody offered to help her, but then neither did anyone ask her to do it. Everyone seemed to concur that she was paid help, but with no pay.

Nancy was too busy to worry about Dorothy; she was in love. She was in love with France, with the cloudless blue sky, with the soft, scented air, with the lazy Mediterranean sea, with the umbrella pines that lined the campsite, with the soft golden sand, with the white seagulls that perched on the telegraph poles and flocked behind the fishing boats as they returned to shore, but mostly she was in love with Nick. He told her she was beautiful, and every night, alone under the stars, he made love to her. He courted her and he spoiled her. He made sure they all knew she was his girl, and never before had she felt quite so special as during that brief summer. Nick laid claim to her from the moment they all met up at Victoria Station to catch the boat train to Paris.

'Sit here, next to me' he said as they bundled into the second-class carriages.

Obediently, she sat next to him, putting her rucksack on the rack next to his. That was the start, her big mistake. In doing what he wanted, she set a precedent that was to take her many years to break.

At first she was happy. The time in France made a great impression on her, and it began to show in her painting. Toby saw it straight away. He encouraged her to develop her own style, to work more freely. Suddenly, getting the degree dwindled in importance. What mattered—all that mattered—was the painting. It was as if love had opened her eyes to the world. The colours were brighter, the light more intense. She lost herself in a world of colour and form, painting with the passion of a madwoman, as if every brush stroke were to be her last.

Toby took the painting of a reclining nude from her easel and studied it closely. 'This is amazing,' he said. 'I'd say you lost your virginity this summer, Nancy.'

She blushed but didn't reply. Was it so transparent?

Toby grinned. 'Something certainly happened to you, young lady. Your work suddenly has so much maturity, so much clarity. It glows. Tell me, who is the lucky man?'

Her tutor waited for her to answer, but she wasn't going to tell him. Her love burned inside her, fuelling her painting with hope and promise. She couldn't speak of it to anyone. How could she put into words the feelings that over-whelmed her? She'd slept next to Nick on the train for twenty-four hours, her body leaning against his, on fire from his touch—so close to each other, and yet so far apart. How could she explain the urgency they had shared, just to get there, to be at last alone, free of their friends' watchful eyes? How could she admit the wait had only increased their passion, that when they were finally alone, just the two of them, lying on a deserted beach in Juan-les-Pins, she had given herself to him freely, without a moment's regret? If she put these feelings into words, the flames that warmed her heart might die, and she would be left with nothing more than the ashes of her memories. The love she felt when she lay in her lover's arms had transformed her, given her confidence, made her see the world through new eyes. That love freed something in her, something transmitted directly to her paintings. She no longer worried about technique and style, or tried to emulate the artists she admired. She was her own woman, now. And she painted what she felt.

Watching her, Toby realized she would keep her own counsel. 'I have arranged for you to put some of your pieces into the Spring Exhibition,' he told her. 'You've got plenty of time to prepare; it's not until March.'

She looked at him in amazement.

'Do you know who is coming to judge the exhibits?' he asked. 'Professor Ramsey of the Royal Academy. I think he'll be bowled over by your work.'

Nancy blushed with pleasure. This was an honour she had not expected. The eminent professor was going to be looking at her paintings. She couldn't wait to tell Nick the good news. When Toby moved on to another student, Nancy put down her brush and slipped out of the room.

The Department of Three-Dimensional Art was on the ground floor, and students often spilled outside into the courtyard to work. She knew that was where Nick would be, and sure enough, there he was, in his usual dusty brown overall, the sleeves of his shirt rolled up to his elbows. He was a strong man. The muscles in his forearms tensed as he lifted a block of wood onto the bench. He didn't notice her at first, he was so absorbed with his task. He was working on something that looked rather like a bird cage but was well over six feet tall.

'Hello,' she said, rather shyly. 'That's nice.'

He looked up, pushing his long, untidy blond hair back from his face.

'Hi there. What are you doing down here? Your class over?' he asked and kissed her on the lips.

'No, I just had to come and tell you my news. Toby's talking about putting some of my paintings in the Spring Exhibition.'

Nick shrugged and turned back to the bird cage. 'Good.'

Disappointment tugged at Nancy's stomach. 'Good?' she snapped. 'Is that all you can say, Nick? It's quite an honour, you know. And Professor Ramsey is one of the judges.'

She knew she sounded like a petulant child, but she didn't care. She'd thought he'd be pleased for her, that he'd realize how much this meant to her. Inclusion in the Spring Exhibition was a sign of merit.

'Oh well, why didn't you say?' Nick sneered, his voice heavy with sarcasm. 'If Ramsey RA is going to be there, then it must be an honour.'

'I thought you'd be happy for me,' Nancy whispered. He had never spoken to her in that tone before.

'I thought you were above such things,' Nick scoffed. 'It's just an exhibition. I thought it was the painting that mattered, not the acclaim.' His blue eyes were like steel, boring into her head.

'It *is* the painting that matters,' she protested. 'It's *always* the painting. It's just ...' Her voice trailed off. What was the point? The moment was ruined.

'I've got to get on,' Nick said. 'This has to be finished by lunchtime.'

She stared at the sculpture, a nest of twisted wire and wooden planks that looked anything but finished, but she made no comment. Nick did not appreciate criticism, especially from her. Nor did he appreciate her paintings, which he considered insufficiently avant-garde. 'Too bourgeois,' he described them.

'See you tonight?' she asked.

'Yeah. See you.'

It was a surprise when Nick asked Nancy to move in with him—she'd never even visited his flat. Sometimes when they wanted to be alone they would wait until Helen was out with her friends and then Nancy would take him back to her room. On other occasions, when the nights were warm, they would go to the park and find a quiet spot, or lie in the shadows under the footbridge to make love. One evening when they were walking along the river bank arm in arm, Nick suddenly stopped. 'It's silly, you paying for that bedsit,' he said. 'You're hardly ever there. Why don't you move in with me and save some money?'

At first she had been too surprised to answer. 'What about Joe?' she asked. 'I thought you shared with Joe?'

'Joe's leaving. His mum's ill so he's going back to Bristol. She's got cancer.'

'Oh, poor Joe. I didn't know. When is he going?'

'Tomorrow. So you can move in right away.'

'Oh.'

'What's the matter?'

'It's not as easy as that, Nick. Helen can't afford to pay the rent on her own.'

'She'll find someone else. Don't worry about it.'

'But what about my parents? They'll be furious if they discover I'm living in sin.'

'Living in sin? Good God, girl, is that what you think of me?'

'Of course not, but my parents are very old-fashioned.'

'Well, make sure they don't find out.'

Nancy hesitated. This wasn't what she wanted. She loved Nick, which was why she'd agreed to sleep with him. She'd calculated that her parents need never know, and one day she would tell them she and Nick were getting married. This new suggestion, that they just live together, came as a shock. Nick had talked of marriage, but never of them simply living together. Her heart was beating so loudly, she was sure he could hear it. What should she do? If she said no, she might lose him. If she said yes, she would have to lie to her parents.

'I don't like lying to my parents,' she said at last.

'Well don't. Tell them the truth. Unless, that is, you're ashamed of me? Maybe I'm not good enough for your family. Is that it? Council house scum, is that what you think of me?'

'No, of course not.'

'So why don't they know about me? Why haven't I ever met them?'

He pulled away and was facing her now, gripping her arms tightly.

'Stop it,' she said. 'You're hurting me.'

They stood close to the weir, and the noise as the river cascaded down to its next level was deafening. For a moment she felt frightened. There was something menacing in the way he looked at her, a harsh challenge in his voice.

'Well?' he asked.

She didn't answer but pulled away and continued to walk along the tow-path, unsure where this new turn of events was leading. A pair of geese, like some strange ghostly apparition, flew overhead, honking noisily. Nick followed behind, and they walked along in silence. 'Okay,' she said, at last. 'I'll tell Helen.'

'Good. When will you bring your stuff over?' His voice was once again light and welcoming.

'Whenever you want, but I'll need some help. I've got a lot of paintings and stuff.'

'Of course. I'll speak to Kelly. He's got a van. You can load it all into that. We'll do it on Saturday.'

Saturday? That was only two days away. Her mind was racing. Why the hurry? Why couldn't they wait until the end of the month?

'There's no point hanging about,' he said, sensing her hesitation.

'No, I suppose not.'

After all, it made sense. At the moment, they had very few opportunities to be alone, and when they were, she was always on edge in case someone caught them. Besides, she was tired of sneaking him into her room the moment Helen went out. She didn't like deceiving her friend. If she moved into his flat they could be together all the time, like a married couple. She felt a thrill of excitement. She was going to live with Nick. She would wake up each morning at his side.

'Saturday, then,' she said with a smile.

Nick pulled her towards him and kissed her, and she responded, as always, with a pleasure that she had never known until she met him. Suddenly she was overwhelmingly happy. Nick was her soul mate, her lover. She no longer cared what her parents would say, nor Helen, nor her friends at college. Her place was by his side. All that mattered now was that they would be together forever.

An old comedy show is playing on the television, the characters mouthing their lines, their faces contorted with silent laughter. Nancy sits up. Her mouth is dry, her head throbbing, and there is a sharp pain in her neck. She shouldn't fall asleep on the sofa, she reminds herself, but she does it all the time. She spends a lot of time sleeping these days, dozing off in front of the television, snoozing in the afternoon—when she wakes in the morning she no longer gets up straight away but lies there drifting in and out of consciousness until the alarm goes off. Just another symptom of growing old, her doctor assures her.

She sighs. The room is dark except for the flickering blue of the television. She switches it off and stares out into the darkness. It is late. The sea is a blackness that stretches out and blends with the starless sky. There is no moon tonight; only the twinkling of lamplights that line the promenade relieve the blackness. People emerge from the bar along the street, illuminated by the warm orange glow of its lights. Three couples by the look of it, and they stand together for a bit, lighting cigarettes and chatting. It is too cold to stay and gossip outside for long. They button up their coats, flick their cigarette butts into the gutter, and set off to their cars. Nancy looks at the sea and shivers. It's time she went to bed.

CHAPTER 6

Ana stares at the computer screen. She is no expert on painting but even she can see there is something strange about Nancy's work. She has found a web page that gives a broad overview of the artist's career: 'Nancy Miller, a Retrospective of her Work.'

She hears the front door open.

'Is that you Andy? Come here a minute, will you?'

'What is it?'

He drops the bread on the table.

'Found something interesting?'

'I think so. Look at these photos. These are Nancy's paintings from 1957 to 1958.'

'They're nice. Remind me a bit of that French chap, Gauguin, is it?'

'Yes, exactly. Very colourful, vibrant, lively. I'd say she was happy, wouldn't you?'

'I suppose so.'

'Now look at these. These are from 1960 to 1965. Look how they become increasingly darker and more violent. The skies are no longer blue. It's all grey skies and dark clouds, sharp edges, even dead animals. What do you think that's all about? It's almost as though they've been done by a different artist.'

'Maybe she didn't paint them.'

'No, she definitely painted them. But what has happened to her?'

'Well maybe it's because she's back in England. You know, grey skies, rains a lot. Perhaps you didn't know that about England?' he says with a touch of sarcasm.

'No, it's more than that. She was only in France for a couple of months, yet she painted all these wonderful happy paintings afterwards. Something happened to change her attitude. But what?'

Andrew, who's been looking rather bored with the conversation, leans over her shoulder. 'You're right' he says. 'Something has happened to her or was happening to her because, look, these earlier ones are not as dark as these later ones. These last three are almost the work of a mad woman. Look at that one, the pain in the woman's eyes is incredible.'

He presses the zoom key and the haunted face of a young woman, made old by sorrow, stares back at them.

'That's not all. After 1965 there is another dramatic change in her style. She starts to paint water: the sea, rivers, lakes, no boats, no people, just water. Even when she reverts to something more like her earlier, less gloomy, period, there is always water somewhere in the painting. It's as if she had become obsessed with it. And look at this. What would you say this was?'

He peers closely, 'A pair of eyes?'

'Exactly. What's that all about?'

'She was probably just trying out different styles. Like you said, we don't know much about painting. What do the experts say about it?' Andrew loses interest again and moves away.

'They are as mystified as we are. But they all agree she is a great painter. Her paintings are worth a small fortune.'

'Well, be nice to her and maybe she'll give you one when you've finished writing her biography.'

'Memoirs. She likes to refer to them as her memoirs.'

'Whatever. Is that all? Only I'm playing paddle in ten minutes.'

The next day Ana calls at the baker's first, and buys two croissants before driving to Nancy's flat. She's later than usual. Maria opens the door.

'*Buenas días*, María. How are you today?'

'*Muy bien, señora.* Come in. Señora Miller has only just woken up. She fell asleep on the sofa last night and now she is complaining of a bad back.'

The maid does not seem very concerned about her employer. She shuts the door behind Ana and goes back to emptying the dishwasher.

'Is she all right? Maybe I should come back tomorrow,' Ana says.

'You can stop talking about me as though I don't exist,' comes a sharp voice from the bedroom. 'I am perfectly well enough to sit and talk to you.'

'Good morning, Nancy. I've brought you some croissants. They're still warm.'

'Well bring them in here and tell that idle woman I'd like some coffee, sometime this side of Christmas.'

María pulls a face and switches on the coffee machine. She obviously has little patience with Nancy. Ana can only assume that Nancy's son is paying María well.

'Come in. Come in. You don't need to hang about in the kitchen,' the old woman calls irritably.

Nancy is sitting up in bed, propped on a pile of blue cushions. She is wearing a silky dressing gown, the sort that people bring back from their holidays in Thailand, and her hair is hanging loose about her shoulders. Ana is surprised to see how long it is. Nancy usually wears it tied back in a neat bun and pinned into place with tortoiseshell combs. Her hair is a mixture of grey, white and reddish streaks and today is uncombed and slightly greasy. Ana is tempted to offer to comb it for her but thinks better of it. Seeing Nancy like this makes her realize how old and frail she really is, despite her bombast.

Ana hands her a copy of the chapter she finished writing the night before. 'I thought you might like to read what I've written so far. See what you think of it.'

'You can sit over there,' Nancy tells her imperiously. 'I'm not well enough to get up today.'

'María said you fell asleep on the sofa last night,' Ana says.

'So, what if I did? What business is it of yours?'

Ana sighs. It's going to be one of those days. She wonders if she should suggest postponing their session, but before she can say anything, Nancy tells her, 'I've received a letter from my agent.'

The old woman pulls an envelope from under her pillow and hands it to Ana. It is an invitation to the retrospective exhibition of Nancy's work that she has seen mentioned on the internet.

'I want you to go with me.'

'But it's in England,' Ana says in surprise. 'At the Modern Art Oxford.'

'Of course it's in England. Where else would it be? You want to see my paintings, don't you? What better way to see them than in a gallery of modern art? If you let my son know when you can go, he'll book the tickets and the hotel.

The exhibition is on for two months but I think we should go as soon as possible.'

Ana doesn't know what to say. On the one hand she is thrilled at the prospect of a free trip to England, but on the other she isn't sure how Nancy will cope with the journey, or how *she* will cope with Nancy.

'Maybe we should wait until you're feeling better,' she suggests.

'Stuff and nonsense. I told you, my back aches because I fell asleep on that dreadful sofa, that's all. It's time I bought a new one. Remind me to speak to Martin about it.'

María comes in with two cups and a jug of coffee. She places them on the table by the bed and pours out the coffee.

'Would you like milk and sugar?' she asks Ana.

'*No, gracias. Solo.*'

'Did you say something about croissants?' Nancy asks.

'Oh, yes. I'll get a plate.'

'And some butter and jam,' she adds.

Nancy might look frail, but there is nothing wrong with her appetite this morning. She soon polishes off both croissants. While Nancy is eating, Ana takes out her digital recorder and rewinds it to the beginning.

'So what do you think?' Nancy asks.

'About what?'

'The exhibition, of course. When are you free?'

Ana is reluctant to admit that she can go any time. There is nothing in her diary at the moment except working with Nancy. 'I'll have to check with my partner,' she says. 'But I expect we could go sometime next week. Would that suit you?'

'Partner?'

'My boyfriend.'

'Oh. Well, ring my son and let him know. Here's his phone number. It's one of those mobile things so you should be able to get him any time. That's what he's always telling me, anyway.'

She wipes her mouth with a serviette and leans back on the pillows. 'Well, we'd better get started. I'm not paying you to watch me eat my breakfast.'

Nancy may be crabbier than usual, but her mind seems sharper. Ana hopes they will cover a little more ground today. She clicks the recorder on and picks up her notepad.

'Right, why don't you tell me about your childhood? You were born in Oxfordshire, weren't you?'

'In a little village in South Oxfordshire,' Nancy corrects her. 'We lived in a converted rectory by the Thames.'

'Sounds lovely.'

'It was. I should never have left there.'

CHAPTER 7

Nancy isn't hungry. She pushes the plate of paella María has brought her to one side. Maybe she will eat it later, or maybe she'll flush it down the loo. She will have to do one or the other because María will be quick to report back to Martin, and Nancy has promised Martin that she will make more of an effort to eat the food her carer brings her.

She opens the fridge, but there is no white wine. That's strange. There should be a bottle of Albariño, unopened. So María has taken to stealing her wine now, has she? Well she won't get away with it. She will tell Martin to dismiss her. She can't have a thief in her house, even he can see that.

There is more wine in a box on the floor but it isn't cold, so she pours herself a glass of sweet Málaga wine and puts a new bottle of white wine in the fridge to cool.

She has read the draft chapter Ana left her. It is well written, and, strangely, Nancy could hear her own voice as she read it. Harry made a good choice with that young woman but then Harry always did know quality when he saw it.

Today's session with Ana has left her drained and morose. Talking about her family has awakened a sense of guilt she thought had been buried under all the other emotions that had assailed her during those early years. Her parents' disappointment in her had never lifted, not even when they heard how well she did at college. She had not conformed. She had gone against the social norms of the time. Even her mother, so free herself, would not contradict her father, and together they had abandoned her to Nick and her fate.

Nancy takes her glass of wine and sits by the window, watching clouds scudding across a grey sky. Today it looks like rain. She might as well be in England. She sips the sweet wine and thinks back to when she took that first fatal step, more than fifty years ago.

Kelly turned up in a white van that he used for a part-time window cleaning job. He had painted KELLY O'HARA WINDOW CLEANER on the side and there was an adjustable ladder tied to the roof.

'Hi Kelly. I didn't know you were a window cleaner,' Nancy said, opening the door to him.

'It used to be my dad's but he's too old to clean windows now, so I took it over. It's grand. I can fit it in around my classes quite easily in the summer. Ah, it's a wee bit more difficult in the winter but I manage. It helps to pay the bills.' He smiled and continued, 'So you and Nick are shacking up together, are you?'

She smiled and said, 'Come in. I don't really have much stuff. It's the paintings that take up the room.'

He looked around the tiny flat and laughed. Her two small suitcases stood by the door and propped around the room were at least two dozen canvases in varying stages of completion. There was also a large cardboard box filled with paints, brushes, old rags, and all the other paraphernalia that a student artist collected, and a smaller box with gaily coloured cups, plates and bowls.

'Right, let's load this up then.'

She liked Kelly. He had a kind and gentle manner about him. She liked his wide open face and his flat, boxer's nose that looked as though it had been pressed up against a window. She liked the way his dark hair hung carelessly over his collar, and his lilting Irish accent. He was a Kerry man, and what she most liked about him was that he was respectful and polite and never caused any trouble. She never said she liked him and she never let anyone else know she liked him, but Kelly knew. She could tell from the way he would lower his head and look at her from under his long lashes. There was a presence about him that made her relax, and she enjoyed being alone with him. If Nick was there, however, she kept her eyes averted from that gentle face and never looked at Kelly straight, in the frank friendly way she did when they were alone. Sometimes she thought that Kelly was in love with her, but, if he was, he never spoke of it. He was Nick's friend. They had shared rooms in college before Nick decided to move out and rent his own place. There was no way that Kelly would betray his friend, no matter what his feelings for Nancy might have been. On her birthday, which Nick forgot, Kelly had given her a piece of blue Wedgwood pottery, a small dish for sweets or trinkets, he said. Nick hadn't commented on the gift but somehow managed to knock it off the shelf and now it lay in pieces. She felt that Nick was jealous of his friend because Kelly had done well in his end-of-term exams and now had an apprenticeship with a major sculptor in London. He was leaving in the autumn. She would miss him.

'Hello there, Helen,' he said as Nancy's flatmate came out from the bedroom. 'How're you doing?'

She stared at him and didn't speak.

'What's up with her then?' he asked. 'She's a quare one.'

'She's angry that I'm moving out,' Nancy whispered. 'She was whinging all night, saying how she'll never be able to pay the rent if I go. I don't know what to do.'

'Oh, is that all,' Kelly said. 'She'll get over it. Pass me that box.'

Men just didn't understand. She had been sharing with Helen for nearly two years, ever since she moved to Kingston, and they had become really close friends. Helen said Nancy was deserting her, but what could she do? For some reason Nick did not like Helen. He made it quite plain that Nancy had to choose between her friend and him. Now Helen wasn't speaking to her.

She moved around her old flat, checking the drawers and the bookshelf to see if she had left anything behind. She had been happy here in this flat. It was the first time she had lived away from home, and if it hadn't been for Helen she would have been very lonely those first few months. The two girls had become inseparable. They went to the cinema together, to college dances, to the local pub, they took the train to London and visited the art galleries. In summer they would go to the seaside and one year she had spent a week in Scotland with Helen and her family. Helen was like a sister to her, they told each other everything—until she met Nick. Now she was leaving. No wonder Helen felt she was abandoning her.

'That's all of it, I think,' said Kelly. 'Shall we go?'

'Just give me a minute, will you?'

She went into the kitchen. Helen was standing at the sink, staring out into the back yard.

'I'm off then, Helen,' Nancy said.

There was no reply.

'Look, I'm sorry about this but I thought you'd understand. It was bound to happen one day. It could just as easily have been you leaving and me left behind. I really don't know why you're behaving like this, Helen. I told you Nick wants us to live together. We love each other. We're going to get married. I thought you'd be happy for me.'

Helen continued to stare blankly out at the yard, with its row of black dustbins and the crates of beer bottles that belonged to the two lads living above them. A ginger cat sat on one of the dustbins and looked at them mournfully.

'Look, if it's about the rent I'll pay for next month's until you get a new flatmate. It won't take long till you find someone else to share with you. There'll be a whole load of new students in September.'

At last Helen turned to face her. Her eyes were filled with tears. 'It's nothing to do with the rent. I just said that to try to get you to change your mind. I don't want you to go.'

'But it's all arranged now, Helen. Look, I'm sorry, really I am, but we can still see each other, go to the pictures or for a coffee. I'll see you at college. We don't have to stop being friends just because I'm living with Nick.'

'You think?' Helen's voice made it clear she thought otherwise. 'Nancy, you're my best friend. I can't bear to see you hurt. Please don't go.'

'What are you talking about Helen? Why would I get hurt? I'm moving in with Nick. He loves me. I love him. That's all there is to it.'

'He'll end up hurting you. I know he will. Please, Nancy, wait until you know him a little better. I've seen him with other girls. He's jealous and cruel. There's no way we can continue to be friends because he won't allow it. He's never liked me because I can see straight through him.'

'No. You don't know Nick like I do, Helen. You've got him all wrong. I know he seems a bit possessive, but Nick would never hurt me.'

Helen shook her head and turned away. 'They say love is blind, and how true that is. But I love you too, Nancy, and I'm not blind. I know what he'll do to you. First he'll cut you off from your friends, then your family, and finally from your painting. He won't stand for anything to come between you. He's a control freak, one hundred percent. Please stay, Nancy, just a few more months, until you can see him for how he really is.'

Nancy could not, would not believe her—Nick, hurt her? No. Why was Helen saying such hateful things? She and Nick loved each other, and that was all that mattered. He had told her so.

'I'm sorry Helen. I've got to go. Kelly is waiting.'

She picked up the last of her bags and looked back at her friend, who continued to stare out of the window. She wanted to grab her and shake her, make her say it wasn't true, admit it was just jealousy on her part, anything but what she had said. Instead she turned and ran down the stairs, the sound of Helen's silence following her.

Nick was out when they arrived at the flat so Kelly helped Nancy carry her belongings into the building and along the narrow passageway that led to her new home. The building was Georgian, converted into a number of one-room flats. Nick's was at the back of the house, overlooking the garden. She unlocked the door with the key he had given her the previous evening. It had been in her pocket ever since, burning with illicit promise. She stepped into a large, square room, its high ceiling edged with white stucco coving, an enormous carved ceiling rose in the centre. The walls were panelled in wood to waist height, but they were grubby, the wood panelling cracked and splintered in places as though something had been thrown at it repeatedly. The floor was covered with grimy, black-and-white-checked linoleum worn in patches, with even a few holes. The faded green sofa by the window was dotted with cigarette burns. This once-elegant room, after years of student letting, had been reduced to a shadow of its former glory.

'Windows could do with a wash,' Kelly remarked, squinting at a tall sash window covered in grime. 'I'll come round and do them for you before I leave.' He pulled back the grubby lace curtain and looked out. 'Nice garden though. Somewhere to sit in the summer.'

Kelly was being kind, but the place was a tip. Nick's clothes were everywhere: draped over the threadbare sofa, on the floor, hanging on the backs of chairs, screwed up into smelly balls in need of a wash. She resisted the urge to sweep them all up and push them into the cupboard. There were ashtrays full to overflowing on the floor, alongside empty beer bottles and half-finished wooden models.

'What a mess,' Kelly said, looking through a small archway into the kitchen. 'You stay here. I'll pop down and get that last box.'

'Thank you,' Nancy said, nearer tears than she wanted him to know. She cleared a space on the sofa and sat down. What had she done? She watched as heavy raindrops trickled down the window panes, cutting a path through the exterior grime, revealing glimpses of thick, evergreen bushes and patches of green lawn. A washing line had been strung between two poles and somebody's wet clothes flapped in the breeze. The grey light of that wet afternoon made the room look grimier and dingier than ever.

It wasn't the south of France, but it was what she had chosen. You always feel like this when you make a change in your life, she thought—it was the same when she first came to Kingston. You'll soon get this place straight and then you'll feel better, she told herself. But she knew there was something more this time; she couldn't deny it. It wasn't disappointment, she hadn't expected Nick to live in a palace; that was not important. It was the feeling of dread that came over her when she realized that this was her home now. She had taken the first perhaps ill-considered step on a new path, unsure of its direction.

'There. That's the last of them,' he said, 'This box is full of dishes and things. Kitchen?'

'Please,' Nancy said, forcing herself to smile.

She followed him into the smallest kitchen she had ever seen. It was dark and dirty. A greasy, burnt chip pan had deposited its contents all over the tiny gas stove, up the back wall and even on the floor. Fat clung to all the surfaces like a sticky overcoat. She sighed. There was no doubt this would be her first job, cleaning up this disgusting mess.

Kelly put the box on the floor. 'Not good when two blokes live together. I doubt this kitchen has been cleaned in years. It's a wonder they didn't get food poisoning.'

'I can't think about it at the moment,' Nancy said with a shudder. She picked up a tea towel blackened with grease and deposited it in the sink. 'Let's inspect the bathroom.'

The bathroom, third and last room in the flat, was reasonably clean, as long as you didn't look at the brown stain in the toilet bowl or the black line of mould edging the sink. Nancy picked up a threadbare towel from the floor and hung it over the edge of the tub.

'Well,' Kelly said, 'it looks like you've got hot water. So you'll be able to have a bath.' An old enamelled geyser hung on the wall above the bath. He turned the bath tap on and the geyser's flame fluttered a moment, then roared into life.

'My God. I thought you'd blown it up,' Nancy said, letting the water run over her hand. 'At least it seems to work. Where's the meter?'

'I noticed it in the kitchen. It takes sixpences.'

'Hey there! Anyone hungry?' The door to the flat was flung open and Nick came in, carrying three bags of fish and chips.

'Nick, you're back,' Nancy said, throwing herself at him. The geyser, the dirt, grime, greasy pans, overflowing ashtrays, discarded towels and clothing were all forgotten in the pleasure of seeing him standing there with a wide grin on his handsome face, in their first home together.

'Hi there, man.' Nick tossed a packet of fish and chips at Kelly.

'Thanks, mate.'

Nick bent to kiss Nancy on the mouth, a kiss that tasted of cigarettes and beer. 'So, my little wife, how are you?'

'Feeling better now you're here.'

'Kelly not been looking after you, then?' he asked with a grin.

Kelly was perched on the arm of the sofa, unwrapping the newspaper. The fish smelled delicious, and suddenly Nancy was hungry. She took a packet and settled down on the sofa. There was a table in the flat, but it was covered in magazines and more wooden models. At the moment there seemed to be nowhere to sit to eat and definitely nowhere for her to paint.

'So, what do you think of the place?' Nick asked, covering his fish and chips liberally in brown sauce.

'It's lovely.'

'Yeah, I like it. It's a bit of a mess but I reckon that you'll soon get it sorted out.'

'There's only one question.'

'Yes?'

'Where do we sleep? There's no bedroom.'

'That's not a problem. Get up a minute.'

Nancy and Kelly stood while Nick converted the sagging sofa into an even more saggy bed. '*Voilá.* Your bed, madame.' He reached up and pulled Nancy down beside him.

'Well I think I'll leave you guys to get sorted out,' Kelly said, screwing the newspaper into a ball. 'Thanks for the fish and chips.'

'No sweat. See you down the pub later?'

'Maybe. Bye Nancy.'

'Bye Kelly and thanks.'

Once they could hear Kelly's long legs bounding along the passage, Nick turned to Nancy. 'Well, young lady, what do you think of your new home?'

'It's fine Nick. I like it just fine.'

'Well I think we should celebrate but first come here. We need to try out the bed.' He pulled her close to him and kissed her. 'I love you, Nancy,' he whispered in her ear. 'I really love you.'

Nancy didn't tell her parents about living with Nick, not at first. She told them she had met a boy she really liked and that he was a student at the college. This seemed to satisfy them for a while and Nick never brought up the subject of meeting them again. She thought it could go on like that forever and never gave a moment's thought to the future. She was happy and Nick was happy. Her previous fears seemed senseless now.

She slipped easily into a routine of going to college, shopping in her lunch break, and cooking for them both in the evening. She even felt a particular satisfaction that she had managed to make a reasonable working area out of the minuscule kitchen. Her painting flourished. Toby's praise encouraged her, and Nick's love inspired her. Life could not have been better.

But the future was not so predictable. It would not let her continue to live each day in the same way. It started to change when Toby chose not one but four of her paintings for the Spring Exhibition. She was so excited, she rang her mother to tell her the good news.

'Darling, that's wonderful. I always knew you had a special talent. You were chosen to take this path you know. Your spirit guide knew what she was doing.'

'Yes, Mum, I know. You've told me before. But hard work has something to do with it too.'

'Well I'm very proud of you. I'm coming to Kingston to see the exhibition. It's time your dad and I had a break. We never go anywhere these days. This is just the excuse I've been looking for. Oh, how lovely for you, to be in a real exhibition. And four paintings. I'm just so very proud of you.'

Her mother rattled on about how proud she was and how much she was looking forward to seeing her only daughter again, and Nancy didn't have the heart to dissuade her from coming. Luckily there was no suggestion of staying with Nancy; her father booked a small hotel in the town and Nancy arranged to meet them there.

She knew her father would not approve of Nick. He was unlikely to approve of any boyfriend of Nancy's. He had always been a strict father, and it had only been on her mother's insistence that Nancy had been allowed to leave home and go to college. Her father had wanted her to take a typing course at the local technical college. In his eyes, young girls were easy prey once they were living away from home, open to all manner of danger and corruption, the worst of all being an unwanted pregnancy. She knew he would think his fears had been confirmed if he found out she and Nick were living together.

What was she going to do? It would be impossible for her parents to be here and not be introduced to Nick; he would be furious to be overlooked and they would be suspicious, maybe even thinking he was black or worse still, a married man. They would have to meet sometime, so she might as well face up to it sooner than later.

Nancy woke first. It was barely light and as she crept out from under the blankets she shivered with cold. There had been no sixpences for the gas meter last night, and they had gone to bed early, huddled together to keep warm. Nick was still asleep, stretched on his back, with one arm hanging out of the bed.

He had been in a foul mood the night before because, he said, she refused to invite her parents to the flat. But she knew it was really because none of his work had been chosen for the Spring Exhibition. He'd expected them to select his birdcage piece which, now it was finished, was more like a birdcage than ever. Even with her rudimentary knowledge of modern sculpture, Nancy knew it was not very good. It looked too utilitarian, not like a work of art at all. She wasn't surprised when his tutor declined to put it in the exhibition, but Nick had been devastated. Then his mood turned surly, and now she was bearing the brunt of it.

Nancy moved quietly around the flat. It felt like home, since she had scrubbed and polished, swept and tidied, and even white-washed two of the walls. Now that Kelly had cleaned the windows and the grubby curtains had been thrown into the dustbin, the light that streamed in was more than adequate for her to paint by, and she had set up her easel in front of them. At last the flat looked like somewhere she could live instead of a place just to crash in. She had even hung a couple of her paintings on the wall facing the window.

She pulled on some clothes, crept into the kitchen, and put the kettle on the stove. Her parents were arriving today. She had arranged to meet them at ten o'clock at their hotel, and Nick was going with her. A wave of nausea washed over her at the thought of Nick meeting her parents; he was so unpredictable. For a moment she thought she was going to be sick in the sink. She hurried to the bathroom and knelt with her head hanging over the toilet bowl until the feeling passed.

'Are you making tea?' Nick called from beneath the blankets.

'Yes. Want some?'

A grunt suggested that he did.

At precisely ten o'clock they were standing in the lobby of the Carlton Hotel. Nancy's stomach was still churning at the thought of Nick and her parents coming face to face. She had tried to tell him as diplomatically as she could how much they would disapprove of them living together, how it was best not to say anything about the flat. But could she rely on him to keep quiet? She had planned her story carefully. She would say that Helen had moved away and that she could no longer afford to pay the rent on her previous flat so she'd taken a room in the same building as Nick. The previous evening she had removed all traces of Nick from their flat, hiding his clothes in the wardrobe and removing his shaving things from the bathroom. If they insisted on seeing where she lived she would have to take them there.

'Darling, there you are. Oh my, how thin you look. I knew you wouldn't eat enough without me there to nag you. And this must be Nick? Hello, young man. How nice to meet you.'

Nancy's mother pulled back from the all-enveloping bear hug in which she held her daughter to look at Nick. Nancy was pleased with the effort her lover had made. He had gone out for a haircut the day before and shaved that morning, not normally a daily occurrence. He wore his best trousers and a freshly pressed shirt. He was a handsome man and today, she thought, even more so. His thick blond hair was carefully combed, and as she looked at his straight, muscular figure, she was filled with desire for all six-feet-two of him. She could see from her mother's smile that she approved of him too, but her father was looking very serious. He held out his hand.

'How do you do,' he said, shaking Nick's hand vigorously.

Her father always said you could tell a lot about a man by his handshake. She wondered what he had learnt about Nick.

'Nice to meet you, Mr. Miller,' Nick said. 'I'm glad you could come to the exhibition.'

'We wouldn't have missed it for the world,' Nancy's mother chipped in. 'And it's given us a chance to meet some of our daughter's friends as well.'

'I take it you're a student here, Nick?' her father said.

'Yes, I'm in Three-Dimensional Art. A sculptor actually.'

'How nice,' Nancy's mother said. 'So you have some things in the exhibition too?' She took her daughter's arm and led her towards the door of the hotel.

There was a brief silence during which Nancy thought she could hear her own heart beating then Nick said, 'Actually I haven't. I'm not interested in the bourgeois idea of exhibitions and prizes. Art should be unfettered. It should be a pure expression of the soul. Art doesn't need to have a purpose. Its beauty is its purpose. Don't you agree?'

He looked directly at Nancy's father, who seemed lost for words. Nancy visualised the birdcage. What was Nick trying to express with that, she wondered. A trapped soul? Freedom? To her it just looked like a birdcage without the bird.

'Oh well, it's nice to meet a friend of Nancy's,' her father said.

'Oh, but I'm not just a friend,' Nick said, smiling at them. 'Hasn't Nancy told you? We live together.'

There was a moment of silence that seemed to stretch forever, then her mother said, 'Oh, of course, Nancy has a room in the same house as you, doesn't she?'

Nick looked at Nancy then back to her mother. 'Not just the same house, we live in the same room. We're living together. You know, like man and wife. I'm her lover.'

The world seemed to stop. Nancy couldn't believe he was saying this—he knew she didn't want her parents to know about their relationship, not like this, not now. Why had he done it? Did he get some strange pleasure from seeing her parents' discomfort? Was he trying to make her father angry?

There was a long, uncomfortable silence then her father spoke, 'We'll talk about this later, Nancy. Now I think we should be getting on to see this exhibition. We've come a long way, and I don't want to be too late leaving.'

His tone was icy and she could see that her mother was on the brink of tears. Her father put his arm around his wife and ushered her into the street, leaving Nancy staring in amazement at her lover.

The sound of the telephone ringing rouses Nancy from her reminiscences. For a moment she is confused. Is it the telephone on the wall or that little thing Martin says she must carry with her at all times? She looks at her mobile lying next to her empty glass, silent and unthreatening. She pulls herself up from the sofa and makes her way to the telephone.

'Hello?' she says. 'Who is it?'

'It's all right, Mama; it's only me, Martin.'

'Who?' she bellows into the phone.

'Martin. It's Martin.'

'What do you want?'

'I just wanted to see if you were okay. I tried ringing your mobile but it has no signal. Have you forgotten to charge it up again?'

Nancy glances across at the table.

'I suppose I must have,' she says. 'I think María has taken the charger.'

'Okay, I'll speak to her about it.'

'And while you're at it, tell her to stop stealing my white wine,' she snaps.

She hears her son give an exasperated sigh.

'Anyway, Mama, I wanted to tell you that I won't be round tonight. I'm sorry. Sara has an appointment with the gynaecologist and she wants me to go with her. I'll see you tomorrow. Ring me if there's anything you want.'

'You go with your wife. Don't worry about me,' she says, but she knows there's a grudging tone in her voice.

'You're sure you're okay?'

'Of course I am.'

'I'll see you tomorrow then,' her son says and hangs up.

That wife of his. What is it this time? Not pregnant again, surely?

CHAPTER 8

Ana has finished typing up the last session with Nancy and is about to turn off the computer when she notices a new email. She clicks it open and reads:

Dear Señorita Álvarez,

I understand that you are helping my mother to write her memoirs and I wondered if I could speak to you some time. As you are probably aware, my mother's memory is not what it used to be and maybe I could help fill in some of the details of her past. I am approaching you directly because I know my mother will say she does not need my help but I am sure you would like to make an accurate account of her life, despite her objections.

I look forward to hearing from you.

Sincerely

Martin Henderson

'Well, fancy that.'

'What?'

'It's an email from Nancy's son. He wants to have a chat about his mother. Says he can help to fill in some of her background.'

'That's good, isn't it?'

Andrew doesn't look up from the newspaper. It's his night off, and they're going to the cinema later.

'Yes, of course. I had been wondering who else I could talk to about Nancy's life. Maybe he can suggest some of her old friends.'

'Does she have any friends? Aren't they all dead?'

'That's the problem. She just clams up whenever I suggest talking to anyone else. She says it's her memoir and there's no need for anyone else to be involved. But it doesn't work like that. Everyone's memory plays tricks on them, and Nancy's is particularly suspect. If I ask her about certain things—Martin's father, for example—she just ignores me and talks about something else. Maybe Martin will be able to tell me more himself.'

'Hey, I thought this was supposed to be a night off? Time you got yourself dolled up if we're going to have a drink before the film starts.' Andrew leans over and kisses the top of her head.

'I won't be two minutes,' she says and snaps the computer closed.

She'll phone Nancy's son tomorrow and arrange to meet him sometime next week. As it happens, she and Martin meet sooner than either of them expected.

'Well, I didn't think much of that,' Andrew says, as they leave the multiplex cinema and head for their favourite bar.

'I thought it was brilliant,' Ana says, her head still full of visions of Matthew McConaughey's extraordinary transformation as the HIV-positive homophobic Texan. They had watched the film in Spanish, and although he will never admit it, she guesses that Andrew had trouble following the fast-moving dialogue.

'Is that your mobile?' he asks.

It is. She flips it open and speaks rather impatiently into it, '*Digame.*'

An agitated voice is talking to her in Spanish.

'Dr Henderson? Is that you? What's the matter? I got your email, by the way, but I didn't think you expected me to reply straight away,' Ana says. She feels annoyed that her evening has been interrupted but continues to listen.

'I tried ringing you earlier but your phone was off,' Dr Henderson says.

'I know. I always switch it off when we go to the cinema.'

'I'm sorry. Are you in the cinema now?'

'No, the film's finished. We're on our way out.'

'What does he want?' Andrew asks impatiently.

Ana holds up her hand for him to be quiet. '*Lo siento*, what did you say?'

'Is my mother with you?'

'No, why should she be with us? I haven't seen her since I left this afternoon, about two-thirty.'

'She's missing. Not in her flat and the door is open,' he says. He sounds distraught.

'I'm sorry to hear that, but I have no idea where she might be. Have you tried speaking to her neighbours?'

'Yes, I've tried everyone I can think of. You were my last hope.'

'What about the police?'

'I'm going to call them now. I know this is a bit of an imposition but do you think you could come round here? Someone needs to stay in the flat in case she comes back.'

'Yes, of course I'll go round to her flat, if you think it will help.'

'I'll wait here for you,' he says.

'I'll see you there.' She rings off and puts the mobile back in her pocket.

'What's that all about?' Andrew asks.

'It's Nancy. She's gone missing. Her neighbour noticed that her front door was open, and when she went inside to see if Nancy was all right, she couldn't find her, so she rang María, then María rang Nancy's son.'

'So what's it got to do with you?'

'He wanted to know if we'd seen her.'

'Well we haven't.'

They have reached the bar and Andrew opens the door for her to go in.

'I told him I'd go over to the flat.'

'But why? There's nothing you can do. They should get the police on it. What use will you be? That María woman will help him.'

'Nancy can't stand María. Anyway I promised him I'd go.'

'How are you going to get there?'

'I'll take the car. Look, I won't be long, and then I'll come back and we'll have a drink together. Don't be like that, Andy, I won't be long, I promise.'

'Oh, do what you want. You always do.'

He pushes past her and joins the noisy crowd jostling to get served at the bar. She notices some friends of theirs at a table in the corner and waves at them.

It takes Ana about fifteen minutes to get to Nancy's flat. The door is still open and when she goes in she sees a man talking on his mobile phone. He looks up and nods at her.

'Let me know as soon as you have any more news,' he says in Spanish and rings off.

'The local police,' he explains. 'They have alerted their patrols but can't do anything more than that. You must be Ana?' He holds out his hand and smiles at her. He is a handsome man, in his early fifties, well dressed with fair, receding hair. His eyes are an extraordinarily bright blue.

'Yes. Dr Henderson?'

'Oh, call me Martin, please. So, Ana do you have any idea where she might be?'

'Not really. We could walk along the promenade and see if she has gone down there for a stroll.'

'But it's nearly midnight and it's cold. Why would she go out in the dark on her own?'

'Do you know what time she left?' Ana asks.

'Well she was here at six o'clock because I spoke to her.'

'What did the neighbour say?'

'She says the door was closed when she went out at ten o'clock. Which was why she thought it strange that it was open when she returned.'

'When was that?'

'About half an hour before I called you.'

'Have you checked to see if she has taken any clothes?'

'Oh, my God, no I haven't.'

He dashes into the bedroom and returns saying, 'Nothing much seems to be missing. Even her coat is still here.'

'That's not good. She'll freeze out there with no coat.'

'We'd better go and look for her.'

'Wouldn't it be better if you stayed here, in case she comes back or the police phone?' she suggests. 'I'll go and look for her. I doubt if she has gone very far.'

He looks sceptical at this but then nods his head. 'Okay. But ring me if you find her and I'll come and help you to get her home.'

'I will.'

'Here, take this,' he says, taking a pocket torch out of the kitchen drawer.

His face is drawn, and she feels sorry for him. He obviously is very concerned for his mother. She slips the torch into her pocket and hurries out into the street.

She is glad she has her thick coat with her. There is a cold breeze coming off the sea. For some reason she remembers Nancy telling her about the swimmer that drowned. She'll start there. The street lamps cast pools of yellow light on the promenade, but between them the shadows are dark and it's hard to see if anyone is there. She shines the torch into the darkest spots, but its beam is weak and wavers as though the battery is about to go out. Today is Monday and many of the bars and restaurants are closed tonight. The beach is deserted, and the few people that are out are not loitering. The wind is too cold for that. Ana hopes Nancy is somewhere warm. A chill at her age could be disastrous. She pulls her coat tightly around her and hurries along, calling out Nancy's name every so often.

'Lost someone, dear?' an English voice asks.

'Yes. I'm looking for an old lady, wandering on her own. An English woman. Have you seen her?'

'No. Sorry, dear. You could try further up. There's a little bar that's open all the year round up there. Maybe she's gone in for a night cap.'

'I will. Thanks.'

Ana hurries on. This is impossible. Nancy could be lying on the beach, injured, unconscious, and Ana would never know. She could walk right past her and not see her. She stops and listens. Nothing. How is she going to find her like this? She carries on along the promenade, shining her torch along the beach, but all she can see are waves breaking on the shore, ripples of white foam. Then she hears a sound—it is faint, hard to separate from the ceaseless murmur of the sea. Yes, there it is again—it is definitely a voice. An English voice.

'Nancy? Is that you? Nancy?'

Ana flashes her torch in the direction of the sound, and then she sees her. She is sitting on the sand, leaning against one of the fishing boats and she seems to be talking to someone.

'Nancy, it's me. It's Ana.'

She runs across to the seated woman. There is no one with her; she is quite alone. Whoever she was speaking to has gone or was never there, but Nancy is still talking in a steady, quiet voice.

'I couldn't trust him. I had to do something,' Nancy mutters, looking straight ahead of her.

She seems unaware of Ana's presence so Ana sits down beside her and says, 'Are you all right Nancy? Is there anything I can do to help you? Are you hurt?'

'I'm not a bad person, you know. I had no choice. You mustn't tell Martin. He must never know.'

'Know what, Nancy? What is it that Martin mustn't know?'

'Promise me you won't tell him.'

'Of course not, Nancy. Now don't you think it's time I took you home? It's freezing here.'

Nancy peers up at Ana, recognising her. 'Oh, hello my dear. Have you come to interview me again? I can't talk to you now; it's far too late. We'll have to leave it for another day.'

'We have been looking for you, Nancy. What are you doing down here at this time of night? Martin is very worried,' Ana adds. She takes out her mobile and rings his number. 'It's okay, Dr Henderson, I've found her. Yes, she seems fine. We're on the beach, not far away,' she tells him. 'Right opposite the Oveja Negra restaurant. Yes, we'll wait for you.'

She turns to Nancy, who seems in no hurry to move, and takes her hand.

'*Dios mio*, you're frozen. We need to get you home. Come along, Martin is coming for us with his car.'

'Martin? I thought Martin had to go to the hospital with that pretty little wife of his?'

'It's late, Nancy. Martin's wife is at home in bed, which is where you should be. Come along now, let's get you back to your flat and in the warm.'

Ana realizes she is talking to Nancy as though she were a child, and Nancy soon picks up on it.

'Don't fuss, girl. I'm not cold. I'm quite comfortable where I am. I like listening to the sea; it's comforting. It's helping me get my head straight. It helps drive the nightmares away.'

Ana sits down again. 'Why do you need to get your head straight, Nancy? Who were you talking to?'

A sly look crosses the old woman's face. 'No one. I wasn't talking to anyone. Have you been spying on me?'

'No, Nancy. I haven't been spying on you. I've been looking for you. We were worried about you. Martin rang me and said you'd gone missing.'

'Gone missing? I'm not a prisoner, you know. I'm allowed to go out whenever I want. I don't have to ask you for permission,' she says. 'Or Martin.'

'Of course not, but we need to go home now.'

'He drowned,' Nancy says, staring straight ahead of her. 'He's under the water now. Gone forever.'

'Who's drowned, Nancy? The swimmer? It's sad I know, but there's nothing you can do about it—it was an accident.'

'No. It wasn't an accident.'

'Yes, it was. They got into difficulties, that's all that happened. It was a tragic accident. These things happen all the time. You mustn't let it upset you so much. Now, come along. We must get you home. I'm getting cold,' she adds, changing tack.

Nancy looks at her and reaching out, touches Ana's face. 'Oh, my dear child, I'm sorry. Of course we must go now. We'll come back again tomorrow.'

'Yes, Nancy, that would be lovely.'

She helps the old woman to her feet and slowly they make their way to Martin's waiting car. He hurries towards them. 'Mama, what are you playing at, going off alone, in the middle of the night? We've been worried sick about you.' The relief is clearly etched on his face.

'Don't fuss so. It was lovely down there by the beach,' Nancy says, walking past him and climbing into the front seat, but Ana can see that she has started to shiver. Her pride may not allow her to admit it, but she is cold now.

Once they have Nancy home, Martin makes her a hot drink and gives her a sleeping tablet.

'What's that?' she asks.

'Just something to help you sleep, Mama. Here, drink your cocoa.'

Nancy is strangely subdued. She takes the tablet and swallows the cocoa without a murmur of complaint. 'I'm going to bed now,' she announces. 'Good night.'

'Good night, Mama. Sleep well.'

Once her bedroom door is closed, Martin turns to Ana. 'I can't thank you enough for tonight,' he says. 'But what made you look for her along the beach?'

'It was something she told me the first time I came here. She watched a man drown from the window, and it seemed to affect her quite a lot. I just thought maybe she had gone down to have a closer look.'

'Well I'm very grateful. If she had been out there all night I think she would have ended up with pneumonia.'

'Has she done this before, wandered off in the middle of the night?'

'No, but she has been getting more and more forgetful and I have to confess I'm worried about her living here alone.'

'Have you spoken to her doctor about her?'

'When I can get her to agree to see him. She is as stubborn as a mule, that woman. I tell her I'm only trying to help but she accuses me of wanting rid of her.'

'Why don't you examine her, yourself? You're a doctor, aren't you?'

'A paediatrician. Not that it matters, she wouldn't let me near her anyway. She doesn't trust doctors. She says that once she starts seeing one, it will be the beginning of the end.'

He sits down at the kitchen table and puts his head in his hands with a weary sigh. 'I don't know what to do for the best. I have suggested sheltered housing, but she's adamant she doesn't need it.'

'Couldn't she live with you?' Ana asks.

'We've even suggested that, but she refuses to leave her own place. She is very independent, you know.'

'Yes, I can see that. Well maybe she needs a full-time carer.'

He lets out a little snort of exasperation. 'You've seen how she is with María. She thinks everyone is spying on her.'

'Don't worry. Maybe getting lost tonight will have changed her mind.'

'Mmn. I'd like to think so.'

'You said you wanted to talk about your mother's past. Would next week suit you?'

'That sounds good. Why don't you come to my house on Wednesday evening? I don't have a surgery on Wednesdays. Shall we say at six?'

'Fine.'

'Here is my address.' He hands her a business card. 'Do you know the area?'

'Vaguely. Don't worry, I'll find you all right.'

CHAPTER 9

Wednesday is a busy day at the hospital for Martin, which is why he has no private patients that day, but somehow he manages to get everything finished and be home in time for lunch at three. As usual Sara has his meal ready for him and she and his two sons are already seated at the dining room table when he arrives.

'*Hola*, Papa,' says Emilio, a boy of almost nine with thick dark hair and large brown eyes. Both his children have inherited his wife's Spanish good looks.

'Can we go to the beach after lunch?' the little one asks; he is only seven. 'Mama says it's all right if you agree.'

Martin hangs up his coat and, after kissing his wife on the cheek, sits down beside them. He pours himself a glass of water and drinks it thirstily.

'I'm sorry boys, but I'm too busy today.'

'But you said we could go to the beach, it's Wednesday. You promised,' wails his youngest. His name is Juan, after Sara's father.

'I know but it will have to wait until the weekend.'

'It's supposed to rain,' his wife comments.

'Well I can't control the weather,' he replies irritably.

He turns to his sons and says, 'If it doesn't rain on Saturday, I will definitely take you both to the beach. How's that?'

'Can we take our scooters?'

'Yes, you can take your scooters.'

'Can we get ice creams?'

'Yes, you can buy ice creams. Now eat up your *puchero* and let me speak to your mother.'

It amuses him how they always like to negotiate with him. The boys exchange conspiratorial smiles and begin spooning the savoury soup that their mother has made into their mouths.

'Ana is coming over at six. I need to talk to her about Mama,' he explains to Sara.

'Ana?'

'The woman who is helping Mama write her memoirs.'

Sara laughs. 'Is that really happening? I thought it was just a passing fancy of your mother's.'

'No, it's really happening. Ana goes to see Mama almost every day. I don't know how far they've got. That's why I want to talk to her, to see if she needs any help.'

Sara reaches across and strokes her husband's hand. 'You're such a softie,' she says. 'Did you get time to ring your mother today? Has she recovered from her adventures?'

'She seems as right as rain. Adolfo said he would pop in and see her again tomorrow, just to be sure.'

'That's kind of him.'

'Well he says she's like family to him.'

'I suppose she is. What is it, thirty years since you've known him?'

'At least that.'

He takes some bread and, breaking off a chunk, wipes it round his bowl. His wife is an excellent cook, a lot better than his mother.

'What about you? Any more sickness?' he asks her.

She smiles and whispers, 'Just a bit.'

He looks at the boys but they are busy chattering about something that happened at school. He and Sara don't want to tell them about the new baby yet, not until they are absolutely sure that nothing will go wrong. Sara's doctor has warned her that this time it might not be so straightforward—she is in her late forties now. Martin hadn't wanted her to take the risk but Sara so wants to have a daughter that he has capitulated.

'Have you told your mother?' she asks.

'Good God, no. You can imagine her reaction. We'll tell her later.'

'Tell her what?' asks his youngest son, who never misses anything. 'What are you going to tell Grandma?'

'That she should have someone taking care of her,' Sara says. 'She's too old to be on her own.'

'I'll look after her,' the boy says, stuffing a piece of bread in his mouth. 'I like Grandma.'

'Don't talk with your mouth full,' Sara says and collects up the empty soup bowls.

Just after six, the doorbell rings. It's Ana. She is wearing a dark-coloured padded coat and has a blue scarf wound around her neck. Her big brown eyes, half-hidden by her spectacles, crinkle as she smiles at him. She looks very young, like a student.

'*Hola*. I hope I'm not late,' she says. 'I know what English people feel about punctuality.'

'Come in,' Martin says. 'You're right on time.' He takes her coat and scarf and ushers her into the lounge. 'This is my wife, Sara. Sara, this is Señorita Álvarez.'

'*Encantada, señora,*' Ana says, rather nervously, he thinks.

'*Mucho gusto*. Well, I'll leave you two alone. I have to make sure the boys are not making a mess of their homework.'

'Your wife is Spanish?' Ana asks, looking faintly surprised.

'Yes, we met in Madrid when I was at medical school.'

The young woman is looking around the room, unsure of what to do next.

'Shall we sit at the table?' he suggests. 'It will be more comfortable if you want to make any notes.'

'Yes, that's fine. Do you mind if I tape our conversation? It helps me to remember.'

'Of course not. Do you want to talk in Spanish or English?'

'English, I think. After all I will have to write it up in English.'

'Fine. We usually speak English at home—it's good for the boys. We want them to grow up bi-lingual.'

They sit at the dining room table, now cleared of the lunch things and covered by a thick, tapestry cloth that reaches to the floor. The round, oil-filled electric heater is still on, and Martin can feel the heat radiating up his legs. Sara wanted to install central heating like her parents have in Madrid, but he prefers the old fashioned *brasero*. It encourages people to sit close together to enjoy the shared heat source. His mother always had one of these under-the-table heaters when he was a boy, but in those days it was fired by live coals instead of electricity. He had burnt himself on it more than once, he remembers.

'This is cosy,' Ana says. 'My mother has a *brasero* at home.' She makes herself comfortable and arranges her notebook and digital recorder in front of her. She looks at him expectantly.

'I thought it might be a good idea to meet,' he says. 'But before we start I want to thank you for your help the other night.'

She smiles and gives a slight shrug. 'What did the doctor say?' she asks.

'Well as you can imagine, my mother refused to visit the doctor so I arranged for an old friend of the family, Don Adolfo, to visit her. He is actually her old heart specialist but he was happy to check her over and said that she seems to have suffered no ill effects from her little adventure. He has arranged for her to have an MRI scan to see if there is any physical reason she is behaving like this, but his general opinion is that it is just a symptom of old age.'

'Well that's good news, then, isn't it?'

'Yes. Of course we won't know until she's had the scan but that isn't for another two weeks.'

'What about this exhibition she wants to go to? Do you think it is wise in her condition?'

'Wise or not, my mother is determined to go.'

'Perhaps we should postpone it. Tell her we will go later, after the scan,' Ana suggests.

He shakes his head. 'I don't think it will make any difference. What will the scan say? That she has dementia? Or Alzheimer's? Whatever the outcome I doubt if anything can be done about it. This is probably her last chance to go to a major exhibition of her work. I don't want to take that away from her. I would take her myself, but I can't afford the time away from the hospital at the moment, not with the new dialysis unit to organise, and anyway it is a wonderful opportunity for you to see a full retrospective exhibition of her work.'

He takes a folder from his briefcase and hands it to her.

'These are your tickets. I've booked you both into the Randolph Hotel in Oxford for three nights. It's probably more time than you need, but I don't want my mother to get over-tired. The flights are booked with Iberia, and I've arranged for a car to pick you up and take you to the hotel. It's a short walk to the exhibition, but if you feel you need a taxi, please feel free to take one. My mother will have plenty of money for the trip, but just in case, here is some extra cash.'

He passes her an envelope with English money and a British passport. 'That is my mother's passport. I have it for safe-keeping. Please don't lose it. I know this is asking a lot of you, but my mother has taken a liking to you, and she is so keen to show you her work. I'm sure it will all be fine.'

'But what if she wanders off in the middle of Oxford? How will I find her?'

'I have put a GPS tracking signal on her mobile. Before you go, I'll show you how it works.'

'It didn't work the other night,' she says.

'Ah, no. She left it in the flat.' He hesitates and then asks, awkwardly, 'Oh, and I don't suppose my mother has paid you anything yet?'

Ana shakes her head.

'I thought not. Well here is the payment for last month. I think that is what she agreed with you.'

Ana checks the money and nods. 'Thank you. That will keep the landlord happy.'

'Oh and of course you'll be paid for your time in Oxford, as well. If you have any questions before you leave for England, just telephone me. My mobile number and the house phone number are in the folder.'

He pushes his chair away from the table and leans back.

'Right, so now that we have all that organised, maybe I can fill you in on my mother's background.'

'Please. There are a few gaps in what she has already told me.'

He smiles. Only a few?

His wife comes in, carrying a tray with two cups of coffee, a jug of milk and a small bowl of sugar. 'I thought you might like some coffee while you were working,' she says, placing the tray on the table.

'Thank you, *cariño*.'

'Yes, thanks,' says Ana. 'I'm dying for a coffee. No, nothing with it, *gracias*.'

Martin pours milk into his own cup and begins.

'Well, I don't know if you realize, but I was only two when we moved to Spain, so my memories of those early years are rather vague, and I can't be sure if I actually remember what happened or whether it's what someone told me had happened. Anyway I'll do my best.'

He sips his coffee. 'We left England in 1963 and I'm sure that my mother must have found life here in Spain very strange. We had been living in a place called Kingston-on-Thames, a small town just outside London, when she and my dad split up.'

'Not in Oxford then?'

'No, but it wasn't far from there. Anyway, after my parents separated, she decided to move to Spain. I think it was probably to get as far away from him as possible.'

'She never mentions your father,' Ana says. 'I take it his name was Henderson, the same as yours?'

'Yes, that's right. Nicholas Henderson. I don't remember him. As I said, I was very small when we left, and my mother refuses to talk about him. She would get this angry tightness around her mouth whenever I asked anything about him. I was just a boy, and naturally I was curious about my father, but she has never relented, not even now. The only thing I remember is her telling me one day that he had died in a car crash. This was when I was about ten and she only said that because I told her we had a school project to do about our families.'

'Was that before you left England, or had the car crash happened later?' Ana asks, sounding rather inquisitorial, Martin thinks.

'I really don't know. As I keep saying, the subject was taboo. It might not even be true; maybe she just said that to shut me up. I was a very persistent child.'

'Mmn. So there were just the two of you?' Ana asks. 'No other relatives?'

'No. I never knew my father's parents, not even where they came from. Mama always said that they had died in the war.'

'And your mother's parents?'

'Yes, I have a vague memory of them. They lived in a house in the country. I can remember a big black dog and some woods behind the house. But there again maybe my mother told me about it.'

'Did you ever see them after you came to Spain?'

He shakes his head.

'No. We never saw anyone. Looking back, I think she must have cut all ties with her past. Except for her agent, Harry. She kept in contact with him. She had to. She needed to make some money.'

'So what do you remember about those early days living here?'

'Well, Spain was very different at that time. You're probably too young to remember. For a start there were no motorways, and the main coast road wasn't even dual carriageway. Not everyone had a car, like today, and many of the local people still used donkeys and mules for getting about. It wasn't even unusual to see ox-drawn carts lumbering along the main road with the traffic backed up for miles.'

'That must have been dangerous. No wonder the N340 got the reputation for being the most hazardous stretch of road in Europe.'

'Yes, but that was later. As I said, when I was a boy it was pretty quiet down here. There were tourists, but it was nothing like today's influx. You wouldn't have recognised the town.'

He breaks off and goes to the sideboard and takes out a battered photograph album. He shows her an old postcard view of Marbella, a white town with traditional red roof tiles. 'You see? Hardly any blocks of flats and so many green spaces. And look at this one of the beach, miles and miles of sand and hardly a house to be seen. This was where we lived, somewhere along there.' He points to a deserted spot to the west of the town. 'It was an old fisherman's cottage on the beach. It's all built up now, of course, but then it was lovely. We could walk straight out the front door and onto the sand. I remember there was a wooden shack on the beach that served as a bar, and my mother would go there to meet some English people. In those days the only English people who travelled were wealthy and that was particularly true in southern Spain; it was always

Lord and Lady so-and-so or Sir whats-it. They were an aris-
tocratic lot, most of them middle-aged I suppose, although
to me they looked very old. They wore Panama hats and
navy blazers and sat in deck chairs sipping glasses of gin. I
remember one old boy wore a monocle and a yellow bow
tie. My mother painted some of them. Have you seen any of
her portraits?'

Ana shakes her head. Her hair has come loose from the
clips that hold it back, and two ringlets hang across her
face.

'They'll probably be on display at the exhibition in Oxford,' he tells her. 'Anyway, life in the cottage was pretty
primitive. The milk arrived in a can and it was goats' milk–
–we didn't have any cows' milk until we moved into the
town. The local shop was small and had a very limited
range of goods. It wasn't even easy to recognise that it was
a shop, as it looked just like a normal house but with a bead
curtain across the open doorway to keep out the flies. Inside
it was like a bazaar, packed with cartons of dried food, tins,
smoked sausages that smelled of garlic, huge wheels of
evil-smelling cheese and whatever fruit and vegetables
were in season. Most of the foodstuffs were loose and
stored in barrels; everything came in bulk and was meas-
ured out to you in paper cones or wrapped in newspaper.
There was no tea, which was a great hardship for my mother, and only local wine, which she soon got used to. I remember that we lived mostly on *chorizo* and fish that we
got straight from the fishermen, usually mackerel or
boquerones. My mother would send me down onto the
beach to wait for the fishermen to come in with their catch.
I became quite good at choosing the biggest, fattest ones,

and I'd carry them home in a bucket. I must have been about four or five by then.

'The local people were very friendly and I used to play with our neighbour's two little girls, that is, until I grew too old to play with girls. At first I had no idea what they were talking about, but it didn't take me long to pick up the language, although it was very rough Spanish that they spoke, and I had to unlearn a lot of it when I went to school. My mother found an Englishwoman who gave her Spanish lessons, so before long we could talk to everyone. Our Spanish neighbours would pop round for a chat, and my mother would speak to them in a mixture of Spanish and English. They were poor people, just like us at that time, but they never came empty-handed. They always brought us a gift, some oranges or some olives, a lettuce from the garden or a few tomatoes. My mother would reciprocate by painting a portrait of their children or their animals.'

He smiles when he remembers the excitement of the children when they saw the paintings. 'Our next-door neighbour had a donkey and several chickens,' he continues. 'You were considered rich if you owned a donkey, and at night our neighbour used to take the animal indoors with him. He always said it was his most valued possession, more valuable than his wife.' He chuckles when he remembers old Arturo, with his leathery hands and his toothless smile. 'Anyway, we lived in the fisherman's house for quite a few years, until I was about eight or nine. Then my mother sold it to the developers and we moved into the town.'

'Is that where your mother started painting seascapes?' the young woman asks. 'When you lived in the cottage?'

'I suppose so. She painted every day. The cottage was full of her canvases and, as you may have noticed, they were mostly of the Mediterranean. I think she was a little obsessed with the sea at that time.' He pauses, then adds, 'It's hard not to be, when you live right on the beach like we did. Then one day she persuaded the manager of the Marbella Club Hotel to let her put some of her paintings up in the hotel lobby. They were a great success. I expect you know that, even then, the hotel's clients were all very rich. There were many Spanish aristocrats, film stars, industrialists, even royalty who came to Marbella in those days. Not as many rich Arabs and Russians as there are today but plenty of wealthy people. That was really what got my mother's name known. She had been supplying a small gallery in the town for some time, but the paintings hadn't been selling well. It was the Marbella Club that changed things for her, and before long she was exhibiting in London and Madrid.'

'And she always used her maiden name?'

'Yes, always.'

'Tell me about her agent.'

'Harry? I never met him. He never came to the house. She used to arrange to meet him in Madrid, but I never went with her. I was at school by then. Then when I graduated I went to university in Madrid and then on to medical school.'

'You never went back to England?'

'No, never. My mother always said you should never look back, always forward. But we travelled. She took me to Rome and Paris; we went to Barcelona, Seville, Toledo, Granada, all over, and always to look at paintings. I became very familiar with the art galleries of Europe. I could recite the names of all the important painters by the time I was ten. I can tell you about the French Impressionists: Matisse,

Monet, Renoir, Degas, about Velasquez, Sorolla, Goya, Picasso—I can identify a Gauguin, a Rubens, a Hockney. She made sure my cultural education was not lacking as far as art was concerned. Not that it did me much good. I haven't inherited any artistic genes from my mother. I must take after my father, I suppose.' He tries to keep his voice steady. 'I'm a more practical type.'

Martin hadn't realized how emotional it was going to be, talking about the past. Just as his mother has always wanted, he has shut out all thoughts of his father. Now he feels it's time to find out more about him. After all, how can he understand himself or his children if he knows nothing of his own father? Was he tall? It's possible. He himself is almost two metres in height. Did he drink? Maybe that was the problem between them. Maybe that was why she left him. Smoke? They all did then. Was he an artist? Did he play sports? So many questions and she has refused to answer any of them. For a moment he is angry with his mother. She has no right to deny him his heritage.

'Is everything all right?' Ana asks, after a few minutes.

'Yes, of course. Would you like some more coffee?'

'No thanks, I'm fine. So, Dr Henderson, what was it like living with a famous painter?'

'Please call me Martin. There's no need to be so formal if you're going to know all the family secrets.'

She laughs and sits there waiting for him to say more. But what can he say? He should try to be objective, but it is his mother, after all; he's bound to feel an emotional involvement. Still, this woman is writing the story of his mother's life. Surely that should be written with warts and all.

'She was a very devoted mother, especially when I was small. I don't remember ever being left with anyone. If anything I think she was probably a bit overprotective, perhaps even too possessive of me. I was with her all the time, either playing outside while she painted or trailing round the galleries while she tried to interest people in her work. It was almost as if she didn't want me to be out of her sight.'

'But she didn't take you to Madrid with her, to meet her agent?'

'No, as I said, I was in school by then, a weekly boarder. I just came home at weekends but that was good because she never let anything interfere with our time together. And when it was the holidays she would take me off around Spain in her little old Fiat. I was about twelve when she became famous. It was one painting in particular that did it. Personally I don't see what all the fuss was about, but the critics went wild.'

'What was the title?' Ana asks.

'Blackwater Lake.'

'Another water picture? Is that the one with the sunrise and what seem to be eyes looking up from below the water?'

'Yes, that's it. Actually I think they're supposed to be some kind of plant, but that's the one. Anyway that painting made her name. After that, everything she painted sold like wildfire. We were rich. We moved out of our small flat and she bought a big apartment in the centre of Marbella, overlooking the beach. Her agent wanted her to move to Madrid but she said there was nowhere better than the south of Spain for a painter, that the light was so clear, the colours so vibrant. She was never going to move. She loved it here. She still does.

'After that she was invited to exhibit internationally, give lectures to art students, and travel more extensively. Sometimes she would be away for days at a time, but mostly she was in her studio, painting. I think she liked the fame and the accolades but her first love was always the painting.'

'What about friends?' Ana asks.

'There were plenty of people about. At the weekends the house was full of friends, hers and mine. She was a very generous hostess. Looking back I'm not sure she was all that happy, despite the money and the fame, or how true those friends were. I think she was happier when we were living in that fisherman's cottage, just the two of us and she could devote herself to me and her work.'

'She never married again?'

'No.'

'No boyfriends?'

'Not that I'm aware of, but you'd have to ask her. I can't imagine she didn't have some romantic affair when she was young; she was after all a very beautiful woman.'

'And rich,' Ana added.

'Exactly. She must have had a few Lotharios after her, but if she did have any affairs, she kept them very secret. She certainly never lived with anyone, even after I'd grown up and left home.'

'What about her agent?'

'Harry? I suppose she might have had a bit of a fling with him. Come to think of it, I remember she did go up to Madrid rather a lot, and it was strange that he never visited us. I do remember that when we had a telephone put in, he was always ringing her. She said it was about work, but I suppose it could have been something more. Again, you'd have to ask her.'

'So she has remained single all these years.'

He nods. It surprises him that he has never found this strange before. Now it seems very odd. Why would she never have another man in her life? It can't be because she loved his father too much to replace him. All the signals he has ever received from her have indicated that she hated the man. Or did she hate all men? No, it wasn't that. She didn't mind flirting with men; she still did it today, much to his embarrassment. She had made poor Adolfo blush when he tried to examine her. He pours himself some more coffee. It makes him uncomfortable speculating about his mother's love life.

'What about girlfriends?' Ana asks. 'If she'd had a romantic liaison with a woman, she would have wanted to keep that quiet, wouldn't she?'

This woman is very direct in her line of questioning, Martin thinks.

'No, I don't think she was gay. And if you suggest that to her, she'll either burst out laughing or throw you out.'

Ana smiles. 'It's quite acceptable nowadays,' she says.

'Maybe, but my mother is definitely not gay,' he says emphatically.

He resists the temptation to stand up and asks instead, 'Now, is there anything else I can help you with? When I was older I didn't see so much of her. I only came home during the holidays when I was at university, and then I worked in a hospital in Salamanca for a few years. As far as I know nothing much changed in her life during that time. She continued to live in Marbella, and she continued to paint. Her later work was never as sought-after as the early stuff, but she continued to be well-respected in the art world.'

He wants Ana to go now. Delving back into the past has been somewhat of an ordeal, and he wants to be on his own, to organise his thoughts a bit, calm these feelings that talking to her has unleashed.

'No, I think I've got plenty to work on for now. Thank you so much for your help, Martin. And thank you for the tickets.'

She offers him her hand, in the English way, but he leans across and kisses her on both cheeks.

'Just ring if you need anything,' he says.

She smiles, picks up the folder and leaves. He goes into the kitchen and pours himself a large glass of cold sherry.

'Has she gone?' his wife asks.

'Yes.'

'What's wrong? You seem upset.'

'No, not really. It's just this business about my father. I'm only now beginning to realize how very little I know about him. Mama never told me anything, not when I was a boy, nor when I'd grown up. You'd think she would have confided in me at some point in our relationship.'

'Well, ask her outright. Tell her you need to know. After all it would be nice for the boys to know something about their English grandfather. And I know you don't want to think about it, but she won't live forever. You need to ask her before she dies.'

'There you have it. I don't even know if he was English. In fact Henderson's a Scottish name but he could have been English, or an American, a Scot, an Australian—who knows what blood runs in my veins. I don't even know what happened to him. She told me he died in a car crash, but she never gave me any details, not even when it happened. Every time I tried to ask her something she just clammed up. She won't be any different now.'

'Well if you don't want to confront her directly, maybe we could find him on the internet. We could use something like *Quien Sabe Donde,* the Spanish website for tracing people.'

'He wouldn't be on that. I'm pretty sure he isn't Spanish.'

'No, but there are English equivalents. Go onto the internet and see what you can find. Or ask Emilio to do it for you. He'd like to help his papa.'

Martin finishes the sherry and pours himself another, ignoring the rather pointed look his wife is giving him.

'I don't know. Maybe it's not worth stirring things up after all these years. What if I do trace him and I don't like what I find?'

'It can't hurt. After all, he's dead, isn't he?'

'That's what Mama says, but can I believe her?'

'Well, think of it like this. Your mother is almost eighty. She has early symptoms of Alzheimer's.'

'We don't know that for sure,' he interrupts.

'No, I know, but my point is this, if you leave it too long you may never get the chance to ask her about him. Don't leave it too late, Martin.'

She goes to the fridge and removes the salad she has prepared for their supper.

'We'd all like to know more about this mystery man. If he exists,' she adds, sprinkling the salad liberally with oil and vinegar.

'Not too much salt,' he says. 'Remember your blood pressure.'

Obediently she replaces the salt on the table. 'You can add it after,' she tells him.

Martin goes outside and sits on the terrace so he can have a cigarette before lunch. He has almost given up smoking, would even go so far as to say, if asked, that he didn't smoke. He knows Sara will be tutting in annoyance, but he doesn't care. She says it's a bad example for the children, bad for their health, that a doctor should know better than anyone what damage it does to your body, and she's right, but at times like this he always reaches for his old crutch.

He wants to remember something, anything, from when he was small. Lots of people say they can recall taking their first steps or seeing a face peering at them over the edge of their pram. He has never had such memories. He closes his eyes and thinks back as far as he can. It is hard to sift his own half remembrances from the things his mother has told him. It is like looking in a broken mirror and seeing fractured images of his childhood: a sandcastle someone kicked over and destroyed, a collection of seashells, paddling through the shallows and his mother screaming at him to be careful, holding her hand as they crossed a busy street, a donkey with matted hair and red ribbons, the time he was sick on the stone floor of their cottage, his mother telling him stories as he lay in bed. These and other oddments float back to him, as ethereal as the cigarette smoke that is drifting into the cool evening air.

He can remember nothing from England. He tries to recall the journey that brought them to the south of Spain. And why here? Never has his mother explained why they have ended up so far from family and friends. There had been a train, he remembers at last. He has always been fond of trains. They had travelled on a train, a long, noisy steam train, exactly like the ones he used to watch going past the end of his road. He can remember it now, his mother stopping the push chair so that he could watch them go by, the huffing and puffing and that whoosh of noise as they pulled into the station. There must have been a station at the end of their road, or at least a railway line. The moment is electric. Maybe, if he tries, he will remember more. But try as he may, nothing else comes to mind. Those days are as closed to him as if they had never existed.

CHAPTER 10

Nancy has barely started to get dressed when she hears a frantic ringing on her doorbell. She pulls on her slippers and heads for the door.

'Who is it?' she asks, pulling back the bolts and undoing the chain. 'What do you want? Go away or I'll get my son to call the police.'

'It's all right Mama; it's me, Martin. Are you going to let me in?'

'Martin? What's wrong?'

She peers round the door. Why is her son here at this hour? She looks at the kitchen clock. Nine o'clock. He doesn't come to see her at nine o'clock. He should be at the hospital. She peers at him again. Yes, it's definitely Martin.

'Mama, let me in, please. I haven't got a lot of time.'

She pulls the door open and studies him closely. 'What are you doing here? Why aren't you at work? Has something happened to the children?'

'No, Mama. I just thought I'd call in and see if you were all right. I didn't want to wait until this evening.'

She turns and walks back into the kitchen, muttering to herself, 'He never comes at nine o'clock. He should be at the hospital.'

'You seem okay,' he says, following her and sitting down. 'I wondered if Adolfo had been to see you again.'

'Why would he do that? I told you, there's nothing wrong with me. I don't understand why you're making all this fuss.'

'Well, you had us all worried, disappearing like that.'

She snorts. 'I didn't disappear. I just went for a walk.'

She can see he doesn't believe her, and the truth is that she too is rather surprised at her actions. She never normally goes out at night, certainly not on her own; she is far too nervous these days. What's worse is that she can't remember why she did it, and although she won't admit it to him, she can't remember how she got there. She is sure it has something to do with the drowning she witnessed the other morning. It must have upset her more than she realized. The image of that swimmer, struggling against the waves, his arms flailing in desperation, keeps coming into her head. What a terrible way to die. What with that and all this dragging up the past, it's bringing everything back to her, things she wants to remain buried, things she wants to forget.

'I've got some news for you,' he says, looking at her and smiling.

What a lovely smile he has, always has had. Her little boy. She reaches out and ruffles his hair, what there is of it nowadays—he is getting rather bald.

'You're going to be a grandma again,' he tells her. 'Sara is pregnant.'

'I expect it'll be another boy,' she says. 'That's all we can produce in this family.'

'We're hoping for a girl.'

'I thought you'd given up on that,' she says. 'I thought Sara was too old.'

'Well she's in her forties, it's true, but the gynaecologist seems to think she'll be fine.'

'Oh, well. Tell her congratulations from me. What do the boys think?'

'We haven't told them yet. Better to leave it a while, just in case.'

He doesn't say any more, but she knows he is thinking of the two miscarriages his wife has already had. That had been a bad time, both in the same year. She thought they had stopped trying after that.

'Do you want some coffee?' she asks. 'I've just made some.'

'No, I must get to the hospital; there's a lot on today. We've just opened a new children's dialysis unit. I'll look in again tonight.'

'All right.'

When he has gone Nancy takes her coffee and sits in her usual place by the window. It is a beautiful day—no wind and the sea is calm and still. A woman is taking her dog for a walk on the beach; the animal races up and down like a mad thing then stops and digs frantically in the sand. She wonders what sort of dog it is. It looks a little like a collie, but she can't be sure. She misses having a dog. They always had one when Martin was young. The first had been a multi-coloured stray who had taken to sleeping on their doorstep every night, waiting for Martin to feed him. Martin had called him Rainbow.

She sips her coffee. So Sara is pregnant. That was the reason she went to see her gynaecologist. Well, she thought as much. She hopes it goes all right this time. Poor Sara had been four months along when she lost the last one. Nancy knows what that feels like, as though your heart has been torn out of you. She leans back and closes her eyes. Pregnancy. Sara and Martin are happy at the news. They want this child. They will plan and prepare and enjoy the experience together. There will be messages of congratulations and baby presents. Martin will go shopping with her to buy the pram and all the other paraphernalia without which the modern baby apparently cannot manage; the spare room will be decorated and furnished appropriately, and everyone will be excited about the arrival of another little Henderson. She sighs. Nancy never had that pleasure. For her, pregnancy was a word laden with doom, something to be kept hidden until the last moment when her swelling body betrayed her shame to all the world. For those unfortunate enough to be unmarried it was the worst possible stigma. It labelled the mother-to-be as a loose woman, a slut, someone who slept around. The circumstances did not matter. No one cared to look beyond the swollen belly and the ringless finger before passing judgement. Nowadays pregnancy is something to be displayed with pride. No longer is it mandatory to wear a tent-like maternity dress that gives no hint of the little body growing within its mother's—those awful garments that made you feel like a shapeless, shambling bear. Now, leotards, mini-skirts and shorts, tight-fitting tops that hide nothing, even, on the beach in the summer, bikinis, all are worn by the young pregnant mothers of today.

She had been so naive. It had never occurred to her that she might be pregnant until Nick suggested that was why she felt sick all the time. He seemed rather pleased about it—a salute to his manhood that he had fathered a child, but she thought the bottom had fallen out of her world. Nick might be happy, but she was not ready for this.

She told Helen, when they sat drinking coffee in the college café, that she had decided not to tell her parents until after the baby was born, reasoning that they might more readily accept an innocent child, their own grandchild, than the news that their only daughter was about to become an unmarried mother. Fortunately her father had been so angry about her living with Nick that he refused to visit her again and, although her mother wrote begging her to come home, Nancy always had a good excuse for postponing any visit to her family.

Nick, on the other hand, made sure that all his mates and many of Nancy's fellow students knew about the baby as soon as possible. It became his new excuse for extended drinking sessions in the pub. He, Nicholas Henderson, was to become a father. But Nancy could not share his joy. For one thing, she was far too ill. The doctor had told her to expect some morning sickness during the first three months but she hadn't thought it would be so bad. All kinds of food and even the smell of cooking would set her off, whatever the time of day. She seemed to spend half her life kneeling by the toilet with her head hanging over the bowl. Her breasts grew large and tender, and there was a slight swelling of her stomach, but because she could not eat she began to lose weight. If Nick had not advertised her condition so widely, she was sure that most of their friends would never have guessed she was pregnant. Helen, whom she only managed to see at college these days as Nick would not let her go out in the evenings without him, had advised her to have an abortion but she knew she couldn't do it and anyway it was too late now.

'I think it's time you told them you're not going back,' Nick said one morning at breakfast.

Nancy was sitting at the table drinking tea and eating dry toast, the only food she could keep down.

'What do you mean? Tell who?'

'Well they must know that you're pregnant by now. You can't continue at college with a bun in the oven, now can you? You have to tell them you're leaving.'

'They can't make me leave. The baby's not due for another two months, and anyway I've got another year to complete or I won't get my degree. I can't drop out now.'

'Well you'll have to drop out once the baby's born, so you might as well get used to the idea,' he said, lighting a cigarette and flicking the match on the floor.

'What about you? Are you going back in September?'

'Of course. This is my career we're talking about.'

'But you know how much I love painting. I can't just give it up because I've got a baby,' she protested. 'It's my career too.'

As he looked at her, he blew smoke into her face, making her cough. Another thing that made her nauseous: cigarettes.

'You can paint at home if you've got time,' he said. 'But remember that being a wife and mother is your career now.'

Nancy knew better than to contradict him. She had said as much as she dared. Of late, Nick had become even more unpredictable, and his mood swings were unnerving. One moment he was laughing and joking, usually when other people were about, and the next he would lose his temper, shout and throw things. She knew she had to tread very carefully.

When she first moved in with Nick, they had continued to see their friends, going to the cinema with Frank, a sculptor friend of Nick's, and his girlfriend Mary, or meeting up in the pub with Kelly and the other students she knew from her trip to France. Now the only person she saw outside of college was Kelly when he came to clean their windows. She had even given up going to the pub in the evenings. The smoky atmosphere made her feel ill, and sensing Nick's eyes on her all evening made her uneasy.

'I've got an appointment at the antenatal clinic this morning,' she told him. 'The doctor is worried I'm not putting on enough weight.'

'Well you don't eat anything, do you? What do you expect?'

'Do you want to come with me?'

'Me? Go to the antenatal clinic with you, with all those fat, pregnant women? You've got to be joking. No, I'm seeing the lads at lunchtime for a pint.'

She picked at the toast. It looked even more unappetising.

'Nick, how are we going to manage for money once the baby arrives?'

He still had another year before he finished his course, and he didn't even have a part-time job. They hadn't bought the pram yet, and all she had as baby clothes were some things the woman upstairs had given her. If it wasn't for the money she made at the newsagents, they wouldn't even be able to pay the rent.

'We'll manage,' he said. 'I'll find a job. Don't worry.'

'There's one going at Grimshaw's,' she said. 'They want a stonemason.'

He stared at her as if she were mad.

'Chipping away at tombstones and things, day in, day out? You're kidding me. No, I'll find something, just don't start nagging. Anyway how did you find out about it?'

'Kelly told me. I met him in town yesterday, and we went for a coffee.'

'You never mentioned it before,' he said, stubbing out his cigarette on the saucer. 'Why was that?'

'No reason. I just forgot.'

He had that look in his eye that made her stomach turn over.

'Oh, I think I'm going to be sick,' she said, leaping up and running into the bathroom.

The toast had not stayed down long. Afterwards she washed her face in cold water and looked at her reflection in the mirror. Her hair was longer now but being pregnant had robbed it of its reddish gloss and it hung in drab, dank strands around her face. Half the time they had no money for the gas meter, so there was no hot water to wash her hair. She ran a comb through it, but it looked no better.

'What are you doing in there?' Nick's voice broke through her reverie.

'Nothing. Just coming.'

As she opened the door his fist caught her on the side of her face. The pain shot through her jaw, making her gasp. The impact took her off balance and she fell back, hitting her head on the edge of the bath. Everything began to spin, and she thought she was going to faint. She could hear his voice, harsh and cruel, 'So you forgot to tell me you've been seeing Kelly, did you, bitch? I suppose you fancy him, do you? A nice bit of Irish rough. Is that what you like? Thought I'd never find out? Well you won't do it again in a hurry, my girl. I'll see to that.'

He pulled her up by her hair and dragged her into the living room.

'Nick, stop. I haven't done anything wrong. Leave me alone.'

'Oh stop, is it now? I bet you didn't say that to Kelly, did you?'

'It was only a cup of coffee, Nick. Kelly's your friend. Why would you think I'd do anything like that?'

She began to cry. He was going to kill her, and for what? Had he gone mad? She put her hand to her head and felt the blood trickling down her face. Then she passed out.

When she came round she was lying on the sofa and Nick was sitting next to her, his head in his hands. He looked as though he'd been crying. She tried to sit up.

'Are you okay?' he asked. 'I'm so sorry, Nancy. I didn't mean to do it. I don't know what came over me. I love you so much I can't bear the thought of you being with anyone else.'

She didn't reply. What was the use? He would take her words and twist them into what he wanted to hear.

'Are you sure you're all right?' he asked.

'I'm fine. I just need to go to the bathroom.'

She locked the bathroom door and sat on the toilet seat, staring at the floor. Why did he do it? He had lost his temper before, but he had never hit her. She began to cry silently, hot salty tears that ran down her face. He mustn't hear her.

Nancy stayed there in the bathroom as long as she dared and, after applying some make-up to her swollen cheek and washing the blood from her hair, went back into the living room. Nick was still sitting there, looking contrite.

'I have to go to the clinic,' she said. 'I've an appointment.'

'I'll come with you,' he said. 'But I'm not going in.'

The doctor had sent her to the antenatal clinic to learn how to look after herself and her baby, but after one visit, she was reluctant to return. She might as well have been a prostitute, she was received with such scorn. The look the receptionist gave her when she said she was Miss Miller and that no, she was not married, and the stares from the other expectant mothers were enough to warn her. The gynaecologist, when she was eventually ushered into his surgery, could not have been more unsympathetic. There was no kind word, no smile, no chat about whether she wanted a boy or a girl. She considered he was unduly rough when he examined her and had to hold back a cry of pain. It was plain that she was an unwelcome intrusion into their world of happy families. It seemed to her that her only sin was in reminding them that, married or not, they had all succumbed to carnal desire, that it was sex that had brought them here with the fruits of their lust growing in their bellies. Only for her, it was much worse because there was no greater sin for a young English woman in 1958 than to be pregnant and unmarried.

The next day she went to Woolworth's and bought herself a brass curtain ring and took to calling herself Mrs Miller.

The week before Nancy was due back in college, she received a letter from her mother saying that she was coming to Kingston. Her father was not well enough to accompany her, so she would only stay a short while. She wanted to meet for coffee.

'What shall I do?' she asked Nick, handing him the letter.

'She'll have to know sooner or later,' he said. 'So tell her.'

'I should have gone to see her before,' she said. 'She will be hurt that I haven't told her about the baby.'

'Do you think she'll care?'

'Of course she will. She's my mother, after all. This will be her first grandchild.'

'You're a stupid bitch. She won't want anything to do with you or your bastard baby. I'm your family now. Remember that.'

She didn't answer. Nick hated it when she spoke about her parents. He was becoming so jealous lately. She hoped he wasn't going to be jealous of the baby.

'So, I can meet her for coffee then?' she asked, meekly.

'I suppose you'll have to. At least it will be over and done with.' Then he smiled. 'She might give you some money. Tell her you need it for the baby. She won't be able to refuse you then.'

Her mother knew Nancy was pregnant right away, despite the loose smock she was wearing. She put her arms around her and whispered, 'Oh, my poor girl, what have you got into now?'

'It's all right, Mum. We're getting married, once the baby's born.'

'When is it due?'

'Two months' time.'

'So soon? You're not very big.'

'I'm fine, really, Mum. Don't worry. How's Dad?'

'Your father's not too good. It's his heart, you know. He's had to give up work. Early retirement, they call it. He says he's been put out to grass and he's not happy about it.'

'What about you, Mum?'

'Oh, I'm all right.'

'I've missed you, Mum,' she said, starting to cry. 'I'm so lonely.'

It was true. Now that she was sitting opposite her mother, she realized how much she needed her. She had been wrong to let Nick come between them. He had separated her from her family and isolated her from her friends, just as Helen had warned. The only life she'd had was at college, and now he said she had to give that up too.

'Don't cry, sweetheart,' her mother said, taking her hand in hers and stroking it gently. 'You'll soon have a lovely little baby to look after. Then you won't have time to be lonely. Come along, let's order some tea.'

Nancy wiped her eyes and gave her a watery smile.

'That's better. Now tell me about your painting. Have you done anything new lately?'

'I've done a bit. The flat's not very big, so it's not easy.'

'But you're back at college next week aren't you? You'll be able to work better there, spread yourself out.'

'Nick wants me to leave.'

'I suppose you will have to sooner or later,' her mother said sadly. 'But that doesn't mean you have to stop painting.'

Her mother reached into her handbag and pulled out her purse. 'Just a little something for the baby,' she said. 'Buy her something nice from her grandma.'

Nancy had not intended to ask her mother for any money, despite what Nick had said, but she took it anyway.

'We don't know it's going to be a girl,' she said.

'Oh yes, I'm sure it will be a girl. A lovely little red-haired girl just like my Nancy,' her mother said, reaching out and patting Nancy's tummy. 'I'm sure of it.'

'Thanks Mum. I do need to buy her a few things.'

All too soon they finished their tea and her mother was talking about catching her bus.

'Your dad doesn't know I've come to see you,' she said. 'He'll be cross if he finds out.'

'Will you tell him about the baby?' Nancy asked.

'Later. Not now.'

She put her arms around Nancy and hugged her.

'You take care my darling,' she said. 'Take good care.'

Nancy walked with her to the bus stop and watched as her mother boarded the bus. She stood there as the bus pulled away and gradually disappeared from view, taking with it her only link with her old home.

It was still early so she decided to walk through the park and down to Kingston Bridge. It was a lovely October morning with the sun gleaming on the Thames and the tree-lined banks that bordered Hampton Court were bright with autumn leaves. She paused, leaning on the stone parapets, and looked down at the fast-flowing river below. A coxed four rowed beneath the bridge, heading downstream to Teddington. She could hear the high-pitched cries of the cox as he bawled out his instructions and the splash of the oars cutting through the water. A heron flew low and fast along the river, landing on the bank with a clap of its huge wings, and perched motionless, waiting for its prey. Close by, on the far side of the river, she could see a young mother with a toddler and a baby in a pram. The mother was teaching the toddler to throw bits of bread to the ducks but the bread kept falling short of its target. The ducks began to waddle towards the child causing him to shriek and hide behind his mother. This family scene made Nancy feel surprisingly sad. Would that be her in a few years' time? Would her world have shrunk to nothing more than feeding the ducks on a sunny morning?

Nick was waiting for her when she returned. She knew he had been drinking. The room smelled of stale beer and cigarette smoke. She walked straight to the window and pulled it open.

'Where have you been?' he asked.

She turned and looked at him.

'To see my mum. You knew I was going to see her,' she said.

'All this time to have a coffee?'

'We had tea.'

'Oh, tea was it?' he sneered. 'Tea with Mummy.'

'We had a lot to talk about. I haven't seen her in months. My dad isn't well,' she added.

'I don't give a fuck about your dad. What were you talking about? Moaning about me, I suppose, telling her what a good-for-nothing bloke you're living with, was that it?'

'No, Nick, nothing like that. We talked about the baby and she told me what had been happening at home. My brother Ted's been posted to Germany. We didn't talk about you at all.'

His hand was raised, about to strike her, but she opened the door and dashed out into the hall to protect herself and her baby.

'Get back here,' he shouted. 'Get back here now or don't bother coming back.'

She ran. There was no way she was going back now, maybe later when he had sobered up, but not now. What happened next she could never quite work out. Her feet were slipping and she was grabbing for something to hold onto and then falling, tumbling through the doorway and down the slippery steps until she landed in a heap at the bottom. Her hands automatically went to her stomach; all she could think about was protecting her baby. She must have cried out because she could hear the doors on the landing above opening and shutting and the anxious voices of her neighbours.

'Are you all right, my dear?' asked Mr Khan from number 2A. 'Shall I ring for an ambulance?'

'She's all right,' said Nick, bounding down the steps. 'I'll look after her. Here, come on, girl, let me help you inside.'

'What happened?' asked old Mrs Brown, hanging out the window of the flat next door.

'She slipped. Probably on some of that shit that gets left on the steps all the time,' Nick said, pushing past old Mr Khan and taking Nancy into their flat.

Nancy was too shaken to object. Her leg hurt and her shoulder was painful where she had landed on it but nothing seemed to be broken.

'I think you should call an ambulance,' Mr Khan repeated. 'After all, she is pregnant.'

'Yes, it wouldn't hurt to have her checked out,' said his wife, who was peering round the door.

'Yeah, yeah. I'll ring the doctor later,' Nick said, shutting the door on his concerned neighbours.

He half-carried her to the sofa and helped her to lie down.

'You shut your eyes for a bit, Nance. You'll soon feel better.'

She touched her head. Miraculously, she hadn't hit it. Her body had taken the brunt of the fall.

'I think they're right, Nick. You should get the doctor. What if I've done some damage to the baby?'

'We'll take you round there later. For now, just rest.'

He was quieter. His rage had died down, but she knew it could easily flare up again, so she did as he said. Maybe if she pretended to be asleep he would leave her alone.

She must have slept because it was dark when she awoke. There was a tremendous pain in her stomach and she seemed to be lying in a puddle. She tried to sit up, but the pain was so severe that she cried out.

'Nancy? What is it?'

'Help me get to the bathroom. I think something has happened.'

Nick got up and switched on the light. That was when she saw the blood. The sofa was covered in it. Nick had turned pale. He didn't need to be told what to do. He said, 'Stay there, I'll ring for an ambulance.'

The last thing she heard before she passed out was him running along the corridor to the public telephone in the hall.

Someone is shaking her gently.

'Señora Miller,' a voice says.

'Have I lost the baby?' she asks.

'Baby? What baby? Wake up, Señora Miller, the doctor is here to see you.'

She opens her eyes and for a moment she does not know where she is. Then she recognises María.

'María, what are you doing here? How did you get in?'

'You left the door unlocked. And now the doctor is here to talk to you.'

She is aware of someone standing behind María, a man in a dark suit.

'It's only me, Mrs Miller, Adolfo. I just wanted to see if you were all right. Martin said he'd tell you I was coming by.'

'Oh, hello Adolfo. I thought you were someone else. Yes, Martin did say something, but really it wasn't necessary for you to come. I'm quite all right, really.'

'I'm sure you are, but I wouldn't be doing my job if I didn't make certain for myself,' he says and sits down next to her. 'Did I disturb you?'

'No, why?'

'You are still wearing your nightdress.'

'That's because my silly son arrived so early this morning, I hadn't finished dressing,' she says, then looks down at her floral nightdress and adds, 'Then I fell asleep. I suppose I ought to go and get dressed now.'

'Later, perhaps. I thought maybe we could have a little chat first.'

She nods at him. Adolfo has been a family friend for many years. Nancy knew his mother, a small, sprightly woman who looked as though she would live forever and then died suddenly of a brain haemorrhage.

'I wondered if you ever played any word games?' he asks.

'Crosswords you mean? No, I never liked crosswords,' she says dismissively. 'They're for people with nothing else to do with their time.'

'No, not crosswords, things like this. Would you like to do one?'

He hands her a piece of paper with the following words printed on it: "FINISHED FILES ARE THE RESULT OF YEARS OF SCIENTIFIC STUDY COMBINED WITH THE EXPERIENCE OF YEARS…"

She reads it and asks, 'What do I do with this?'

'Just count the number of Fs.'

'Is that all?'

'Yes.'

'It's easy. Three.' She looks at him. 'Well am I right?'

'There are six actually.'

'Are there?' She snatches the paper back and counts them slowly. 'Of course, so there are.'

'All right. What about this. Can you read this?' He hands her another piece of paper: "Teher rwee ahrdly nya cras ni hte raea nad hwenvere ew wnet pu nito hte ihlls ot edliver hte enwspppaers…"

'Are you mad? This is gobbledegook. Of course I can't read it. María, where is my breakfast?' she calls, realizing that she hasn't had anything to eat yet this morning.

'You said you didn't want any,' María says, reappearing with some fresh coffee. 'Would you like a coffee, doctor?'

'*Si, por favor. Solo.*'

María pours him a small black coffee and looks at Nancy.

'The same for me,' she says.

'What about this one?' he asks, handing her a paper grid covered in letters of the alphabet. 'Can you read any words there?'

'It's a jumble. How am I supposed to find any words in that mess?'

'Okay, try this one. Here's a list of the letters of the alphabet. How quickly can you think of words starting with each letter?'

'What, are you trying to teach me to read now?' she asks, feeling more and more irritated. 'A is for apple, B bacon, cat, dog, eat. Oh this is silly.'

'Okay, just relax. Let's try these instead.'

He hands her sheet after sheet but none of them make any sense to her.

'I'm too old for this nonsense,' she says, annoyed by her lack of success.

'Don't worry about it,' Adolfo says. 'What I'd like you to do is come along to my clinic next week so that I can do a few tests, just the usual routine things: blood pressure, blood analysis. I can send an ambulance for you or we can get Martin to bring you along. Whichever suits you best.'

'All this just because I went for a walk without telling anyone? I'm not mad, you know.'

'I know that, Mrs Miller. I'm just trying to be thorough.'

She smiles and says, 'I understand. Thank you, Adolfo. You arrange it with Martin.'

They drink their coffee and chat about inconsequential things, the weather, the latest comedy on the TV, and then Adolfo says, 'Thank you for the coffee, Mrs Miller. I must be going. I'll see you later in the week, then.'

CHAPTER 11

Martin has arranged to meet his friend Adolfo and his wife Estrella in a restaurant near the beach. They are making an evening of it, and Sara is with him. She has asked a neighbour to babysit for them. It is a long time since they have been out without the children, so he is looking forward to an evening uninterrupted with trips to the toilet, requests for ice cream, and the incessant beeping of electronic toys.

'Where are we meeting?' Sara asked.

'La Barca, near the beach. You'll like it—they have *langosta*. That won't be too rich for you, will it?'

She laughs and says, 'Absolutely not. It's my favourite.'

When they arrive, their friends wave across to them from where they are already sitting at a table on the terrace. '*Buenas noches*. Have you been waiting long?' Martin asks, greeting his friends in the traditional way with a hug and a kiss to each cheek.

'Hello, Sara, you're looking radiant. Pregnancy obviously agrees with you,' Adolpho says. 'You know my wife, Estrella, don't you?'

'Yes, of course. How are you?'

'Very well, thank you,' Estrella says, smiling.

She is Adolfo's second wife and is at least twenty years younger than him. They have only been married a year and according to Adolfo have no plans to have children. This doesn't surprise Martin as his friend already has four children by his first wife.

'I've ordered some white wine. Is that all right for you?' Adolfo asks.

Martin grins. 'For now,' he says. He looks around the restaurant. 'You certainly know the places to eat, Adolfo. This looks splendid, if a bit expensive.'

He feels his wife dig him in the ribs. She hates him making remarks about the cost of things.

'So you saw my mother again?' he asks Adolfo.

'Yes, briefly. I did a few little tests to see if she might have Alzheimer's, but I really need to get her to come to my clinic to be sure.'

'You'll be lucky.'

'Well, actually, she has agreed to you bringing her along. I want to arrange a day when we are both free, this week if possible.'

'How long will the tests take?' Martin asks. He has had to take quite a bit of time off work lately, what with checking up on his mother and Sara's pregnancy.

'About four hours, maximum, maybe less. A morning would do it. Of course she will have to go to the hospital for the MRI scan, but as I said, we have to wait a few weeks for that. I could try to hurry it up, but there is a lot of demand for the scanner, and it's only urgent cases that get moved up the list.'

'What are the tests for?' Sara asks.

'Well the MRI is to make sure she doesn't have a tumour or a blood clot. It's easy to confuse the symptoms of either of those with Alzheimer's.'

'If it was that, then you could operate?'

'Yes, probably. It depends on what we find, but there is a lot more that has to be looked into as well. One of my colleagues would do some of the tests, as he is much more experienced than I am in this particular area.'

'So what other tests are you going to do?' Martin asks.

He already has an idea of what is involved but doesn't want to put his mother through any unnecessary trauma.

'First, we need to look at her history to see if she has had a prior illness or an accident that could be causing the confusion or if she has any allergies to her medicines.'

'I don't think any of that applies. I don't remember her having any head injuries and I'm pretty sure she has no allergies,' Martin replies.

'What about anyone else in the family?'

'Didn't you tell me that your grandmother had to go into a home? Did she have Alzheimer's? Is that why she was there?' Sara asks.

'I'd forgotten about that. Yes, that's right—my maternal grandmother had some sort of dementia and they had to put her in an old folks' home. When we went to see her, she never recognised us. My mother told me that she always thought I was a neighbour's child.'

'Well, she may have had Alzheimer's. They weren't so good at diagnosing it in those days. As I say, there are so many things that can cause memory loss, especially in old people. We have to get the possible physical causes eliminated before we can start looking at the neurological ones. What we'll do primarily,' Adolfo continues, 'is give her a physical examination, check for diabetes and take blood samples. If nothing shows up there, then we will move on to a neurological examination: co-ordination, motor skills, sensory responses.'

'What if the tests are all negative? My mother-in-law seems pretty healthy to me,' says Sara.

'Well, we also have to do some cognitive tests.'

'So what are the signs of Alzheimer's, apart from memory loss?' Sara asks.

'Memory loss is the one that everyone identifies with Alzheimer's but memory loss can be linked to many things. We have to look for more signs, such as mood swings.'

'She has those all right,' Martin chips in.

'The inability to look after herself, wash and dress herself. I noticed this morning that she was still in her nightdress at midday, for example. Then some patients get very confused and suspicious of people around them.'

'Like her paranoia about María,' Martin adds.

'They can find that their ability to make logical decisions or to reason is impaired.'

'There's nothing wrong with her in that area; she's still as sharp as a button.'

'What will be more difficult to find out is whether she has any insight into her condition.'

'How do you mean?'

'Well does she know she is confused and forgetful? This can tell us how far down the road she is.'

'I don't know, but she makes lots of lists and the kitchen is covered in yellow post-its,' Martin tells him.

'Yes, and she relies on her diary a lot. She writes everything in it,' Sara adds.

'Well, that suggests that she is aware that she is forgetful and is taking counter measures. That's a good sign. Has she said anything to you about her little excursion the other night?'

'No, she just maintains that she wanted to go for a walk.'

'But you don't believe her?'

'She never goes out at night. She never goes out anywhere unless it's with me.'

'Do you think something happened? Did something upset her?'

'Well Ana, she's the woman helping Mama write her memoirs, told me that my mother saw a man drown the other day. And in fact that's where we found her, on the beach where it happened.'

'But she didn't know this man,' Sara says. 'So I can't see how it can be connected.'

'Did you say she's writing her memoirs?' Adolfo asks. 'That could have stirred up some memories that are upsetting her. Has she said anything?'

'My mother? Say anything about her past to me? No. She hasn't said a word. I don't think she has said anything to Ana, either, or she would have mentioned it.'

'Still it's possible. Remember how upset you were the other evening after talking to Ana about your childhood. Adolfo could be right. It could be dragging up the past that is bothering your mother,' Sara says. 'Maybe there are things that she would rather forget.'

'Like my father, for example.'

Adolfo signals for the waiter to come over.

'So how are you going to determine all this, whether it is just something emotional or whether she really has got something wrong with her?' Sara asks.

'A lot of it will be through observation, talking to the family, like we're doing now and doing some simple tests. It will take a while to get a result.'

'Are you ready to order?' the waiter asks.

'Yes, I think so, Marcos. What do we fancy? *Langosta* for everyone?'

CHAPTER 12

Nancy is angry. She can't find the remote control for the television anywhere. She has pulled out all the cushions, moved the chairs, searched through the jumble of books and papers on the table, but there is no sign of it.

'María,' she calls. 'María, what have you done with the remote control? María, where are you?'

María comes out of the bathroom, where she has been cleaning the bath. She looks hot and annoyed at being shouted at, but Nancy doesn't care. It's time this woman understood that Nancy knows what she is up to.

'What is it, Señora Miller?' María asks.

'The remote control. It's missing. What have you done with it?'

'Sorry. I haven't done anything with the remote. I never use it.'

'But it must be somewhere. Find it for me.'

Nancy knows she sounds overbearing and bossy, but she is convinced that her carer is up to something. Maybe her plan is to make it seem that Nancy is no longer capable of living on her own. Perhaps Martin has put her up to this. Well, Nancy is not stupid. She is not going to be manipulated by them, least of all by a fat woman in an apron.

'Have you looked in the sofa?' María asks. 'It could have fallen behind the cushions.'

'What, what did you say? Speak in English.'

María gives her one of her long-suffering looks and goes back into the bathroom. Well, if she won't help her, she will find it herself. She goes back to the television corner and begins to pull everything out. Soon the place is a mess, everything piled up in the middle of the floor, but still there is no sign of the remote control.

'Señora, what are you doing?' María cries when she sees the mess that Nancy has created. 'I don't have time for this. I have to take my daughter to the doctor this morning.'

She bustles about, replacing the cushions and picking up the papers and books that Nancy has scattered across the rug.

'Look, you sit down and I'll make you a nice cup of tea, something to calm your nerves,' she says.

'There's nothing wrong with my nerves,' Nancy snaps, but she sits down anyway.

She can hear María moving about in the kitchen, filling the kettle, getting out the cups.

'In a teapot,' she calls. 'Make it in a teapot. None of those dreadful tea bags.'

'*Si, Señora.*'

She looks up. María is standing in front of her, the remote control in her hand.

'Is this what you were looking for?' she asks. 'It was in the cutlery drawer.'

'What? Who put it there?' Nancy asks.

María shrugs and goes to fill the teapot. It's a plot to muddle her; Nancy is sure of it. Why on earth would she put the remote control in with the knives? It doesn't make sense. She knows she's getting a bit forgetful but she doesn't do silly things like that. . . or does she?

'Thank you María,' she says, as her carer hands her a cup of tea.

'You rest for a bit, Señora. I have to leave now but your son will be here later,' María tells her. She already has her coat on, ready to go. Nancy sips her tea and tries to relax. It was silly of her to get so angry over a missing remote control. The sun is warm through the window and she begins to feel drowsy.

As soon as she opened her eyes, she was aware of a bright light shining straight at her. At first she didn't know where she was—then she remembered the blood. A nurse in a blue uniform was leaning over her; her white starched cap sat straight and stiff on her dark hair. There was a man in a white coat at the end of the bed, looking at her in a concerned but kindly way. He had a folder in his hand, and he was talking to the nurse in a low voice.

'Where am I?' Nancy asked. 'What happened?'

'You're in Kingston District Hospital,' the nurse said. 'You fell.'

'The baby? Is the baby all right?' she asked.

The man with the folder moves closer to the bed and looks down at her, then addresses the nurse, 'So, what's her name?'

'Nancy Miller. She's nineteen years old and unmarried.'

'Has she been taking anything?'

'Not that we're aware of.'

'Drinking?'

'No sign of alcohol on her breath.'

'So what happened?'

'Her boyfriend said she slipped on the front steps.'

'Was it an accident?'

'I think so. He said there were witnesses. He said it was an accident.'

'Six months pregnant, I see. Well let's have a look at what's happening.'

'She's lost a lot of blood, and her waters have broken,' the nurse informed him.

'I see. But she's having contractions?'

'Every three minutes.'

As though to prove the nurse's words true, Nancy let out a frantic cry as the pain tore through her body.

The nurse put a hand on her shoulder and whispered, 'It's all right. It won't be long now. Just relax, the doctor needs to examine you.'

She lifted Nancy's legs up and placed them on the cold, steel stirrups.

'Just relax, Miss Miller, this won't take long,' the doctor said.

The baby was born at four o'clock in the morning. The nurse informed her it was a little girl but she was so tiny they had to keep her in a special incubator. A little girl. Her mother would be pleased. She had been right after all. What about Nick? He had never said if he wanted a girl or a boy. It didn't seem to matter to him. She wondered if he realized what was happening to them. Did he understand that when the baby was born there would be a new little person in their lives, someone whom they would have to love and care for? She still felt woozy from the gas and air that they had given her and lay there, drifting in and out of sleep. Visitors were not allowed until the afternoon, so she had plenty of time to rest. They had put her in a general ward now, and she was aware of new mothers feeding and nursing their equally new babies. Sometimes there was the sound of crying from the nursery and a mother would be called to attend to her offspring, but mostly the women sat on their beds, chatting to their neighbours. The curtains were still half-drawn around her bed so no one spoke to her, and for this she was glad. She didn't feel up to talking to anyone. She just wanted her baby.

'Nurse,' she called as one of the nurses scurried past. 'Can I see my baby? They took her away so quickly I never got to see her; I only had a quick glimpse of her immediately after the birth. Can you bring her to me, please?'

She remembered seeing a wrinkled red face and fuzz of ginger hair, and then her little girl was gone, wrapped in a blanket and whisked away by the matron.

The nurse picked up the notes at the end of her bed and said, 'She's very weak. Maybe in a couple of days.'

'Can you tell me anything about her?' Nancy asked, trying to hold back her tears. 'Will she be all right?'

The nurse stopped and moved closer to her bedside. She was older than the other nurse and her hair, scraped back under her cap, was tinged with grey, but she had a kind face.

'She's a lovely wee girl with lots of red hair, just like yours,' she explained. 'But she's only five pounds. That's very small. We have to keep her in the incubator until she is stronger. But you'll be able to see her soon, when you're feeling better. Don't worry now, she's in good hands.'

She looked at Nancy's milk-stained nightdress. 'It looks as though you're a bit uncomfortable. I'll be back in a minute to get you to express some of that milk so we can feed her.'

Nancy sniffed and wiped away a tear. Perhaps it was the gas and air, but she still felt slightly drunk and distinctively weepy.

'Can't I go and see her today?' she asked the nurse. 'Just for a minute?'

'No, dear. It's not a good idea. Maybe tomorrow. You won't be able to hold her—you know that. The risk of infection is too great.'

Nancy couldn't hold back her tears any longer and began to sob. This wasn't how it was supposed to be. The baby should be with her, not alone in some antiseptic chamber, fighting for her life.

'Now then, there's no need to cry; we're doing all we can for her,' the nurse said, her voice soft and comforting. 'Tell me, have you thought of a name for her?'

'Geraldine, after my Mum,' Nancy said, swallowing hard at the thought of her mother.

'That's a lovely name. I'll make a note of it in case the vicar has to christen her.'

'Christen her? Why would he do that?'

'Oh my dear, it's not certain that she will make it. As I told you, she is very weak.'

Nancy felt numb. After all this, was she to be deprived of her child so soon? Was the poor little mite going to die? This was all her fault. If she hadn't tried to get away from Nick, she wouldn't have fallen and the baby wouldn't have been premature. She would never forgive herself. She buried her face in her pillow and wept. Where was Nick? Why didn't he come to see her? Where was her mother? Did she know Nancy was in hospital? Did she know about the baby? Why didn't someone come?

Three days later she learned that Geraldine had died, and now she, Nancy, could go home. She had seen her baby only that once, and never again. It was not allowed. The nurse said it would only upset Nancy to see her like that, and although she begged them and cried for her baby, they would not take her to see her little daughter.

When the doctor came to discharge her, he warned her that she might experience some depression, but this would be quite natural. She was to go to her GP if she was concerned. But in the long weeks that followed, it wasn't depression Nancy suffered, it was anger. Anger that the child had to die before her life had even begun. Anger that her mother never knew she had a granddaughter, albeit for only four days. Anger that she never got to hold her baby in her arms, that she would never get to know her own child. Anger that Nick had not even let her mother know she was in hospital, and anger at herself, that she did not have the strength to leave him.

She wrote to her mother, telling her what had happened, a long, emotional letter stained with the tears she could not hold back. If it caused her grief to unfold her misery to her mother in that way, it caused her even more grief when she received the reply.

'*My darling girl,*

I am so sorry to hear about the baby but at least now you will be able to get on with your life, which most surely would have been ruined by having a child before you were ready. Your innocent daughter will now be in heaven and the angels will be watching over her. There is nothing more you can do for her.

I know you didn't want me to tell your father but I had no choice. He is my husband after all. When I told him what had happened he was naturally very angry. He says that if you want to continue to be his daughter you must leave that man and return home. If you stay with him, he says he will have nothing more to do with you.

I have prayed to God to give me guidance and I truly feel that it would be best if you were to leave him and return home. You know we love you. Your place is with us.

Your loving mother.

Nancy tore up the letter and burned it in the ashtray, then flushed the ashes down the toilet. If Nick found it he would fly into a rage and she would suffer even more. He was at college that morning so she was on her own in the flat. It would be easy to put a few clothes in a case and get the train to her mother's. She would be free of his possessiveness, his jealous imaginings, and his temper. It would mean leaving Kingston, but there were other art colleges. She groaned and put her head in her hands. If only it were that easy. Her parents' house was the first place Nick would look for her. He would follow her there and he would not leave until she went with him. Her father was an old man in poor health—he could do nothing to help her, even if he wanted to —and her brother Ted was in Germany. If she waited until Ted came home on leave, what good would that do? As soon as he went back she would be vulnerable again. No, she knew how violent Nick could be. She wasn't going to involve her parents in her problems. Something would turn up. Maybe Nick would calm down. He had been kinder to her since the baby died, so maybe being a father had changed him.

She picked up a pen and wrote:

Dear Mum,

I was very sad to receive your letter. I understand that Dad is angry with me but I never planned this to happen. I foolishly fell in love and my life began to change. I know I made a mistake but that doesn't make me a bad person. I am still my father's daughter. It breaks my heart to think that he doesn't want any more to do with me.

I can't come home. My place is here with Nick. My only regret is that you never got to meet your granddaughter before she died.

I hope you will continue to write to me, Mum, but I will understand if you decide you cannot.

Your loving daughter

Nancy

If she hurried, she could get it posted before Nick came home. Then she would go to the college and ask Toby if she could resume her classes. Nothing was going to bring Geraldine back to her, but her own life could continue. She was going to paint. She was going to pour all her sorrow and anger into her work. That way she would avoid madness.

'You're having a bad dream, Mama,' Martin says, leaning over her and gently shaking her shoulder.

'Oh, Martin. Was I? No, not bad really, I was dreaming about my mother.'

She sits up and rubs her eyes. She is always falling asleep nowadays—it must be her age. She no sooner sits down and picks up a book then her head begins to nod and she is asleep.

'Why are you here?'

'Have you forgotten? We're going to look at *El Paraíso* today.'

'So I'm off to paradise am I?'

'Very funny. Come on. Do you want me to help you get dressed?'

'Certainly not.'

She goes into the bedroom and takes out a brown cashmere sweater and a pair of cream trousers. There's no way she's going to that old folks' home looking like some old biddy.

'Don't take too long, Mama,' her son calls from the sitting room.

'Just doing my make-up,' she says.

She must be careful not to put on too much; she puts on her spectacles and inspects her face in the mirror. Yes, that's better. She doesn't want to look like an old has-been, with bright blue eye shadow and crooked lipstick.

'Ready,' she says, grabbing her handbag and keys.

'You look nice, Mama. Very smart.'

'One has to look one's best to go to paradise,' she says, happy that he has noticed.

The residential home is only twenty minutes outside Marbella but it is inland. It is a large white building surrounded by green lawns and carefully manicured gardens. The borders are filled with pink and red hibiscus bushes, and she can hear the constant hum of bees as they flit from flower to flower. A number of small bungalow-type structures have been built in the grounds, in the same white finish as the main house.

'I can't see the sea from here,' she says as soon as she gets out of the car.

'Yes, I'm sure you can. Just wait until you get inside.'

Martin has parked on the gravel drive in front of a flight of white stone steps that lead up to a pair of double doors, studded with copper nails in the Andalusian style. The entrance looks ominous, as though once you pass through the doors, you may never come out again.

'Plenty of room to get the coffins in and out,' Nancy says.

'Mama, please behave,' Martin says, but he can't hide a smile.

She has always been able to make him smile, even when she annoys him.

The door is unlocked, and he steps aside to let Nancy go in first. A man in a suit comes bounding across to greet them.

'Good morning. Dr Henderson, isn't it? And you must be Nancy?'

'Mrs Miller,' she says in an icy tone.

'Of course, Mrs Miller. Welcome to *El Paraíso*,' he says, his smile never wavering. 'My name is Tubbs, George Tubbs. I am the manager here.'

'Good morning, Mr Tubbs,' Martin says, ignoring his mother's hostile stare. 'It's good of you to see us on such short notice. My mother is going to the UK next week, and I wanted her to have a look at your facilities before she leaves.'

'It's no problem, Dr Henderson; in fact it's a pleasure. Now where would you like to begin? A coffee perhaps, or a cup of tea?'

He looks at Nancy who stares back at him, unsmiling.

'Or should we get right on with the tour? Perhaps the leisure complex. Or would you like to see our self-contained, secure, one-person accommodation?'

'*Dios mio*, it sounds like a prison,' Nancy says. 'Here I thought I was going to paradise and I'm off to the penitentiary.'

'Mama.'

Mr Tubbs throws her a look of unconcealed hostility. Maybe she should try to be a bit more friendly, just in case she does end up living here.

'I assure you, madam, that our accommodation is quite unlike a prison. Each unit is separate and secluded but quite secure.' He turns to Martin and adds, 'I'm sure you would agree, Dr Henderson, that security is very important.'

'Indeed. Please forgive my mother; she is upset because she can't see the sea from here. She is an artist, you know. Such things are very important to her.'

'Really. Well, we do have a vacant unit on the north side of the grounds. It is an elevated situation and has a splendid view of both the sea and the Sierra Blanca.'

'What happened to the previous tenant?' Nancy asks.

'He passed away.'

'I told you—a quick route to paradise,' Nancy mutters.

'The gentleman concerned was ninety-three,' the manager tells her, looking offended that there might be any suggestion that the man's death was somehow his responsibility.

'That sounds all right. Why don't we start there?' Martin says, looking at her for confirmation.

'Whatever you say, my darling.'

'Would you like a wheelchair? It's quite a walk,' the manager tells them.

Nancy does not reply.

'I think we'll manage, thanks,' says Martin.

The discrete, bijou accommodation that the manager has in mind is indeed on high ground, and Nancy pauses outside, drinking in the view, before she follows them into the bungalow. The sea is no more than a couple of kilometres away and today it is a milky blue, calm and still, the horizon blending seamlessly with a cloudless sky. Fishing boats drift lazily by, barely disturbing the tranquil water. A view from paradise, that's what it is. She turns to where the men are patiently waiting for her, outside one of the six identical bungalows that are grouped around a central open-air patio. The patio, designed in a simplified Andalusian style, is cool and shady, with potted geraniums, sago palms, and a fountain with running water. It is gay and colourful with blue and white tiles on the floor, matching umbrellas and cane furniture, but it is communal. She sees two elderly people sitting there. One is reading a newspaper, the other is knitting some tiny pink garment.

'Very nice,' Martin says. 'I should have asked Sara to come with us; she's much better at this sort of thing than I am.'

Nancy knows he is wishing Sara had come instead of him.

'Shall we go inside?' the manager asks.

Nancy shrugs but follows him through the front door. Bijou is an apt description; it is small but it is elegant and well designed. There seems to be plenty of storage space, and, although there is no separate room in which she could paint, the lounge is large and has an alcove where she could stand an easel.

'It's very nice,' she says, 'a bit small but adequate.'

'That's just what I was thinking, Mama,' Martin says, smiling encouragingly at her. 'Once you have your paintings hung up, the place will look just like home.'

'There are panic buttons in every room,' the manager says, pointing to a red button on the wall of the lounge, 'even the bathroom.'

He opens the door of a small bathroom and says, 'There is no bath but there is a shower especially adapted for elderly people, so that they can get in and out more easily. And this cord here will summon help if you were to be taken ill. Someone can be here to take care of you within two minutes of pressing a panic button or pulling this cord. We have people on duty twenty-four hours a day.'

He gives a mock tug at the cord. Nancy wants to turn and run out but she knows she wouldn't be running from him, nor from this safe, secure, bijou residence, but from her own old age. How pitiful it is to grow old. You are either ignored or you are treated like a child. She prefers the first. Better to be ignored than have your weaknesses exposed to the world. So maybe she is a bit forgetful from time to time; maybe she does lose things, and it's likely she was the one responsible for putting the remote control in the cutlery drawer. Perhaps she doesn't move as quickly as she used to do and her skin is as wrinkled as a dried prune, but inside she is still the same Nancy. She doesn't drive anymore; she doesn't have the strength to clean her house, and saddest of all, she doesn't have the energy to paint. This is what old age has done to her—it has robbed her of her ability to express herself.

'So, what do you think?' Martin asks her.

'Shall we look at the main house now?' She has no intention of living in this establishment. She is doing this to please Martin, but that is as far as it goes. For all George Tubb's smarmy talk, Nancy knows that once she signs on the dotted line she will be signing away her independence and she will never get it back.

CHAPTER 13

Ana knocks on her landlord's door and waits. The building is identical to many others in the street, built in the seventies and now in need of a good facelift. The owner bought the building some ten years ago. He has kept the whole of the top floor for his own family and lets out the rest of the flats. Ana and Andrew rent the one on the floor below.

'*Buenas días*, Ramon,' she says when he opens the door. 'I've come to pay last month's rent.'

'*Buenas días*, Señora Ana.'

He is still in his vest and looks as though he has just got up. He is unshaven and, by the strong smell of body odour, also unwashed. Ana waits while he counts the money and writes out a receipt for her.

'And the month before?' he asks. 'When will you pay that?'

'What do you mean? We only owe you for one month. I can pay this month's rent next week, when my boyfriend gets paid, if you want.'

'You own me seven hundred euros,' he says. 'And that doesn't include this month.'

'But I'm sure we've paid you,' she protests.

'Do you have the receipt?'

'I'll speak to Andrew. He must have it somewhere.'

'Yes, you speak to him.'

He closes the door and leaves her standing on the landing, feeling foolish.

Andrew is still asleep when she goes back into the flat. He was supposed to pay it. She remembers quite clearly that he said he would pay it last month because she had no money. She pours herself a cup of coffee and sits down at her computer.

Nancy's memoirs are progressing quite well, thanks to Martin's help, but his perspective has been that of a child and, as such, is rather patchy. What she would like is to find some of Nancy's contemporaries, someone who knew her before she was famous. She hopes that this trip to England will turn up someone who knew Nancy back then, although given Nancy's age, it is doubtful if many of her old friends are still alive. But the trip might help to jog Nancy's memory a little and she will get some more facts from her. So far her research has turned up very little. Despite being famous, Nancy has led a reclusive life and Ana cannot find much more than the official version of that life on Google, a version readily available to anyone. That in itself is strange, as Nancy does not seem a shy woman. But then maybe she was, when she was younger. After all, people change.

'Morning. Any more coffee?' a sleepy Andrew asks.

'Yes, it's fresh,' she says, thumbing through her notes.

'Still working on that artist?' he asks.

'Yes. I'm not half-way there yet'.

She closes her notebook and turns to face him. 'I went up to pay Ramon the rent,' she says.

'Oh, good.'

'No, not good. He says we didn't pay for last month.'

'Oh, I was going to tell you about that. You see I had to get the bike fixed and I owed some money to Pepe. I meant to pay it before you found out, but I didn't get time. Don't worry, I'll give him some money next week.'

He leans over and kisses her. He hasn't shaved yet. 'I'm sorry,' he says, stroking her hair as though she was a cat.

'You should have told me, Andrew. I felt such a fool. You know what Ramon is like, he treats women as some lower life form. It's all he can do to accept the money from me. God knows what his wife sees in him.'

'Don't worry about him. I'll go up later and speak to him.'

'I'm going to England next week,' she says.

'Really. Why?'

'Nancy wants me to go with her to an exhibition of her work. It's in Oxford. We'll only be gone a few days.'

'Have you been to Oxford before?' he asks, adding the sugar to his coffee and stirring it vigorously.

'No. I'm looking forward to it. I hope there'll be time to look around the colleges.'

'Is she paying? Make sure she pays you for all the hours you put in. After all it's not as though she can't afford it.'

'Her son is paying for everything: the flight, the hotel, everything. And he's going to pay for my time, so you don't need to worry about that. He's very generous.'

'So there'll be no problem with the rent when you get back?'

'I suppose not.'

Ana is irritated with his attitude—all he can think about is the money. She flicks through her notes aimlessly.

'What is it? I thought you'd be really excited about a free trip to England.'

'Oh, I am, but I'm worried about Nancy. What if she wanders off when we're there? I can't be with her twenty-four hours a day, and I can hardly lock her in her room at night, can I?'

'Look, this guy Martin, he knows what his mother is like. He's a doctor, after all. If he is willing to trust her to you, then you've nothing to worry about. The worst that could happen is that she ends up wandering around the hotel in her nightdress.'

'*Dios mio*. Don't say that.'

'Anyway, aren't you going round to see her today?'

'Yes, but I've arranged to go this afternoon. I want to get some more notes written up first.'

'Well, I'll leave you in peace.'

He heads back to the bathroom and a few minutes later she can hear the shower running.

Ana needs to prepare her questions carefully. She is convinced that Nancy's odd behaviour is not only to do with dementia, or whatever it is that she is suffering from. Nancy has a secret and Ana is determined to find out what it is. Her behaviour at the beach the other night was very strange. Why was she talking about the drowned man as though he was someone she knew? Has this got anything to do with her fascination with the sea? Has she suffered a near death experience or drowning or something? And what about this agent of hers? Was she having an affair with him, and where is he now? It would be good to meet him. Surely he would be able to tell her something about Nancy's past. Despite talking to Martin, she is still no closer to knowing anything about his father and his mysterious car crash. Perhaps if she asks Nancy right out, she might let something slip.

Ana has changed her appointment time because she wants to see if Nancy is more alert in the afternoon. She needs a lot more information from her if this book is to work.

'Who is it?' Nancy asks when she rings the doorbell.

'It's Ana.'

The old woman goes through her usual routine of pulling back chains and unlocking the door. She is dressed in a sky blue wool dress, and her hair is pulled back in its usual bun. She has put on some make-up but it has not been very carefully applied and her lipstick is crooked, making her mouth look lopsided.

'You look nice,' she says. 'Are you expecting someone?'

'Only you, my dear. I've decided that I've been letting my appearance go a little of late. That happens when you get older. So today I have made more of an effort.'

'Well you look lovely,' Ana says, trying not to stare at her bright red mouth.

'I wasn't sure about the lipstick,' she says. 'Do you think it is too bright?'

'Maybe a little bright for the day-time,' Ana says gently.

Nancy goes to the mirror and stares at her reflection.

'Yes, you may be right. Better for going out at night,' she says, rubbing it off with the back of her hand. 'Just a minute. I'll be right back.'

She disappears into the bathroom and returns after a few minutes. The lipstick is gone but the rest of her make-up remains.

'Are you excited about going to England?' Ana asks her as she spreads her papers out on the table.

'I think I must be,' Nancy says. 'I haven't been there for fifty-one years.'

'Things will have changed,' says Ana. 'Do you think any of your old friends will still be there?'

'Friends? No, my dear. I never kept in touch with any of them. You have to realize it wasn't like today with all these mobile phones and computers and cheap flights. No, I never saw any of them again after I came to Spain, not a single one. I made new friends.'

'But you kept in touch with Harry.'

'My agent? Of course. That was business. He would come to Madrid to see me.'

'He never came to Marbella?'

'No.'

'Why not? I would have thought he'd have liked a trip down to the south of Spain.'

'I didn't want him to. I liked to keep my private life separate from my public image. That's how it was then, not like today when all the most personal details of a celebrity's life are splattered over the newspapers.'

'So you only saw him in Madrid?'

'And occasionally at other exhibitions. Have you packed yet?' she asks.

'No, I'll do that the day before we go. You'll have to advise me what I should take. I've never been to England at this time of year.'

Nancy looks at the wall clock and says, 'Mmn, October. It could be cold. You'd better take a coat and a cardigan. And something smart. We may get invited to a reception or two.'

Ana smiles. 'Are you letting them know that you will be there?' she asks.

'Who, dear?'

'The organisers of the exhibition. Do they know you will be attending?'

'I haven't replied to them. Do you think I should? I thought that Harry might have done it.'

'Have you written to Harry to say when you're going?'

'No.'

'Well maybe you should write to him as well. It will be nice for people to see you.' She almost says 'to see you're still alive,' but stops herself in time. Instead she says, 'They will be interested to hear about your memoirs. It will be good publicity.'

'Do you think so? Very well, I'll write to them both to-morrow. Now are we going to get started?'

Nancy certainly has more energy today. Ana isn't sure whether it is because it is the afternoon, because she is excited about the trip to Oxford, or because the doctor has perhaps changed her medication.

'I thought you'd like to tell me a bit more about your family, your brother for example,' Ana says.

'Ted? Why would you want to know about him? Where was he when I needed him?'

'It would make the book more complete if we had some details about your family,' Ana says, patiently.

'Oh, very well. There's not much to tell. We haven't been in touch for years. Ted was two years older than me and the apple of my father's eye. Ted and I were not at all alike. He was all about down-to-earth common sense, a man's man. He had no interest in art or music or any of the things my mother and I enjoyed, he was much more like my father in that respect. He loved football, cricket, any sport. My father used to take him fishing at the weekends, or sometimes to a match. They got on well together. When he left school, which was as soon as he possibly could, he joined the army. My mother was a bit upset about it because she would have liked him to have a safe job at home, but my father couldn't have been happier.'

'Did you get on well?'

'When we were small, yes, but as we got older we grew apart. As I said, we just didn't like the same things. We had completely different interests; he joined the sea cadets and the local football team and I wasn't interested in sport of any kind. Then he went in the army and a couple of years later I moved to Kingston. After that we never saw much of each other.'

'Do you have any photos of him?'

'Some of when we were young and one of him in uniform, I think. Wait a minute.'

She gets up and takes down another battered photo album. She leafs through it for a moment then hands it to Ana.

'That's Ted.'

She points to a gangly youth in a military uniform. He is grinning at the camera. Ana glances at the other photos, all of Martin as a little boy, on the beach, at the zoo, feeding a donkey. She turns the page and asks, casually, 'No wedding photos?'

Nancy's mood changes instantly. She snatches back the album and snaps, 'Ted wasn't married.'

'He never married?' Ana asks, as if that was what she had meant all along.

'I don't know about that. The last time I saw him he said he had met someone and was planning to get married but I never saw him after that.'

'So you didn't go to the wedding?'

'No. I would have liked to have seen him get married,' she says. 'I would have liked to have met the girl.'

'So why didn't you go?' Ana asks.

'I'd moved away by then, and we'd lost touch.'

'That's sad.'

'Why is it sad? He had his life and I had mine. We weren't a close family, really. If we had been, I suppose we would have made more of an effort.'

She gets up and goes into the kitchen and comes back with a bottle of wine. 'Would you like a glass of wine?' she asks. 'I usually have a small glass at this hour.'

It is half-past six. Perhaps Ana should join her. It might encourage Nancy to open up a bit more. 'Yes, but only a small one. I have to drive home later.'

The old woman pours out two substantial glasses of white wine and brings them back to the table.

'Why did you say that your brother wasn't there when you needed him?' Ana asks, mentally bracing herself for Nancy's angry reply.

However, instead of snapping her head off, Nancy says, 'When I was small I worshipped my brother. I always believed that if I was ever in trouble he would come running to my rescue, but life isn't like that. It was a childish dream. When I was grown-up and could have done with a brother's support, he was away in Germany. It wasn't his fault that he never knew what happened to me. How could he have? He had his life and I had mine.'

She holds the photograph close to her face so that she can see it better, and Ana thinks she is going to cry.

'So what did happen to you?' Ana asks.

'Life happened, that's what. Until then I had lived a sheltered life, loved and cared for by my family. I thought that was all there was. Then I learned about passion and despair.'

She replaces the photo and closes the album.

'Why don't I prepare you for the exhibition?' she says. 'Have you been to an exhibition before?'

Nancy is obviously not going to say anything else right now. Maybe later she will be more forthcoming.

'Not one of any importance,' Ana says. 'I'm looking forward to it.'

'Well, when we get there, we must buy the catalogue, so that you can understand what the paintings are about.'

She laughs and drinks some more wine. 'What I should say is, so you can read what the critics *think* the paintings are about. But you will have an advantage. You will have me to explain them to you.'

'Do paintings have to be about something?' Ana asks. 'Can't they just be paintings?'

She is remembering what Martin told her about his mother painting her neighbour's chickens and the donkey. Surely the critics wouldn't be able to find anything very profound in them.

'You are more intelligent than you look, my child. Of course they can. But if you want to sell a painting for thousands of pounds, you need to have a good back story and if there isn't one, then someone will invent one.'

'You sound very cynical, Nancy.'

'I am, but I have made a good living out of my paintings so I shouldn't complain about how my agent presents them.'

Ana has her laptop with her. She opens it and calls up the file on the exhibition. 'We can look at what they're exhibiting here; it's all online,' she explains.

'Well, fancy that. Let me see,' says Nancy, moving her chair closer to Ana. 'Yes, you're right. That's my exhibition.'

Ana has to be careful how she words her next statement; she hesitates and then says, 'They seem to have divided the paintings into time periods. Look, these are your earliest works.' She clicks onto a small icon and the screen is filled with colourful paintings.

'They're a bit small,' Nancy mutters. 'How can anyone appreciate them when they're so small?'

Ana clicks on one of them and it fills the screen.

'That's better. Yes, I painted these after I came back from the south of France. I was very young then, still at art school.'

Ana clicks on one of the later ones and says, 'What about this one? Where were you when this was painted? It's very different from the earlier ones.' The painting is sombre and angular.

'I was just trying something out,' she replies. 'I think it's probably better if we wait until we are at the exhibition. You can't get the real impact looking at them like this.'

She is bored now, and Ana knows that it will be hard to get her to say much more about them. However the look on Nancy's face when she saw the last painting tells her there is more to it than that. Maybe she was just trying out new techniques, as she says, but there has to have been a deeper reason for such a dramatic change in style. She hopes the visit to Oxford will reveal more.

Jenny has already changed and is waiting for Ana when she arrives. Tuesday is their day for going to the gym together.

'Hi. I was beginning to think you weren't coming,' she says. 'The class is about to start.'

'Sorry, I was with Nancy.'

'The painter? How's it going?'

'Slowly. I might be able to put something together for her, but it isn't easy. She doesn't want to tell me anything about herself, only about her paintings.'

Ana removes her shoes, then pulls down her trousers and replaces them with a pair of stretchy shorts.

'She's old. Old people can be a bit funny,' Jenny says.

'It's not that. I agree she is rather forgetful at times, but it's more than that. I'm sure she is hiding something. The more I see her, the more I'm convinced that something happened to her back in England, before she came to Spain. When we talk about Spain her memory is fine. She remembers people's names, places, things that happened to her son, all sorts of little details. But when I ask about England she changes the subject or just clams up. Something's not right. And I still know nothing about her husband, other than his name.'

'Mysterious. Well, if you can find out what her secret is, you'll probably have a best seller on your hands. For all her success no one knows much about Nancy Miller. You'd be the first to open that box.'

Ana laughs.

'Yes, but what if it's Pandora's box? How do I get the genies back in again?'

'You know what you could do,' Jenny says.

'What? Ask her outright what happened to her husband?' Ana says, struggling into her gym shoes.

'Yes, that too. What I mean is that you could look him up on the internet.'

'Who, the husband? How would I do that when all I know about him is his name?'

'There are lots of web sites dedicated to that sort of thing. I've been trying to find my Irish grandmother online and you'd be amazed at what turns up. It seems that she was part of a large family from Mayo that went to England in the forties. Her father, my great-grandfather, went to Liverpool to look for work and got a job on the roads. Then he sent for his wife and kids. I've found relatives I never knew existed, some even my mother hadn't heard of.'

'So how do I start?' Ana asks.

'I'll send you the links. Once you have those, it's all self-explanatory. I should use Martin as the base—after all, she did give him his father's name.'

'Are you two ready? We're waiting to begin,' the instructor calls through the door.

'Just coming,' Jennie calls back.

'I'm going to England with Nancy next week, so maybe I'll learn something new there,' Ana says. 'I'm sure that's where the key to the mystery lies.'

CHAPTER 14

Martin hasn't been to see her since their visit to *El Paraíso*; he has been too busy to do more than telephone each day from work. It's Sara. She has been unwell, and Martin is worried about her. Nancy appreciates his concern. It is risky for his wife to be having a baby at her age, and he wants to be certain that nothing goes wrong. When he telephoned this morning, he said he would try to pop in some time to-day. He wants to make sure she remembers what to pack for the trip to England.

Nancy takes the plate of *paella* that María brought this morning and puts it in the microwave. She is not very hungry, but María will tell Martin if she doesn't eat it and then he will nag her. She thinks about putting it in the rubbish bin but the last time she did that, María found it. Now her carer makes a point of checking the bin for food each morning when she comes to clean up.

Ana was here again today, asking more questions about Nancy's family. Nancy knows she agreed to write her memoirs, but now she is wishing that Harry had never mentioned it. Sometimes she feels that Ana's questions are too intrusive. Why does she keep asking about Martin's father, for instance? By now she must realize that even Martin doesn't know anything about his father, only what Nancy has told him, and most of that is lies. It isn't simply that she doesn't want to talk to Ana about her past, it's that she finds it physically impossible. It is so long since she has spoken about those days that now the words stick in her throat. She is still overwhelmed with feelings of shame and guilt. When Ana asks about Nancy's family, Nancy feels that old resentment and sense of abandonment rise to the surface again. She doesn't want to talk to Ana about her parents because she doesn't want her to know she still harbours such ill feeling towards them. She knows that she should put it all behind her, and in fact, that is what she had done until she started these damned memoirs. What is worse is that Ana has a way of dragging information out of Nancy that she doesn't want to give her. She should have realized the skeletons wouldn't stay locked away forever, that once the cupboard door was open they would come tumbling out, screaming to be heard. Still no matter how hard Nancy tries, it is difficult not to feel that her parents let her down. If they had stood by her, things might have turned out differently, and no one would have had to die.

She pours herself a glass of wine and sits on the sofa to wait for her food to heat.

She shouldn't blame them; life was different then, and they had acted like any other middle-class parents would have at the time. But if only they'd had the strength to ignore social taboos and say, 'To hell with what people think.' If only they had put her first. It's hard to believe that social acceptance was more important to them than family, but that's how people were, in those days. Her parents were no exception. With hindsight, she can see now how petty her crime really was. For her transgression, her parents abandoned both Nancy and her child. But not her brother, she was wrong to blame Ted. He didn't know what she was going through because she never told him. She never told anybody except her parents, and they would never have mentioned it to anyone. They were too ashamed.

At first Nick had been kind to her. She thought that the shock of losing the baby had changed him, but she was wrong. If he had felt any guilt for what happened to her and their daughter, it soon evaporated, and he returned to his old ways.

Things were not going well for him at college and he was struggling to get good grades. His tutor knew about the baby—everyone knew—and at first, he was very considerate to Nick. But his patience ran out when Nick failed to complete one assignment after another. That was not just bad news for him, Nancy was made to suffer too. Every time he received a bad assessment, Nick came home in a rage, shouting and throwing things around the flat. It was everyone's fault but Nick's. He blamed his tutor for his inability to see what he was trying to express through his work. He blamed the quality of the materials the college provided. He blamed his tardy assignments on the fact that he had a part-time job. But most of all, he blamed Nancy. She could do nothing right. He was jealous of every move she made and everyone she came in contact with. Life became impossible for her. She had to think twice before she spoke, in case she said anything he could construe as criticism. She dared not look about her when they went out, or lift her eyes in case they happened to fall on some unsuspecting man. She was frightened to speak to, or even look at, their own male friends. Time and again he accused her of smiling encouragingly at someone in the street and, before she could deny it, sent her reeling from one of his casual backhands. His violence, which she originally thought was kindled through some provocation on her part, became customary, an automatic reaction to anything he didn't like. She began to realize that he did not love her, he despised her. He used her as a punching bag for all his frustrations; he humiliated her, dominated her life to the extent that she could no longer hold an opinion of her own. In the end she hardly spoke and walked with her head down, staring at the ground beneath her feet. Even at college he tormented her, running up to the third floor and bursting into her classroom, demanding to know what she was up to. Eventually, Toby banned him from their department and threatened to tell the Principal of his actions if he continued. That was when Nick decided that Toby was in love with her.

'Don't be so ridiculous,' she said. 'Toby is just trying to help me.'

'Oh, yes, and I know how he intends to do that. I've seen him leaning over you, putting his hand on your shoulder. I know men like him. They like to use their positions of power to flatter their silly little students into thinking they are special, when all along it's just a way to get into their knickers.'

'Toby's not like that. He's married, for God's sake.'

'As if that mattered. Now he knows you're as good as a whore, he'll think he's in with a chance.'

'What's that supposed to mean?' she asked, but she knew what he meant. It wasn't the first time he had suggested that she'd been with other men. The accusations started soon after she moved in with him, and although she told him over and over that she loved him, he did not believe her and, in the end, she did not believe it either. Nick was violent, lazy and abusive but he was not stupid. He knew his behaviour was slowly killing their love, but he didn't seem able to do anything about it. She could see that behind all his jealousy was a real fear that she would leave him, and she knew in her bones that he was never going to let that happen. He would kill her, rather than let her go.

'You were quick enough to drop your knickers for me, so what's to say you hadn't done it before,' he sneered at her.

'You're insane,' she said, turning away.

'Don't turn your back on me,' he shouted and grabbed her arm.

She wrestled with him, trying to pull away, but his grip was like iron. The more she struggled the more he twisted her arm. She could feel the tendons stretching and cried out in pain, begging him to let her go. Then she heard a click. A startling flash of pain shot up her arm and across her collar-bone. She screamed. Nick let go and she fell to the floor, crying with agony.

'You've dislocated my collarbone,' she wept. 'Oh God. How could you? Why do you behave like this? I've done nothing to deserve it.'

'Don't be ridiculous. I didn't touch you.'

He picked up his coat and headed for the door.

'Where are you going?' she asked.

'To the pub.'

'Don't leave me,' she moaned. 'I need to see a doctor.'

'Rubbish. It's just a sprain. Don't make such a big drama of it.'

She lay where she was, curled up on the linoleum floor, moaning quietly. What had she got herself into? A wave of self-pity swept over her, and she began to weep. What was she going to do? She couldn't put up with his temper for much longer.

There was a timid knock at the door, and her neighbour from across the hall asked, 'Nancy, are you all right? Can I do anything to help?'

Nancy swallowed hard and wiping her eyes with her sleeve said, 'I'm fine thanks, Mrs Brown. Just had a bit of a tumble.'

'Are you sure there's nothing I can do for you?' the old woman asked.

'No, really. I'm fine.'

She wasn't going to let Mrs Brown see her like this, so she waited until she heard her go back into her flat and close the door, then she put her coat around her shoulders and set off for the local cottage hospital. It was as she had suspected, a dislocated collarbone.

'So how did you manage to do this, young lady?' the doctor asked. 'Did someone twist your arm?'

'I just fell.'

He was looking at the bruises on her chest and arm. 'Quite a fall. Is that how you got all this bruising?' he asked, running his hand down her back and feeling for any other damage. 'Does this hurt? Or this?'

'No, just the collarbone.'

'Good. Well there doesn't seem to be anything broken, but you should be more careful next time.'

She nodded and tried to smile at him. Her entire body was aching, and she felt she was going to be sick.

'I'm sorry but this is going to hurt. It won't take long,' he said. 'Just relax and it'll soon be over.' He had barely finished speaking when she felt an excruciating pain, and her collarbone was back in position.

'The nurse will put your arm in a sling and in a few days you should be as right as rain. Take some aspirins if the pain continues, and if you have any problems come straight back. Ask for me, Dr Reed. Any problems at all.'

She could see from the way he looked at her, with an expression that was both kind and exasperated, that he guessed what had happened; he had seen the signs before. She could feel herself blushing with shame, but she was not going to admit it to him.

'Thank you, doctor.'

He smiled at her and patted her head, as though she was a young girl. For a minute she struggled to hold back her tears. She wished her mother was there—she needed a hug, as she sometimes had when she was a small child. A hug and some love, maybe a kiss on the bruise or a rub on the offending limb, that was all that was required to make her better then. Now, she needed a miracle.

Nick wanted her to leave college. Embarrassing her was one of his ways of making her life there unbearable, but she was determined to stick it out. All she had left was her painting. If she gave that up, she would have nothing.

'What's the matter with you?' Nick asked.

'I feel a bit sick,' she said, climbing over the bed to get to the bathroom.

'Not pregnant again, are you?' he called, not bothering to get up.

The Principal had thrown him out of college the previous week, this time for striking one of the staff, and they were not taking him back. He had blustered about it not mattering, but she knew his pride was hurt. Nobody liked being expelled, not even Nick. So now he lay in bed all morning until the pubs opened.

Pregnant again? She groaned. He could be right. This felt exactly like last time. Maybe she was. It was quite possible. Nick refused to use any protection, and because they weren't married, she couldn't get any family planning help. She was in an impossible situation. If she pleaded tiredness or a headache, he took no notice. If she tried to refuse, he accused her of seeing someone else. So she lay there and prayed that it would be over quickly and that she would not get pregnant again.

'I'm fine,' she said, fighting back the sensation of nausea.

'Come back to bed.'

'No. I'll be late for college.'

There was no reply so she had a quick wash and got dressed. She wanted to get out before he thought of a reason to stop her.

'I'll see you this evening,' she said, grabbing her bag and painting things and climbing over the bed again.

'Spoilsport,' he said, making a half-hearted attempt to pull her down into the bed. 'You'll have a lot more fun here with me.'

'I know, but it's important. Toby has hired this new model for us for Life Drawing. I don't want to miss it.'

The words were out of her mouth before she could stop them. Nick sat up, his eyes blazing, still holding her arm. 'What sort of model?' he asked, his voice icy with menace.

'I don't know, but he's supposed to be good. He's been working for the Royal College of Art for some time.'

'A male model? Nude?'

'It's Life Drawing, Nick. He could be. I don't know. Toby didn't say.' She kept her voice as light and casual as she could.

'So that's his game, is it? Gets you excited drawing some guy in the buff, then he can make his move.'

'Don't be silly. It's just a drawing class. We all have to do them; they're part of the curriculum. I don't remember you getting upset when you had nude models in your class.'

She stopped. Nick was out of bed now, and he was angry. She thought he would hit her. Oh God, please don't let him hit her again, she prayed. It was so humiliating, having to lie about the bruises on her face and arms. She knew nobody believed her, and their pity was worse than Nick's cruelty.

'You're not going back to that college again, ever. It's time to make a decision, Nancy. It's me or the college.'

'Nick, don't be like this, please. You know this is my last year. I only have one more term to finish the course. If I leave now I won't get my degree. Don't make me do this, please.'

She started to cry. If she defied him, he would strike her, she was sure of it.

'Look, I won't go in today but I have to go back. I just have to,' she said.

'I don't see why you want to go there anyway, not after the way they treated me,' he said.

'But you hit the Deputy Principal,' she said, without thinking. 'You punched him, and he had to be taken to hospital.'

'Don't tell me what I did,' he said and smashed her in the face with his fist.

Nancy screamed. Blood was pouring from her nose, down her clean shirt and onto the bed. Why didn't she just keep her mouth shut? She had promised herself, after the last incident, that she would say nothing to provoke him, and here she was again. She climbed off the bed and staggered to the bathroom, her head ringing. Her nose would not stop bleeding. The blood dripped down her blouse and onto the floor. She ran the cold tap and mopped at her face. Already an unpleasant dark swelling was visible on her cheek but it was her nose that had taken the brunt of his blow; it looked as though it was broken. Well she wasn't going to the hospital again, not to see the pity in the nurses' eyes and listen to their questions.

'Nancy, are you all right?' Nick called.

He was up now. She could hear him moving about.

'I'm sorry, darling. Really I am. I just can't bear to think of you with another man. It drives me insane. Please come out and tell me you forgive me,' he said.

The door handle moved. She would have to go out otherwise he might decide to break the door down.

'Just a minute. I'm on the toilet,' she said.

She dried her face, patting her nose as carefully as she could. The bleeding had stopped now but the swelling was more evident. She pulled the toilet chain and unlocked the door. He stood there, smiling contritely. And in that moment she knew just how much she hated him. It rose in her throat like bile and threatened to choke her.

'Come here, darling. Let me see. Oh, it's not too bad. You'll be fine; just change your blouse,' he said, pulling her towards him and hugging her. 'I love you, Nancy.'

She could not say anything. She could not trust herself to open her mouth.

She wrote to the college and said that for personal reasons she would not be able to carry on with her classes. She did not expect to receive a reply, but one morning when she had just finished tidying the flat, there was a knock at the door. To her horror, it was Toby.

'What are you doing here?' she gasped. She looked up and down the corridor. If anyone saw him and said something to Nick, he would surely murder her.

'I just wanted to speak to you, Nancy. The Principal told me that you had written to him.'

'Look Toby, I was just about to go out.' She had to get him away from the flat before anyone saw him. She grabbed her coat and bag and pushed her way past him. 'I have to go to the shops,' she said, pulling the door shut behind her. 'And I'm in a hurry.'

'That's all right. I'll walk along with you. I have a class in half an hour anyway.'

He looked surprised at her abrupt manner. Nancy liked Toby, and they had always got on well together. Normally she would have been delighted to see him but not today, not here. He followed her along the passage and into the road.

'I must say I was very surprised at your news,' he said. 'It's a shame that you couldn't just continue for a few months more. You know you would have got your diploma with no problem; you're already well above the standard for a pass. You're a very talented painter, Nancy—you mustn't give up.'

She looked over her shoulder to see if anyone was watching them, but the street was empty. Nick was at work and wasn't due home for a couple of hours, but she couldn't rely on that. He often just appeared at the flat, for no reason other than to check up on her.

'Is something wrong? You seem nervous, frightened almost. Is there anything I can do?'

They were out of sight of the flat now, and Nancy began to relax a little. The tightness in her stomach loosened, and she felt able to speak.

'No, Toby, it's all right. I'm just a bit tired. Look, I'm sorry about leaving college, but I have no choice. It's not working out. That's just the way it is.'

'I don't understand you, Nancy. What's not working out? Are you talking about your painting? You are by far the best student I have. You've never missed an assignment, and the quality of your work is improving with everything you do. You have real talent, don't you understand that? Is this a confidence thing, Nancy? We all get our doubts, you know; it's part of the creative process. Believe me, you have nothing to worry about. Nothing.'

If only she could tell him the whole story, but what good would that do? If Nick felt challenged, he would certainly hit Toby; all he needed was an excuse. She was fond of Toby. Why drag him into her squalid life? Best to let things stay as they were.

'Thanks, Toby, I'm glad somebody believes in me. But trust me, it's for the best. I have to leave.'

'Well I'm sorry to hear that, but please promise me one thing.' He pushed his straggly, greying hair off his face and smiled at her. His round, black-rimmed glasses made him look like an ageing schoolboy. What a kind, supportive teacher he had been to her over the years. How could Nick think that there was anything going on between them? Toby was the same with all his students, male and female. He just wanted to help them paint.

'Yes,' Nancy said, 'if I can.'

'Don't give up painting. Even if you can't come back to college, continue painting. I know someone who will buy your work. He's a friend of mine, with a small gallery in Eton. He has a great eye for new talent, and he saw some of your work one day when he called in to pick me up. He won't pay a lot, but you might be interested.'

He handed her a small leaflet. It said: '*The Aquarius Gallery, The Bridge, Eton — paintings bought and sold — oils, watercolours.*'

She put the leaflet into her coat pocket and said, 'Thanks Toby, for everything. Say goodbye to the others for me, will you?'

Then she crossed the road and went into the library, the one place she could sit and think and have nobody bother her.

Nick seemed genuinely pleased that she had left the college. He didn't complain when she moved the table closer to the window and shoved the rest of the furniture up against the opposite wall. This was her makeshift studio, where she spent most of her time, painting. He didn't seem to mind that she had created a wall of silence in her head. She tried to ignore Nick, pretend he did not exist, and spoke to him less and less. He didn't mind that she was nothing more than a compliant partner when they had sex. She couldn't think of it as love-making any more—for that you needed love. He had her there, in the flat, in front of him most of the day; that was what he wanted. He always knew what she was doing and where she was. He could monitor her every move. If she went to the shops, he knew how long it normally took, and he timed her. She had no friends, she had hardly any contact with the outside world. Her only respite from his watchful eyes was when he went to the pub or was asleep. So she painted. She entered her own world of colour and form. She created canvas after canvas, and when she ran out of canvases, she painted on top of old ones. Then one day, just when she thought she had found a way to live with her misery, he proposed.

'Nancy. I think it's time we got married. What do think, darling? Mrs Henderson,' he said, rolling the name around his mouth as though it were the sweetest thing he had ever tasted. 'Yes, I like the sound of that.'

He beamed at her.

'Well? Nothing to say? We can't live in sin forever you know, so it's time I made an honest woman of you. After all if I don't, who will? Who's going to want an old slapper like you?'

She thought it was a joke because, for once, he had a smile on his face. But Nick had long since stopped playing jokes. No, he was serious.

'It's an idea,' she said.

'It's an idea,' he sneered. 'Is that all our little Picasso can say? I'm offering to marry you and that's all you can say?'

'I'm sorry, Nick. You took me by surprise. I thought you were joking.'

'Well, I'm not joking. I want to marry you. I've told you often enough how much I love you, and that's what people do when they're in love. They get married.'

'Yes.'

'What do you mean, yes?'

'I mean yes, I'll marry you,' she said, as enthusiastically as she could.

'Next month,' he said, pulling her towards him and kissing her. 'As soon as possible.'

'We have to post the bans first,' she said.

'I'll see to it tomorrow. Now all you have to do is think about what you will wear, because I intend to have the most beautiful bride in Kingston.'

He picked up his jacket and made as if to leave.

'Where are you going?' she asked.

'To the pub. Want to come?'

'No. I've got the dinner to prepare,' she said. 'Have a good time.'

He would be gone at least two hours, maybe longer as he had something to celebrate today. The pub he frequented, The Black Cat, did not close until three o'clock; she would be gone before he realized it.

As soon as the door shut she took out a bag from the cupboard and threw some clothes into it. She couldn't take everything, just the essentials. She stopped and looked longingly at her paintings. No, she would have to leave them behind; they were too bulky to carry. She retrieved her post office savings book from its hiding place under the bath and tucked it into her handbag. She had ten shillings in her purse, more than enough to get her a train ticket to Reading. From there she'd take the bus to Wallingford.

Somebody is sitting on the sofa beside her. Nancy sits up and looks around her.

'Ted, is that you? Why aren't you wearing your uniform?' she asks.

Her brother is in the army. He's stationed in Germany, that's what her mother told her. So why is he here? What does he want?

'It's me, Mama, it's Martin.'

'Martin?'

She peers at him. Of course. She has been dreaming again.

'Oh, I thought it was Ted,' she says, rubbing her eyes and replacing her spectacles.

'Ted's probably dead by now, Mama. It's me, your son.'

'I know it is. What do you want, waking me up like that? And how did you get in?'

Her son holds up his key.

'Grandma, have you got any chocolate milk?' a little voice asks, and her youngest grandson jumps up onto her lap.

'Careful, Juan,' his father warns him. 'You're too heavy to be jumping up on people nowadays.'

'He's fine,' she says, delighted to see her little grandson. She cuddles the boy against her chest and presses her face into his hair. He's so like his father, despite his dark colouring.

'Where's your big brother?' she asks.

'I'm here, Grandma,' says Emilio.

'Well this is a nice surprise. Now let me get up and I'll see if I can find any chocolate milk for you. I'll tell you what I do have, some chocolate chip cookies. Do you like them?'

She can see from their faces that they do. She pours the milk into two glasses and spoons in generous helpings of Cola Cao.

'Hot or cold?' she asks.

'Hot, please Grandma,' Emilio says.

She opens the microwave; the *paella* is still there. Martin is busy talking to his elder son, so she takes it out before he notices and hides it in the cupboard with the plates.

'No school today?' she asks.

'Grandma, it's Saturday,' the boys say together.

She looks at the clock—they are right. It's six o'clock on Saturday, 12th October. When is it she's going to Oxford? Soon. She knows it's soon. She feels nostalgic for those grey skies and the cool, damp grass. The river that flows past her old home also passes through Oxford. Childhood memories come flooding back, of fishing for newts on the riverbank and messing about on an old punt, moored and neglected for as long as she could remember.

'I wanted to see if you needed anything for your trip,' Martin says. 'Do you have a decent suitcase, something lightweight?'

'I have the suitcase I've always had,' she says. 'That will do fine.'

'But, Mama, it's old and it's heavy. Why don't I buy you a nice, new, lightweight one with wheels, and then you don't have to carry it.'

'We've got one like that, Grandma. It's amazing.'

'We've got one each. Mine's blue,' says Emilio. 'Papa let me put stickers on it. It's cool.'

She smiles and takes the cookies out of the cupboard.

'Well I don't think I'll be putting stickers on mine unless they say *"Beware, bad-tempered old crone!"*' she says.

'What's a crone, Grandma?' asks Juan.

'It's an old woman,' she says. 'A bit like a witch.'

'Are you a witch, Grandma?' he asks, his eyes opening wide.

'What do you think?' she asks, bending over and scowling at him.

'No. You haven't got a long nose and a pointy hat,' he says, giggling nervously.

'And you haven't got a cat,' says his brother. 'All witches have cats. They're called a familiar.'

'Well, you do know a lot about witches,' Nancy says. 'But you don't think I qualify? What if I were to cast a spell on you both and turn you into toads? Would you believe it then?'

She mutters some nonsense, raises her arm, and points at them. The boys scream with delight and run back into the living room. How marvellous children are, she thinks, so full of life and energy. What a shame they have to grow up.

'Okay, boys, calm down,' Martin says.

He turns to her and says, 'You do realize that it will be Ana who will have to carry your case. I doubt you will be able to manage it. At least let me get you a new one, for her sake.'

'Don't keep nagging me, Martin. All right, if you want to buy me a new case, go ahead, but nothing flashy, mind.'

'No Mama, nothing flashy.'

'Which day is it we go?' she asks, as casually as she can.

'On the 16th.'

'Plenty of time to get ready,' she says.

So, next week she will be back in England. Which ghosts will be waiting to meet her, she wonders.

CHAPTER 15

Ana decides she will take Jenny's advice. As soon as she gets home that afternoon she sits down at her computer and opens up Google. There are plenty of web sites to choose from, but she goes straight for the one Jenny recommended. It's not free, but neither is it very expensive. She logs in and soon has the options open to her. There are a number of Nicholas Hendersons, but only one that fits what little she knows of him. The first document she opens is his birth certificate, giving the names of his parents and where he was born. Jenny has explained how it works. You sometimes have to go back in order to find what you want. So she looks up his parents, discovers they are indeed dead and that there was a brother, also now dead. Then she finds Nicholas Henderson's marriage certificate. This is a surprise. So Nancy was married after all. But why is she so reluctant to tell her? Ana had begun to believe Nicholas Henderson didn't exist, that whoever Martin's father was had been a one-night stand at a time when people were becoming more liberated in their sexual attitudes, that Nancy hadn't known who was the father of her child. But no, there it is in black and white. She had known him. She'd married him.

After an hour's work and a total expense of twenty-five euros, she has as much information as the system is inclined to give her. Nancy's mysterious husband was born in London in 1937, which made him two years older than

Nancy. He was the elder of two sons, his brother was called Patrick, and his parents were June and Fredrick. His mother died when she was only forty of, according to the death certificate, a heart complaint. His father remarried, to a woman called Agnes, and it seems that they had no children. According to various census records the family resided in north London, where Fredrick lived until at seventy he died of sclerosis of the liver. The younger son, Patrick, died in an accident at the age of thirty-five. He seems to have been unmarried. It is so easy to find the information that Ana is surprised that there is no trace of a death certificate for Nicholas Henderson. Can this mean he is still alive? She puts his name in for a general search and there he is again but it is not his death certificate that comes up—this time his name appears as the named father on two birth certificates. It's definitely him, there he is, the father of Martin Henderson, male, born in the Kingston Maternity home in 1961, mother Nancy Miller. The other birth certificate puzzles her. The father is a Nicholas Henderson, occupation student, and the mother's name is Miller. The year is 1958. Can it be Nancy? The baby is female, a girl named Geraldine. Nancy has never mentioned having another child, and Martin never spoke of a sister. Is this the secret Nancy has been hiding from them?

She prints out copies of all the documents and puts them in her folder. She has a fuller picture of Nancy's husband now, but two questions remain. Is Nicholas Henderson still alive? Who is Geraldine and what happened to her?

She is tired, but her mind is buzzing. She has to speak to someone about what she has found, so she rings Jenny. A sleepy voice answers after a couple of rings.

'Ana, is something wrong?'

'No, I just wanted to talk. Are you busy?'

'No, I was asleep. Do you know what time it is?'

Ana checks her watch; it's almost midnight.

'Oh, I'm sorry; I didn't realize it was so late. I lost track of time. I've been on the computer all evening.'

'That's okay. I'm awake now. So what is it? What did you find out?'

'You were right about the internet. It's amazing what you can turn up about people.'

'Is this about that Henderson chap?'

'Yes. I think he could still be alive.' She hears her friend yawn and adds, 'Look, I'm sorry. I'll tell you all about it tomorrow.'

'No, you won't. I'm wide awake now, and Pepe is still snoring away beside me. Tell me what you've found out.'

'It's more to do with what I haven't found, actually. He appears on all the usual things, even the census returns, but there is no death certificate.'

'Maybe he died in another country. Have you contacted any of the consulates? Here in Málaga, for example.'

'No, I didn't think of that.'

'Or France? Didn't you tell me that he and Nancy spent some time together in the south of France?'

'Yes, but that was when they were students.'

'Still, it was a place he liked. He might have gone back there.'

Ana feels a bit deflated. 'Okay, tomorrow I'll contact all the consulates.'

'And check for a death certificate in Spain.'

'Right. I'll let you know how I get on.'

'And what about the car crash? Have you turned up any details of that?'

'No. I thought if I could get a date of death then I could search the local papers but at the moment I have no idea when he died. And I found something else as well.'

'What?'

'Nancy had another child, a girl. I found the birth certificate.'

'And she never mentioned it?'

'No. Martin thinks he's an only child.'

'That's a difficult one to handle. So what are you going to do with all this information when you've finished?' Jenny asks.

Ana hesitates. 'I don't know. Tell the son I suppose.'

'Shouldn't you speak to Nancy first, especially about her daughter?'

'She won't tell me anything.'

'If you show her the documents, she'll have to speak about it.'

Jenny always makes things sound so easy, but she has never met Nancy. If Nancy doesn't want to discuss something, then that is that. Ana doesn't want to be fired because she is enjoying the job and the money is very useful. Martin is very prompt at transferring her money each month. She will miss it when the book is finished.

'I'll see what her son says first. He's much easier to talk to.'

'Okay.' Jenny yawns. 'Now, I'm going back to sleep before Pepe wakes up and thinks it's his birthday.' She laughs and hangs up.

The next morning Ana is up before Andrew is awake. She has made a plan. She will drive to the British Consulate in Málaga and ask them to make a search for Nancy's husband. She'll say he's a distant relative and her aunt wants to know if he died while living in Spain because she can't find any trace of his death in England. That's ninety percent true anyway.

'Hey, sleepyhead. I'm going into Málaga. I won't be too long—I'll be back for lunch,' she tells Andrew.

'Mmmn. Okay, I'll take you out somewhere. I got paid last night.'

'That's good, but I'd sooner you paid the rent.'

'Fine. Whatever.' He rolls over and pulls the covers over his head.

'I'll phone if there's a problem.'

'Okay.'

When she arrives home, Andrew has prepared lunch, and he has paid the back rent, so they are broke again. 'How did it go?' he asks, passing her a bowl of *callos*—tripe and tomato are one of his favourite dishes.

'I've drawn a blank,' she says. 'There is no death certificate for Nancy's husband in Spain, either. The assistant consul was extremely helpful, but he couldn't find any trace of him.'

The young man had even extended the search to Madrid and all the other consulates on the Iberian peninsula but not only was there no death certificate, there was no indication that Nicholas Henderson had ever lived in Spain and if he had, he had not registered with the British Consulate. This, the assistant consul had assured her, was not an unusual occurrence.

'So you've been barking up the wrong tree,' Andrew says, dunking a chunk of bread into his stew.

'What?'

Andrew likes to test her with uncommon English phrases. She thinks quickly. It's obvious.

'Yes, I've been barking up the other tree.'

'*Wrong* tree, you wally.'

'Anyway, you're right. It looks as if he never came to Spain at all.'

'What about divorce papers, anything there?'

'No. Maybe they never divorced. Maybe she just left him.'

'Or he left her. That would explain why she hates him so much.'

'What makes you think she hates him?' Ana asks.

'She has wiped him out of her life so completely even his own son doesn't know anything about him. Hardly sounds like a woman who loves him, does it?'

He is right, of course. Something terrible must have happened for Nancy to have held on to that hatred all these years. Most people's feelings mellow with time, but not hers. 'It's strange. I should be able to find some trace of him, a death certificate at least.'

'Maybe you're right. Maybe he's still alive. Maybe she doesn't want you to find him in case he has a claim on her money. If they never divorced, then he has a legal right to half her wealth. It could be that simple.'

Money again, Ana thinks. 'I'm sure there's more to it than that,' she says.

'Well you should ask her outright. Just think, if he did disappear under mysterious circumstances it could turn your book into a best seller. Then you'd be inundated with offers to write other books.'

'I'm not worried about that, but I do have a job to do,' Ana says. 'How can I write a comprehensive book about her life if a major player, her husband and the father of her son, is never mentioned? It would look sloppy. Suspicious.'

'Well there you have it. It is suspicious. Something strange happened, and she doesn't want anyone to find out.' Andrew pours more wine into his glass.

'No, no more wine for me, thanks. I need a clear head.'

'So you're working again this evening, are you?'

'I'm going to visit her son. It's time I spoke to him about his father.'

'Oh God, Ana, when will you learn? The woman hasn't told her son anything about him. It's *her* you have to work on.' Andrew pushes back his chair in exasperation.

Perhaps he's right, Ana thinks, but she can't rely on Nancy's story alone; it has too many holes in it. Something is wrong, and she is determined to find out what it is.

CHAPTER 16

Nancy opens the suitcase Martin bought for her. It is made of a soft green fabric, quite discreet, nothing she can complain about. And it's roomy, with far more space than she needs, and especially light. Arnos Superlite, the label says. She zips it up and wheels it around the room. Yes, it's perfect. There is even a small matching purse that hangs from a leather strap. She lifts the case onto the bed and opens it again. What should she take with her? Martin has suggested María help her pack, but she doesn't want that woman snooping around her bedroom, rifling through her cupboards. She opens the wardrobe, looks at the clothes hanging there, pulls out a blue wool suit and lays it on the bed next to the suitcase, then a red dress, a brown skirt, and a checked jacket she's particularly fond of. What will the weather be like? It could be cold. She takes two sweaters from the chest of drawers and a heavy black cardigan. Maybe she needs some trousers—two pair. Black cords and camel flares join the pile. What if they are invited somewhere smart? Does she have anything suitable? It's been years since she went to a posh restaurant. Martin suggests every year that they go to Villa Romano for her birthday, but she always declines, and they usually end up at El Barco, where the fish is fresh and delicious, they know the waiters well, and she doesn't have to dress up. Black. That's the answer, her black cocktail dress. She finds it at the back of the wardrobe, hanging under a cellophane wrap with a dry-cleaning logo on it. She may have grown old and have more than her fair share of wrinkles, but she hasn't put on any weight. She takes the dress out of its wrapping and holds it up against her. Yes, it will still fit her. Now what about shoes? October. Yes, it's bound to be cold—she'd better take her boots and a pair of court shoes. She sorts through the untidy pile of shoe boxes at the bottom of the wardrobe, and pulls out a pair of red, high-heeled sandals. She had forgotten she had them. She'll take them as well, to go with the red dress, and the beige suede ones with the low heel, much easier for walking. She places them on the bed with all the rest and stands back to survey the scene. Black shoes. She must take black shoes, and her black handbag. Gloves, too—she might need gloves, and a hat. It can get very cold in Oxfordshire, she reminds herself, thinking of how the wind blew down from Christmas Common across the vale. Her father had taken them there to fly their kites one Christmas but Ted had let go of his and they stood and watched it hurtling through the sky until it became a tiny red dot far above them. She remembers Ted snivelling all the way home. They say there are real kites there now, red kites reintroduced from Spain, so completely at home that the farmers complain about them. Oh, and a scarf. The blue is nice, pure cashmere. Now does she have an adequate coat? She opens another wardrobe where she keeps her outdoor wear and takes out a mink jacket. It is soft and sleek beneath her fingers, perfect for going somewhere special, but she must take something else for the journey, something more durable in case it rains. She remembers Martin telling her once that fur was frowned upon these days, that someone might throw a can of red paint over her. But why anyone would be walking about with a can of red paint on the off-chance of spotting a real fur coat, she cannot imagine. Still, the world is a strange place these days, and England one of the strangest if the BBC news is anything to go by. She pushes the case to one side and lies down on the bed. All this packing has tired her. She closes her eyes and begins to doze.

Nancy's heart was pounding as she opened the door to the third-class compartment of the Reading train, and it did not abate until the train pulled out of Kingston station and she was sure Nick would not suddenly appear on the platform to drag her back home. She'd had enough of him. She could not—would not—put up with more of his violent outbursts. She held a handkerchief to her nose. It was still painful but the bruising was going down. Until recently, Nick had been careful where he hit her, making sure that the bruises did not show, but now she had to put up with the added humiliation of people seeing that he was knocking her about. Surely her parents would not turn her away when they saw what he had done? She would explain to them that she had made a mistake and that she was sorry. She would tell them she wanted to come home.

Nancy placed her bag on the luggage rack and took an empty seat next to the window so she could direct her attention outwards and not have to speak to anyone in the compartment. The train was half-empty, her only companions a young girl in a school uniform and a middle-aged woman with half a dozen bags of shopping. The girl was reading a magazine called *Jackie* with a picture of Cliff Richards on the cover. The woman was already dozing, head back, clutching her handbag to her bosom. Neither of them took any notice of her.

The journey was slow, the train stopping at every station, but Nancy didn't care. The slow pace of the journey gave her time to think about her life, time to revert to being herself and not the frightened, cowed woman Nick had turned her into. She did not want to marry him. Marriage would mean that she would be tied to him forever, until death parted them, and she could not face that. She was very clear about that in her mind, but on her own, she knew, she would be unable to dissuade him. If she raised any objections it would lead to a row, and she would suffer the consequences. There was only one solution, to leave him before they were married. But to do that she needed help.

For a while, she had held out hope that Kelly would come to her rescue, but he never spoke up in her defence, and whenever Nick got into a rage, he excused himself, saying he had to leave. She was sure Kelly liked her, but it seemed clear he liked a quiet life even more. Since he'd left Kingston, they saw him rarely. She had only one alternative: to go home. If she promised never to see Nick again, she was sure her parents would help her. After all, that was what they had demanded from the start, that she have no more to do with him. Just thinking about it made her feel dizzy and nauseous.

'It's really stuffy in here. Do you mind if I open a window?' she asked the girl.

'Nah.' The girl looked up from her magazine. 'Are you going to be sick? You're as white as a ghost.'

'I don't know. I feel a bit faint,' Nancy said, getting up and heading for the passage. 'Can you watch my bag for me?'

'Yeah, all right.'

Nancy staggered along the passage to the toilets. It was as she feared. As she vomited all her breakfast into the void below her, she wished she could disappear as easily. She touched her breasts and she knew—she was pregnant again.

It was exactly six o'clock when she arrived at her old home. She knew her parents would be in because their evening ritual began with the six o'clock news broadcast. She rang the doorbell and waited, imagining her father getting up from his armchair, grumbling at being disturbed at this sacrosanct hour, and her mother's querulous voice wondering who it could be, so late in the day.

Her father opened the door, took one look at her, and returned to the radio.

'Who is it, Richard?'

'It's your daughter.'

Nancy's mother's bewildered face appeared in the doorway. 'Darling, what on earth are you doing here?' She held out her arms, and before she could stop herself, Nancy was sobbing out all her problems.

'All right, my love, it's all right now. Come inside and tell me all about it.' She led her daughter into the kitchen and closed the door.

Watching her mother go through the usual routine of warming the teapot, carefully measuring the tea—one spoonful per person plus one for the pot—pouring in the scalding water, was restful. The simple ritual took her back to her childhood, where such things were the norm. Nothing in her life was normal now, not even making a simple cup of tea. Only two days ago Nick had hurled his tea across the room, smashing the cup and staining the carpet.

She couldn't even remember what she had done to provoke him.

Although she could not have missed the ugly swelling on her cheek and the fact that Nancy's once perfectly straight nose now had a definite kink in it, her mother made no comment.

Nancy took a deep breath and said, 'I've left him. I want to come home.' It was done. It was that simple.

'I knew you'd see sense eventually,' her mother said. She placed three cups on the table and poured out the tea.

The telephone rang as Nancy's as parents were about to go to bed. Her mother answered—it was Nick. Nancy looked at her mother. What would she say to him? Would she accuse him of mistreating her daughter? Would she tell him that she had seen the bruises on her face, her crooked nose––would she say she knew about the dislocated collar bone?

'Who?' her mother asked, adopting the rather useless tone she always used when faced with any technology. 'Nick? Nick Henderson?' There was a pause, then she replied, 'No, she's not here, Nicholas. No, we haven't seen her for months. Of course, I'll let you know if she contacts us. Just a minute while I get a pencil.'

Nancy watched as her mother rooted around in the sideboard until she found a pencil, then wrote down the number he dictated.

'Yes, I will,' her mother said firmly. 'Goodbye.' She put down the telephone.

'He wants you back, Nancy. He said to phone this number and leave a message with Jim.'

Nancy laughed. Was that the best Nick could do, leave her the pub landlord's number? 'I'm not going back,' she said, her voice on the raw edge of hysteria. 'He'll kill me. I know he will.'

'Darling, don't be so dramatic,' her mother soothed, sounding, to Nancy's ear, every bit as false as Nick himself. 'Of course he won't kill you—he's just worried about you.'

Nancy's temper flared. 'He's worried that I've left him, that's all. He always said he'd kill me if I left and he means it.' A note of terror crept into her voice. 'You mustn't tell him where I am. Please, Mummy.'

'Of course not, darling. Now you get off to bed. I've put clean sheets on for you. And tomorrow we'll see the doctor, to find out what he can do to help you.'

Nancy's room had changed very little. The pink walls had a new coat of paint, and her posters had been removed. The Walker brothers no longer hung above her bed and Bob Dylan was gone, along with Elvis and Jerry Lee Lewis, but her mother had left the curtains—frilly pink muslin too fine to keep out the early morning sun or the light from the street lamp outside. As a child Nancy had found it comforting to fall asleep in that half-light. Her bookshelf still stood in the corner, her favourite stories leaning side by side: 'Black Beauty,' 'Robinson Crusoe,' 'The Lion, The Witch and the Wardrobe,' 'Tales of a Thousand and One Nights,' 'The Blue Fairy Book'—they were all there, as were her ancient rabbit with its torn ear and two raggedy dolls.

Nancy undressed and slipped into the cold bed, stretching her legs to feel for the hot water bottle her mother had slipped under the covers just before she said goodnight. How strange it felt to be back in her old room, so much the same but so very different. She felt she was seeing it with new eyes. She was no longer the girl who had lived there before—too much had happened. Nancy inched the hot water bottle up from the foot of the bed and pulled it against her chest. When she had told her mother about her suspicions about being pregnant again, her only reaction was to sigh sadly and make an appointment with the doctor. How wonderful it would be if Nancy could stay there forever, in her childhood room, in her little pink bed—if she and the baby could stay there with her mother.

At six o'clock the next morning Nancy woke to the sound of the telephone ringing. This time her father answered. She could hear his voice, raised in anger. 'What the hell do you want, ringing at this time of the morning?' he asked. Then, 'Don't speak to me like that my lad. You don't frighten me, I'll have the police on you.' She heard him swear as he slammed the telephone down and padded back into his bedroom.

'It's that yob again. God knows why she ever got involved with him in the first place.'

'But she's left him now,' her mother replied. 'She wants to come home.'

'Oh, does she.'

Nancy pulled the covers over her head. She didn't want to hear what else her father might say, not now, not yet.

Nancy was embarrassed about going to the clinic. Dr Marsh had known her since she was a child, attending to all the usual winter ailments. He had treated her for chicken-pox and measles, even took her to the cottage hospital in his car when she fell off the swing and broke her ankle. How was she going to face him now, a young woman, unmarried and pregnant? What would he say to her? But she needn't have worried. He was brisk and professional, his usual kindly, avuncular self.

'What scrape have you got into now, young woman?' he asked, showing her into his surgery.

The room hadn't changed at all. It still smelled of floor polish and antiseptic. The brown leather couch for patients to lie on still stood against one wall. An eye-test chart, yellow and curled with age, was pinned to the wall opposite, behind a weighing machine and the wooden measuring rod he had used to record her height for as long as she could remember. The articulated skeleton that used to give her nightmares still swung from a coat stand in the corner, and the doctor's wooden desk, which had always seemed so huge, was littered with assorted oddments left by pharmaceutical reps: out-of-date calendars, jotters, fountain pens bearing the inscribed names of pharmaceutical companies, boxes of paper-clips, a glass globe that rained artificial snow onto a miniature Santa Claus—all the things that had fascinated and distracted her as a child.

Dr Marsh sat down in the leather chair behind his desk and picked up her file.

'Will you just give her a check-up please, Dr Marsh. She's been irregular,' her mother said brightly.

'Irregular? In what way.'

Her mother blushed. 'It's her periods,' she clarified. 'She's missed one.'

'Two actually, mother,' Nancy said, quietly.

'I see.' The doctor looked at Nancy over his glasses. 'Well, just go behind the screen please, Nancy, and slip off your dress.'

If he noticed the bruises, he never said. He felt her breasts and her abdomen, asked a few personal questions which Nancy hoped her mother could not hear, then as if he were informing her that she had the flu, he said 'Yes, it seems you're pregnant. Six to eight weeks, I'd guess.'

Nancy said nothing, but pulled on her dress and went to face her mother.

'Well, Mrs Miller, it seems that you're going to be a grandmother,' Dr Marsh said, beaming at them both.

'Oh no. Richard won't stand for it.' Nancy's mother stood up in her agitation, dropping her handbag on the floor.

'I'm afraid there's very little he can do about it,' the doctor replied, dryly.

'What about an abortion? Can't she have an abortion?' she wailed.

'I'll pretend I didn't hear you say that, Mrs Miller. You know it's against the law.'

'I don't want an abortion, Mum,' Nancy protested. 'I want this baby.' In a perverse way she was glad she was pregnant. In the end something good would come of the mistakes she had made. This time, she would make sure her child lived.

But her mother continued to lament. 'Oh my God, what will your father say?'

The doctor ignored her and turned to Nancy. 'Here's the address of the antenatal clinic. You should go along there as soon as you can. They'll give you all the advice you need. And if you decide you don't want to keep the baby, they'll put you in touch with someone who can help you with adoption.'

Nancy looked at him, her chin up and her eyes clear. 'Thank you, Dr Marsh.'

'Be sure to make the right decision, Nancy—it's a big step to take either way.' He smiled at her. 'Take care of yourself. And good luck.'

Nancy had almost convinced herself Nick wouldn't find her, that she had actually broken his hold on her, that she was free, when he arrived on the doorstep. It was a Sunday morning and the street where her parents lived was quiet, most of the neighbours taking advantage of the opportunity to stay in bed a few extra hours. Only the man who lived opposite was in his garden, clipping away at his beech hedge, when Kelly's van pulled into their drive. Nancy had been lying in bed, halfway between sleep and waking, when she heard the squeal of brakes. She knew immediately who it was and crept to the window to peer from behind the curtain at the scene below. Nick, his face contorted with rage, was marching along the path towards the house. The van door was open and an anxious-looking Kelly was getting out. The man opposite stopped cutting his hedge and stood to watch, probably wondering what these two men were doing at his neighbour's home at that hour on a Sunday morning.

There was a loud banging on the front door.

'Who the hell is that?' Nancy's father asked. She could hear him moving around his room, imagined him putting on trousers and a clean shirt, maybe his tie, which he always wore even on a Sunday. There was a pause while he tied his shoelaces, and she could hear her mother's quiet voice: 'It could be him. Don't get angry now, Dickie, will you? If it's him. Try not to lose your temper. It won't do any good.'

'*If* it's him? Of course it's bloody him. Who else would be trying to break our door down at this time of the morning?'

The banging was worse than ever. Nancy was sure their front door would cave in with the force of it. She pulled off her nightdress and got dressed as quickly as she could, then peeped out from behind the curtains again. The man opposite had moved out onto the pavement, his hedge forgotten. Curtains were twitching at upstairs windows on either side of him. A neighbour's dog, alerted by the disturbance, was barking madly, jumping up and down at his fence. Kelly was standing on her parents' lawn now, trying to reason with his friend—and then suddenly, the banging stopped.

Before Nancy could move away from the window, Nick had stepped back and was looking straight up at her. She leapt back into the room, horrified. He had seen her. It was no use her father denying she was here. Nick had seen her. She would have to go down and face him.

By the time she reached the hall her father had already opened the door.

'What the hell do you want?' he demanded. 'If you don't stop making all that noise and clear off, I'm calling the police.'

'Where is she? Let me see her.' Nick sounded angry, nearly out of control.

'She doesn't want to speak to you, now or ever,' Nancy's father told him. 'Go away. You've ruined her life enough as it is. You're a bloody animal. Getting her pregnant once wasn't enough for you, was it? No, you had to go and do it again. Well, you're not having her or the baby. She's getting rid of it and going back to college. So clear off before I have the law on you.'

Nick looked straight past her father, directly at her. 'Pregnant? Are you sure, Nancy?' His anger was suddenly gone, had evaporated, leaving him radiant. 'We're going to have another baby? You have to come home now. We'll get married. I promise I'll look after you both. I'll love and cherish you. I'll get a proper job. Please, Nancy, give me one more chance. You can't have this baby on your own. Come home with me.'

'This is her home, you moron,' her father thundered, pushing Nick away. He never saw Nick's fist, which landed squarely on his chin. With a sound like the air leaving a punctured tyre, Nancy's father crumpled, and fell to the floor.

Nancy screamed and rushed to help her father. 'Daddy, are you all right?' she cried, bending over his unconscious body. 'Speak to me, Daddy. My God, Nick, what have you done? You've killed him.'

A shriek behind her told Nancy that her mother had joined the scene and was now pummelling Nick's chest as hard as she could. 'You bastard, what have you done to my husband? You bastard.'

Nick held her away from him. 'He's all right lady, he's just knocked out. He shouldn't have pushed me.'

'Nancy, ring for an ambulance and get the police,' her mother shouted. 'Nick's killed him.'

But Nick had grabbed Nancy's arm and was pulling her into the garden. 'Come home, Nancy, please,' he pleaded. 'I can't live without you. The flat is so empty without you— please come home. You know how much I love you. I'm begging you, come home.'

'Leave her alone; she's staying here,' her mother cried.

For a moment Nancy thought Nick was going to strike her mother as well. Apparently, so did the neighbour, who had come across to see what was happening and still had the shears in his hand. He was a big man, not the sort to step back from a fight.

'Okay now, boyo.' Kelly put his hand on Nick's shoulder. 'This isn't going to solve anything. Let's all try and calm down.'

Nancy's father moaned, sat up, and looked around him, dazed and groggy. He staggered to his feet. 'Get out of my house,' he shouted, looking straight at Nancy. 'Get out, all of you. And take that slut with you.'

Nancy felt her knees go weak. She couldn't believe her father would treat her like this. He was throwing her out.

'Daddy…' she whispered.

'Don't "Daddy" me. You've brought this on yourself and now you want to drag us down with you. Well it isn't going to happen. You're not bringing any bastard child of his into this house, ever. And that's final.' He took his wife by the arm, pulled her inside, and slammed the door on all of them.

Nancy heard the bolt slide into place with a loud clunk. Even the man from across the street looked surprised at this turn of events and, without saying a word, went back to his own garden. The others stared at the shut door in astonishment. She was stunned. Her father didn't want her any more. She'd said she was sorry and sought his help, but he abandoned her. Again. Just like that. Her own father. A slut, he had called her, a slut, in front of everyone. That hurt. And her mother, who had always supported her, who had encouraged her to become an artist, who had wanted her to be a free spirit, had said nothing, had not defended her. Instead she had meekly followed her husband inside, not even turning to look at her, the daughter she claimed to love.

Nancy knew, now, that she had no option but to leave with Nick. Without her parents' help how was she to support herself and a baby? She had nowhere to live and no money to live on. She stared up at her bedroom window through tear-filled eyes. She would not come back to this house, ever.

The front door opened a crack and for a moment Nancy hoped her father had relented, but then her bag sailed across the lawn and landed at her feet, and the door slammed shut again.

So it was up to her now. She was on her own. Well, she would hold Nick to his promise to marry her. At least that way their child would be legitimate and would have a home. She would do this for her baby. And she would find out about this new pill everyone at the antenatal clinic was talking about. There was no way she would become pregnant again, ever. If she had learned one thing, it was that no one, not even your own family, had time for an unmarried mother.

Nancy and Nick were married the following month at the Kingston registry office. It was a simple affair—one of Nick's friends from the pub was best man. Nick had asked Kelly, but he said he would be away. She knew from his silence as they drove away from her parents' house that day that Kelly wanted no more to do with Nick. She would have liked a moment to speak to him alone, to tell him that it didn't matter, that she had made her decision for the sake of the baby, but there was no opportunity. Kelly had stood by Nick for years, for the sake of their friendship, but even he could see Nick's behaviour was out of hand. She was disappointed in her friend, even though she knew she was being unfair. There was no reason why Kelly should come to her defence; after all, she had brought it on herself.

Neither her mother nor her father attended the wedding, though she sent them an invitation. Nick's father and his new wife were not invited, but his brother came down from Sheffield for the occasion, got drunk and left without saying goodbye. That night, after the reception at The Black Cat was over and the landlord had called time, the newly-weds returned to their flat. Nick was drunk and sentimental. Now he had what he wanted. Nancy was bound to him legally. There was no escape.

'Come here, Mrs Henderson,' he slurred and pulled her towards him. 'How's my lovely little wifey?'

What a travesty. Nancy had just lied before witnesses, promising to love, honour, and obey Nick as her husband. But she did not love him and could not honour him, though she knew if she did not obey him, she would suffer.

Nick leaned over her, his breath thick with beer fumes and pickled onions, and kissed her. She wanted to wrench herself away from him, tell him how much she hated him, run out the door and never come back. How was she going to survive life with a man she had come to detest? Never before had Nancy realized she was capable of such intense feelings as those Nick brought out in her—disgust, loathing, revulsion, fear, and yes, even hatred. Hatred. She had married a man she hated. Nevertheless, it had been her choice. So she took his arm and said, as sweetly as she could, 'Time for bed?' If she was lucky, he'd fall straight asleep, which would give her one night without him lying on top of her. She would meet the rest as they came. Something had changed in her. From now on, she was going to take control of their lives, but in such a way that Nick would not even know he was being manipulated. If she couldn't change her life, she could at least try to manage it.

Nancy wakes with a start, her back aching. She must have fallen asleep on the bed. Why are there so many clothes everywhere? She sits up, puzzled, and then she sees the suitcase. Someone has been packing her clothes. But why? Where is she going? Has Martin arranged for her to go into a home? He has been talking of nothing else lately. She must ring him. She has to tell him that she's not going. She is staying in her own apartment. She doesn't want to share her home with a lot of senile old biddies. He can't do that to her.

There is a knock at the door. Nancy doesn't move. The knock is repeated, then a voice calls, 'Nancy, are you there? It's me. It's Ana. Can you let me in?'

Ana? She's the writer. Of course. She has come to talk to Nancy about her paintings. She moves slowly towards the door. Her key is already in the lock, so she turns it and peers out.

'Hello Nancy, are you going to let me in? It's Ana.'

Nancy opens the door just enough for the woman to squeeze through.

'Is something wrong? You seem upset.'

'My son is moving me to an old folks' home,' she says. 'He thinks I don't know about it but I can see through his scheme.'

'Are you sure? He never mentioned it the last time I spoke to him.' Ana takes off her coat and sits at the table.

'Well he wouldn't, would he? Look, come with me. Look at this. Clothes everywhere. What's this all about, if he's not moving me to a residential home?'

'It looks as though somebody's been packing for a trip,' Ana says.

'Exactly. Now why would he be packing my things?'

'Are you sure he did this?'

'Who else could it be?'

'Well, Nancy, you told me yourself that you were going to pack for our trip to Oxford. Have you forgotten? That's why I came round this evening, to give you a hand.'

Now it becomes clear—of course. She and Ana are going to the exhibition in Oxford. How could she have forgotten that? She is looking forward to it. She glances at Ana, feeling embarrassed at her outburst, but Ana is busy collecting items of Nancy's clothing from the floor and replacing them on the bed.

'So what do you think?' Nancy asks, pointing to the motley collection of clothes and shoes.

'I think you'll have a hard job getting all that to fit in one small case. Why don't we go through it together and see what you really need to take. And you can advise me on what I should take, as well. I've never been to England in the autumn. My sister and I only went in our summer holidays.'

'It will be colder in October,' Nancy says. 'But English weather is very unpredictable, you know.'

'I'm sure it is.' Ana laughs, lifting up the sleeveless red dress. 'But not that unpredictable.'

Nancy laughs too. 'I suppose I have got a bit carried away. All right, let's go through this mess together.'

She is relieved that she is mistaken about the nursing home. Still, she will speak to her son anyway, just in case he is planning a surprise for her. And she must be more careful to write everything down so that she doesn't get so confused. She hopes Ana will not mention this to Martin.

CHAPTER 17

Martin switches off the car radio and parks his car as close to their house as he can. The boot is full of shopping he has picked up from Mercadona. This is not his usual task, but Sara is having a hard time with her pregnancy and has been told to stay in bed for at least a week. He can't help thinking about the previous miscarriages. Her gynaecologist, a good friend of his, has told them to be very careful this time. Although he didn't say in so many words, the look on his friend's face when he learned Sara was pregnant again told Martin how risky he thought it was. Martin is fully aware of this, but Sara has been very insistent that this time everything will be fine. Nevertheless, he has insisted that she give up her job as a dentist's receptionist and that her mother come to stay for a while. 'It will be good for your mother,' he argued, 'and you will be forced to take things easier with her around.' To his surprise she has agreed to both.

Her mother arrives later this evening and has asked him to pick her up from the bus station at eight. She refuses to travel by train since her husband died ten years ago. His death affected all the family very badly. He had been on train 21431, pulling into Atocha Station on 11th March when three consecutive explosions blew up the train, killing him and a number of other passengers. Martin remembers with horror listening to the news that morning and learning of the dead and dying in Madrid, one hundred and ninety-one passengers, one of them his father-in-law.

'Isn't that the train your father takes?' he had asked his wife as they stood, glued to the television, unable to believe what was unfolding before their eyes. Four trains and ten explosions in less than five minutes. It was like something in a horror film. When they rang her mother, she was still asleep in bed, unaware of the tragedy. They tried ringing his father-in-law's mobile, but there was no reply. They tried ringing his office, but the stunned secretary knew no more than they did. Still they waited and hoped that he was among the lucky few, the injured rather than the dead, or the traumatised who staggered from the twisted carriages unable to believe they were still alive. The day dragged on, carrying no more than a shadow of normality, and that adopted only for the sake of the children. Martin had attended his patients at the hospital as usual, but his receptionist cancelled his evening clinic. Sara called the dentist's surgery and said she was sick. All day she sat by the phone, waiting to hear from her mother, ringing and re-ringing her father's mobile and listening to the stomach-churning message that the number was unavailable.

When the news finally came that her father was one of the casualties and that his body had been identified at the temporary field hospital at the Daoiz y Velarde sports complex, Martin drove Sara straight away to be with her mother, her brothers and sisters. His wife, normally so bubbly and vibrant, seemed diminished by the news, shrinking inside herself so that she appeared somehow small and frail. It has taken her a long time to come to terms with the fact that her father had been ripped from their lives by a terrorist's bomb.

Sara's family is large and closely knit. He has watched how the brothers and sisters interact with each other, the jostling good humour, the casual affection, the quiet rivalry between the brothers and the brothers' wives, the cheerful intimacy between the sisters—and he realizes this is something he has never experienced. Sara's siblings are all married now, the youngest having wed earlier that year, and when they are all together the house is a riot of noise and laughter. Family gatherings include not only Sara's siblings and their spouses, but uncles and aunts, cousins, nieces, even great-uncles and great-aunts. Everyone is invited, everyone is welcome, and they all arrive with some offering: home-made wine in stone jars, baskets of grapes from their vines, a pumpkin or two depending on the season, tomatoes, jars of olives, flasks of olive oil. Each brings something to add to the feast. The grandchildren are numerous. They range in age from a twenty-year-old—Sara's brother's oldest child—to a six-month-old baby, and there always seems to be another one on the way.

As a child, it did not matter to Martin that he had no brothers and sisters. He was happy having his mother's undivided attention, not having to share her love. But now, since he has known Sara, he understands what it is to have a family to love and support you. His mother-in-law is a kindly soul who dotes on her children and grandchildren—on all her family—and she has welcomed him wholeheartedly.

Like him, Martin's mother-in-law was an only child, an unlikely occurrence in those days when contraception was against the law. Her life has been a tragic one. Her own parents were killed in the civil war when she was very young, and she was brought up by an elderly aunt. Martin has sometimes felt this may have been the reason why she wanted so many children herself. In a country where family is such an important aspect of life, it is a tragedy to be alone.

'Come on, Juanito, grab that bag, the blue one, and you take this one, Emilio.'

The boys pick up the bags of shopping and run off down the road. Martin hums a few bars of Enrique Iglesias's latest song and follows them, smiling at their enthusiasm. It seems impossible for them to do anything slowly; everything must be done at top speed. Emilio is the leader in whatever they do, with Juan trotting behind, desperate to keep up. Rangy for his age, Emilio has just finished a growing spurt and now is all arms and legs, angular corners, and knobbly joints. Juan, on the other hand, is what Martin's mother would call a bit of a bruiser—stocky, with chubby arms and legs that wouldn't look out of place on a sumo wrestler. Yet they are very similar boys. Both have the same liquid brown eyes as their mother and her slow, inquisitive way of looking at you, tilting her head just a little to one side.

'Careful now, don't break anything,' he calls. 'And slow down.' But they take no notice. The bags are swinging madly to and fro, and he fears the shopping will end up on the pavement, but before the handles go completely, the boys are at the door and ringing the bell.

'Stop that. Your mother's in bed,' he shouts. 'Just wait for me.' But the door opens and there stands Ana, his mother's assistant, as he has come to refer to her. 'Ana? What are you doing here?'

'Hello, Dr Henderson. I rang to see if I could have a word with you, and your wife kindly invited me to come round. She said you were picking up the children from school.'

'Yes, she's not too well,' he says. He doesn't feel like discussing his wife's condition with someone he hardly knows.

Ana is looking very pert today, like a bright little sparrow, with a white shirt and a short red jacket. Maybe it's a robin he's thinking of. Yes, a robin, alert and inquisitive. He wonders what she wants. He thought they had covered everything last time they spoke.

'Take the bags into the kitchen, boys, I'll be along in a minute,' he says and turning to the young woman asks, 'So, Ana, what can I do for you?'

'I have a couple more questions for you, and I also have information about your father.' Ana says, taking a blue folder out of her bag.

Martin feels his stomach start to churn. Is this going to be something he wants to hear? All this talk about his father is unsettling. 'We'd better go into my study,' he says. 'Just give me a few minutes to see if my wife is all right and get the boys settled, and then I'll be with you.'

He opens the door to his study and watches her go in and sit by the window. Despite his preoccupation he can't help noticing what lovely legs Ana has. Today she is wearing a short denim skirt instead of her usual blue jeans.

'Will you be all right here?' he asks.

'Yes. You just do what you have to.' Ana smiles and opens her notes. 'I'm in no hurry.'

The boys have spread the shopping out on the kitchen table and Emilio is perched on the stool, taking the items little Juan hands up to him.

'It's okay, Papa, we'll put the shopping away,' Juanito says with a chocolate smile.

They have already opened the milkshake and a packet of crisps. This is a treat for them. Sara is very strict about what they eat, but today he wants to make an exception. They don't know about the baby yet, they just think their Mama is tired.

Looking at the boys' chocolate-smeared faces, Martin laughs. 'Try not to eat everything in one go,' he says. 'And not too much chocolate. I'm making lunch in a minute.'

'When's Mama getting up?' Emilio asks, tottering on the stool as he stretches to put the coffee on the top shelf.

'Careful now, don't fall,' he says, then adds, 'The doctor says Mama needs to rest for a few days.'

'So we can't go to the park with our skateboards then?'

'Yes, of course you can. I'll take you later this after-noon, after you've done your homework.'

'Yeah,' cries Juanito, almost knocking his brother off the stool in his excitement.

'What did I just say about being careful?'

'Sorry Papa.'

Sara is dressed, lying on the bed with her feet on a cushion. The doctor has said she must rest as much as possible, and by that he means staying in bed. This is not easy for Sara, who is a very active woman and finds it hard to sit still.

'How are you, darling?' Martin asks, bending to kiss her. She smells of jasmine and honeysuckle, the new sham-poo she is using. Her hair is loose, spread out on the pillow like a fan. He sits on the bed beside her and strokes it, let-ting the shiny black strands slip through his fingers. 'Still feeling sick?' he asks tenderly.

'No, I'm okay now—it's better when I lie down. Did you get everything?'

'Yes, the boys are putting it away for me.'

'*Dios mio*! You know what that means—I'll never be able to find a thing.'

'I see Ana is here again,' he says.

'Yes, she was very insistent about seeing you before she and your mother go to England. I know it's your free afternoon, but I thought you wouldn't mind.'

Martin runs a general paediatric clinic three afternoons a week, and just lately has had so many patients that he is considering making it four. It's all down to Sara, really—she is the one who suggested he put in toys for the children. She has decorated his waiting rooms, converting them into a children's paradise, a fairytale land of sparkling lights and painted walls. His little patients and their parents love it. They come early for their appointments so that the children can play while the parents relax with a coffee from the machine Sara installed. There are tiny pushchairs, dolls, teddy bears, plastic motor cars, Wendy houses for them to play in, video games for the older children, cartoons, colouring books, jigsaws—Sara had a great time buying it all. It is a clever idea, something she picked up from the dentists' surgery. If the children are happy and relaxed before they come in to see him, it will make his job easier and the patients will be less stressed, she said. And she was right.

'Well, I'll go down and speak to her, and then I'll get you some lunch.'

'A sandwich will be fine. I'm not that hungry.'

'It's a good job your mother is coming tonight. She'll make you eat.'

'Go on, go and see Ana. Then you can come up and tell me about your day. It's pretty boring up here on my own.'

'That's what it's supposed to be, boring and restful.' But he goes downstairs anyway, stopping by the kitchen to see what his sons are up to and then, satisfied that they can be left for a while longer, prepares himself for whatever news Ana has brought him.

'How can I help you?' he asks her again.

'It's just a couple of questions.' Ana's teeth are very white and even and when she smiles there are dimples in her cheeks.

'I've been trying to fill in some of the background to your mother's past. She seems very vague about everything that happened before she moved to Spain.'

'Yes, well, I did tell you that her memory is not so good these days.'

'I know, but I would have thought she could remember something about your father, for example.'

Here she goes again; she is determined to find out about his father. Why is it so important?

'Do you have any idea why your father didn't come to Spain with you and your mother?' Ana asks.

'No, she never said. I expect they had broken up by then, and she came here to start a new life.'

'Yes, that's what you said before, but it doesn't make sense. Did you know that your father had been planning to live in Spain?'

'No.' This is a surprise, and he can see she has registered that from the look on his face. Increasingly uncomfortable with questions about his family, and especially about his father, Martin wishes Ana wouldn't go poking into their business. Still, he is intrigued. His mother has never suggested for one moment that his father had considered joining them. She has always behaved as if he didn't exist.

'Yes,' Ana says. 'I went to the notary's office in Marbella yesterday and I found your old house listed. It was bought from a fisherman, as you said, but it was your father who bought it. Don't you think that's strange?'

'I don't know anything about that. I don't think I was even aware that we owned the house until my mother sold it. As I keep telling you, I was just a little boy. You'll have to ask my mother,' he says.

'But why would he buy a house and then not go to live in it? Can't you remember anything about that time?'

'Maybe he changed his mind when he split up with my mother. Maybe he bought it for my mother. Ana, I don't know anything at all about my father. I was only a toddler when I last saw him.'

'But even young children can remember something about their lives. Can't you remember anything?'

Martin is getting irritated, but he answers politely, 'No, not really.'

'Did you know that you had an uncle?'

'Uncle Ted, you mean?'

'No, Patrick, your father's brother. He died in an accident at work. He was only thirty-five. Did your mother never mention him?'

'No.'

Ana opens the folder and hands him several documents. What are they? Birth certificates?

'I found your father's birth certificate and your parents' marriage certificate,' she tells him.

'So?'

'I couldn't find a death certificate. Do you know if your father is still alive?'

Martin's stomach leaps. 'He died years ago, as far as I know. What is this? Do you think I'm lying to you?'

'No, no—of course not. It's just that I can't trace him. There's no death certificate for him in the UK and no mention of him living, or dying, in Spain.'

'Maybe there's a mistake in the records. Maybe he moved to Ireland. My mother told me they had a close friend from Ireland.'

'Maybe.' She writes something in her notebook and then says, 'And it looks as though you have a sister, older than you. Did you know about her?'

Martin looks at the birth certificates in his hand. One is his own; he has seen that before and has the original tucked away somewhere with the other family papers. The other birth certificate is for someone named Geraldine. He examines it closely. It seems genuine, and there are his parents' names. This birth has even been registered in the same registry office as his own. But if this is his sister, where is she now, and why hasn't his mother mentioned her? Suddenly he is angry with Ana. His hand is trembling. 'No, I didn't know I have a sister, but I can't see what business this is of yours. My mother didn't employ you to start muck-raking. You're supposed to write what she tells you.'

'I'm sorry if I've upset you,' Ana says, blushing scarlet at his words. 'I thought you'd want to know about your father.'

'Of course I want to know about him, but I prefer to do my own investigations when it comes to personal matters. So I'd be obliged if you would stop searching for a man who was never part of my life and concentrate on my mother and her paintings.'

'Of course, if that is what you want.'

'And don't mention anything about this supposed sister to my mother. Her health is fragile enough as it is.'

'As you wish.'

'Now, Señora Álvarez, I really must see to my family.'

'Of course, Dr Henderson. I'm sorry to have troubled you.' Ana gathers up her things and bundles them into her bag. 'I'll see myself out.'

Martin has offended her, that is obvious, but he couldn't help himself. He is angry that she has been nosing around in his mother's life looking for some scandal or other. Does she think the book will sell better if she can unearth some juicy facts about his mother's past? It was the sixties, after all. Lots of celebrities were into free love and drugs in those days. Does she think his mother was one of those? Why can't she just leave things as they are? He knows there is something strange about his mother's life, but if she wants to keep secrets from him, what can he do about it?

He pours himself a large glass of sherry and sits down. The boys are in the lounge now; he can hear the television. They're not allowed to watch television so early in the day, but he can't be bothered to go and remind them. Something is niggling away at the back of his mind. So it was his father who bought the fisherman's house, was it? He tries to think back to that time.

Ana's insistent questioning has rekindled his memory. It is not true what he has told her—he does have some memories from those days in England, only they are not very nice ones. He remembers his mother crying a lot and his father getting angry. He has vague recollections of his father. He can remember a tall man, with rough hands, who would grab him and throw him into the air with a roar and a huge, belly-shaking laugh. There was always a sweet, sickly smell about him. Now he realizes it was probably the smell of beer or some type of alcohol because he has smelled it since on the breath of the drunks that loiter in the plaza, begging for money. What else can he remember? Then it comes back to him, his father's voice: 'Off to Spain, Martin, my lad. You'll like that. Sun and sea. Sea and sun. Off to Spain, my lad.' He had made it into a song, and he'd sing it to him as he drank his tea over breakfast, waving the rolled up newspaper like a baton in time to the words; it was something like: *'We're off to Spain, my lad, with a hey, nonny-no. No more work, my lad, hey nonny-no. Sun and sea and sea and sun, sing hey nonny-no, my lad.'*

Martin had sung it with him—he thought it was fun. Of course Martin had no idea what Spain meant, but he understood sea and sun, so he had smiled and clapped his hands as his father sang. Ana was right then, his father had intended to move to Spain. So what happened? Despite his annoyance with Ana, he is intrigued. Why had his mother brought him to Spain on her own? What happened to his father? And if, as Ana says, his father was the owner of the house, how did his mother manage to sell it? There were a lot of questions that needed answering, but could he face asking her?

He decides to call in on his mother on the way to the bus station to collect his mother-in-law. He knows if he doesn't do it straight away, he will never do it. He recounted to Sara what Ana has found out and she has told him that he must confront his mother and ask her for the truth. If only it were that easy. His mother has such a clever way of sidestepping any questions she doesn't want to answer. He knows exactly how it will go—first, she'll ignore what he has said and change the subject. If that doesn't work, she will pretend that she is tired, that her memory is failing her, that it is too stressful to think back to those days. And if that doesn't work—and he persists—she will tell him it's not worth dragging up the past. He sighs. He doesn't really feel up to a battle of wills with his mother, but neither does he feel like returning to Sara and telling her that he didn't have the courage to ask her. He is caught whichever way he falls.

He rings the bell and waits. He can hear his mother shuffling up to the door.

'Who is it?'

'It's me, Mama. It's Martin. Let me in.'

The door opens and she peers round at him. Her hair is loose, as though she is about to go to bed, and her face is shiny with night cream.

'Am I disturbing you, Mama?' he asks, quite ready to kiss her goodnight and take his leave.

'No, no, darling, come in. I'll make you some cocoa.'

She is in her nightdress, with a blue dressing gown round her shoulders. The flat is baking hot.

'It's very hot in here, Mama, would you like me to adjust the central heating?' he asks, moving towards the controls on the wall.

'No, thank you, darling, I've got it just right.'

'But it's set at 35,' he says. 'That's rather high, you know.'

'Not for me, it isn't. I'm a hothouse flower, always have been.'

He takes off his coat and scarf and sits down in the kitchen, watching her prepare the cocoa. She is in a good mood and seems a lot brighter than usual.

'I've just been watching an old film,' she tells him. 'With Paul Newman.'

'Which one?'

'Oh, I don't remember, the one by Tennessee Williams, you know, with Elizabeth Taylor.'

'*Cat on a Hot Tin Roof?*'

'Yes, that's it. He was a troubled young man,' she says. 'Drank too much. And of course the heat brings out the passions in people.'

He nods, trying to look interested. The truth is, he barely remembers the film. It was years ago when he watched it, and then only because Sara said it was a classic. They'd watched it dubbed in Spanish, he remembers.

'Is that why you came to Spain?' he asks. 'For the heat?'

'What a strange question. I suppose it was. That and the light. The light is wonderful here for painting, so clear. All those grey, cloudy skies aren't good for painters, you know. We need to see the sun.'

'It didn't seem to matter to Turner and Constable,' he says.

'Pouf! You know what I mean.' She stirs the cocoa into the hot milk and passes it to him. 'There you are,' she says, 'just like I used to make for you when you were a little boy.'

'Why didn't my father come with us?' he asks, watching carefully for her reply.

'Is it too hot, dear? Would you like a little cold milk?' She opens the fridge and takes out a carton of milk.

'When we moved to Spain, why didn't my father come too?' he persists.

'I don't remember, dear. It was such a long time ago.'

'Of course you remember, Mama. You know perfectly well. You just don't want to tell me.'

'Ana didn't come today. I'm sure she said she would come today. I have it in my diary.'

'Don't keep changing the subject. I want an answer. I deserve an answer. After all these years, the least you can do is tell me why he didn't come with us.' Martin is trying not to let his voice rise. He doesn't want to push her too hard.

She sits down and looks him right in the eye. 'It's a mistake, this thing with the memoirs. A big mistake. Harry should never have suggested it; that man never knows when to leave things alone. All it's done is rake up the past. I never wanted this. I wanted to leave the past in the past,' she says and her face is sad. 'Your father didn't come with us because I didn't want him to. Our marriage was over. I just wanted to get as far away from him as possible, and Spain seemed as good a place as any.'

'But it was his idea,' Martin says—he is relentless. 'It was *his* idea to move to Spain. I remember him singing silly songs about it.'

'You remember that, do you?' she laughs. 'Well, fancy. Yes, it was his idea at first, but then he didn't want to come here anymore. So I decided to take you and live in the house he'd bought. It was my money he'd used anyway, left to me by my father.'

'I wonder why he didn't follow you here?' he asks. 'Since it was technically his house.'

'I told you, it was my money that bought it.'

'But later, didn't he try to contact you? Didn't he want to see me?'

He can't imagine how he would feel if Sara took the two boys and left him, moved to a strange country and never contacted him again, not a phone call, not an email, not even a photo—he would be distraught. It seems such a terrible thing to have done to his father, cutting him out of their lives like that.

'No,' his mother says. 'He never contacted us again.'

'But he knew the address. He knew right where we were. He could have written.'

'Look Martin, I know it must be hurtful for you, but he never got in touch with us again.'

'So he didn't want us?'

She makes it sound as if it was his father who abandoned them, and maybe it was, because surely he could have traced them if he had wanted to see them again. He looks at his mother. She stirs her cocoa and sips it slowly. There is a chocolate stain above her lip just like the boys.

'But how were you able to sell it? I remember you selling the house. I must have been about ten at the time. Then we moved into the town. He must have known then. Did you contact my father to get him to sign the papers?' He's trying to get some sort of timeline in his head.

'My solicitor sorted it out. Something to do with "power of attorney." I don't remember much about the details. I left it all to Harry and the solicitor.'

He sips the cocoa. It is so reminiscent of his childhood, sitting here sipping cocoa, his mother in her dressing gown. He feels five years old again.

'What is it, Martin? What's bothering you? It's something more than the house, isn't it?'

He looks up at her. Her eyes are wide and clear; there is no trace of the mists of forgetfulness clouding them now. She remembers it all. But will she tell him? There is no easy way to ask this.

'Do I have a sister?' he blurts out.

He can see she is startled by the question. She puts down her cup and stares at him.

'How did you know?' Her voice is quavering. 'How did you find out?'

'Ana came up with her birth certificate. Geraldine, that's right?'

'My mother's name,' she says. 'I called her after my mother.'

'What happened to her?'

'She died, just a few days after I gave birth to her.'

'But you never said.'

'Why would I? It was before you were born, before I was married. Then later, what was the point of telling you? You were a little boy. How could you understand? We had come here to make a new life. Why drag up the past? It never does any good, you know. I watch these television programmes where they put people together and get them to reveal their secrets—it never does any good. It's a destructive process, Martin. People aren't capable of forgiving so easily. It's best they don't know.'

She sighs and repeats, 'I knew it was a mistake to start these memoirs, a big mistake.'

CHAPTER 18

She is here again, asking her endless questions, making Nancy feel harassed, although she tries not to show it. Nancy is tired, having slept badly. She has tossed and turned all night, beset with dreams from her past. Her mother in particular kept appearing. She was wearing her gardening apron and gloves, and had one of those wide brimmed floppy hats that Englishwomen wore at the first glimpse of sunshine. Her shoulders were mottled with tiny squares of light where the sun shone through the coarse weave. 'If I stay perfectly still, do you think I'll be permanently covered in brown squares?' she asked Nancy and laughed her familiar, tinkling laugh. Then later, another time, her mother wanted to know why it was so hot and then, when was Nancy coming home and why hadn't she brought the baby to see her yet. Nancy had woken, sweating and distressed. It's Martin's fault, all those questions last night, interrogating her like a criminal.

'You look tired,' Ana says as she sits at the table and sets up her recording machine.

She looks cool and efficient today in a dark blue trouser suit. It has become a routine which, despite the intrusive questions, Nancy has come to enjoy. It has brought some meaning to her days. She no longer wakes, thinking of the day stretching before her, empty and useless. Now she has a task to do, information to record for posterity, for her grandchildren. For the first time in quite a while she is considering getting out her watercolours and painting again. Portraits, that is what she will paint, first one of Ana and then the boys. She will paint a watercolour of the boys playing on the beach or paddling in the sea. And she'll give it to Sara when the baby is born.

'I slept badly,' she replies. 'Would you like some coffee? María has just made a pot.'

'Please. I didn't have too good a night, either.'

She doesn't explain, so Nancy doesn't ask. Maybe she has had a row with that boyfriend of hers or maybe it's the opposite, maybe they were up all night making love. She smiles at the thought.

'Shall we start?' she asks. 'What do you want to know?'

Ana seems more hesitant today; instead of beginning with a whole stream of questions which tend to leave Nancy dazed and confused, she says, 'What do you want to tell me?'

This throws Nancy for a moment. What does she want to tell her? She knows what she *doesn't* want to tell her and that seems to be the part Ana is trying to unearth. What can she say?

'About what?' she asks.

'About your life, your friends, what it was like growing up at that time,' Ana says, gently. 'Tell me what you'd like me to write for you.'

'Well, let me think,' she says. 'Life was so different then. People talk about the "swinging sixties" but I was already twenty-one by the time the sixties began, and then Martin was born. I was a boring mum and housewife. There was no money and no time to go to wild parties. Then I came to Spain, and there certainly were no "swinging sixties" in Franco's Spain. My God, no—no bikinis, no short skirts, no women in trousers, no free love, films, music, everything was censored. A lot of the girls still had chaperones. They couldn't even go out with their fiancés unless an aunt or some female relative accompanied them. Anyway I think that the "sixties" phenomenon was limited mostly to London. People know more about it now than they did at the time.'

'But you lived quite close to London, didn't you?'

'About fifty miles. But I don't remember being aware of much going on; it probably all happened later. Even Mary Quant hadn't come on the scene by then, although I do remember wearing drainpipe jeans—a craze Audrey Hepburn started. Do you know whom I mean? I was a great fan of hers; a pretty little actress she was, very famous in her day.'

'Yes, I've heard of Audrey Hepburn.'

'You have to remember I was born at the start of the war. It was a time of great austerity for everyone, both during and afterwards. We had very little of anything when I was a child. Everything was rationed: food, clothing, shoes. Then rationing ended. I don't recall the year exactly but I was still at school. I remember coming home one day, and my mother had bought some bananas for tea. I'd never seen a banana before. Actually I didn't much like it. I preferred the sandwiches she used to make with brown sugar. After that things got better. My father had a good job working in a bank. He bought his own house, not something that many people could afford to do then, so I suppose we were lucky. You don't really take much notice of those things when you're a child; you just take them for granted. Anyway, I suppose I could say I had a happy childhood.'

She pours herself some more coffee and looks at Ana to see if she needs a refill, but her cup is untouched. Suddenly it seems it was only yesterday when she was hurrying to get ready to go to the Majestic with Janet, her lipstick tucked into her bag alongside her dance pumps, pretending they were off to the pictures, the excitement whizzing around in her stomach as they waited for the bus. Then the Majestic itself, with long queues to get in, teddy boys with their DA haircuts and velvet collars, their thick crepe-soled shoes, flick knives tucked in their back pockets, the girls, squealing and chattering like starlings, pony-tails and full skirts over starched petticoats, tiny sack dresses that showed your bottom if you bent over, the smoke-filled dance floor, glittering chandeliers, and bright lights that dimmed when the music was smoochy. They lived for Saturday nights. 'Of course, my parents didn't know we were going to the Majestic; they thought Janet and I were at the pictures,' she says aloud.

'Sorry?'

'Janet, my best friend. We'd been friends since primary school.'

She realizes she hasn't explained herself very well and says, 'We used to sneak off to the Majestic on a Saturday night, for the dancing. It was the best around. Live bands that played everything: pop, rock and roll, and look-alike crooners who sang like Frank Sinatra and Perry Como. There were Bill Haley and Elvis impersonators and sometimes well-known singers such as Jimmie Young and Alma Cogan would be there. We saw Lonnie Donegan once. On another occasion we saw Cliff Richard live at the Odeon. What an experience that was. The crowds were screaming the whole time. We sat in the front row and I never took my eyes off him. Janet couldn't go with me that time. I went with a boy called Andrew Peachey. He was sweet on me—a nice boy. I'm sure my mother would have approved of him. He had curly blond hair and glasses.'

'Was he your first boyfriend?' Ana asks.

'Oh, no. I wasn't allowed to go out with boys; my father would have killed me if I said I had a boyfriend,' she tells her. 'He never knew where we went or who we were with– –he'd have stopped me going out altogether if he'd found out. I sometimes think my mother guessed what we were up to, but she never said anything. No, I didn't start going out with boys until I was at college and by then I was eighteen.'

'What about Janet? Did you keep in touch with her?'

'Not really. We exchanged letters for a few months and then we drifted apart. She became a nurse and the last I heard of her she was living in Edinburgh.'

'Any other friends? What about at college? Surely there was someone you kept in touch with?'

'Of course I had friends,' she snaps, irritated by the change in Ana's line of questioning. 'I just don't remember any of them.'

'Not one?'

'There was a girl called Helen. We used to share a flat when I first went to Kingston. But I haven't heard from her since I moved to Spain.'

'Helen? What was her last name?' she asks.

'Brown, or maybe Jones, I don't remember.'

'No others? What about boyfriends? Can you can remember anyone special? Martin's father for example, did you meet him in Kingston or did you already know him?'

Now she sees where Ana is going with this. So she wants to know about Nick. Well Nancy isn't going to tell her.

'I still have some of my original drawings from school,' she says instead. 'Would you like to see them? I was only sixteen when they were done.'

'I'd love to.'

She goes into her bedroom and takes out an old suitcase from the back of the wardrobe. Inside are a few of the things she has saved. How strange it is when she looks back. She had taken very few things with her when she left England, but she had packed all her sketches, even the school ones, simple exercises in anatomy: faces, torsos and drawings of her own feet. She looks through them. There is Andrew Peachey, immortalised in pencil, and Janet with her cropped hair. There is the boy from the First Year, whose hands they had to draw but whose name she never knew, and Amanda Jones, who was the best tennis player in the school, and there is the elderly Miss Skinner, who consented to sit for them one summer afternoon, her white hair pulled into a bun on top of her head and her half-moon spectacles slipping down her nose. She had smacked Nancy across the legs with her ruler on many occasions. Yes, she remembers them all, but the person she cannot remember is herself. Whatever happened to Nancy Miller, that innocent sixteen-year-old, preparing for her O-Levels?

Nancy was on her way home from shopping when she saw Helen crossing the road, pushing an empty wheelchair. She was about to turn away and pretend she hadn't seen her when she realized that here was someone she could talk to––the only person she could talk to— so she hurried across the road and called out to her, 'Hey, Helen.'

Her old flatmate stopped and smiled in surprise. 'Why, Nancy. I haven't seen you in ages.'

She let go of the wheelchair she was pushing and hugged Nancy. She seemed so pleased to see her that it was all Nancy could do to hold back her tears. She swallowed hard. Was she really so starved for affection?

'And who's this little chap? Hello there,' Helen said, bending down and tickling Martin's cheek. 'I didn't know you had a son, Nancy. How old is he?'

'He's two and a half.'

'He's a bonny wee thing. Look at those lovely blond curls.'

'Nick says I should get them cut. He says they're too babyish.'

'So you're still together?' Helen asked, looking at her wedding ring. 'When did that happen?'

'We got married just before Martin was born.'

'Congratulations. I'm happy for you.'

'Can we talk?' Nancy asked, her voice cracking a little as she spoke.

'Of course. Is something wrong?'

'I just need to talk to someone,' Nancy said. 'Do you have time for a coffee or something?'

'Well look, I have to return this wheelchair to the Day Centre. I borrowed it for my grandmother, while she was staying with me for a few days. Walk along with me. It's not far. Then we'll go and have a coffee at Guilio's.'

Guilio's used to be their favourite hang-out. What a long time ago it seemed, in another lifetime almost. She looked at Helen; she seemed different, more confident, and she was wearing an engagement ring. Her hair was longer now, backcombed and lacquered into the latest bouffant style, ash blond with a hint of pink. Who would have thought Helen would be so fashion conscious. She wore a black and white sack dress that stopped above her knees and heels so high that she tottered behind the wheelchair as if she needed it for support.

'So you're engaged?' Nancy said. 'Who is it, someone I know?'

'You noticed,' she said, holding her hand in the air so that the ring sparkled in the sunshine. It was a sapphire, surrounded with tiny diamonds. 'That's why Granny came down; she wanted to meet my fiancé. You might know him; he works at the Westminster Bank in Kingston. Tall, good-looking, a bit like Buddy Holly with thick rimmed glasses.'

Nancy shook her head. 'No, I never go into that bank. Congratulations, anyway. You must be very happy.'

'I am. He's wonderful. We're getting married next year, just as soon as we can find a house. I thought we'd probably rent for the first few years but Tom says no, the bank offers its employees such good terms it isn't worth our while to wait.'

'So you're looking for a house?'

'Yes, nothing too grand but big enough for a family. Tom wants lots of kids.'

She bent down again and chucked Martin under the chin. The child gave her his biggest grin and she was delighted. 'What a gorgeous kid. I can't wait to have some of my own.'

Helen chattered on, telling Nancy about their plans for the wedding and how Tom had planned a surprise honeymoon for them, but she had seen the brochures in the boot of his car, so she knew it was to be Malta. 'Of course I haven't let on that I know. If he wants it to be a surprise I can go along with that.'

'Are you still painting?' Nancy asked.

'Not really. You know I was never very good anyway, not like you. I only enrolled at Kingston because I thought I'd meet some fun people and it wouldn't be as boring as a shorthand and typing course.'

Nancy remembered how Helen had struggled with some of the course work. She had been a pretty competent drawer but completely useless with a paintbrush. No matter what she tackled, it always came out looking a fairly uniform mud colour.

'Did you finish the course?'

'Yes. I thought, well I've done all that work so I might as well stay and get my degree. I didn't get great grades but I managed to scrape a pass.'

'Good for you. So what do you do now?' Nancy asked.

Helen blushed and said, 'Well actually I've got a job in a local office. You know the sort of thing, receptionist, a bit of typing, filing, making the tea, general dogsbody really. But I've given in my notice. Tom says I don't need to work. He says that I can stay at home and look after him.'

'Won't you get bored?' Nancy asked. 'Or lonely on your own?'

She didn't have a job either. Nick would not allow her to work. Luckily he allowed her to paint, but that was only because she could sell the paintings—it was what he called his 'beer money.' So that was how she filled her days, looking after Martin and painting. Yes, she knew all too well about loneliness.

'I don't think so,' Helen said. 'Working is boring, all those men expecting me to run around after them and not even a word of appreciation. If I'm going to wait hand and foot on someone, I want it to be Tom. Anyway we're going to start a family as soon as we can. Then I won't have time to be bored.' She looked across at Martin and beamed.

They had arrived at the Day Centre so Nancy waited outside while Helen returned the wheelchair and chatted briefly to the matron.

'It's a great system,' she said, as she rejoined Nancy. 'I don't know how we would have coped without it. It meant we were able to take her to the church, and when I went for my final fitting, she came with me. She enjoyed that.'

'Is she very old?'

'Eighty-three. She's very fit really but has a problem walking. Hardening of the arteries, they say. Come on, let's go and have some coffee.'

It was a short walk to Guilio's. Nancy hadn't been there for years, but the moment she stepped through the door that warm, yeasty smell of the homemade bread, the salamis hanging behind the counter, the pungent cheeses and, above all else, the strong aroma of fresh Italian coffee took her back to her first days at college. This was where she had met Nick. If only she had known what was going to happen she would never have gone there.

'Mummy, dinner,' a little voice said.

No, that wasn't true. She would never take those years back, dreadful though they had been, because then she would not have had Martin, and he was the most important thing in her life.

'All right darling. What would you like, an iced bun?'

'Here, let's sit by the window and we can see who goes by,' Helen said.

'No, no. I prefer to sit over there,' said Nancy, pointing to a table in the corner, at the furthest point from the door and the window, where fewer people would see them. She could not risk Nick wandering past and seeing her with Helen.

'Whatever you say.'

They arranged themselves at the table in the corner, squeezing the pushchair in between them and waited until the waiter had brought them two frothy cups of coffee, a chocolate milk for Martin and a plate of iced buns and tiny Italian biscuits.

'Is that nice?' Helen asked Martin, who was slurping the chocolate milk through a stripy straw.

He didn't answer but nodded in contentment.

'He doesn't talk very much yet,' Nancy said. 'He's rather a quiet child, actually.'

'He's gorgeous,' Helen said with a big smile for the boy. 'How are things between you and Nick, anyway? I have to admit I am really surprised to hear that you are still together. I don't think he's ever stayed with anyone more than a few months before. You must have made some impression on him. I won't say love because I, personally, don't think he is capable of such feelings. Well, only for himself. He loves himself well enough.' She stopped and blushed.

Nancy could see that she thought she had gone too far because then she added, 'Sorry. He's your husband after all, the father of your child. Still, it's good. Everyone can change, they say. I'm glad it's worked out for you, Nancy.'

She leant across and squeezed Nancy's hand. That was too much. Nancy fumbled about in her bag and eventually pulled out a large handkerchief and blew her nose loudly.

'That's just it, Helen. It hasn't worked out. Life with Nick is a living nightmare.'

She pulled her long hair to one side so that Helen could see her neck. It was covered in purple bruises.

'My God, did he do that?'

'That's nothing. He throws me around the flat. If I say anything he doesn't like, he hits me, and nowadays it's with his fist. At first I used to go to the hospital but now I can't bear the sympathetic looks the nurses give me. They can't do anything anyway. He's very clever, careful not to break any bones and he mostly hits me where it can't be seen. Helen, I don't know what to do. I know he will kill me one day. I try not to antagonise him, really I do, but it's so hard. He watches me all the time, hoping to catch me out in something, a lie, a complaint, anything. I am afraid to go out anywhere with him. If he saw me in here with you he'd go mad. He'd accuse us of all sorts of horrible things.'

She looked hastily towards the door, expecting him to storm through at any minute. It had started to rain and the doorbell jangled as an elderly man came in, shaking his umbrella over the floor.

'What about the police?' Helen asked. She was whispering now, picking up on Nancy's fear, her head inclined as far towards Nancy's as possible.

'They won't do anything, and if they came round it would only make things worse. He really would go mad then.'

'Why don't you leave him?'

Nancy looked at her in amazement and said, 'Do you think I haven't thought of that? The thing is where could I go? He'd find me and then it would be worse than ever. I went back to my parents once, before Martin was born. He followed me there and when my Dad told him to leave he punched him. I can't do that to them again. Anyway, my father's dead now. He died back in January, a heart attack.'

'I'm sorry to hear that. You certainly are having a bad time of it. Look, if you're afraid to go to the police, why don't I go and tell them what he's been doing to you? There must be hospital records to back it up.'

'No, Helen, you mustn't get involved. You know what he's like; he wouldn't rest until he got back at you. No, you're about to get married. You don't want to get mixed up in my problems. Don't worry, I'll sort it out somehow. I have to. I can't spend the rest of my life like this.'

'What about Martin?' Helen whispered. 'Does he hit him?'

'No, thank God. He says he likes kids, although he doesn't actually spend much time with Martin. He's always saying that we should have more children, but I think it's just his way of binding me to him even closer. But I've taken precautions.'

'How?' asked Helen, wide-eyed.

'I went to the family planning clinic the moment that Martin was born. I'm on the pill.'

'Really? So he doesn't know?'

'No. My God he'd kill me if he knew, but I had to do something.'

'Is it safe?' Helen asked.

'Safer than having a kid every year, I'd say.'

'Look, if you need money, I can help you,' Helen said. 'At least let me do that.'

'Really Helen, it's very kind of you, but I have some money. I've been selling my paintings and keeping some of the money for myself. Nick doesn't know about it. Yes, he knows I'm selling the paintings. In fact it was his idea that I continue to paint at home and sell them to make some extra money, but he doesn't know I'm keeping some back for myself.' She laughed bitterly and added, 'It's funny, he's always saying I should charge more, that I'm virtually giving them away.'

'Is he working?'

'Sort of. He has a job at the stonemason's on the Richmond Road, but he's always skiving off, telling them he's sick when he's really down the pub with his layabout friends. I'm surprised that they haven't sacked him, but he says he's good at what he does. I think it's because the owner, Bert Grimshaw, is an old man and he's frightened to get rid of him. Anyway the money's not all that good, so he's grateful for what I can get for the paintings, although he spends most of it down the pub. I give him half in cash and I put the rest in my post office savings account.'

She gave a dry little laugh and said, 'That's it, you see; he thinks I'm too frightened of him to go against him and to a certain extent he's right, but he doesn't realize just how desperate he's made me. You can only push people so far.'

'Be careful, Nancy. Nick's a nasty piece of work. I did try to warn you.'

'I know, but I thought I was in love. How quickly all that changed. This is the one I love now.' She wiped the chocolate from Martin's face, and he smiled as she bent down and kissed his cheek.

'All right darling? Do you want anything else? Some water?'

'No, Mummy.'

'Good boy. We'll be going home soon.'

Helen had finished her coffee and was looking at her watch. 'I'm sorry, Nancy, but I really have to go. I'm meeting the caterers at four o'clock and it's twenty-to already.'

'We must go anyway,' Nancy said, picking up her coffee and drinking it quickly.

'We'll do this again. How about next week? Same time?' Helen said.

'I'll try but I can't promise.'

She couldn't be certain about anything in her life because she had no control over it. It had been lovely talking to Helen. For a few minutes she had felt relaxed, but now, as soon as she thought about returning home, not knowing what she would find, wondering whether Nick would be in a good mood or whether she'd have to tread on eggshells all evening, the old tightness gripped her stomach and she felt sick. Seeing Helen had reminded her how abnormal her own life had become. This wasn't married life, it was a life sentence. She wasn't going home to her husband but back to prison, to her jailer.

Someone is shaking her. Nancy sits up with a jerk that makes her head spin. For a moment she doesn't know where she is and panics.

'What is it? What's happened?' she cries. 'Is Martin all right?'

'Martin's fine. I'm sorry I frightened you, Nancy. You fell asleep. I just wanted to let you know that I'm going now. I'll see you tomorrow.'

She peers at the face bending over her, unable to make out who it is at first then she remembers. It's Ana.

'Ah, Ana. Was I sleeping? I'm sorry. You should have woken me sooner. I've been dreaming.' She dreams a lot these days, vivid, colourful dreams so realistic that when she wakes they are still with her.

'Don't worry. It gave me time to write up my notes but I really have to go now,' Ana says.

Nancy sits up and stretches her back, feeling the joints complain as they slip back into place with more creaking than she would like.

'I'll see you tomorrow then, Nancy.' Ana picks up her bag and heads for the door.

'Yes, all right my dear. Did you get all that you wanted?'

'Yes, thanks. Don't get up. I'll let myself out.'

Nancy listens as the door closes and the apartment is once more in silence. The dream is still with her and even the smells that she associates with Guilio's continue to linger. Thinking of Helen's friendship, knowing that she could contact her if she needed her, had helped to sustain her during those following months. But would Helen have stood by her if she knew what Nancy had been forced to do?

CHAPTER 19

The class has already started by the time she arrives. She can see Jenny in the far corner, bending and twisting in time to the music. Their instructor, a muscle bound young man with the face of an angel is calling out instructions as he bounces and stretches, bends and twists and, unlike the leotard-clad women in front of him, all in perfect synchronisation. The session has just begun, and already he is looking bored. Their aerobics class is the last one of the day and he must be tired of shouting the same instructions to the same music to the same women he sees every week. Jenny spots her and waves. Ana slips into the back row and does her warm-up exercises, then after a couple of false starts she picks up the rhythm and begins her weekly workout. The best part is that she cannot think of anything else while she is doing it. If she lets her concentration slip, she misses the beat and is immediately out of step. Nancy, her mysterious husband, Andrew, the rent, all of it can wait.

The session ends as usual with them all lying on the floor, letting their heartbeats slow and their breathing return to normal. Now her thoughts drift back to the morning with Nancy. It had started well enough. Nancy was in a talkative mood for once and Ana began to get a feel for what she had been like as a young woman. Nancy had wanted to show her some of her early drawings and while she went into her bedroom to look for them, Ana had rewound the recorder and checked on a couple of points that needed clarifying. But when Nancy didn't reappear, Ana had become worried and went to see if she was all right. She found the old woman fast asleep on her bed, the drawings still in her hand. Reluctant to leave her like that, Ana had sat down beside her and written up the morning's notes. At first Nancy snored, and then she began to talk in her sleep—odd words that Ana could not make out, muttered under her breath. Ana turned off the recorder and tried to listen carefully, but all she could make out was the name 'Helen' and 'hospital'; the rest was unintelligible.

'Hello there, what happened to you? You're not usually late,' Jenny says, coming over and sitting down beside her.

'I was busy with the book and lost track of time.'

'How's it coming along?'

'Not bad but every time I try to get some more information out of Martin or Nancy, they clam up tight. It's almost as if they're sorry they started it.'

'That might be true. These things always seem a good idea until you start poking about in the dirty washing, then nobody wants to help.'

'That's exactly it. Martin was very unpleasant when I told him I'd found out about his sister. He literally said I was to keep my nose out of his business. If it wasn't for all the effort I've already put into it, I think I'd tell them to go to hell.'

'There has to be a reason for it. It's clear there's something that they're hiding, that they don't want you to find out. The thing is to find out what it is,' Jenny says.

'I think it has to do with Nancy's husband. If I could find him, then it would all become clear.' Ana stretches slowly and gets to her feet. 'I asked her about any friends she had but she was very vague. All she said was that there had been a flatmate called Helen.'

'Well, try to find her and see what she can tell you. It can't be that difficult. Go onto Facebook, put in her name and anything else you know about her and see what comes up. Everyone's on Facebook these days.'

'But I don't know anything about her except that she's called Helen.'

'Surname?'

'Possibly Brown, possibly Jones but she could have married since then. How will that help?'

'Put in Kingston College of Art, people usually have their schools and colleges listed. Maybe something will come up. Are you coming for a drink?'

'No, not this evening. I think I'll go home and see what I can find about the flatmate. If I can track her down on the internet then maybe I can arrange to see her when I'm in England.'

'Good idea. Okay, I'll see you next week.'

Andrew has already left for work so she has the flat to herself. She pours herself a glass of wine and sits down at her computer. She is not a great Facebook fan but she does have an account so she logs in and, ignoring all the messages she has received over the last month, types 'Helen' into the search box. *Dios mio*, Helen must be the most common girl's name in England; there are hundreds of Helens on Facebook. So she amends it to 'Helen, Kingston-on-Thames' and waits to see what comes up. Three women are listed, two of them are in their forties and one has not stated her age. She clicks on to the latter, a Helen Wilson. There is no profile photo of her, but there is one of some young children and yes, this Helen went to Kingston College of Art. She clicks on the button asking to be her friend and, as Jenny has told her that the best way to get in contact is to send a private message, she clicks on the message box and writes: *'Hello Helen, You don't know me but I am helping Nancy Miller write her memoirs and I wondered if you could tell me anything about the time when you were friends at college. Ana'* Of course she could be waiting forever. If this woman is like Ana, who hardly ever logs on to Facebook, then it will all come to a dead end. She sips her wine and sits, staring at the screen and trying to work out what else she can do. There are dozens of social networking sites on the internet, but somehow she can't imagine a seventy-five-year-old woman being on many of them. Her aunt likes Facebook because she can see what her grandchildren are up to, but doesn't use it for much else. She certainly isn't on Twitter or Google or any of the numerous other social networks.

There is a ping as a small box appears on the screen. Amazingly, Helen Wilson is on line at the moment, and she has agreed to be friends with Ana. Instantly, Ana is able to access her page and there it is. Helen was definitely a student at Kingston Art College in 1957 and her name used to be Helen Jones. A minute later the following message appears: *'Hello. What a shock to hear Nancy's name. I haven't heard from her in years but we were good friends at college. What do you want to know?'*

Ana doesn't want to jump straight in with questions about Nicholas Henderson, so she writes: *'Nancy and I are coming to England next week to see an exhibition of her work in Oxford. Is there any chance we could meet?'*

Helen's reply is swift. *'I live in Henley, now. Not far from Oxford. Here is my telephone number - 01491 574646 - contact me when you get here. I'd love to catch up with Nancy.'*

Ana cannot believe her good fortune. At last she has found someone who knew Nancy in the old days and who is happy to talk to her. She copies down Helen's telephone number and writes back: *'Thank you. We will be there from 24th to 27th October. I will ring you first.'*

She reads through Helen's Facebook profile to see if there is anything useful but most of the entries are to do with her grandchildren, so she logs off and telephones Jenny. There is no answer so she leaves a message: 'Hi, Jenny. It's Ana. You were right. I've found Helen and I'm going to see her in England. Brilliant idea of yours to use Facebook. Thanks. See you soon.'

At last she is getting somewhere. If Helen and Nancy were flatmates, then Helen must have known about Nicholas Henderson and maybe even about baby Geraldine.

CHAPTER 20

Martin and Ana are coming to collect her at eight o'clock. She has been ready for almost an hour, sitting on the sofa in her cream wool coat, waiting. Martin has convinced her that taking a mink to England is a waste of time and luggage space. It's a pity because this is probably the last chance she will ever get to wear it. What should she do with it? Nobody wears fur coats in the south of Spain, and who else is there to leave it to when she dies? She won't admit it to him but she is very excited about this trip. Nancy has not been back to England since she left in 1963, not even to her exhibitions.

1963: that was the year when everything came to a head. It started with a letter from her brother, Ted, saying he was coming to see her. She could hardly believe it. The last time she had seen him was at her father's funeral and he had been cold and distant. He had barely spoken to Nick, other than a terse greeting when Nick had offered his condolences. He was probably still thinking about the occasion when Nick had punched his father. Luckily Ted was not easily roused, and no doubt her mother had warned him beforehand. The last thing anyone wanted at the funeral was an argument between those two testosterone-fuelled men. So now her brother was coming to see her. Why? Had something happened to her mother? She was suddenly filled with guilt. She hadn't been in touch with her mother since her father's funeral.

It had been a dreary affair, and although she had cried a few tears when they had lowered his coffin into the ground, they were more for the father she had known in her child-hood than the man who had turned his back on her. If any-thing her grief was for her mother, who stood there in the rain, pale and wan in her widow's black coat, tears running down her cheeks. She knew she should have made more effort to see her, but it was all she could do to keep Nick on an even keel. She dreaded to think what he would do if she told him she was going to stay with her mother for a few days.

She re-read the letter, hoping to find a clue to Ted's visit or at least a phone number so that she could ring him and tell him not to come, but there was nothing, not even the date of his arrival. She felt sick. Nick was not going to like this. What if her brother arrived when Nick was at home? How would he react? She had often wondered if her hus-band was a bit of a coward at heart. He was brave enough with her, but would he take on a six-foot-two squaddie? She slipped the letter into the pocket of her apron and resumed ironing Nick's shirt. Whatever happened, it would be her who received the brunt of Nick's anger. A wave of help-lessness swept over her. What life was this when the thought of a visit from her own brother left her quaking with fear?

She was just folding up the clean clothes and putting them in the chest of drawers when there was a knock at the door. Her heart seemed to stop. Surely this wasn't Ted al-ready?

'Mummy, door.' Martin said, looking up from his colouring book.

'Thank you, darling. I'll see who it is.'

She took off her apron, had a quick glance at herself in the mirror to check she looked respectable and opened the door. A tall, young man in a striped suit stood there and, for a moment, she didn't recognise him.

'Ted? But where's your uniform?' she asked. 'And what are you doing here?' She glanced quickly up and down the corridor; none of her neighbours was around.

'Hello, Nancy. Not much of a greeting. Aren't you pleased to see me?'

'Ted. Yes, of course, it's just that I only got your letter today.' She stared at him blankly.

'Well aren't you going to invite me in?'

'Mummy?' a little voice called.

'It's all right, Martin. It's just your uncle Ted. Come and say hello to him.' She stepped back so that her brother could enter and waited while he bent down and swung Martin up in the air.

'Hello there, young fellow. My, you've grown since I last saw you. I don't expect you remember me, do you?'

Martin shook his head, shyly.

'Cat got your tongue?'

'No,' he whispered.

'He's a bit on the nervous side,' she explained. 'He doesn't know many men except his dad. Come and sit down. Would you like some tea?'

She knew Nick was not due home until the evening, but still she was worried that he might make a surprise appearance. He had done it before. She would have liked to ask her brother to leave, but the truth was that she was very pleased to see him. His face had filled out since she last saw him and a narrow moustache adorned his upper lip. His hair was no longer cut close to his head according to army regulations, and she could now see a strong resemblance to their father.

'Yeah, a cuppa would be fine.'

'So why no uniform?' she asked, filling the kettle and putting it on the gas hob.

'I've been demobbed. That's partly why I'm here. I've got a job interview in London tomorrow and I thought I'd kill two birds with one stone, so to speak.'

She placed two cups on the table in front of him and sat down. 'It's nice to see you, Ted. We didn't get much time to talk at the funeral. How's Mum?'

'Well, that's one of the things I wanted to tell you. She's not good. She's been going downhill since Dad died and last month she moved into a nursing home. They're not sure what's the matter with her, but whatever it is, it's affected her mind. She doesn't recognise me anymore; she thinks I'm Dad. It's Richard this and Richard that and did I have a hard day at the bank—it's impossible to have a conversation with her anymore.'

'Does she ask after me?' Nancy asked.

'Not really. She thinks you're still at school and keeps rattling on about what a clever girl you are and how you're sure to pass your eleven-plus.'

'Oh, that's terrible. Poor Mum.'

'Perhaps you could go and visit her one day. It's in Goring. I'll leave you the address. She seems happy enough there; they're good to her and she isn't even aware that she has a problem. It's the rest of us who are suffering.'

'Is that why you left the army?'

'Partly, that and the fact that I'm getting married in a few months. Angela isn't keen on being an army wife.'

'Oh, Ted, that's wonderful. Do I know her?'

'No. I met her when I was stationed up north. She's a Yorkshire lass. You'd like her. It'd be nice if you could come to the wedding.'

Nancy felt her eyes fill with tears. Her mother was in a nursing home, her brother was getting married, and all she could think about was whether Nick was going to walk in on them at any minute.

'You seem very nervous, Sis. Is everything okay? Is Nick treating you right?' He was staring at the bruise on her neck and instinctively her hand went up to her collar and tugged it higher.

She forced herself to smile and said, 'Everything's fine. Nick's got a job at the local stonemason's. He's been there almost a year now.'

'I hope he's not knocking you about.'

'No, of course not.'

She glanced at her son, but he had taken out his building blocks and was playing with them on the floor.

'Because you could leave him, you know. You don't have to stay here. You could get a job and start a new life.'

'Everything's fine, Ted. Really it is.'

Leave Nick? If only it were that easy. But how could she live? What sort of job could she get? She didn't even have her art diploma. And who would look after Martin? Even if she managed all that, she knew Nick would find her, no matter where she went. No, she was better where she was.

'Well, once we're married I'll send you my new address. You can come and visit us. You're still painting then, I see,' he said, looking at the canvases stacked against the wall.

'Yes. It brings in a bit of extra money. These are ready to take to the gallery later,' she said, picking up some of her work and passing it for him to see.

'They're good. You always had a talent for art, even at school. Not like me, don't know one end of a paintbrush from the other.'

The kettle's high-pitched whistle made her start, and she went into the kitchen to make the tea.

'I like this one. Can I buy it from you?' Ted said, holding up a pretty little watercolour of a church and a river-bank. 'It reminds me of Wallingford.'

'Well spotted. That's where we used to go fishing for newts. Do you remember?'

'So how much do you want for it?'

'Have it as a wedding present,' she said. 'I can paint another one.'

'Thanks. Angela will love it. She's into art in a big way.'

'Does she paint?'

'No, but she likes dragging me around the art galleries, all those old masters and stuff.'

'She sounds a nice person.'

'Yes, you'd get on well. I do hope you can make the wedding. I'll send you an invitation.'

'Yes, do that,' she said, trying to sound positive about it.

'Anyway I've something else to tell you,' he said, pulling his wallet out of his pocket. 'I've sold the house, Mum and Dad's house. There was no point in keeping it, and besides, we need the money to pay for Mum's nursing home.'

She felt unbelievably sad at the news. Everything was changing. She had lost her father, her mother had dementia, and now her childhood home had been sold. It was all she could do not to burst into tears.

'That's a real shame,' she said. 'What did you do with all our things? The photo albums?'

He pushed a canvas bag across to her and said, 'Here are a few things I rescued from your bedroom but everything else has gone, sold with the house. All the furniture, carpets, the lot. One of the charity people came and took Dad's clothes and the things that Mum will never wear again. I took her the photo albums; she likes those. Sits and looks through them over and over. I'm not sure if she recognises many people, but every so often she will start talking about someone from her past. So, yes, it's all gone. Pretty sad, really. But what else could I do?'

'No, you did the right thing. What's the point of hanging onto stuff just for sentiment's sake?' she said, although that's exactly what she would have liked to have done. She opened the bag and smiled at Ted. There was her old rabbit with its tattered ear, her Brownie badges, some swimming certificates and old school reports.

'Mum hung on to all of it. There was a similar collection of my old things too. I think your passport's in there somewhere.'

'Well I don't think I need these,' she said, pulling out the school reports and putting them to one side. 'But thanks for thinking of me and thanks for this.' She hugged the rabbit against her and thought of her parents.

'Wabbit, Mummy.'

'Yes, sweetheart, it's a rabbit. It was Mummy's when she was a little girl. Here, you can have it now.'

Martin beamed at her. He sat the rabbit on the pile of bricks he had built.

'That's not all. There's some money.' Ted put a cheque on the table in front of her. 'Dad was a wily old thing. He'd saved quite a bit and he had some shares in the bank. So, with his savings and the money from the house, there is more than enough to look after Mum. I've put what she needs into a bank account, and you and I are sharing the rest. It's what they would have wanted.'

She didn't know what to say. She picked up the cheque. It was made out to cash for six hundred pounds. She was stunned.

'I thought you might need it,' he said, looking around at the poky flat, with the camp bed in the corner for Martin and the clothes piled on top of the chest of drawers. 'This must be a bit small for you now, with a growing son.'

'Thank you, Ted. I'm so grateful. This will make such a difference to us. We'll be able to get somewhere with a separate bedroom, maybe even two bedrooms. It will be lovely. Thank you.'

She leant over and hugged him. Just when she thought that nothing good could ever happen to her again, here was her brother bringing her an unexpected windfall.

'I had them make it out to cash because I didn't know if you had a bank account,' he said, looking a bit embarrassed by his sister's outburst of affection. 'Anyway what about that tea?'

After her brother had left she sat staring out of the window, her mind in a turmoil. Her heart ached at the thought of her mother alone in a nursing home, with no friends and family around her. She had promised Ted that she would go and see her, but how she would be able to manage it she had no idea.

'Dinner, Mummy,' Martin said. 'Biscuit?'

'Oh, sweetheart, I'm sorry; there're no biscuits. Here I'll make you some bread and butter. Daddy will be home soon and then we'll all eat together.'

She had taken to keeping Martin up late so that he could eat with them. Nick was less inclined to pick a row if Martin was sitting there. She knew it wasn't fair on the child to use him in that way, but he enjoyed seeing his father before he went to bed. She had made a shepherd's pie and had it in the oven on a low heat.

She was just putting the plates to warm when she heard her husband at the front door. As usual her stomach began to churn and she could feel every nerve in her body grow taut with fear. He was later than usual. Please God he was in a good mood.

The minute he came in she could smell the beer on him. He was smoking a cigarette and smirked at her as he stubbed it out in the sink.

'So, how's my little boy today, then?' he asked.

'Man,' said Martin, smiling up at his father, his innocent face full of excitement. 'Man.'

'What man? What's he talking about, Nancy?'

'It was just my brother, Ted.'

Martin clapped his hands and said, 'Ted.'

'Just Uncle Ted, was it?' Nick's voice was icy as he turned to Nancy. 'What did that brother of yours want?'

'He came to tell me that my mother is in a home. She has dementia.'

'Well she always was a bit batty. Like her daughter. So how come I didn't know he was coming here?'

'He wrote,' she said, holding up the letter, 'but I only received it today and the next thing I knew he was knocking at the door.'

'Knocking at the door, was he?' he mimicked her timid voice and took the letter from her. 'Doesn't say much, does he?'

She looked at Martin. It was impossible to keep anything hidden with a child in the house. Still she would have liked to have kept the news to herself for at least a little bit longer. What a shame Ted had not given her cash.

'He's sold my parents' house and he brought me my share. Six hundred pounds.'

That took him by surprise. Whatever he had been expecting, it wasn't that.

'What, he brought you six hundred pounds? In cash?'

'Not exactly, it's a cheque but made payable to the bearer. It's as good as cash. I thought we could use it to buy our own place, something a bit bigger.'

'Something bigger, in case we have any more children you mean? That doesn't seem very likely. How old is the lad now? Two and a half? Nearly three? And still no more on the way? I think I married a barren old cow, didn't I.' But though his words were harsh, she could tell he was thinking more about the money than her fertility.

She handed him the cheque. 'It's a lot of money,' she said. 'It could change things for us. We could move out of here.'

'Yes, you're right. This could make quite a difference to our lives. So this is your share. How much did he get for the house then?' he asked, going to the fridge and getting himself a beer.

'I don't know. He kept some back to pay for my mother's nursing home and he split the rest between us.'

'So you don't know exactly how much it was?'

'No. But I wouldn't have even known he'd sold the house if he hadn't told me. I'm sure it's fair.'

She expected him to start quibbling about the amount, but instead he smiled and said, 'Very nice. Yes, very nice indeed.'

He pulled out his wallet and slipped the cheque inside.

'I thought we'd open a bank account,' Nancy said. 'Until we decide how to spend it.'

'Yes, good idea. I'll look into it tomorrow.'

'Nick, I'd really like to go and visit my mother. She's not far, just in Goring. I can get the train to Reading and then on to Goring-on-Thames. I'd be back before you get home. You wouldn't even miss me. I thought I'd take Martin with me. She might like to see her grandson.'

'Yes, why not. Now, what's for my dinner?'

She hadn't seen him in such a good mood for a long time. He even said he would stay at home that night and watch the football instead of going straight out to the pub again. Watching him stretched out in front of the television, cigarette in one hand and a glass of beer in the other, she couldn't help feeling that this was just the lull before the storm. Something was going through his mind and, whatever it was, it wasn't going to be to her advantage.

'Mama, wake up. It's time to go to the airport.'

Nancy opens her eyes and, for a moment, cannot make out where she is. Martin is leaning over her and Ana is standing behind him, with Nancy's suitcase in her hand.

'Martin. I was asleep.'

'I can see that, but we've got to get to the airport. Are you ready?'

'I've been ready for ages,' she snaps. 'That's why I fell asleep, waiting for you.'

'Do you have everything?'

'My passport?'

'Ana has that and your ticket.'

He helps her up and ushers her to the door.

'Don't rush me. Where's my handbag? I can't go without my handbag. I need some money or has Ana got that too?'

'Don't get yourself upset, Mama. I'm just trying to help you. Here's your handbag.'

'Hrmph. That's what you always say. Bullying me, more like.'

She opens her bag and checks that her money is there; she has euros in one compartment and the sterling that Martin brought her, in the other.

'Will I need my credit card?' she asks.

'I should take it just in case, but Ana has quite a lot of English money. Now, is there anything else you need?'

'What about the apartment? Should I turn off the electricity? Who will water my plants? Oh, I'm not sure this is such a good idea. The place could get burgled while I'm away.'

Her son sighs, in exasperation she thinks, and says, 'Better while you're away than when you're here, Mama. María will be in later today to see to everything and lock up. So don't worry. You just have a wonderful trip. Remember this exhibition is in your honour. I want you to enjoy it.'

She follows him out to the car and waits as he locks the door behind him. This time tomorrow she will be in England, an England that she hasn't set foot in for over fifty years. What will she find? What ghosts will be waiting for her when she lands?

CHAPTER 21

Martin has spared no expense. He has booked them into the MacDonald Randolph Hotel, right in the centre of Oxford. The Victorian-Gothic entrance of this imposing building is like something from an old English film. Ana half expects Sherlock Holmes, complete with pipe and deerstalker hat, to come marching through the heavy oak doors at any moment. It is quite unlike anywhere she has ever stayed before, and she feels slightly intimidated by the liveried footmen and the oh-so-efficient receptionist. Nancy, on the other hand, is quite at home here and rather imperiously instructs the porter to take her luggage up to her room.

'I need to have a lie down,' she tells Ana. 'Will you be all right?'

'Yes, I'll just put my things in my room, and then I might have a wander around as it's such a lovely afternoon.'

'Yes, you do that, my dear. You must see something of the city while we're here.'

'You'll be all right?' Ana asks.

'Of course I'll be all right. I'm not completely senile, not yet anyway.' She smiles at Ana and adds, 'Run along now.'

'Don't forget we're going to the preview tonight. They're sending a car for us at six o'clock.'

Nancy raises her eyebrows and gives her a look that says, 'Do you think I'd forget?'

'Okay, see you later then.'

The Ashmolean Museum, in the heart of the medieval city, is right next to the hotel and only a short distance from its famous colleges. Ana zips up her jacket and winds a scarf around her neck. The autumn sun is low in the sky and throws warm patches of amber light on the stone walls of the college grounds, but the wind is cold. Through elaborately carved arches and gateways manned by uniformed porters, she catches glimpses of green lawns and walled quadrangles. Vivid red and gold Virginia creeper climbs up the stone walls, birds fly in and out of bushes laden with bright berries: cotoneaster, buckthorn and pyracantha; the petals of late flowering roses litter the lawns, and students ride bicycles or lounge on the grass, their books spread in front of them.

Nancy has already explained to her that Oxford is a city university. It doesn't have one main campus but instead lots of separate colleges. It is very different from the university Ana attended in Badajoz. The *Universidad de Extramadura* was built in the seventies and, although it probably has just as many students as Oxford, she remembers it as being much smaller. Here it seems the city is the university, and the university is the city, no division between the two. As she passes groups of chattering students, college scarves dangling from their necks, knees poking through worn jeans, some wheeling their bicycles, others carrying heavy satchels of books, she feels nostalgic for her own university days, so carefree and untroubled.

She walks for about an hour and then returns to the hotel. It is interesting to see Nancy in her own country. Maybe here she will be able to understand her employer better.

Nancy is already waiting for her in the reception area when Ana comes downstairs. The sleep has refreshed her and she is in a good mood. She has changed into the black cocktail dress she brought with her, tied her hair back in a French pleat and redone her makeup. She is no longer the crabby old woman living alone in an overheated apartment, paranoid that her maid will steal from her. No, she is a famous artist staying in an expensive hotel, and she is determined to act the part. She is even wearing some of her jewellery, the diamond earrings that are usually locked away in the wall safe, and a gold Jaeger Le Coultre watch. Ana is amazed at the change in Nancy. 'You look very nice,' she says. 'Will you be warm enough?'

Nancy holds up a black and gold wool wrap. 'I have this and my coat. I think I'll be fine. Harry phoned to say they're sending a car for us. It should be here by now.' She looks at her watch. 'I bought this in Zurich, many years ago, after a very successful exhibition. I thought it might bring me luck tonight.'

'I'm sure you won't need any luck. It will all go fine. Look, here's the car now.'

The preview is limited to a few local dignitaries, the press, critics from the art world and, Ana presumes, patrons of the arts, people with money to spend. Attendance is by invitation only and there is a sense of exclusivity about it. Nancy's paintings are very impressive, hung in groups according to the period when they were painted. From what she has seen on the internet, Ana can immediately identify the different styles.

The curator of the Oxford Modern comes to greet them, a beaming smile on his face. 'Nancy Miller, my dear lady, this is indeed an honour. I am delighted to meet you. I've been an admirer of your work for many years.' He shakes Nancy's hand vigorously. 'I hope you had a pleasant journey. And haven't you been lucky with the weather? You've brought the sunshine with you.'

A tall, casually dressed man in his mid-forties, wearing rimless glasses that he is constantly pushing back on his nose, the curator admits he was 'very surprised' to get Nancy's letter. 'Very surprised indeed. We knew you'd retired to Spain, but we didn't really expect to get a reply. How fortunate that you were available to come over. I have been considering putting on a retrospective exhibition of your work for some years now, but as you know, these things take time. Most of your paintings were in private hands but the owners have been very generous in lending them to us––and so here we are.' He waves his arms enthusiastically, his gestures encompassing the gallery and Nancy's paintings in particular. 'Your agent tells me you are writing your memoirs,' he says.

'Yes that's right. This young lady is helping me with them.' Nancy pulls Ana forward.

'How very interesting. Let me get you both a glass of champagne, and then I can introduce you. Everyone is dying to meet you. You are a legend, you know.'

He steps away, and Nancy whispers to Ana, 'They thought I was dead. That's why they didn't let me know. Lucky that Harry heard about it. Affects the price, of course.'

'What does?' Ana asks.

'If you're dead. The paintings would jump in value if I were dead.' Nancy smiles and accepts a glass of champagne from the curator. 'You have arranged a very select *vernissage*,' she says. 'Are there any art critics here?'

'Of course. Herbert Small himself has come down from London. He wrote accepting our invitation as soon as he knew you would be attending.'

'He wants to see for himself that I'm still alive,' Nancy says with a touch of her old malice.

'He's a great fan of yours,' the curator mumbles.

'He wasn't such a fan when I had that exhibition in Paris, in the eighties.'

Ana is amazed to see the change in Nancy. She is in her element here, her memory as sharp as her tongue.

'What's a *vernissage*?' she whispers whilst the curator is seeking out people to introduce to Nancy.

'It's just a posh word for a private viewing. French. They don't seem to use it so much these days. Get me another glass of bubbly, would you dear? I think I'm going to need it.'

The curator returns with an elderly man wearing a black velvet jacket and a red and black spotted bow tie. His white hair is thick and reaches his collar. Ana assumes he must be the art critic.

'My dear Nancy, what a wonderful surprise,' he says, holding out his arms to her.

'Hello Herbert. You haven't changed much, I see.'

'A little older, darling.'

'Perhaps a little wiser, too,' she says but allows him to hug her and kiss her on both cheeks.

'What have you been up to? Nobody has heard from you in years. I was beginning to fear that you were dead.'

'Still very much alive, Herbert. Sorry to disappoint you. So you're still scribbling?' she says.

'Have to do something to pay my creditors.'

'Ex-wives, you mean?'

He blushes. 'You don't forget much do you, Nancy. Still, it really is good to see you again. Here, let me top up your champagne and introduce you to a few people. Anthony St John Thomas is here—he's a great fan of yours. I believe he has lent three of your paintings for the exhibition. Come with me. You'll like him.'

Herbert takes Nancy's arm and leads her towards a group of people eating canapés and drinking Moët & Chandon. Ana, no longer required, helps herself to a second glass of champagne from the table and decides to have a closer look at Nancy's paintings. She starts with the oldest, the ones Nancy painted in college. How fresh and vibrant they are, so different from photographs of them. Now she can understand why people love them. They are the paintings of someone who is in love with life, full of vitality, youthful, joyous even.

'They're good, aren't they?' a voice says.

She turns around to find an old man standing next to her. He is staring at the paintings with a look of awe.

'I used to know her, you know. The artist. We were at college together. Many years ago now. Even then we all knew she had something the rest of us lacked. It was all so easy for her. Whatever we had to do, form, colour, perspective, it didn't matter; she was a natural at it.'

'You were at Kingston with her?'

'Yes. I was in her class, back in 1957.'

'So you're a painter, too?'

He laughs. 'Of sorts. I changed to graphic design. There was more money in it. I was never going to be famous, like Nancy.'

'Were you a friend of hers?' she asks, excited that at last she has found someone who knew Nancy at college.

'Not really. We were in the same class for a couple of years and then she dropped out. That was a shock. The best pupil in the whole college, and she just gives it up. We were all really surprised, especially Toby, our art teacher. A nice fellow and a good artist. He acted like it was his fault, kept saying he should have done more for her. We knew it had nothing to do with him, it was that bloke she was seeing. Next thing we heard, she'd got married to him. I couldn't understand it. We knew him from the pub. A strange one, always boasting about how he was going to be rich and famous one day.'

'So you knew her husband. What was he like?'

'It was a long time ago. I suppose he was good looking––certainly all the girls thought so––but he had a terrible temper. I remember once, in the pub, he knocked Nancy clean off her feet. The landlord threw him out and said if he saw him hitting her again he would bar him.'

'So what happened to him?'

'Nothing, as far as I know. He got a job at the local stonemason's, and the next thing I heard was that he was planning to go to Spain. He'd bought some old place off a guy in the pub and was going to set up an artist's colony there. He was always spouting off with crazy ideas. I don't suppose it ever came to anything. He wanted to know if any of us were interested in going in with him, but no-one wanted to get involved. We knew what he was like.'

'And Nancy, did you see her again?'

'No. I never saw either of them after I left college. Nancy hardly ever came to the pub with Nick after that incident. I think she preferred to stay at home with the kid. But then Nick dropped out of sight, too, so we assumed that he really had gone to Spain and taken them with him.'

'Do you know Nancy is here tonight?' Ana asks. 'She's over there talking to that guy with the bow tie.'

'Good God. She's really here? I can't believe it, after all these years. I'm sorry,' he says. 'Do you mind? I must speak to her.'

Ana notices that he is blushing. 'Of course not. You should take advantage of the opportunity.'

'I don't expect she'll remember me, but I had such a crush on her when I was in college. Many of the boys did. She was a really pretty girl and so talented. Will you excuse me?'

'Of course. It was nice to talk to you.'

Ana watches him greet Nancy, who obviously does not remember him but smiles politely and shakes his hand. So, she thinks, Nancy's husband was violent. And he was thinking of setting up a commune in Spain. Was that why he bought the house? But what happened? Where did he go, and where is he now?

She is wondering whether to have another glass of champagne when an elderly man approaches her. He is tall, with a mop of untidy grey hair tied back in a ponytail. He wears tinted glasses and looks slightly Indian.

'Hello,' he says, holding out his hand. 'You must be Ana.'

'Yes. Do I know you?'

'I'm Harry, Jenny's uncle. She told me you were coming with Nancy, and as you are the only beautiful young Spanish girl in the room, I thought it must be you.'

Ana feels herself blushing but can't help laughing at his open flattery. 'Nice to meet you, Harry. I'd like to say that

I've heard a lot about you, but the truth is that Nancy is not very forthcoming about her past. You're her agent, aren't you? I was planning to get in touch with you to see if you could tell me anything about Nancy's early days.'

'Any time, my dear girl. Any time. I'm sure I can help fill in some of the blanks for you. Agent, manager, secretary, friend, father-confessor, suitor, lover—I've been them all in my time. Never persuaded her to marry me though.'

She sees that he is a little drunk.

'Have you spoken to her yet?' she asks. 'She's over there talking to an old student from her college days.'

'Not yet. I am waiting for her to do the rounds, then I'll catch her. She hasn't lost it, has she? She still can work a room like the best of them.'

He is looking at Nancy admiringly, and Ana follows his gaze. He's right. Nancy knows exactly how to meet and greet people, then move on to the next admiring fan. She must have spoken to almost everyone in the room. Ana is amazed she has the stamina.

'She seems to be enjoying herself,' she says.

'My dear young lady, you have no champagne. This will never do. *Camarero*, two glasses of your finest champagne, *por favor,*' he tells the startled waiter.

The preview closes at eight and by then Ana's feet hurt. She has drunk far too much champagne and not eaten nearly enough canapés to stop her head from spinning. Harry was an amusing companion, but after a few words with Nancy, he left early, promising to see them again the following evening. Nancy looks as though she could go on all night, but luckily the curator says he has sent for their taxi.

'What a shame, I was just starting to enjoy myself,' Nancy says.

She has been talking animatedly to a group of the gallery's patrons for most of the evening and bathing in their admiration. It has been like a blood transfusion for her. She is a new woman, younger, more animated, and not at all like the woman she is in Spain.

'Well, it has been a delightful evening,' she says to the curator. 'I hope you have lots of visitors.'

'We expect a good turnout. Quite a few schools and colleges have already booked group tickets, and individual sales are excellent. You may be surprised how popular you have become. Your paintings are very fashionable now, very sought after.'

'Thank you,' Nancy says, shaking his hand.

'No, thank you, for coming all this way to grace us with your presence. Will we see you at the dinner?'

'Of course.'

Nancy flings her wrap around her shoulders and walks out to the taxi, as elegantly as any film star, not even wobbling in the dangerously high-heeled shoes she insisted on wearing. Ana brings their coats from the cloakroom and trots after her.

Ana has arranged to meet Helen in the Ashmolean Dining Room for afternoon tea. Such an English notion. Andrew told Ana to be sure to have a traditional afternoon tea while she is here, but in actual fact it was Helen who suggested the Ashmolean.

The top-floor restaurant is crowded. Most of the tables are taken by students and foreign tourists, the latter easily identifiable by the cameras slung over their shoulders and the guide books sticking out of their pockets. She notices a number of older people, shoppers just finishing their lunch, or maybe visitors to the museum taking the weight off their feet. Perhaps one of them is Helen, but how is she going to recognise her? She is thinking that she should have sent her a photo, or at least some sort of description, when a woman sitting outside on the terrace, smoking, waves at her.

'Hello, are you Ana?' she asks.

'Yes. You must be Helen. How kind of you to see me.' She holds out her hand in greeting.

'Do you mind if we sit outside? It's such a lovely afternoon and we don't get many of them at this time of year,' Helen says. 'Also, these days I'm afraid I am one of the pariahs.' She waves her cigarette in the air to emphasise her point. 'I've been going to give up for years but somehow I've never managed it. Not big on will-power, I'm afraid. I had a husband who spoiled me too much. He's dead now, more's the pity. No one left to spoil me so I have to do it myself.'

Helen is rather a plump woman; her hips hang over the edges of the cane chair and she has a pretty face with hardly a wrinkle. Her hair is snow white and cut short so that it curls around her ears. She looks wealthy. There are heavy gold bracelets on her wrists and numerous rings on her fingers. Ana notices a Louis Vuitton handbag hanging carelessly on the back of her chair.

'So you've come to see Nancy's exhibition?' Helen says. 'I looked it up when you told me about it. I hadn't realized she had become so famous. She was always a good painter though, head and shoulders above everyone else in our college. But to be honest, I never thought she'd make it. That husband of hers was so jealous of her talent. He was at our college too, you know, a sculptor but a pretty poor one, always resentful of her success.'

'She never talks about him,' Ana says.

'I'm not surprised. He was a bit of a bastard.'

'She continued to paint, though, despite her husband' Ana says. 'I've seen some of her early work.'

'Nick didn't like her being at the college, although he didn't mind her painting at home, but only because she could sell her work and he could spend the profits down at the pub. A disgusting man. I never knew what she saw in him.'

'Maybe she loved him?'

'I doubt it. I think she was frightened of him. He could be pretty violent when he'd had a drink. And jealous. He was so obsessed with her, he wouldn't let her out of his sight.'

'So you think he knocked her about?' Ana asks, thinking back to what the old man had told her at the exhibition.

'Without a doubt. I've seen the bruises. Not just bruises, either, but cuts, and once he broke her nose.'

'Didn't she go to the police?'

'You didn't do that in those days, my dear. All the police would say is that it was a domestic matter, between husband and wife. They never liked to interfere in things like that.'

'But if he was violent, surely something could have been done to stop him?'

'Maybe, but she didn't have any faith in the system. If she had complained and the police didn't protect her, then she would have been even worse off. No, she kept it to herself, didn't even tell her friends. I only knew about it after she was married. She had Martin by then, just a toddler. We bumped into each other one day in town just before I got married. I think she was at the end of her tether—it all came pouring out, what he'd been doing to her, how lonely she was, how frightened.'

She stubs out her cigarette and lights another one. 'Do you want one?' she asks Ana, offering her the packet.

Ana shakes her head and says, 'Shall we order some tea?'

'Yes, of course.' Helen waves across at the waitress and orders the set tea for two.

'I used to go out with him, you know. Not for long, just for a few months when I first went to college. He was handsome but too possessive for me. One day I was just chatting to a boy in our class when he came up and gave the poor lad a good hiding. Told him to keep away from "his girl." That was enough for me. I packed him in. Luckily it was just before we broke up for the summer, and by the time we were back at college, he had already started dating someone else.'

'What about Nancy, did she know you used to go out with him?'

'No. I didn't move into Nancy's flat until afterwards and by then I was going out with another boy, so it never came up. When she started seeing Nick I tried to warn her what he was like, but she wouldn't listen to me. She was too much under his spell by then.'

'So he wasn't a very pleasant man?'

'That's an understatement. He was a real bastard, pardon my French, but there's no other word for him. I'm only glad she managed to get away from him in the end, before he killed her.'

The waitress brings a pot of tea, together with a plate of scones, two slices of Victoria sponge, and tiny sandwiches filled with smoked salmon.

'This looks nice,' Helen says, stubbing out her cigarette in an ashtray etched with a royal coat of arms. 'I've not been here before, but it's supposed to be good. A friend recommended it. She comes shopping in Oxford. Shall I pour?'

'Did you go to Nancy's wedding?' Ana asks, picking up one of the tiny sandwiches and popping it into her mouth.

'No. She didn't invite any of her old friends. I knew about it because a lot of us had kept in touch after we left college. I was disappointed, but I understood. She had to get married of course, she was expecting Martin. I didn't see her for a long time, you know, my best friend. I blame him for that. We were flatmates for two years and got on so well, then he came on the scene and bit by bit he stopped her from seeing me. He isolated her from all her friends. It was such a shame; everybody liked her. She was a very popular girl.'

'What did you think when she told you they were moving to Spain?' Ana asks, accepting a cup of tea from her companion.

'She didn't. She never said she was going to Spain. She did say something about Nick having a crazy idea of setting up a commune for painters somewhere in Spain, but I thought it was just another of his mad schemes. I never really paid it much attention. People were always setting up communes for something or other in those days. One day when she arrived she was hopping mad at him. Her brother had given her some money so they could get a bigger flat, and Nick used it to buy a car.'

'Did Nancy drive?' Ana asks. She has never heard her mention driving a car.

'I don't think so. She went everywhere on the bus or by foot. There weren't that many cars on the roads in those days.'

'So you didn't know she was leaving England.'

'No. She met me one day as usual, a hurried cup of coffee in Guilio's, and her looking over her shoulder the whole time. I felt so sorry for her. Living with Nick had changed her personality. She was so nervy, jumping at any sudden sound, looking away if anyone, especially a man, spoke to her—and she hardly ever smiled. We had started meeting for coffee when Nick was at work, usually once a week. Anyway, this day she said that she had had enough of him and she was leaving. I wasn't surprised. I don't know how she had put up with him for so long. I asked her where she was going but she wouldn't tell me. She said it was best I knew as little as possible. I suppose she expected Nick to go round to all her friends asking about her. I really wanted to help her, so I asked her if she needed any money but she said she had saved some from the sale of her paintings. I'll say this for her, she wasn't so downtrodden that she couldn't think for herself. She seemed to have it all planned out. We said our goodbyes, a few tears, as you can imagine, and that was that. She said she would write when she was settled, but I never heard from her again.'

'So she left him and went to Spain.'

'If you say so. I'll tell you what was strange, though.'

'What was that?'

'I never heard from Nancy again, but that didn't surprise me. She was so scared of her husband that when she left him I was certain she would cut all her ties with friends and probably even family. I knew when we said goodbye that I would probably never see her again, and it quite upset me, I can tell you. She wanted to disappear completely. She was terrified that he would find her. No, it didn't surprise me that Nancy never got in touch, but what did surprise me was that Nick never came round banging on the door and asking where she was. I was all prepared for it, I can tell you; I even told my fiancé. He wanted me to move out and go back to my mother's. But nothing. I have never heard a word from Nick, not in all these years.'

'So where do you think he was?'

'I've no idea. Maybe he realized there was nothing more he could do. Maybe he met some other woman and decided Nancy wasn't worth it. Maybe he drank himself to death on Nancy's inheritance. I really don't know. I was just glad that he never knocked on my door.'

'Just one more thing, did Nancy have any other children?' Ana asks.

'Not that I know about, just Martin. Did she get married again then?'

'No, she never remarried. At least I don't think so. I mean before, before Martin was born. Was there a girl?'

'Oh yes, now you come to mention it, I do remember her saying she was pregnant. She was only nineteen at the time. The baby died, I think, a girl and premature. It happened in the summer holidays so I didn't see much of her— I was away in Scotland with my family. Then when she came back to college, she didn't want to talk about it. It had really upset her.'

'Would you like more hot water?' the waitress asks.

'No, we're fine.'

'I really ought to get back to the hotel,' Ana says. 'Nancy will be worried that I've got lost. Thanks for seeing me. It's been nice talking to you.'

'I'll come with you. I'd love to see Nancy again. I wonder if she will remember me after all these years.'

'Actually, her memory is a bit poor. Some days she is absolutely fine but others she drifts off into the past.'

'Well that's all right then, I'm part of that past. I'll get this.' Helen takes money from her elegant handbag and lays it on the table.

Nancy is sitting in the hotel bar, drinking gin and tonic. She has no trouble recognising her old friend and is delighted to see her again. Ana tries to imagine the scared young wife who moved to Spain with her infant son, running away from a brutal and jealous husband. She can appreciate why Nancy doesn't want to talk about that part of her life, but she feels it is crucial to include something about this period of her past in the memoirs. How can people understand Nancy's paintings if they don't know about the person who painted them?

'I'll leave you two to catch up with old times,' she says. 'I need to write up a few notes.'

'It was nice to meet you,' Helen says, holding out her hand to Ana. 'Good luck with the book. If you ever want to come to England just give me a ring. I've plenty of spare rooms. You'd be more than welcome to stay with me.'

'Thank you, Helen. You never know, I might just do that. I'll see you later, Nancy. Don't forget we're going to dinner this evening. Harry's picking us up,' Ana says, wondering if Nancy is all right to be left. It seems a bit early to be drinking gin and tonic, but she knows better than to comment on Nancy's drinking habits.

'I'll be ready. Don't worry.'

Once Ana has left, Nancy turns to Helen and adds, 'She does fuss so. I think Martin has told her to be my body-guard. We've even got adjoining rooms. I ask you. I'm a grown woman. I don't need someone to look after me.'

'Sons are like that,' Helen says. 'They become protective of their mothers, especially when they are widows. My son, before he went to Canada, was just the same. Now he doesn't have the time to worry about me. He has an ex-wife, a new girlfriend, and six children to keep him busy. But he keeps in touch, calls me on Skype every Sunday.'

'I didn't know you had grandchildren,' Nancy says. She has already forgotten about Ana.

'I have two grandsons, lovely boys, just like their father.'

A waiter comes across and asks Helen, 'Would you like tea, madam?'

'Tea? No she doesn't want tea, bring her a gin and tonic, and another for me. We're celebrating. We haven't seen each other for fifty years,' Nancy tells the waiter, confidentially.

She leans back and smiles at Helen. 'So, are you still with that bank manager?' she asks. 'What was his name, Terry?'

'Tom. He died ten years ago. He was a good man. We had a happy marriage, and he left me well provided for,' she said, twisting her gold wedding ring round her finger. 'I was lucky.'

Nancy does not reply. She is thinking about her own sorry marriage and how she too is lucky—lucky not to be still trapped in it.

'Ana tells me you're writing your memoirs' Helen says. 'What fun. I expect you could tell a tale or two.'

'It's not working out as I planned,' Nancy tells her. She feels she wants to unburden herself to Helen even though she has not seen her for many years. After all Helen is the only one she has ever been able to confide in. Helen knew what Nick was really like. She would understand.

The waiter arrives with two gin and tonics and a small bowl of crisps.

'Thank you. Please put it on my room number,' Nancy says. 'Room 144.'

No, she cannot confess, not to Helen, not to anyone. The ramifications would be too great. But how wonderful it would be to have someone to share her burden, this secret she has carried with her for so many years.

'Not working out? Why is that?' Helen asks.

'Ana is a nice young woman and very thorough. If anything, she is too thorough. She goes poking about in things that are best left alone. And all this talk about the past upsets me, brings it all back, and I don't want to remember those days. I want to forget them.'

'You're right,' Helen says. 'Ana is taking this very seriously. She asked me about Nick. I'm sorry if you didn't want me to say anything; I was just trying to help. She wanted to know what had happened to him.'

'What did you tell her?'

'Not a lot, honestly. I said I didn't see him after you left,' she says. 'He never came round to look for you, which surprised me. Did you ever hear from him again? Do you know where he went? Did he meet someone else?'

'No, I never heard from him and I didn't want to. The plan, if you remember, was to disappear so that he couldn't find me.'

'Of course. I did tell her that he had a hot temper and sometimes he took it out on you. I'm sorry. I thought it wouldn't matter after all this time.'

'Oh God, I hope she isn't going to put that in the book. I mean, why would anyone want to read about that?'

'It's all to do with your painting, Nancy—she explained it to me as we were walking back to the hotel. She has a theory that you have been telling the story of your life through your paintings. She's particularly interested in a painting called "Blackwater Lake." Do you know the one she means?'

'Yes, I know it. Well, Ana is just being fanciful. I admit my moods changed over the years, but that's hardly the same as telling my life story.'

Nancy feels a tightness in her chest, as though everything is pressing down on her. What exactly has Ana found out? Is she going to expose her? The thought that Martin would learn her awful secret makes her feel faint.

Helen is concerned. 'Are you all right, Nancy? You've gone very pale.'

'I've got this pain in my chest. I'd better go and lie down for a bit, otherwise I'll be useless this evening.'

'Of course, my dear. Ana says you're not leaving for a couple of days—we'll catch up later, when you're feeling better.'

'Thank you, Helen. You've always been such a good friend to me.'

Nancy is desperate to get away, to get back to her room and lie down. The tightness in her chest is getting worse. She manages to stand and kiss her friend goodbye, then she heads for her room.

The key card doesn't work. For a moment she leans her head against the door and waits for the dizziness to pass, then she swipes the key card again. This time she hears a click and opens the door. There are black spots before her eyes and she feels herself swaying. A couple more steps and she can lie down. She reaches the bed and falls onto it. By now the room is spinning and she thinks she is going to faint.

Ana takes out her notebook and begins to write. For obvious reasons she has not been able to use her recording machine, and she needs to write everything down before she forgets it. What a break, meeting that old guy the night before, and now Helen. She hasn't really told her anything new about Nancy's husband, but she has corroborated the old man's story. Harry, when she spoke to him, hadn't been much help at all; it seems he knows as little as Ana about Nancy's early life. So that just leaves Martin. She wonders if he knows what a swine his father really was. Is it because of his behaviour that the mood of her paintings changed? She has checked the dates. Nancy's dark period coincides with the time Martin was born. Now that had always surprised her. She would have expected Nancy to have been happier than ever with a new born baby, but if the paintings are to be believed, that's not so. Rather than happy, Nancy seems to have been depressed, even frightened, and certainly angry at that time in her life. Is her violent husband the reason? It seems quite likely. She needs to visit the exhibition again and have another look at the later paintings.

CHAPTER 22

When Nancy wakes she has a terrible headache and her mouth is dry. She should never have had that second gin and tonic with Helen; it made her feel quite ill. Still it was nice to see her old friend again after all these years, and that was thanks to Ana.

Ana. What is she going to do about her? The girl doesn't realize what a hornets' nest she is attempting to stir up, but Nancy can't confront her now, not here in Oxford with everyone's eyes on her. She'll have to wait until they are back in Spain. She stretches and feels her muscles protesting. She is still in her blue suit, now crumpled from where she's been sleeping. She will have to have it pressed before she leaves.

Her thoughts drift back to her conversation with Helen. Perhaps she is reading too much into it. After all, how could Ana know what happened back then? It is all speculation on her part. It will be best to just wait and see what she writes in the book, then if Nancy doesn't approve she can pay Ana for her work and destroy it before Martin reads it. It was never her idea to write these bloody memoirs in the first place. She should never have listened to Harry.

'Blackwater Lake'—it's probably just a coincidence that Ana has been asking about that particular painting. It was stupid of Nancy to give it its proper name. Why hadn't she just called it 'The Lake'? There was no need to mention Blackwater. But that is typical of her—she has kept everything hidden away so long, it's almost as if it never happened. She has lived these last fifty years in denial, telling herself that what she did was done for Martin, that she is not a bad person, that it was the only solution she had. She has been so convinced nobody would ever discover her crime, that now it has become unreal, as if it all happened to someone else, not to her, not to Nancy Miller.

She looks at her watch. It's late. She needs to shower and dress for this damned dinner. She sighs. It used to be so easy. She had loved cocktail receptions and fancy dinners when she was younger, all that glitz and glamour, but now she finds them an imposition, something she is obliged to do. Still, she will see Harry again. He has promised to collect them himself at eight o'clock.

Harry. All these years he has been the love of her life. She remembers the day she first met him as clearly as if it were yesterday, a moment she still holds dear, deep in her heart. It was her first exhibition in Paris, in the Musée d'Arte Moderne. Harry was working for the organisers of the exhibition, his job to look after this promising new artist and make sure she had everything she needed. Well, he certainly did that. It had been love at first sight. He was tall and wiry, with long black hair he tied back in a ponytail. His mother was from Sri Lanka, and he had inherited her creamy, smooth skin. He was gorgeous and still is—slightly fatter, considerably older, and with iron grey hair, but still the same warm smile and gentle, caressing voice that thrilled her then and continues to do so.

She steps under the shower and soaps herself carefully. If only she had met him when she was young, before she met Nick, how different her life might have been. Harry had wanted to marry her. He proposed to her one night when they were at an exhibition in Venice. How romantic that had been, drifting in a gondola, under the Bridge of Sighs. She laughs quietly to herself. My God, that was every girl's romantic dream, and she had turned him down. She hadn't been ready to share her life with anyone. How could she? If you loved someone, then you had no secrets from them. But how could she have told Harry her secrets? How could she tell anyone?

She towels herself dry and puts on her underwear. There is a faint knock at her door.

'Yes, who is it?' she calls.

'It's just me, Nancy. I wondered if you were awake.'

'Of course I'm awake. We're going out to dinner in half an hour, aren't we?'

'Sorry. I was just checking.'

That girl is beginning to get on her nerves. Does she think Nancy is completely senile?

'You get yourself ready and I'll see to myself. It will be a posh do tonight, so make sure you have something smart,' she tells her, rather unnecessarily.

She takes a green silk dress off its hanger and slips it on. It still fits perfectly. She tries to remember the last time she wore it—many years ago, she is sure. Perhaps at that dinner in Madrid, the last occasion when she had gone up to meet Harry. When was that? 2000? No, 2001. The year after his wife died of cancer. She could have made her move then, because he was still in love with her, but it was too late. Too many years had passed, and her secrets had to remain buried.

Nancy puts the finishing touches to her makeup and sprays herself with perfume. For old time's sake, she is wearing an emerald ring Harry gave her. It no longer fits her third finger because her knuckles are too swollen, so she has slipped it onto her little finger. She rests her hands in her lap and looks at it. The stone is tiny, but the colour matches her dress perfectly.

Another knock at her door, this time even more timid.

'Come in, Ana. I'm ready.' She picks up her coat and her evening bag. She is ready to face them all.

The next morning Nancy goes down to breakfast early. Last night's dinner was much more fun than she expected, thanks to Harry. He had collected them from the hotel, just as planned, and insisted she sit in the front of the car next to him. He had steered her through the fawning guests at the reception, then, when dinner was announced, took her arm and led her in past the mayor and other dignitaries, and ignoring the carefully arranged place cards, seated her at his right hand. The curator glared at them, but nothing was said. After all, she was the guest of honour and could sit where she chose. She sighs. It is unlikely she will ever see Harry again. He took the early train back to London this morning.

She orders coffee and helps herself to a croissant from the buffet. Today is their last day in Oxford, and she wants to make the most of it. Ana is seated by the window, talking to someone on her mobile. She's always on that mobile. What does she find to talk about?

'Good morning,' Nancy says, sitting down opposite her.

Ana smiles, continues speaking in Spanish, then after a few minutes says goodbye and hangs up. 'Sorry,' she says, 'that was my boyfriend, Andrew. I just wanted to know how he was.'

'And how was he?' Nancy asks with a touch of sarcasm in her voice. 'Any different from yesterday?'

'He's fine. He just wanted to know what time we're getting home.'

'Checking up on you?'

'Not really. Well maybe. He's always complaining about me working. He says I should chill out more. He says I take life too seriously.'

'Doesn't he have a job?'

'Yes, but he works in a bar, so he's out most nights and home during the day, whereas I work during the day and like to sleep at night.'

'Doesn't sound very compatible to me.'

'It is a bit difficult. I sometimes think he resents me trying to make a career for myself. I mean, it's hard enough finding work these days. It would be nice to have a little support from him occasionally. He used to work in a bank, you know, when he was in England. Then he just gave it all up and started travelling.'

'How long have you been together?'

'About a year.'

'Are you going to get married?' Nancy asks.

'He never talks about things like that. He doesn't like permanence, he says.'

'Sounds a bit of a drifter. I'm surprised, Ana—he doesn't sound quite the right man for you. You're a bright, intelligent girl. Why are you wasting your time on someone like that?' Andrew sounds a bit too much like Nick for her liking. She wonders if he knocks Ana about.

'It's just that he's not very ambitious. He can't help that, can he?'

Nancy refrains from making any comment. She likes Ana, but who is she to give anybody relationship advice?

Ana puts her mobile phone back in her bag. 'I think he might just pack up and go travelling again one day.'

'Probably the best thing that could happen. Then you can get on with your life before it's too late.' Nancy spreads butter on her croissant.

'Maybe you're right. The truth is, I don't know how I would feel if he left. I think I might just be relieved.' Ana picks up the jar of strawberry jam and opens it. 'I asked for some olive oil for my toast, but they looked at me as if I were mad.'

'That's far too foreign for a place like this,' Nancy says. 'You'll have to make do with English jam. By the way Ana, I meant to thank you for getting in touch with Helen. It was really lovely to see her again after all these years. She's going to my exhibition today, and even spoke of buying one of my paintings. I don't suppose she will—I doubt she realizes quite how expensive they have become. Even I couldn't afford to buy one. Isn't that funny? I can't afford one of my own paintings.'

'You'll have to paint some more then,' Ana says, pouring herself some coffee and taking a bite of her toast.

'I'm going to do some shopping later,' Nancy says. 'Would you like to come with me?'

'I'd love to, but I'd also like to make another visit to the gallery. I didn't really get a good look at your paintings at the preview, and I'd like you to tell me something about them.'

Nancy hopes that she isn't going to ask her any awkward questions, especially about Blackwater Lake, but she smiles and says, 'Yes, of course. We'll go there first and then we'll go shopping. I'm sure you want to buy some things while you're here.'

Ana finishes off the last of her toast and says, 'I'd like to get something for my mother. She is a great anglophile.'

'Very well. The gallery doesn't open until ten, so we'll go then. I'll meet you downstairs just before.'

'Good idea. I'll see you then.'

She watches as Ana makes her way through the crowded dining room then pours herself a second cup of coffee. She has been drinking a lot of coffee lately. Perhaps that is what has been making her so dizzy.

Try as she might, Nancy can't stop thinking about her past. Seeing Helen again has made it all so vivid. She remembers that night as if it were yesterday, and even now she can't believe she was ever capable of doing such a terrible thing. Where did all that hate come from, to make her do it? Well, she tells herself, everyone has a breaking point, and Nick had pushed her past hers.

It was the money that started it. She probably would have gone on putting up with his temper until…when? Until she was dead? She should never have told him about the six hundred pounds. With hindsight, it was obvious what he would do.

After Nancy told him about the money Nick had been in a good mood, joking and playing with Martin, and not even complaining when she said she was going to visit her mother. Was that all it took to make him happy? A few hundred pounds and he seemed like a normal husband and father. She prayed it would last.

Then one day Nick came home at lunchtime as usual and said, 'Come outside and see what I've got for us.'

He was bubbling with excitement. It was the old Nick, the one she had fallen in love with. What had happened? He took her by the hand. 'Close your eyes. It's a surprise.'

She closed her eyes and let him lead her outside—then she heard Martin cry out in excitement, 'Car. Look Mummy. Blue car.' She opened her eyes and stared in amazement: it was a battered old Ford Prefect. The paintwork was a dark blue, the colour mismatched where it had been repaired. The front bumper had an ugly dent in it but otherwise the car looked all right.

'Can I get in? Please Daddy.'

'Of course you can, son. We're all going for a drive. Here, you get in the back and your mum can sit in the front with me.'

'Whose is it?' she asked.

'Ours, of course. Come on, get in.'

'But how could we afford it?' she asked, dreading the answer she knew would come.

'We have your kind old dad to thank for that,' he said.

'But that money was for a better place to live,' she said, her throat thick with emotion, the words almost refusing to come out of her mouth. 'How could you spend it on a car?'

'Don't be an old sourpuss. It's second-hand, cost me only fifty pounds, a real bargain. And there's plenty of money left.'

Fifty pounds—that was half a year's wages. What was he thinking?

'Are you coming or not? If not, me and Martin are off for the afternoon. I thought we'd pop down to Brighton and have a paddle. What do you think about that, son?'

Martin obviously thought it was a great idea. He was already climbing into the passenger seat.

'What about your job?'

'They won't miss me for one afternoon. Are you coming?'

Reluctantly, she got into the car. No way could she let Martin go with Nick on his own. The last time he had taken Martin out, her son had spent the evening sitting in the porch of a local pub while his father played darts with his friends. No, like it or not, she would have to go along.

The next week he bought a shotgun. A snip, he said, too good a bargain to miss. He would soon get the money back with all the rabbits and pheasants he was going to shoot. A mate had told him exactly where to go, right next to Richmond Park—crawling with them, it was. She'd held her tongue, said he must put it away, well out of Martin's reach. Maybe it wasn't so bad, she reasoned to herself. If he had the car and the gun he could go out every weekend shooting with his new friends, and she wouldn't have to see him. Better than him coming home drunk from the Black Cat every Sunday lunchtime.

Then one evening he came back from the pub bursting with such excitement, she thought he had won the football pools.

'What is it?' she asked. 'What's happened?'

'Sit down, Nancy, you're going to love this.'

'What is it?'

'Sit down. Sit down. Have we anything to drink? We need to celebrate.'

'There's a bottle of beer in the cupboard and some sweet sherry.'

'You stay there. I'll get them.'

He came back, handed her a glass of sherry, and took a good hard drink of his beer.

'Well what is it?' she asked. She was getting nervous. What had Nick done to make him so pleased with himself?

'You know you wanted to get out of this flat?'

'Yes.'

'Well, that's exactly what we're going to do. I've bought us a house.'

'You've bought a house?' She couldn't believe what she was hearing. What house? With her father's money? Without telling her? And where? Her mind was spinning with questions but all she asked was, 'When did this happen?'

'Tonight. In the pub. It's going to be great, Nancy. You're going to love it.'

'You bought a house in the pub?' she said, unable to keep her astonishment hidden.

'Yes, don't worry. It's all legal and that.' He took her hands and continued, 'This is just what we need, to get away from it all. Remember when we were in Juan-les-Pins? Wasn't that wonderful? You and me? We were happy then, weren't we? Well, it'll be like that again. We'll have a carefree life, no slogging day after day, carving pathetic sentiments onto people's gravestones, no choking on stone dust, no one shouting orders at me all day long, plenty of fresh air and sunshine. It will be paradise.'

Nancy felt as if she had been dumped in a cold bath. Her stomach was churning, and she thought she was about to be sick.

'Where is the house?' she asked, at last.

He laughed and hugged her to him. The smell of his body made her want to heave.

'You'll never guess. It's in Spain. I've bought a house in Spain, right on the beach. I've got photos of it, and all the paperwork. It's all kosher. I know this guy. He wouldn't pull a fast one on me. He wouldn't dare.' He handed her a faded black and white photograph of a small white house with a palm tree in front of it. There were pots of geraniums sitting on the doorstep. 'Pretty, isn't it? I knew you'd like it the minute I saw it. It's a house made for someone with your artistic temperament.'

'Have you actually bought it?' she managed to ask, at last. What was happening to her? She was stuck in a nightmare from which she couldn't wake. Just when she thought things were starting to improve for them, he spends all their money on a house that neither of them have even seen. In Spain, of all places.

'Yes, look, here is the bill of sale. He's going to give me the deeds next week as soon as he gets them from his solicitor.'

'But don't we need a solicitor too? Someone to check that the house actually exists?'

He frowned at her. She was not supposed to criticise his wonderful plan. 'Now don't spoil it, Nancy. I've said that there is nothing to worry about. What, do you think I'm a fool?'

She shook her head and tried to look enthusiastic.

'He said if we paid in cash we could avoid all those legal fees. It's not like in England, you know. As long as you have a bill of sale and the original deeds to the property, nobody gives a damn.'

She felt dizzy, and it was hard to concentrate on what he was saying. Bill of sale? Deeds? Nick had spent her father's money on a house in Spain. All her inheritance had gone.

'It's ours. We can move straight in, no fuss, no red tape, just like buying a second-hand car.'

He continued to speak, but she couldn't hear. There was a buzzing noise in her head and she thought she would faint.

'Nancy. Are you listening to me?'

'Oh. Yes, Nick. It's just such a surprise. So what did you pay for it?' she asked, praying that he hadn't wasted all their money on this new venture.

'Four hundred pounds. He wanted four hundred and fifty but I told him that was all I could manage and he was happy with it. Come on. You don't seem very pleased. I thought you'd be happy. This is what you wanted, isn't it, a new house, the chance to start a new life, more room to paint? You'll have all that and more.'

'Yes, but Spain? We never spoke about moving to Spain.'

He stood up and stared down at her. His eyes seemed to see right through her, read her thoughts.

'That's right, throw a damper on it like you always do. God, there's no pleasing you Nancy. You wanted to move, and here I've bought us a new house, and it's not good enough for you. What *do* you want?'

His stance had become menacing. She could see he was working himself up into a temper, so she smiled and said, 'No, it's good. Really. It's just such a surprise, and you know I'm not used to surprises. Let me have a look at the photo again.'

He passed the photograph to her and she studied it carefully, not because she was interested in what little information it offered, but because it gave her something to concentrate on and helped her hold back tears of despair. He had spent all her money, and now he wanted to take her to a foreign country, where she would be as far away as possible from her friends and family—and totally at his mercy. Could her life possibly get any worse?

'Are you ready to go, Nancy?' Ana asks, sitting down in front of her and waking Nancy from her reverie.

'Ana, you were quick. Yes, I'm ready. Just a minute, while I put my coat on. They say it's going to rain, you know.' She is already missing the Spanish sunshine.

Ana is dressed in her blue waterproof jacket and has tied her long hair back into a ponytail. She winds a scarf around her neck and hoists her usual capacious bag, with its ever-present recording machine and notebooks, onto her shoulder. Nancy gives the young woman a smile. 'Let's go and give you a lesson in painting,' she says. She is enjoying being in Oxford. In fact she is enjoying being the centre of attention again.

The gallery is almost empty but then, as Ana reminds Nancy, it is only ten o'clock in the morning. The curator is not about, but one of his assistants recognises her and comes across to see them.

'Hello, Mrs Miller. How are you today? What can I do to help you?'

'Nothing, my dear, but thank you,' Nancy said. 'I just want another look at the exhibition. There were so many people to talk to at the preview that I really didn't get enough time to look at my paintings. Some of them I haven't seen for fifty years, you know.'

'Of course, please take all the time you need. I'll be in the office if you need me. Would you like to leave your coats in the cloakroom?'

Ana hands over her jacket and scarf, and Nancy removes her coat. She is wearing her blue wool suit, freshly pressed, and has abandoned the high heels for more comfortable boots.

'Well Ana, where would you like to start?' Nancy asks.

It is surprising how at home she feels here, surrounded by her own work. She doesn't remember experiencing this feeling of belonging at other exhibitions, maybe because Harry was always there, moving her from one prospective buyer to another. But this time it's a retrospective exhibition, not just for others to enjoy but for her as well.

'I had a good look at your early work during the preview. What surprises me is the change in your style over here,' Ana says, directing Nancy to a wall of dark and sombre paintings. 'What happened to make you paint like that?'

Nancy looks at them for a while before answering. She remembers exactly what was happening to her during that period, but she doesn't want to share it with Ana, not in any specific way, at least. However, she does want Ana to understand her paintings.

'People always think that the artist is trying to convey some message or other,' she says. 'It's not always the case. But it is often true that the artist's feelings are transmitted through his painting. I don't recall exactly what the problem was at that time, but I remember being very depressed, and now that I look at these paintings I can see it reflected there in my work. It was a dark time for me, and it shows.'

'You seem to have liked painting water scenes,' Ana says. 'Look, almost all these have water in them somewhere.'

'Those were painted later. Oh, my goodness, these belong to the Earl of Rochester,' she says, reading the typed label at the side. 'Must be the son, or the grandson. I can't imagine the old man buying my work. He's far too much of a traditionalist for that. Yes, what was I saying?' she asks, looking at Ana for encouragement.

'You said they were painted later, the water ones.'

'Yes. It's not easy to paint water. Seas and skies are very difficult for a water colourist. You can't keep adding layers of paint until you get it right, like you can with oils. You learn to paint quickly. Freely, my tutor used to call it. "Keep it free," he'd say.'

She thinks back to Toby and those early days. He wouldn't let them use any black or white paint. They had to build up the picture without them. And he insisted that they use just one brush, a big one with a very fine tip, even to paint the most delicate details. It was important to develop the skills, he always said. She wonders if he ever knew that she had become a success. Part of her is disappointed that he never got in touch with her when she started to become well-known, but she knows she would never have answered any letters even if he had written to her.

'I suppose I was perfecting my techniques.'

Ana walks over to one of the paintings. 'What about this one? It has always fascinated me. What's this below the water? If I look at it one way it looks like spotlights. And this—is this a hand stretching upwards?'

This is the painting she'd asked Helen about, 'Blackwater Lake.' Obviously Ana thinks she has discovered something sinister in it. Well, Nancy isn't going to confirm her suspicions one way or the other.

'An Irish pop star owns it,' she tells her. 'I understand he has it in his house in Malibu.'

'But does it have any significance? The lights?' Ana persists.

'All art is open to interpretation,' Nancy says. 'True, it is about communication, but what the artist is trying to convey is not necessarily what the spectator is seeing. It is a two-way process. I put my ideas down on paper, but you, when you look at them, see them through your eyes, your perception of the world. You bring your own prejudices, your own experiences to it, and therefore what you see is coloured by your life. It is a mingling of the artist's experience and the viewer's.' She is repeating something she once said at the opening of an exhibition in Vienna and is pleased that she has remembered it so clearly.

'So none of your paintings are particularly significant?' Ana asks.

'Significant? In what way? Do you mean informative, revealing? What would they reveal?'

'You mentioned communication. I just wondered if you were trying to say anything through your work.'

This was what Helen meant—Ana thinks she is confessing something in her painting. Oh, why doesn't she leave it alone? Nancy feels weary. She would just like to be on her own with her paintings, but nevertheless she must give her some sort of answer or she will become even more suspicious.

'All artists try to communicate through their art—that's the nature of the beast. But was I trying to tell a particular story? No, I'm not aware that I was.'

'What about a painter like Picasso and his painting of "Guernica"? Wasn't he trying to make a point there?'

'Yes, of course he was. Sometimes artists want the viewer to see a particular message in their work. Do you know David's painting of "The Assassination of Marat"?'

Ana shakes her head.

'It's very famous. Marat was one of the leaders of the French Revolution, and he was murdered in his bath by a woman. David wanted to show him as a martyr to the revolution's cause, so he painted him as a rather noble figure. All artists have something in mind when they work. Remember that many of the great artists had patrons, and they were expected to paint pictures that would please those patrons: portraits in particular, family scenes. But even then the artist can slip in something that is solely his. Take Velasquez's "*Las Meninas*" for example.'

'I know that one,' Ana says. 'It's in the Prado. I've seen it.'

'Then you will understand. It is a portrait of the King's family, yet the manner in which Velasquez has painted it has transformed the scene into much more. Art critics have been discussing what Velasquez's intentions were for many years, and I'm sure they will go on discussing them for many more. One famous art historian suggested that Velasquez's message was that art, and therefore life, is an illusion, hence the mirror reflecting the King and Queen. Are they the ones he is painting or are they merely spectators? You see everyone has their own personal taste in art, their own interpretation of what the artist is trying to achieve. Some people like art to be as realistic as possible, to others that is anathema. Some expect art to be progressive. Take the entries for the Turner prize for example: unmade beds and cows in formaldehyde. It is all a question of taste. Art truly is an illusion.'

Nancy knows that Ana is very perceptive. The young woman realizes that the key to Nancy's past lies in the paintings, which is why she keeps asking about them, but she will get no more help from her today. It is all too evident to Nancy now, when she looks at her own paintings, that Ana has guessed correctly. They tell the story of Nancy's life.

CHAPTER 23

The visit has been a great success. Nancy wishes that Martin had been with them to see the esteem in which her work is still held. He will be proud of her when she tells him about it. She has saved a couple of the national newspapers which mention the exhibition in a positive light. She knows he will smile when he reads of the general surprise that she actually attended the preview—indeed, that she is still alive. She's not that old, why does everyone think she should be dead?

Apart from an annoying dull pain in her chest, she feels invigorated by the trip. At home in her flat, she spends most of the day reading or sleeping. While she was in windy Oxford she had found much more energy. Yesterday morning, while Ana shopped for ornate tea caddies and souvenirs, she went into Broad Canvas on Broad Street, and bought brushes, paints, and two watercolour pads. She'll show them that she's not dead yet.

'Can I get you anything?' the stewardess asks her.

Martin has booked them business class seats and it is nice to be able to stretch out and enjoy the view. They are flying over the Channel at the moment, and behind them the Isle of Wight recedes into the distance, the last she will see of England for some time, if ever.

Nick had handed in his notice. They persuaded him to work until the end of the month. She was surprised that he bothered to tell them he was leaving, but then she realized he would lose his holiday pay if he just walked out. He never stopped talking about what a wonderful life they were going to have, and when she didn't reply, he addressed himself to Martin. Her little son, too young to understand what it was all about, nevertheless caught his father's excitement and badgered her every day with questions: 'Today, Mummy?' 'Today Spain?' even 'Car Spain, Mummy?' She answered his questions as well as she could and held back her tears.

One good thing was that Nick was making no objections to her weekly visit to see her mother. It was a long journey by train and bus, and when they arrived, her mother didn't recognise her and thought Martin was some child of an old neighbour of theirs, but it made Nancy feel better to see her. She took her chocolates and sometimes flowers. Her mother would eat the chocolates but ignored the flowers, which upset Nancy. Her mother had always been such a keen gardener and now she didn't have the slightest interest in a simple bunch of flowers. The nurses said her condition was stable, but it was unlikely that it would ever improve. She was happy, they said; she wasn't aware anything was wrong with her. Nancy wanted to howl with pain when she heard this. Only the presence of Martin had held her anguish in check. How dreadful not to even know you were ill. She held her mother's hand and whispered to her about the plans to go to Spain, about the weather, about Martin, about her latest painting, about seeing Ted, about anything that might possibly find its way through the confusion that was clouding the old woman's brain, but there was no response.

*

The week before they were due to move, Nancy was in bed with Martin snuggled up beside her when the door to their flat was suddenly thrown open. Nick switched on the light and strode straight to the bathroom. He had been to the Black Cat and was drunk. Nancy could hear him pulling things out of the bathroom cabinet and throwing them on the floor. She was too petrified to move. What had happened? What was he looking for?

'Where are they, you whore?' he shouted, coming back into the room. He reached up to the top of the wardrobe and took down the shotgun and pointed it straight at them. She felt Martin stir and hugged him against her.

'What are you talking about Nick? Where are what? I don't know what you're talking about.' She was terrified. She had never seen him so angry before. He was like a mad man.

'You know very well. You think I'm stupid, don't you. Bill was telling me all about them. One little pill each day and no risk of getting pregnant, that's what he said. Pills. You've got them, I know you have. That's why you're not pregnant, isn't it? You let me think it was my fault, that there was something wrong with me, and all the time you were deceiving me. You bloody cow.'

He was standing over the bed now, the twelve-bore pressed against her chest. She could feel the cold steel through her nightdress. Gleaming gun-metal blue, the shotgun fascinated her as much as it frightened her. The walnut stock was carved to fit a human hand, shaped and smoothed, oiled by a craftsman— a thing of beauty that held the power to destroy their lives. She could not tear her eyes away from it. The metal was engraved with a country scene: a bird in flight, a snipe possibly. She had never really looked at it before. Where had this despicable man got such a beautiful object? She was numb with fear, but still she could not stop looking at the gun.

'Nick, be careful. Martin's here,' she said, her voice trembling. 'Don't wake him. You don't want to frighten him, do you?' All the time her brain was focused on the gun. Was it loaded? She thought not, but she couldn't be sure. He was mad enough to leave it loaded. He was mad enough to shoot both of them and then spend the rest of his life regretting it.

'Where are they?' he repeated. 'Where have you hidden them?'

'In my handbag,' she said. 'They're in my handbag.'

At last the shotgun was lifted from her as he grabbed her handbag and tipped the contents onto the bed. There, amid the usual assortment of keys, handkerchiefs, hair-clips, compact, lipstick and comb, was the aluminium blister with its tiny pink pills. He looked at her with undisguised hatred. 'You cow.' He picked up the pills and strode into the bathroom. She heard him flush them down the toilet.

He had left the shotgun propped against the door. She wanted to pick it up, point it at him, shut her eyes and pull the trigger, but she remained lying there, staring at the gun, tears streaming down her face, admiring the elegant lines of the instrument with which he had threatened her.

'Where did you get them?' he asked, when he came back into the room. 'Who gave them to you?'

'I went to the family planning clinic,' she said, pulling herself up into a sitting position and wiping her eyes with the hem of her nightdress. 'I thought you'd be happy. We could have intercourse without worrying.'

'Intercourse? What sort of word is that? You're my wife. We don't have intercourse, we make love. And what gives you the right to decide whether we have any more children? I am the breadwinner. I say whether we can afford to have more children or not. Well that's the end of it, no more pills, ever.'

She thought he was going to hit her, but instead, he put the gun back on top of the cupboard and sat down.

'Oh, Nancy. I thought we were going to start a new life. How could you deceive me over something so important? Well you won't be able to when we're in Spain. The pills are illegal there. Bill told me all about it. It's a Catholic country, contraception is against the law. Oh, Nancy, I can't understand you at times. You know Martin needs to have a little brother or sister. Why would you do this?'

He leaned down and picked up his son and put him back in the camp bed, then he pulled off his clothes and climbed in beside her. 'We're going to have more children whether you like it or not. And there's no time like the present.' He pulled up her nightdress and climbed on top of her.

That was when she made her decision, lying there cold and impassive, thinking about the shotgun while her husband thrust and grunted on top of her. He had gone too far now. The Rubicon had been crossed.

The next day nothing was said about the pills. Nick smirked at her as he left for work. How she hated him. Despite what he said, he did not love her. She wondered if he had ever loved her. If that was love, she wanted none of it. All he wanted was to control every aspect of her life. Well, her decision had been made; there was no turning back, but she would have to move quickly if she was to put her plan into practice. There were only five days left before they were leaving for Spain.

'Come on Martin, let me put your coat on. We're going to see Granny.'

'Train?' he asked. 'Whoo whoo.' Martin loved trains. Going to see Granny was a big treat for him because he got to travel on two trains and a bus.

'Yes, on a train. Now hurry up and put on your shoes.'

She had to see her mother one last time. That the old woman wouldn't know she had been there was immaterial. Nancy needed to say goodbye. She popped a pink pill into her mouth and washed it down with some water. Nick might have flushed her pills down the toilet but he hadn't found them all. She had always dreaded him finding out she was taking them, so each time she got a new packet, she split it into four weekly allocations and hid them in different places. These had been hidden underneath the bath, wrapped in a plastic bag.

'Ready?'

'Yes, Mummy.'

'Let's go and see Granny, then.'

The nurse was surprised to see them. 'Hello, Mrs Henderson, you're early this week. Isn't it Thursdays you normally come to see your mother?'

'Yes, but I'll be busy this Thursday, so I thought I'd come today. Is that all right?'

'No problem. She doesn't know which day of the week it is anyway.'

The jolly West Indian nurse had come to England as a child in the fifties. Nancy liked her. She was gentle and very patient with her mother, although she could see that her mother often had difficulty working out who she was. There hadn't been many West Indians in rural Wallingford, and her mother insisted on referring to her as the African. Luckily, Blossom, as she was called, didn't object and said she'd been called much worse things in her time.

'How has she been?'

'She's been all right. Doesn't sleep too good, but the doctor has given her some stronger sleeping pills, so she'll sleep better now.'

'Hello Mum. How are you?' she said, bending down and kissing her mother.

Her mother was sitting in a chair staring out of the window. She looked up at Nancy and smiled. 'Hello dear. Have you come to see Mrs Biggs?'

'Mrs Biggs has gone, Mrs Miller,' the nurse said. 'She left last week.'

'Oh, has she?'

The nurse turned to Nancy and added, 'She died, poor soul, but then she was ninety-eight.'

'It's Nancy, Mum. We've come to see you. Look, here is your grandson, Martin. You remember Martin?'

'Hello dear. Have you come to see Mrs Biggs?'

'Yes, Mum.' There was no point insisting that she recognise her. If it was going to happen, it would. 'I've brought you some Cadbury's chocolate,' she said instead.

'Cadbury's. That's my favourite. How did you know that? Well that is very kind of you, whoever you are.'

'I'm Nancy, your daughter.'

Her mother looked at her and smiled. 'No, dear. Nancy is at school. She'll be home soon for her tea. If you wait a bit, you'll meet her. She's a lovely girl. Very artistic. You should see her paintings.'

'I'll leave you to it,' the nurse said. 'Just ring that bell if you need anything.'

Once she'd gone, Nancy leaned closer to her mother and held her hand. 'Mum, I'm going to go away. I won't be able to come to see you anymore.'

Her mother looked at her and touched Nancy's face. 'Don't worry, my dear,' she said. 'Don't cry. It's going to be all right. Everything will be all right, in the end.'

For a moment Nancy thought her mother recognised her, but then her mother said, 'Wait a bit longer. Nancy will be home soon, and Ted. I must get some tea ready for them. They are always so hungry when they get home from school.'

It was no use, her mother's memory was trapped in a bygone age. 'Bye bye Mum. I love you,' she said, tears still streaming down her face.

Martin was sitting on the floor, playing with something. 'What have you got there, sweetheart?' she asked.

'Sweeties.'

She opened his hand. In it was a bottle of sleeping tablets which he had taken from the nurse's trolley. 'No, they're not sweeties, darling. This is Granny's medicine. Give it to Mummy and go and give Granny a kiss goodbye.' She was about to replace the sleeping tablets on the trolley when the idea hit her. She was going to need them. Checking that the nurse was not in sight, she slipped the tablets into her coat pocket.

A plan was slowly forming in her head. It was outrageous, but she was sure it would work. It had to work. It was her or Nick. If her plan failed, he would surely kill her, if not today then one day soon, and then what would become of

Martin? It was the thought of Martin that gave her strength. She could do it. She just had to make sure that she had not overlooked anything.

Nick had already told the landlord they were leaving very early Saturday morning. He planned to drive to Folkestone and get the ferry across to France. From there they would drive down to Spain. He couldn't stop talking about it; she hadn't seen him so excited about anything for a long time.

It was already Thursday, only two days to go, and the strain was beginning to take its toll on her. She hadn't slept for nights, and her insides seemed to have turned to water. Luckily, Nick thought that, like him, she was just experiencing the excitement of moving and didn't enquire any further.

'Martin, I want you to stay with Mrs Brown for a little while. Mummy needs to go out. I won't be long.' She gave him his colouring book and his favourite toy train and took him next door to her neighbour.

'Hello Nancy,' the woman said when she saw Nancy and Martin standing at her door. 'Is something wrong?' Nancy rarely called on her neighbour for anything.

'No, nothing's wrong. I just have to pop out and get some things for our journey, and I wondered if you would look after Martin for me. I'll be no more than half an hour.'

'Of course, my dear. Come in, Martin. I see you've got your train with you. Are you hungry? I'm just taking some sponge cakes out of the oven. Do you like sponge cakes?'

At the mention of food, Martin overcame his shyness and followed her into the flat. Nancy didn't like leaving Martin, and she knew Nick would be angry if he found out, but today it was essential that she went alone.

She walked down the passage and out into a silvery morning, sunshine gleaming on wet leaves, reflecting in the puddles in the road, catching the spray from a passing bicycle. It had been raining all night, but now the clouds were clearing to reveal a watery sun that was warm on her face. Would life be very different in Spain? Would she miss the English weather with its constant surprises: snow in August, Indian summers in September, the light, sometimes so grey and then suddenly shot through with sunbeams, summers too hot to sit outside and others too wet? What would it be like in Spain? Nick said it was hot, far hotter than in France. He said it didn't rain, that it was never cold, that the sun shone all the time. A painter's paradise, he called it.

The bus was just coming round the corner as she got to the bus stop. She would be back long before Martin started to miss her.

'A return to the Day Centre, please,' she said to the bus conductor.

'You're a bit young for the Day Centre, aren't you, young lady?' he said with a laugh.

'Just visiting a friend.' She smiled at him, already feeling that she was at last taking control of her life.

By the time they arrived at the Day Centre, it was starting to rain again. A few other passengers were headed for the same destination, all old and white-haired, so she waited patiently for them to get off the bus and go into the hall then followed them inside. A large room had been set out with card tables, and some of the elderly pensioners were already seated, playing whist with their friends; others were gossiping and drinking tea from white china mugs while a couple of others had set up easels and were painting. Nobody took any notice of her. She spotted a small office at the back of the hall, where a woman sat at a desk half-buried under manila folders.

'Good morning,' Nancy said, tapping on the open office door.

'Yes, can I help you?'

'I wondered if I could borrow a wheelchair? My elderly aunt is coming to stay with us for the weekend. I'm not sure how I'm going to get her about. I'm happy to pay, if there's a charge.'

'There's no charge, as long as you bring it back on time. The question is, do we have one available?' she said.

She picked up the brown ledger that lay open in front of her and skimmed down the page. 'Yes, one was returned last night, so you should be in luck. Wait here and I'll see if I can find it.'

Nancy sat down and waited, her stomach churning with anxiety. Her plan hinged on borrowing a wheelchair. What would she do if there wasn't one? After five anxious minute, during which time all her doubts and fears returned to spin relentlessly round and round in her mind, the woman returned, pushing a collapsible wheelchair.

'Here it is, a bit battered,' she said, breezily. 'I think the last person who borrowed it let their kids take rides in it. Still it will be all right for what you want.'

'It's perfect. I am very grateful.'

'Can you just sign here for it and put the date you'll be bringing it back.'

Nancy hesitated. This was the first step in her plan, but it wasn't irrevocable. She could easily return it if she decided not to go ahead, so she accepted the pen and signed *Geraldine Miller* in the brown ledger.

'I'll bring it back Monday morning after I've taken her to the station,' she said.

'That's fine. Have a nice weekend with your aunt. Maybe the rain will let up for you.'

'Thank you.'

The wheelchair was a bit stiff but quite light. She thought she would be able to manage it very well. Once she got to the bus stop she folded it up and waited for the bus to take her home.

Martin was busy with his colouring book when she knocked at her neighbour's door. She had left the wheelchair in the passage, tucked in a corner where she hoped it wouldn't be seen.

'Done all you needed to do?' Mrs Brown asked, handing her Martin's toys. 'He's been a little angel. Never any trouble.'

'Thank you, Mrs Brown. I'm glad he behaved.'

'I'm going to miss you,' the old woman said. 'It's nice having some young people in the building. I hope you know what you're doing. It's a long way to go, is Spain.'

'So do I.' Nancy smiled. 'Thanks again.'

She bent down and kissed her son. 'Well, darling, did you have a nice time?'

'Yes, Mummy. Cakes and pink icing.'

'Cakes with pink icing? Well, aren't you the lucky boy? Would you like to go out now? It's stopped raining. We could go and see the trains.'

'Yes, please, Mummy.'

When Nick came home that evening, the first thing he noticed was the wheelchair. 'Who's left a bloody wheelchair in the passage?' he asked. 'I nearly fell over it.'

'I think the people across the hall have someone staying with them. It's his.'

'Well I've a good mind to go and tell them to move it. It's not a bloody parking area. It was bad enough when that kid started leaving his bike out there.' He moved towards the door.

'Why bother? We won't be here after tomorrow. They can leave what they like in the hall,' she said. 'We'll be on our way to Spain.'

'Spain?' Martin asked, his eyes widening with excitement. 'Morrow?'

'Not tomorrow but the next day.'

'Next day,' the little boy repeated. 'On the train?'

'No, we're going in the car,' Nick said and picked up his son and sang, *'We're off to Spain, my lad, with a hey, nonny-no. In a bonny blue car, my lad, with a hey, nonny-no. No more work, my lad, hey nonny-no. Sun and sea and sea and sun, sing hey nonny-no, my lad.'*

'Sun and sea,' Martin repeated in a sing-song voice. 'Blue car. Blue car.'

'That's it, Martin. So you need to get to bed early and have plenty of sleep. We are going on a long journey,' Nancy said.

He was already in his pyjamas and needed no further encouragement to jump into his little cot. She kissed him goodnight and went into the kitchen to see to Nick's food.

'Is everything packed?' he asked, cutting the bacon into strips, laying it on his bread then placing the fried egg on top. He put a second piece of bread on top of the egg and pressed it down so that the yolk ran out and on to his plate. It made her feel sick watching him.

'Yes. You just have to load it into the car. I haven't bothered with the cutlery and plates. It didn't seem worth it.'

'Quite right. Most of it was here when I moved in. What have you done with your paintings?' he asked, biting into his sandwich with evident pleasure, oblivious of the egg running down his chin.

'There weren't many. I'd sold most of them, and I haven't had time to do much lately. I just packed my paints and our clothes and a few things of sentimental value.'

'Just as well. We don't want to overload the car. I'll fill it up with petrol after work tomorrow.'

He wiped his mouth with the back of his hand.

'What about the passports and tickets?' she asked.

'They're all here in the drawer,' he said. 'I haven't bought any tickets for the crossing. Bill says it's easier to buy them at the port. Remember to put some blankets in, the heating's not very good in that car, and we may be sleeping in it for a couple of nights.'

'Yes, I'll put them ready tomorrow.'

She was no longer nervous. In fact, an icy calm had taken hold of her. Her mind was focused on her plan and nothing else. All doubts, all arguments, all her fears had vanished. Her mind was clear. Right or wrong, she was doing this for her son.

'Fasten your seat belts, please,' a woman's voice tells her. 'We'll be landing in a few minutes.'

Nancy opens her eyes. Are they in Málaga already? She must have slept the whole way. The seat next to her is vacant. Then she sees Ana making her way towards her.

'Sorry,' Ana says, sitting down and buckling her belt. 'I couldn't wait any longer. Did you sleep well?'

'My neck's stiff,' Nancy says. 'And I could do with a drink.'

'The bar's closed now; they've packed everything away. We'll be home soon.'

Home. Spain is her home now. 'Is Martin meeting us?' she asks. She really wants to see her son again. She has missed him.

CHAPTER 24

Martin and his sons are waiting at the airport for her. It was Sara who suggested he take them along to meet their grandmother.

'Is that Grandma's plane,' Juan asks, looking up as an Airbus comes hurtling along the runway.

'No, Grandma's already landed,' his brother tells him.

'She should be coming into the arrivals hall any minute. Come on now, or we'll miss her and then she might panic,' he tells them.

He takes the boys by their hands and leads them towards the lift. When they step out, there are Ana and his mother scanning the crowd, looking for them. Ana already has her mobile in her hand.

'We're here, Grandma,' Juan calls and, pulling away from his father, runs towards her. 'Over here.'

His shrill voice reaches her, and she turns towards them with an enormous smile on her face. 'There you are, darlings. What a nice surprise.' She bends and sweeps them into her arms.

Sara is right. His mother is very fond of his sons. Not exactly a doting grandmother but a loving one, nevertheless.

'Martin, thank you for coming to collect me,' she says, kissing him on the cheek.

'Did you bring us a present from England?' Juan asks.

'Juan, don't be so rude,' Martin says.

'No, it's all right, Martin. Of course, I brought you each a present, but you'll have to wait until I get home because they're in my suitcase.'

'Did everything go well with the exhibition?' he asks.

'Oh, Martin, I wish you had been there; it was like old times. The exhibition was a great success; they all said it was.'

'Maybe I'll take Sara and we'll go for the weekend,' he says.

'Yes, it doesn't finish until the beginning of December, the ...' she hesitates, trying to remember the date.

'The fourteenth,' Ana prompts her.

'That's it, the fourteenth. I'll look after the children for you,' she adds. 'You go. You could do with a break.'

Martin is astonished. She is so animated that he hardly recognises her. Never has she suggested babysitting for them, let alone looking after the boys for a whole weekend. Of course, now it is out of the question—she is barely able to look after herself. Still it makes him happy to see her so positive.

'So you enjoyed yourself?' he asks.

'Yes, I suppose I did, although it was a bit strange seeing some of my paintings again. The curator had done a good job collecting them all together.'

'That's wonderful,' he says. 'What about your agent? Was he there?'

'Of course. You don't think Harry would miss my swansong. All the daily papers were there, and you'll never guess who also came along?'

He shakes his head.

'Herbert Small.'

He looks blankly at her.

'The art critic, well, art historian really, but he fancies himself as a bit of a critic as well. You must have heard me speak of him?'

'Sorry, Mama, I can't say I remember the name.'

'Herbert Small,' she says slowly, enunciating every letter as if he were a child again.

He shakes his head.

'Hrrmph. Waste of time trying to educate you,' she mutters. 'Are we going home now? I need a drink.'

He smiles. Now he recognises her.

Martin decides to telephone Ana the next day to ask her how it all went and to apologise for his earlier behaviour. He is sorry that he reacted like that, but he can't deny that raking up the past has affected him much more than he expected. He now finds that memories he didn't realize he had are coming back to him. Her probing into his past has unlocked a few doors. It has also made him understand that trying to remember who his father was is no longer a betrayal of his mother. It doesn't matter anymore. His father is dead, and if his mother continues to hate him, then that's her decision. He doesn't have to go along with it.

What has become clearer in his mind is a long journey on a train. It must have been through France and then into Spain but, as a child, all he remembers is the excitement of stopping at stations, watching them refill the engines with water, the passengers waiting on the platform jumping back as the train pulled in wheezing and belching steam, the women with trays of food and drinks for sale and people getting down from the train to buy *pinchitos,* slices of *tortilla* or wedges of juicy, red water melon, the trucks loaded with black, glistening coal parked in the sidings, and the shrill whistle and wonderful acrid smell of the smoke as they took off again each time.

And the windmills. He remembers seeing windmills. That must have been somewhere in the middle of Spain, La Mancha, probably. His mother had told him a story about the windmills, something she had made up about a little boy who lived in one. He remembers her telling him lots of stories on that journey.

These are real childhood memories, he is sure, not something his mother had recounted later. But are they of their journey to Spain or of some other time, some other place? Whenever it was, he is certain that his father was not with him on the train, only his mother. The last memory he has of his father is him sitting at the table in the kitchen singing a silly song about going to Spain. What had happened? Why didn't he go to Spain with them after all?

'*Hola,* Ana,' he says, when he hears her voice. 'How are you? I'm sorry I didn't get much chance to talk to you yesterday. Did you enjoy the trip to England?'

'Dr Henderson? Oh, yes, thank you very much. You are very generous. The hotel was wonderful, and we were treated really well by everyone.'

'That's more to do with being with my mother, I expect. Anyway, I'm glad you enjoyed yourself. So my mother was all right? No wandering off in the middle of the night?'

'She was perfectly fine. In fact, I'd say she was much better than she normally is. She wasn't so forgetful, and she was interested in everything that was happening. She was also in a good mood, which was a blessing. You should have seen her at the preview. She was a star. She even wore those high heels you said she wouldn't need.'

'Probably just to prove me wrong,' he says, but he feels proud of his mother. 'I will say this for her, she knows how to rise to the occasion.'

There is a short silence on the line, then Ana says, 'Rise to the occasion?'

'Behave correctly when it is needed, I suppose. She wasn't going to play the batty old woman with an audience of admirers watching her. I know my mother.'

He thinks back to the days when he had accompanied her to exhibitions. She had been magnificent. Men used to crowd round her, offering her cigarettes, cocktails, each wanting to be the one photographed by her side. As a boy, he had been so proud of his mother—she was the prettiest mother in the whole school, and she was famous. He loved it when she came to the school's open days or to a parents' evening and he would see his friends' fathers looking at her with barely disguised admiration. Yes, his mother knew how to make a man's blood race.

'I've almost finished the memoirs,' Ana says. 'I don't suppose there is anything else you have remembered?'

'Not really. The only thing that has come back to me is the train journey. I think we may have travelled by train.'

'The journey to Spain?'

'Yes.'

'So you didn't travel by car?'

'No, I'm pretty sure we came here on a train. Well, it might have been a number of trains. As I said, I'm not too clear on the details but it was just me and my mother. No one else.'

'Really?'

Her tone irritates him again, but he says, 'Yes, I'm sure that's how it was, just me and my mother.'

'We met your mother's old friend Helen in England,' she says. 'That was a happy reunion. They had a lot to catch up on.'

'She didn't mention it. Who else did she see?'

'Oh, lots of people from the art world, her agent, some famous art critic—I don't know all their names. She seemed to know a lot of people.'

'I bet they were surprised to see her.'

'Yes, she kept saying things like, "You see, I'm not dead," and embarrassing everyone.'

He laughs; it is so in character.

'What about her paintings? What did you think of them?' he asks.

'They were very interesting. I have to admit I don't know much about art, but your mother tried to teach me. I think I understand them a bit better now.'

'So what do they tell you about my mother?' he asks, not expecting a meaningful answer, but Ana takes it as a serious question.

'I think that she is telling the story of her life in her paintings. You can see how she changed from being a happy, carefree young woman, someone in love with life, into a completely different person. There is one group of paintings that suggest she went through a time when she was depressed, worried, maybe even frightened. Then her painting gets lighter again. It's only my theory, and beyond that I don't know what to say.'

'Did you ask my mother about it?'

'She says that people see what they want to see in a painting, that it's not just about what the artist is trying to portray, it's also what the viewer wants to see.'

'In other words, don't read too much into her work?'

'Yes, I suppose so.'

'Well thank you for taking care of her. I'm glad you enjoyed your visit to Oxford.'

He hangs up and goes into his clinic. He would like a drink but his first patient arrives in ten minutes, so he pours himself a glass of water and sits at his desk.

'Everything all right, *cariño*?' his wife asks. 'Can I get you a cup of coffee?'

'No, I'm fine. I was just talking to Ana. I wanted to thank her for looking after Mama.'

'Did she have a good time?'

'Yes, I think so. She's very persistent you know, she keeps on about my childhood and our journey to Spain. She asked me again just now if I was sure that we came by train. She seems to have an idea in her head that we came by car.'

'Really. Did you even have a car in those days? Not many people did. My father had an old Ford but that wasn't until I was in my teens.'

He looks at her in surprise. 'Yes, we did. My God, I had forgotten all about it. We had a blue Ford Prefect. I can remember my mother packing all our things into the car ready for the journey.'

'So what happened to it? Why did you end up on the train?'

'I don't remember. I just remember lying down on the back seat and my mother telling me to go to sleep and that when I woke up I'd be in Spain.'

'Maybe it broke down.'

'But my dad must have been driving, because my mother couldn't drive.'

'Maybe you're mixing it up with another journey,' Sara says.

'No, I'm sure we were going to Spain. What happened? Was there a crash? Is that the crash that my father died in? Oh my God, I have to know. She owes it to me to tell me what happened to him.'

'Don't get upset, Martin. You can't do anything right now. Your first patient has just arrived. Go over and see your mother tomorrow evening and tell her what you remember. If she thinks you know most of the story, there's no reason to hold the rest back, is there? Just calm down, *cariño.*'

He nods at his wife. She is right. There is no need to let this upset him. He has lived without any knowledge of his father for fifty years so he can wait a little while longer. Maybe Ana is right. Maybe the paintings hold the key to his parents' past. He too has often wondered about his mother's change in painting style. It was one of the first things Sara said when he showed her the retrospective display of Nancy's work on the internet. Seeing the paintings grouped together like that did make it seem his mother was telling a story. Well, if she was, then it's time she shared it with him. He knows it's likely she will not tell him the truth, even if he challenges her, but he has to try. Whatever she is hiding, she ought to tell him. What harm can it do, after all these years?

CHAPTER 25

It is nice to be back in her own home but Nancy is very tired. The journey has taken a lot out of her, and she barely has the energy to unpack the new paints she bought. She sits in her usual chair by the window and looks at the sea. There is a stiff breeze blowing, and the usually calm Mediterranean is crashing on the beach in cascades of white foam. The seagulls shelter on the sand, serried ranks of black and white soldiers, their backs to the waves. She sips a little wine, then puts the glass back on the coffee table. The heaviness in her chest has returned, and now there is a pain in her arm. She rubs it gently.

It was Nick's last day at work. He said he wanted to say goodbye to his mates and have one last drink with them, so he'd be a bit late. Surely she understood that. She told him, 'Yes, of course I understand. I'll have your meal ready when you get home.'

She still had things to prepare, and in a way she was glad to postpone putting her plan into action until the very last moment. She put Martin in his pushchair and they set off for the town. Her first stop was the chemist shop at the far end of the high street, a chemist she had never visited before.

'Can I help you?' a young man with tortoiseshell spectacles asked her.

'Yes. My mother has been prescribed some sleeping tablets, but she has lost the prescription and I wondered if you could tell me what the correct dosage is,' she said, handing him the bottle of sleeping tablets she had taken from her mother's room. 'I've been giving her one tablet a night but she still lies awake for hours.'

'Ah, yes. Well, really you should be asking her doctor for that information.'

'I know, but I can't get an appointment until tomorrow. I want her to get a good night's sleep, but I don't want to give her an overdose.'

'Well, let me see.'

He opened a book and looked up the name of the drug then said, 'Of course, it depends on the patient, but the recommended dose is 10 mg.'

He looked at the bottle and added, 'That's one tablet. So one tablet when she goes to bed. It's quite a strong drug, so make sure they are kept out of reach. You don't want her forgetting she's taken one and then taking another. It sometimes happens when people are half asleep, and that would not be good for her.'

'So I can't give her two tablets, or one and a half?'

'I wouldn't recommend it.' He handed her back the bottle and added, 'You should check with your doctor if you are still concerned.'

'Thank you. I'll do that.'

The next stop was the library. She was very familiar with Kingston Public Library, so she knew exactly where to look for what she wanted: Medicine and Pharmaceuticals. Sure enough there was a book on the shelf entitled Barbiturates. Most of it was technical and way beyond her comprehension, but she found a section relating to overdoses and symptoms. Would these tablets do what she wanted? Her head was beginning to swim with names such as phenobarbital, amytal, pentothal, seconal. She took the bottle from her pocket and studied the small print but it gave her no clue as to what the tablets contained. How stupid of her. She should have asked the chemist for the name of the ingredients, but then that might have looked rather suspicious. She looked down the page. Marilyn Monroe had died from an overdose of a barbiturate called Nembutal. She turned the page again and then she saw what she wanted, 'The Dangers of Drinking Alcohol While Taking Barbiturates.' The effects of an overdose in those circumstances were severe: death or a coma. With a shiver, she closed the book and put it back on the shelf.

'Mummy,' Martin said. 'Mummy.'

'What is it darling? Are you tired, my sweet? Just one more place to go, and then we'll buy something for Daddy's dinner.'

Her next stop was the post office. She took out all her savings and closed the account. She was not going to need it again. Then she went to the off-licence and bought a bottle of Spanish wine.

'Mummy,' her son whinged. 'Mummy.'

'All right, darling. Shall we go and feed the ducks on our way home?'

'Ducks,' he said, his face brightening. 'Bread, Mummy.'

'Of course, we'll buy some bread first, and then we'll go and feed them.'

Poor little lad, this would be his last time feeding the ducks at the river. What future lay ahead for him in Spain? A better life, she hoped.

She had prepared everything. Martin, bubbling with excitement, had been persuaded to go to bed and lay there, on his back, arms above his head, fast asleep. Now she waited. She was not nervous—for once she was completely relaxed, her mind only on the task in hand.

The sound of the car pulling up outside alerted her to Nick's arrival. Slowly she took the bottle of wine that she had bought at the off-licence and uncorked it. Then she turned up the heat on the casserole that was simmering gently on the stove.

'Well, there's no going back now,' her husband said, coming in and throwing his coat on the sofa. 'Collected my P45, not that I'll need that again, and my money. Said my goodbyes, and now I'm ready for anything.'

He had been to the Black Cat to have a farewell drink or two and, uncharacteristically, was in a good mood that evening. To show it he put his arms around her and kissed her neck. She didn't want him to be nice to her. She didn't want anything to weaken her resolve. If she was to carry out her plan, she needed to stay strong and remind herself that no matter how pleasant he was now, he could turn at any moment, and next time it could be Martin that got hurt. That was what she had to concentrate on. She was doing this for her son.

'This is going to be a new life for both of us,' he said, pulling her round to face him. 'You'll see. You'll love it in Spain. Neither of us were cut out for this country with all its rules and petty regulations. We need space, freedom to do our own thing. You'll be able to do all the painting you want, and I think I might try my hand at writing. I've always fancied writing a novel, a detective story maybe.'

'Your dinner's almost ready,' she said.

'Good. I'm starving. What's this?' he asked, picking up the bottle. 'Wine?'

'Yes, Spanish wine. I thought we should make a special evening of it as it'll be our last night in England for some time.'

'Yes. Why not? That's a good idea, Nancy. Look, I'll load the car with the luggage and you pour us some of that Spanish wine.' He picked up two of the bags and carried them out to the car then came back for the remaining two.

'Don't forget my paints,' Nancy said.

She poured the wine into two glasses, put one on the table and took a sip from the other. It was rather strong in flavour, just right for what she intended. The sleeping pills had already been finely crushed and she slipped them into his glass and stirred it carefully until there was no sign of them. She heard the car door slam and his footsteps returning along the hall.

'That's it then. All done,' he said. 'We're packed and ready to go.'

'Did you fill the car with petrol?' she asked.

'Yes, I did that on my way home. Now, is there anything else?'

'The map? Did you buy a map?'

'Yes.' He took a map out of his jacket pocket and spread it on the table.

'Have some wine,' she said, handing him the glass.

He held the wine up to the light and looked at it. For a moment she thought he could see the pills and realized what a risk she was taking. If he found out, he'd surely kill her.

Then he said, 'Not really a wine drinker, you know that Nancy. I'd prefer a beer. And, anyway, I need to keep a clear head for driving. We want to be on our way before six.'

'I know, but it's a celebration, after all. You know I don't drink beer.'

'Okay. You're right. I suppose we should drink it, as it's open. It would be a shame to waste it. Anyway, I'll have to get used to drinking wine once we're in Spain, because I don't expect the local beer will be up to much. Right then, here's to our new life,' he said, emptying the glass in one go. 'Funny tasting stuff, wine. Don't know what people see in it. Give me a nice draught of beer any time.'

'So where are we heading for?' she asked, pointing to the map.

'We're here,' he said, stabbing at the map with his finger. 'We'll take the A25 to here and then pick up the A20, all the way to Folkestone. It's a piece of cake. Then we get the ferry to Dunkirk and drive down through France. Maybe buy some French wine on the way,' he added, filling his glass with more wine. 'This stuff grows on you. It's not so bad after all.' He folded up the map and placed it next to the file containing their passports and the details about the house.

'I've made you a lamb stew,' she said.

'Hey, you're spoiling me. That's my favourite. We haven't had that in ages.'

'Well, I did say it was a celebration, and I doubt if you've eaten much today.'

'I had a packet of crisps in the pub after work, so yes, you're right, I am pretty hungry.'

Nancy ladled the stew onto his plate and heaped some mashed potatoes alongside. She had put some more of the pills in the stew. She hoped she had got the dosage right.

He was a big man and she had calculated that it would take at least three times as many pills as her mother took, in order to knock him out. In the end she had made it four times, just to be on the safe side.

'This is lovely, Nancy. I don't know if they have lamb in Spain, but, according to Bill, they do have goats so you might have to learn how to make goat stew.'

'I expect it's much the same,' she said, pouring herself a little wine. She was amazed at herself. There was no fear and little hesitation on her part.

'You're not eating,' he said.

'I had some with Martin, earlier. You know I'm not a great lover of lamb. It's a bit too fatty for me, especially at this time of night.'

'You don't know what you're missing. This is great. Is there any bread?'

She handed him the bread basket and watched as he mopped up every morsel of the stew, wiping the plate clean.

'That was something else,' he said. 'Here, give me a bit more wine.'

'Should you be drinking so much? I thought you wanted to keep a clear head?' she said.

'This is nothing. Gnat's piss. I couldn't get drunk on this if I tried.' Neither the wine nor the tablets were having any effect on him. Maybe she should have given him a bigger dose.

'I'm just going to the bathroom,' she said. 'Then I've got some apple tart for you.'

She had made every effort to get him into a good mood, and it was working. He positively beamed at her and leaned back in his chair contentedly.

Nancy retrieved the sleeping tablets from under the bath where she had hidden them and took out four more and crushed them up as finely as she could. She put them in a screw of paper and hid them in her pocket. Somehow she would have to get some more into him if her plan was to work.

'Hey Nancy, all the wine has gone. Did you buy another bottle?'

'No, sorry. I wasn't sure you'd like it. Would you like a beer instead?'

'Yes, that sounds good, a nice refreshing beer is just what I need and a slice of your apple pie. What more could a man ask for?'

It was easy. She put the powdered tablets into the glass and poured the beer on top of them. 'It might not taste as good after the wine,' she said.

'Beer not taste good? You're joking, aren't you? Here, give it to me.'

She could see that her husband was well on the way to being drunk now, but so far was still very conscious of what was around him. She handed him the beer and watched as he took a long, slow drink from the glass.

'Lovely. Nothing wrong with the taste,' he said. 'Now where's that apple pie?'

As she was cutting the pie, she heard a thump as Nick slumped forward on to the table. At last. She went across and lifted his head. He was out cold. It was almost midnight. She would wait until one o'clock, and then she would leave. In the meantime, she brought in the wheel-chair and with great difficulty, lifted the unresisting body of her husband into it. She collected the passports and papers and packed them in a bag with the clothes she had already put aside for her and Martin, then she took Nick's wallet, emptied it of money and identification and put it back in his pocket. She went into the bathroom and pulled another plastic bag from under the bath. This one contained the savings that she had withdrawn that morning. She had more than two hundred pounds, which together with Nick's wages and holiday pay would last them for some time. The owner of the gallery had been surprised that she had so many paintings to sell, but she explained to him that they needed the money because they were buying a new house. Always keep as close to the truth as possible, she told herself.

There was still more than half an hour to go and she was tempted to leave there and then, but she forced herself to stick to the plan. Leaving now was a bad idea. There could still be people around, and somebody might see her. No, she would wait until she was sure everyone was home and asleep. In the meantime she made herself a cup of tea, washed up the dishes, making sure she left no trace of the sleeping pills, and flushed the remains of the lamb stew down the toilet. Then she sat down at the table with her tea and a slice of apple pie. She spread the map in front of her and studied it carefully. She knew exactly where she was heading. They had passed it a couple of weeks before, one Sunday when Nick had insisted on taking them out for a drive in the country. She wouldn't have noticed it if Martin had not said, 'Mummy, trains. Trains, Mummy.'

Nick had looked to where his son was pointing and said, 'No, don't be silly, Martin. That's an old quarry. But it's not used anymore. It looks deserted to me.'

'Corry,' the child said.

'Yes, that's right, son. It's a quarry, just a big hole in the ground. No trains.'

Blackwater Quarry. It was just off the main road. She had marked the place in her mind, and now she looked for it on the map. Yes, there it was, probably about a couple of hours' drive away. She studied the early part of her route and memorised it. She didn't want to be distracted when she was driving. She had no driving license, but she knew how to drive a car. At least she thought she did. Ted used to take her with him when he was learning to drive, and sometimes they would go to the football ground, and he would let her drive around the car park. She had always intended to take her test, but there wasn't time when she was at college, and when she suggested it to Nick, he had at first laughed at her and then become suspicious. Why did she want to drive? Where did she want to go without her husband? She had dropped the idea. But when he bought the car, she began to take more interest in driving and watched him carefully whenever they went out. Now she knew the car as well as he did.

She folded the map and placed it in her handbag. Martin was still asleep, so she took his push chair out to the car and put it in the boot, along with their bag of clothes, his toy train and his colouring books. It wasn't much, but it was all she would be able to carry, and she didn't want to draw too much attention to herself. That done, she sat down again and drank her tea. She could still hear the people upstairs moving around and a baby crying. What would her neighbours say if they came in and saw Nick, drugged and sitting in a wheelchair? That was never likely to happen. Nick had made it quite plain to all their neighbours that they were not welcome in his home. For once she was glad of his antisocial ways. She looked at her husband, his head slumped on his chest. Asleep, without that permanent sneer on his face, he looked more like the man she had fallen in love with. A pang of conscience struck her. This wasn't right. Surely there was another way of getting away from him? Perhaps she should have taken Helen's advice and gone to the police. No, who was she kidding? They wouldn't have done anything to help her; just another domestic, they would have said and sent her on her way, or if they had decided to investigate and then dropped the case, Nick would have been furious and punished her. She had to face it—this was the only way out. Somewhere a church clock was striking. She could hear the bells. It was one o'clock. Time to leave.

She opened the door and looked outside. There were no lights coming from any of the other flats, and apart from a baby crying somewhere on the first floor, there were no other sounds. She wheeled her husband out to the car and pushed and pulled him until she had him resting on the passenger seat. She picked up his legs, swung them round, and tucked them inside the car. She was sure he was going to wake up. Her heart was pounding so hard, she thought the noise of it alone would rouse him, but he never moved. His head lolled strangely to one side and his mouth hung open, a dribble of white spit running down his chin.

She leaned in and felt for the pulse in his neck. At first there was nothing, then she detected a faint beat. He was still alive. For a moment she thought she had given him too many sleeping pills. The image of the dead Marilyn Monroe came into her head, and she shuddered. Carefully, she closed the door and went back to get her son.

Martin still slept soundly, so she picked him up gently and carried him out to the car, where she laid him on the back seat and covered him with his blanket. Luckily, once Martin was asleep, a bomb could go off and he'd never hear it. Almost done. She put the wheelchair back in the hall, checked that everything was switched off in the flat, left the keys on the table, and pulled the door shut. The landlord would collect the keys later that morning. Nothing would look out of the ordinary to him. He knew they were moving to Spain to live. Everyone knew that. Nick had broadcast their plans to all and sundry. She looked at her watch. It was half past one. It had not been easy to get Nick into the car. He was a big man, and asleep he seemed even heavier, so it had taken longer than she planned. She looked up and down the street. The wet pavements gleamed in the light from the street lamps, but there was no one about, only a solitary cat patrolling its territory. She took one last look back at the building where she had lived for the last five years, a place she did not even want to grace with the name of home, because it had never been that to her; then she got into the car and drove in the direction of the A25.

When she wakes, Nancy feels refreshed. The pain in her arm is still there but is not so intense. She goes into the bathroom and takes a couple of aspirins, then puts on the kettle. She wants to start painting again before she loses her enthusiasm. She takes one of her new watercolour pads and selects some paints. Her old palette is wedged under the sink, and she bends down to pull it out. Her easel is in the wardrobe. She pulls the coffee table out of the way and sets everything up by the window, overlooking the beach.

The sea is magnificent today, an oily grey, the breakers topped with white horses. White horses. She used to tell Martin that, once, long ago when Spain was invaded by the Muslims, the Christians sent an army of knights on white horses to free the land and how, even today, you can see those white horses racing towards Spain to set it free from tyranny. She smiles. It was a lot of nonsense, but Martin liked it.

CHAPTER 26

Ana takes her notes and sits down in front of her computer. The trip to England had been interesting and very useful, particularly seeing Nancy in an environment other than her stuffy apartment. Now it is easier to imagine how she was when she was a younger woman, someone at the top of her field, respected by everyone. She had been a different person at the exhibition, lively, funny, even flirting with the men who came up to talk to her. It was if she had been transported back into her past, and she loved it.

Ana had taken a gamble getting in contact with Helen, but it had worked out well. She had expected Nancy to be furious with her, but instead she was grateful that she had brought the two friends together again. Now she can understand why Nancy never wanted to talk about her husband. He sounds a jealous and violent man. She should have guessed that it was something like that. She is always reading in the newspapers of cases of domestic abuse. What, does she think that it is only Spanish men who beat their wives? Although Nancy has never admitted it and probably never will, Ana is now certain that her employer had run away from her husband and taken Martin with her. But how can she put that into the story without upsetting Nancy and, more importantly, Martin?

The manuscript is piling up beside her, a neat stack of double-spaced A4 pages. She looks at it with pride; it is turning out quite well, despite Nancy's recalcitrance.

'All done?' Andrew asks, handing her a glass of wine and sitting down on the sofa.

'Almost. What a great feeling it will be to have it finished. I thought at one point I'd have nothing to write about, but going to England has helped a lot. I'm managing to fill in quite a few blanks.'

'So have you worked out her dirty secret then?' he asks.

'I have a theory,' she says. 'But I'm not sure I can put it in the book.'

'What is it?'

'Well, according to her friend Helen, Nancy's husband used to beat her up. He made her leave the art college, and he stopped her having any contact with her family and her friends. He was a control freak and really jealous.'

'So why didn't she leave him?'

'Well that's the thing. Helen said that Nancy told her she was going to leave him. She was going to take Martin and disappear.'

'Go to Spain.'

'She wouldn't tell Helen. She was frightened her husband would go round and cause trouble, but here's the really strange thing. It wasn't her idea to go to Spain, it was her husband's. He even bought a house here and gave up his job. Helen said he wanted to set up an artists' colony. You know, some kind of hippy artists' group.'

'Yeah. A commune. There was one in Castellar de la Frontera. They say the place used to be full of hippies. Don't you remember it? We stayed there one night when we were driving from Cádiz to Marbella.'

'Yes, now you mention it, I do remember the place. They moved all the inhabitants out into a new town in the seventies, and the old town was abandoned.'

'That's right—and that's when the hippies moved in. I think there are still a lot of artists living and working there now.'

'There was an old castle,' she says. She can picture it clearly. Andalusia has many beautiful old villages, but this one was special with its narrow cobbled streets and a fourteenth-century castle perched on the hillside, overlooking a lake and surrounded by forests of cork oak. It was the perfect place for an artist to work, serene and picturesque. 'Yes, I remember buying a carved box there. Well, anyway, yes, I suppose her husband wanted to start something like that, but I can't find any evidence that he ever came to Spain. It's odd, don't you think?'

'Maybe he decided that France was a better place for his commune.'

'But he'd already bought a house here. Why would he go somewhere else? And why did Nancy and her son come here alone? Where was he? That's the big question.'

'So have you come up with an answer yet?'

'Not really. There's something else. They had a car. Helen told me that he bought a car not long before he disappeared. Now why didn't they bring the car to Spain? It would have been much easier than travelling by train. Then there's this obsession she has with painting lakes and the sea. There has to be something to that.'

'So what are you saying, that Nancy Miller killed her husband and pushed him and his car into the sea then caught a train to Spain? It would definitely make it a best seller if you wrote that. She might sue you for libel, but it could be worth it,' Andrew says, a little too casually she thinks. This isn't a joke.

'But it's possible, isn't it?'

'Anything's possible. She had a motive, and she probably had the opportunity, but did she have the means? I can't see a woman of her weight and size overpowering a grown man and killing him. Then she had to dispose of the body, and all that without anyone seeing her. And there's her son. Where was he, while she was chopping up his father? It's an exciting theory, but a bit far-fetched.'

'Far-fetched?'

'Beyond belief. I don't think the old girl was capable of it.'

'But she wasn't old then. She was in her twenties.'

'Even so, Ana, I think you're letting your imagination run away with you. Maybe you should turn it into a crime novel instead.'

He's right. Was Nancy actually capable of murdering anyone, let alone her own husband, the father of her child? It seems unlikely, but there's something about it that won't let her rest. The answer is there in the paintings, she knows it.

'So I've been thinking,' Andrew says, coming over and sitting on the edge of her desk. 'If this book is almost finished, it would be a good time to do something new.'

'What do you mean? A new book?'

'No. I mean you and me. I've been thinking for some time that I'd like to visit North Africa. Why don't we give up this flat and take to the road again? We could cross over to Morocco, then move across to Algeria and then, who knows, maybe Italy or Greece. Yes, Greece sounds good. So, what do you think? Are you up for an adventure?'

'Oh, Andrew, I can't think about anything like that right now. I want to get this book finished first.'

'Okay, okay. Just think about it will you? I don't want to be stuck in a dead-end job as a barman all my life, and it's not as though you've got much keeping you here. You could write wherever we were.'

'I'll think about it. Now let me get on. I've got a lot to write up before I forget it.'

So she is right. Andrew has the wanderlust again. She knows he will go, with or without her. Is trekking through North Africa really what she wants for herself? Nancy's words come back to her. Is she right? Is Ana wasting her life?

CHAPTER 27

Nancy has been painting all afternoon. It is going well. She got up early this morning to paint the sunrise, and she is pleased with the result. She'll show those critics that she is still very much alive and kicking. She hopes that this painting, fishing boats coming home after a night at sea, will be more cheerful than the previous one. It must be all this reminiscing that's bringing this dark mood to her painting. She doesn't want that. She wants something happier, something she can give to Sara. Martin is coming round after he finishes work. He says he wants to talk to her about something important. What can it be? She hopes it's nothing to do with the baby. How dreadful if Sara has had another miscarriage. She washes out her paintbrush and sits in her usual place by the window. The last rays of the afternoon sun has bathed the Sierra in gold and turned the Mediterranean into a glittering mirror of light.

Nancy stalled the car a couple of times until she got used to it, and each time it happened, she looked across at Nick, terrified he would wake and ask her what on earth she was doing. Still, driving was not as difficult as she had imagined it would be. The steering was stiff, but the car ran smoothly. Even so, she was tense. She sat hunched over the wheel, her hands gripping it tightly, her eyes staring into the dark night, terrified something would go wrong. Luckily, there was no traffic on the road. She passed a couple of vans, a street cleaner pushing his cart, and a parked police car—otherwise the streets were deserted.

She turned a sharp corner. Nick slipped down in his seat and banged against the car door. Everything about him looked odd. His position was unnatural, his head lolled about as though it didn't belong to his body, and his face gleamed white and clammy in the weak light that lit up the car each time they passed a street lamp. She wanted to stop and check if he was still alive but was frightened she would have trouble starting the car again, or somebody would see her and come to investigate, so she drove on into the night, trying not to think about what she had done.

The pharmacist had said one tablet was sufficient for her mother. Two or three at the most would have been enough to send Nick to sleep, but she had given him how many? Five? Six? No, in her panic she had given him eight. Good God, there was no turning back now. He was probably dead already. She shuddered at the thought of what she had done. Don't panic, she told herself, keep calm. She had done this for Martin. After all, it was only a matter of time, and Nick would have hurt him as well as her. Nick was already becoming jealous of all the attention she gave their son.

The car was running well now, but each time she took a sharp left hand bend, Nick lurched towards her, his head flopping against her shoulder, and when she pushed him back so that he leant against the car door, his body felt colder to her touch.

At last they left the A20 and joined the A25, following the signs to Folkestone. Now there was a lot more traffic, mostly lorries heading for the continent, heavy, noisy machines that thundered past her in the outside lane, dousing the car with spray and temporarily blinding her. She could hear Martin, moving restlessly on the back seat.

'Go back to sleep Martin,' she said, soothingly.

'Mummy?' he asked in a sleepy voice. 'Spain? Sea?'

'Soon darling. Soon.'

Poor child, what would he think if he knew what his mother was about to do? When he woke up would he wonder where his father was? How much would he remember of tonight and their old life? He was after all very young, but what about when he was older? Would he want to know what had happened to his father, and what would she tell him? That she had done it for him? Somehow it did not seem enough. She began to wonder if she was doing the right thing.

She drove on, the windscreen wipers beating madly back and forth, the rain lashing at the car, forcing her to slow down. It was dark and hard to see. Her eyes ached from the strain of peering into the darkness. Lifting her husband into the car had hurt her back, and it was throbbing relentlessly. She was unsure where they were and was beginning to think that she had made a mistake about the location of the quarry or had driven past the turning while momentarily blinded by a passing lorry, when she noticed the public house on her right.

The Royal Eagle was a well-known roadside pub, and though it was closed at this hour, the lights in its car park were bright enough to pick it out clearly. They had stopped there that day so that Martin could go to the toilet and Nick could have a beer. She remembered that the turning to the quarry was only a few yards further on. She sighed with relief. They were almost there.

A few minutes later, she had turned off the main road and was driving slowly down an unlit narrow track. The rain was stopping, and a sliver of moon came out from behind the clouds. It would soon be dawn. Already the horizon had a silvery tinge to it, and as she turned a bend in the road, she saw it spread out before her. The quarry wasn't just a hole in the ground as Nick had told Martin, it was an enormous lake. Whether it was underground springs, rainwater, or aquifers, something had filled the disused quarry with water and now it lay in front of them, glimmering in the pale early morning light. She drove a little further and stopped, the headlights illuminating a wooden sign that read DANGER KEEP OUT and underneath, in smaller print: DEEP WATER NO SWIMMING.

Martin was still asleep, and there was no movement from Nick. She turned off the engine and got out. The car stood on a slight incline, close to the edge of the quarry. She walked forward and looked down into the shimmering lake. It was a sheer drop, the stone cut away by the quarrying machinery to form a steep cliff face. If she hadn't stopped the car when she did, they would all be at the bottom of the lake. She felt sick at the thought. Nobody would ever have known what happened to them. Nobody would even be looking for them. As far as anyone knew, they had gone to Spain to start a new life.

The sun rose slowly, casting its pale rays across the water, turning it first to silver then pink then gold. A pair of ducks flew across the lake, squawking loudly. It was a beautiful autumn morning with that slight chill in the air that always reminded her of roast chestnuts and walks in the park with her parents. A new life, that's what this was about, a new life for her and Martin. What right did Nick have to take her future from her, to own her, to dominate her? Did being her husband give him the right to destroy all her hopes and dreams? No. It was up to her to change things. She was the only one who could do it. Her family had abandoned her. Society had abandoned her. If anything was going to save her, she alone would have to make it happen. Now she was going to take control of her life.

She opened the boot of the car, removed the pushchair and her bag, then very carefully, so as not to wake him, she lifted Martin out of the car and placed him in the pushchair. He grumbled a little in his sleep but did not wake. She bent over him, kissed his soft cheek, and murmured, 'It's all right, my darling, just go back to sleep.'

Nick had not moved. He lay slumped in the passenger seat, his head forward, a dribble of spittle running down his face. She opened the car door and looked at him, then reached across and felt in his neck for sign of a pulse. A tiny flicker told her he was still alive, just. Now was the moment to draw back. There was still time. She could run to the pub and get them to call for an ambulance. She could tell them he had drunk too much. It wouldn't have been the first time he had passed out through drink. But then their lives would continue as before and maybe be even worse. Who knew what he would remember? Even if she told him he had asked her to drive because he was feeling unwell, that they had stopped by the quarry for a rest, that she had been worried about him, would he believe her? He never believed her when she told him the truth. She doubted she could get away with such a blatant lie. Or she could leave him there in the car for someone to find, and she and Martin could carry on with the second part of the journey, but then what? Her plan hinged on the house he had bought for them in Spain. How could they go there if he was still alive? He would know where they were, and he would find them. No matter where she went she would spend all her life in fear, looking over her shoulder, expecting any moment to hear his voice. Nothing would ever change. She would always be at his mercy. No, it was his life or theirs— hers and Martin's. She reached out and touched Nick's face—it was like ice. Once more she placed a finger on his throat looking for a pulse. This time there was none. It was too late to go back now. Nick was dead.

Her husband was dead, but she felt no regret—nothing but the urgency to complete her task. There was no time to examine her conscience; she could deal with that later. Her mind was as cold and clear as the icy lake. She closed the passenger door, walked round to the driver's side and got in. She picked up Martin's toy train off the floor, then opened the car windows slightly, slipped the gears into neutral and released the handbrake.

Almost immediately the car started to move forward. She jumped out, slammed the door shut and stood back as the car rolled towards the edge. At first it seemed to be moving in slow motion, and she had the illusion that there was still time to stop it, reverse all of it, turn back time. She watched, mesmerised, as the car continued to move forward, relentlessly. Now the enormity of what she was doing hit her. She was about to commit murder. In fact, she already had. It was too late. Even if she managed to run after the car and somehow stop its hurtling descent into the quarry, what was the point? She was sure Nick was dead. As these conflicting thoughts collided in her mind, paralysing her, the car gradually gathered speed, and then it really was too late. The blue Ford Prefect seemed to leap into the air, went over the cliff edge and disappeared, with a colossal splash, into the lake.

The deed was done. Nancy could not move. She stood looking at the spot where their car had been. There was no sound. Even the ducks were quiet, and the silence hung in the air like a cold mist. Time seemed to have stopped. Still she stood there, her emotions twisting and turning inside her, pulling her in every direction. She had done it. She was free of him at last. But to do that she had become a murderess. She had taken a life. Slowly she walked to the edge of the quarry and forced herself to look at the result of her actions. There was nothing to see but a few bubbles—the car had sunk like a stone. For a moment she thought she could see him, just below the surface, looking up at her, his arm raised. No, she told herself, that was impossible. Nick was in the car and the car was at the bottom of the lake. It was over. It was as if Nick had never existed. She had made him disappear, and now she would erase all memory of him from their lives. Looking down into the flooded quarry, she felt no sorrow, no guilt. Her mind was empty, her heart suddenly still. She had done what she had to do.

She walked back to Martin, who despite all that had happened, was still fast asleep. She pulled the blanket tighter around him, balanced her bag on the back of the pushchair and set off back down the lane, the way they had come. She had already checked and knew that outside the Royal Eagle there was a bus stop; they could catch a bus that would take them directly to the train station. They would be there in half an hour, and then they would be on their way to Spain.

Nobody would miss them, nobody would look for them, and that was all thanks to Nick. It was he who had cut them off from the world, and now the world would not know he was no longer around. The hesitation she had felt, the doubts about her actions, all melted away. It was Nick who had made her close in on herself, made her distance herself from her emotions in order to survive. Now she felt nothing for him or for what she had done. He was dead and she was free, that was all that mattered. The sun climbed higher in the sky, illuminating them, mother and son, trudging up the lane alone. Nancy felt neither elation nor regret, nor grief nor joy. She was numb.

The pain is worse and making Nancy feel sick. She searches for the emergency button that Martin has insisted she have with her at all times but can't find it. Her head is spinning, and she thinks she is going to faint. Where is her mobile phone? She must phone Martin. She manages to open the drawer of the coffee table, and there it is. She presses the pre-set number and waits. It is an answer machine. God, what does she do now?

'Martin, it's Mama. Can you come, please? Now.'

The phone drops from her hand, and she thinks she is falling. Everything is going dark and there is a roaring sound in her head. Martin, where are you?

CHAPTER 28

Ana has not slept. Her mind was racing all night: chapters of the book repeating themselves in her head, a confession from Nancy, Martin refusing to pay her, threatening her with court. Ana has woken at six, her mind befuddled, and her head aching. She pads into the kitchen and puts on the coffee machine. Andrew is dead to the world. He didn't get home until almost four o'clock and has been sound asleep ever since.

A thousand questions race through her head. What is she going to do? How is she going to finish this book? She has a duty to write the truth but can she be sure that it is the truth? Maybe she is letting her imagination run away with her. After all, what is she basing her theory on, the fact that Nancy refuses to talk about her abusive ex-husband? That's not surprising. Anyone in that position would want to forget her past and start a new life. Is it that Nancy's paintings show a number of dramatic swings in her mood? This can be explained by the fact that she was in an unhappy marriage. And then there is her obsession with painting water scenes. Does that really tell her anything more than that Nancy liked to paint the sea? When she lays out her evidence clearly, it is obvious that there is no case to be made. And yet she cannot shake this feeling that something terrible happened to Nicholas Henderson, and that Nancy was somehow involved.

The coffee stops percolating. She pours a cup and sips it slowly—it is very hot. There is no other way; she will have to talk to Nancy again. She'll make it like a joke. Say something like, 'If you won't tell me anything about your husband, then I'll start to believe you murdered him.' Ha, ha. No, that won't work. Perhaps she can ask her about the car and see what her reaction is to that. She sighs and tries the coffee again.

It's no good. Ana knows she won't get any more out of Nancy than she has already. If Nancy really did murder her husband and push him and his car into the sea, she certainly isn't going to confess to Ana. Maybe she should take Andrew's advice and turn it into a novel.

She swallows the last of the coffee and picks up her manuscript. She will read through it once more, and then she'll telephone Martin later, when he's home from the hospital, and ask to see him, to find out what he wants her to say about his father. After all she is writing this book for the family—her duty is to them. What will Martin think if she reveals her belief that his mother is a murderess? What about his sons? Does she want them to find out one day, when they are older, that their grandmother killed their grandfather? Is that what she really wants? Is telling the truth worth all that pain?

Ana spends the day reading through the manuscript, going over different ways to bring in the mysterious Nicholas Henderson without upsetting the family. In the end she decides she cannot do any more until she has spoken to Martin. It is gone six o'clock by the time she rings him and her call is diverted to voice mail. At first she thinks of hanging up then she says, 'Hello, Dr Henderson, this is Ana. I've finished the memoirs but before I give them to Nancy, there are a couple of things I'd like to speak to you about. Can you call me, please?'

She logs onto her computer and starts correcting some of the typos she has found in the manuscript. Martin still owes her money, but once these memoirs are finished, she will have no more work. She wonders what she will do. She is tired of not having a regular job, just picking up bits of casual work, translating the occasional business letter or acting as an interpreter for English people who need to speak to their solicitors or visit the doctor. The pay is poor and the work is boring.

Spending a few days in Oxford with Nancy has opened her eyes to other possibilities. She would enjoy working in England for a few years. It wouldn't be forever, just until the economic situation in Spain improved, and it would help her accent, she is sure. She finds herself going through the benefits of making such a move as though she is explaining it to Andrew.

Andrew. That is the problem. He will not want to come with her. He has set his sights on visiting North Africa and he wants her to go with him. But she doesn't have his wanderlust. Yes, when she was younger, it was fun to travel, but now she wants stability, a decent job with regular wages. She wants challenging work, something that will look good on her CV. Her mobile phone starts to vibrate and she picks it up.

'*Digame.*'

'Ana? It's Martin Henderson.'

'Dr Henderson, I wondered if I could come round to talk to you sometime,' she says.

'It's not convenient at the moment,' he says. 'I am with my mother at the hospital. She has had a heart attack.'

'*Dios mio*, I'm so sorry. Is there anything I can do?'

'No, thank you. I have to go now but I'll let you know how she gets on.'

He ends the call and leaves her looking at her phone in a stunned silence. A heart attack. How is that possible? Nancy was so well in England, no sign of tiredness, no pain. Ana wasn't even aware that she had a heart problem. The journey must have been too much for her.

She looks back at the computer screen and reads the last paragraph she typed. It says: '*And of course, the whereabouts of Nancy Miller's husband remains a mystery. Nick Henderson disappeared in 1963, the year that Nancy and her young son moved to Spain. There is nothing to suggest that he ever came to Spain with them, but he was never seen again.*'

She reads it again then highlights the paragraph and presses delete. She closes the file and shuts her computer. She suddenly feels very tired. She goes into the bedroom and lies down beside Andrew.

The next day she receives a call from Sara, Martin's wife. She sounds rather distressed.

'Ana?'

'Hello Sara, I was going to ring later to ask how Nancy was.'

'I'm sorry to tell you this, Ana, but Nancy died last night. Martin asked me to call you. He's very upset. We all are.'

'I'm so sorry. I just can't believe it. She was fine when we were in England. I'd never seen her so lively.'

'I know. The doctor says it could have happened at any point. She has had a heart murmur for years. It seems that recently she has suffered a number of small heart attacks, which we weren't aware of, and they weakened her heart. He wanted to know if anything had happened to upset her, if she had been under any stress. We told him about the trip to Oxford. Maybe that was more of a strain on her heart than we realized.'

'But she seemed fine, and she was very keen to go to her exhibition. You can't blame yourselves.'

'You're right. We knew about the heart murmur, but she has lived with that for years. We thought she was in good health, except for her memory problems. You can imagine how shocked we all are,' Sara says, and Ana can hear the tears in her voice.

'Yes, of course. I really am sorry to hear about it. When is the funeral?'

'This afternoon. At the *Iglesia Mayor de la Encarnacion* at four o'clock.'

'I'll be there.'

'Oh, Martin says that if you'd like to come round to the house tomorrow he will pay you for the work you've done and you can give him the memoirs. Would six o'clock suit you?'

'Yes, I'll do that.'

She can't believe Nancy is dead. It is unreal. As she reads through the memoirs Nancy dictated, she finds herself thinking, 'I must check on that' or 'I must ask Nancy what she means by that' and each time she is hit with the realization that Nancy is no longer there to give her an opinion or clarify an event. Nancy is dead. It is so final. Ana has never had anyone she knows die. This is a new experience for her. Now she wonders how Nancy felt when her new little baby died after only four days, how she felt when her father died. Ana is too young to have experienced any of this. Her parents are young, alive and well in her home town, even her grandparents are living.

'What is it?' Andrew asks. He is showered and shaved but still dressed in the tee shirt he usually sleeps in.

'That was Dr Henderson's wife. She says Nancy has died.'

'What, the old woman who was writing her memoirs?'

'Yes. She had a heart attack.'

'I'm sorry to hear that. You'd become rather fond of her, hadn't you?'

'Yes, I had. She was a crabby old woman at times, but I liked her. She was special. I just can't believe this has happened.'

'Well she was getting on a bit, wasn't she? People don't live forever.'

He sits down beside her and picks up the manuscript.

'Still, it's sad. And she never got to see the finished memoirs,' Ana adds.

'So they're finished now, are they?' he asks, flicking through them casually. 'Will he still pay you?'

'Yes, of course. That was one reason why his wife rang. He wants me to go round tomorrow to settle up.'

'Does this mean that you've decided to tell him about your theory? About the old woman murdering her husband?'

'Yes, I've made up my mind what to do,' she says. 'Look, the funeral is this afternoon. I feel I should go. Do you want to come with me?'

'What time is it?' he asks.

'Four o'clock.'

'Sorry, Ana. I can't. I've arranged to meet Paolo and then I'm going straight to work.'

'It doesn't matter; you didn't know her anyway.'

But did she—Ana—know her either? She has spent the last six months visiting Nancy, talking to her, writing about her life, and yet she feels she doesn't know her any better than she did the first day she met her.

Martin opens the door to her. The house is quiet. His wife has taken the children to visit her mother, he tells her. He appears strained. There are bags under his eyes, and he looks as though he has not slept in days. He leads her into his office. 'The boys are very upset. They loved their grandmother.'

'Of course,' she says. 'I was very sorry to hear about your mother's sudden death. It must have been a dreadful shock for you.' Ana feels rather awkward, and is unsure how to respond to his grief. Everything she wants to say sounds rather trite.

'Yes, we weren't expecting it. She seemed so well after her trip to England, so energetic and full of life.' His voice falters, and for a moment she sees him draw back into himself, but then he takes a deep breath and says, 'She wasn't the easiest of women as she got older, but I loved her. She was a wonderful mother. She brought me up all on her own, you know.' He looks at her and adds, 'Of course, you know that. You know all about my mother.'

She is tempted to admit that it is not true, that she knows no more about his mother than he does.

'She must have confided in you about many things,' he says. 'Things she would never speak to me about.'

'Your mother was a very private person,' Ana says. 'She only ever wanted to talk about her painting.'

'Her paintings, yes. I have something for you.' He goes to his desk and takes out a small watercolour in a gilt frame. 'She wanted you to have this,' he says. 'It's a painting of the house we used to live in.'

Ana takes the watercolour from him and looks at it, too overcome to speak. It is a scene by the beach, of a small white house with the traditional red tiles on the roof. A donkey stands outside, and some chickens. A small boy is playing with sea shells, and there, in the background, is the sea. It is beautiful and instantly recognizable as a Nancy Miller watercolour.

'I don't know what to say.'

'Do you like it?'

'It's lovely, really lovely. How kind of her to give it to me.'

'She said some time ago that she wanted you to have that painting when you had finished her memoirs. I think she was very fond of you, in her way. You know my mother—it wasn't always easy to know what she was thinking.' He blinks away his tears and says, 'Well I suppose I must owe you some money.'

'I wrote it all down,' she says, handing him her bill.

'Have you brought the manuscript?'

'Yes, it's finished. I made you two copies, and there's another copy on the flash drive.'

She opens her bag and takes out the copies of the memoirs and hands them to him.

'I hope you approve. I tried to keep to what Nancy wanted.'

'I'm sure it's excellent. Forgive me if I don't read it right away. I think I'll leave it for a couple of days, until I get used to the idea that I won't be seeing my mother again.'

She hears his voice crack as he says this and waits for a moment before asking, 'What will you do with it? Will you have it published?'

'Yes, I think so, eventually. I'll probably speak to her old agent and see what he advises.'

'Well, I'd better be going,' she says. 'If you want me to do any revisions to the book, let me know.'

'Yes, of course. I mustn't detain you. Just one more thing. My mother left a request in her will that her ashes be scattered at sea. We are going to do it on Saturday. I wondered if you would like to be with us.'

'Yes, I'd like that.'

'Good. I'll ring you with the time.'

He takes out his wallet and counts out the money he owes her. 'I hope this is enough,' he says. 'You'd better check it. I'm not thinking very clearly today.'

'I'm sure it's fine,' she says, folding the notes and putting them in her bag. 'I'll see you on Saturday, then.'

Somehow Nancy's death makes it easier for Ana to make a decision about Andrew. He is a nice man and she is very fond of him, but he is not someone she could spend the rest of her life with. If she is honest with herself, she knows he will soon get bored with her. He wants adventure and she wants security. The money Martin has paid her means that she can make a break. She'll give Andrew her half of the rent and she'll go home to see her parents.

Maybe later, she will phone Helen and take her up on her offer.

It is a beautiful clear morning when they meet on the beach in front of Nancy's apartment. All the family are there, the two small boys, Sara, Sara's mother, Martin, Harry, who has flown over to be there, and even María, who seems so consumed with grief that she cannot stop crying into a large cotton handkerchief.

'Ana, I'm glad you could make it. You know my wife, of course, and this is her mother,' he says, presenting them formally, one by one. 'My sons, Juan and Emilio, and María you've met, and Harry, who tells me he met you in Oxford.'

She smiles and kisses each in turn. She had seen his wife at the funeral when she paid her respects but hadn't stayed to talk to anyone else. She had been too upset. It had surprised her to see the church so crowded. She hadn't realized Nancy had known quite so many people in Marbella. Many of them were people of Nancy's age, but there were a lot of younger ones, new fans of her work, and there were the waiters from the restaurant where she liked to eat fish, women from the hairdressing salon, shop assistants who remembered her from her more active days, her regular taxi driver—everyone who had had some contact with Nancy over the years was there. The RTV television crew parked outside the church panned the crowd with their cameras while the local reporters scribbled in their notebooks. Nancy had been a local celebrity, and the Spanish love celebrities. Everyone had wanted a chance to say farewell to her.

'We can get the boat down there,' Martin says, pointing across the beach to where a small motor launch is waiting.

'It's all arranged. I expect my mother would have preferred that we go in one of the fishing boats, but I don't think Sara could stand the smell of raw fish at the moment, and anyway I'm not sure I could persuade any of them to take us out.'

Ana notices that he is carrying a small casket, presumably Nancy's ashes, and they all follow him across the road and down to the jetty.

'I have asked Pedro to take us along to the beach where my mother and I lived when we first came to Spain. As you know, it is built up now, but I think she would have approved of us going there.'

Everyone climbs on board the boat. The boys are excited about the trip along the bay, and their mother tries in vain to keep them quiet. María looks very nervous. She keeps crossing herself and muttering what could be prayers or supplications to God to keep them safe. Only Martin is calm. He stands in the bow of the boat, looking at the sea.

'This is a lovely idea,' Ana says. 'Your mother loved the Mediterranean.'

He turns and looks at her and says, 'I've read your manuscript.'

She waits for him to say more, but he continues to stare at the horizon.

'So, is it all right?' she asks.

'It's very good. My mother would have approved. You obviously listened to her very carefully.'

'I tried to make it a clear reflection of the woman and her work,' she says.

'I see that. And you didn't mention anything about my father. Why was that?'

This is the opportunity but how can she tell him what she suspects happened to his father? What good will it do? And anyway there is always the possibility that she is completely wrong. Maybe Nicholas Henderson is alive and well. Maybe he died peacefully in bed in some other country. She will never know, so why put such awful thoughts in the minds of Nancy's family?

'I wrote what your mother told me. That was my mission. She never spoke of your father, so there was nothing for me to write.'

'I see.'

He looks at her sadly and, for a moment, she feels that he would have liked her to have told him more about his father.

They are opposite the beach now. Pedro stops the motor and they rock gently to and fro on a Mediterranean sea as blue and calm as a millpond. They are about half a kilometre from the shore, close enough to see the long stretch of beach lined with palm trees. It is, as Martin said, a place of bars and restaurants now, rows of white apartments and expensive villas where once there had been fishermen's cottages. The Sierra Blanca looms in the background, sheltering the beach from the north winds. This was where Nancy lived as a young woman. This was where she painted the watercolour which now hangs above Ana's bed.

'I don't intend to make much of a speech,' Martin is saying to the assembled group. 'My mother was not a religious woman, but she was a person who saw beauty in everything around her and, above all, in the sea. She once told me that what she loved about the Mediterranean was its changing moods, one moment like today, blue and calm, deceptively innocent, and the next turbulent and treacherous. It was her request to have her ashes scattered here, and so as I do that, I would like you to think of my mother, Nancy Miller, and remember her in your own way. She was a special woman, a great artist, an understanding mother-in-law, a loving grandmother, my beloved mother, and my friend. I will miss her.'

He steps to the side of the boat and, opening the casket, carefully drops the ashes into the water. Sara leans over to scatter rose petals on top of them.

'And me, Papa,' says Emilio.

The boys step forward and throw a handful of petals each, then one by one the others do the same. A scarlet carpet of rose petals floats beside the boat and gradually, as they watch, sinks below the surface.

Thank you for taking the time to read my novel PALETTE OF SECRETS. If you enjoyed it, please consider telling your friends or posting a short review on Amazon. Word of mouth is an author's best friend and much appreciated.

Thank you, Joan Fallon

Palette of Secrets

Lightning Source UK Ltd.
Milton Keynes UK
UKHW020644030822
406784UK00009B/1147